Holding Their Own V:
Bishop's Song

By

Joe Nobody

ISBN 978-0615924113

Edited by:
E. T. Ivester

Contributors:

D. A. L. H.
D. Allen

www.HoldingYourGround.com

Published by

www.PrepperPress.com

Other Books by Joe Nobody:

- **Holding Your Ground: Preparing for Defense if it All Falls Apart**

- **The TEOTWAWKI Tuxedo: Formal Survival Attire**

- **Without Rule of Law: Advanced Skill to Help You Survive**

- **Holding Their Own: A Story of Survival**

- **Holding Their Own II: The Independents**

- **Holding Their Own III: Pedestals of Ash**

- **Holding Their Own IV: The Ascent**

- **Holding Their Own V: The Alpha Chronicles**

- **The Home Schooled Shootist: Training to Fight with a Carbine**

- **Apocalypse Drift**

- **The Olympus Device: Book One**

Prologue

Nick lowered the binoculars and sighed. Glancing over at Bishop, he announced, "I guess that's our answer. Doesn't look like Fort Bliss intends to capitulate."

Bishop snorted, lowering his optic and staring at his friend. "When the council decided to ask for Bliss's surrender, you didn't really think they would just give up, did you?"

"No, I guess not. It sent a strong message though."

Adjusting the rifle hanging across his chest, Bishop was optimistic. "Like you said, we have our answer. But I'm not giving up hope just yet. We still might be able to avoid a war. If we can keep this convoy from reaching Bliss, they might change their tune."

"Oh, it's not getting past us today, and I'm sure they'll change their tune. The next song they play, the one that accompanies the next convoy, will include a rhythm section complete with air support and heavy armor. We run out of dance moves when that music starts playing."

Nick raised his glass, returning to study the distant line of military trucks, tankers and escort Humvees. Turning to Sheriff Watts, he asked, "Are you ready?"

The lifelong Texas lawman nodded, looking resplendent in his best dress uniform, complete with Stetson hat and shined boots. "We're good to go."

The acknowledgement sent Bishop and Nick scrambling for the rocks, climbing quickly to reach their pre-assigned position.

It was all up to the commanding officer in charge of the approaching procession now. The men from the Alliance of West Texas were prepared.

While they waited on the lead unit of the convoy to appear, Nick recounted how they had arrived at the current situation.

The ex-Green Beret understood the military mind, especially when it came to command. His years in Special Forces had provided a unique education into how his country's leaders dealt with the problems associated with guerrilla forces and irregular opposition. Now, he was on the other side.

Supply was the lowest common denominator, the need for beans, bullets and diesel fuel drummed into the mind of every regular officer. West Point, the assorted war colleges, and day-to-day training hammered home the importance of logistical assets. If a unit didn't have food or ammo, the soldiers couldn't fight.

This foundational strategy was two-fold. On the one side, the American military machine was built to deny the enemy these critical assets. US troops spent years scouring the Iraqi countryside, seeking caches of weapons and ammunition - a strategy designed to eliminate the foe's access to these all-important tools of violence.

The same overlying objectives shaped the war efforts in Afghanistan, the mission there focused on enemy supply routes coming across the border with Pakistan.

On the other side, US forces didn't deploy without proper supply. Significant investment was made to ensure what was bad for the goose didn't happen to the gander. Every major combat unit was equipped with extensive refueling capabilities, as well as a fleet of supply trucks.

Nick understood this basic premise of his foe, and thus concentrated his forces to the east – the direction from which the supplies must originate in order to reach the units stationed at Fort Bliss.

While Bliss, to his west, might have the armor and infantry, they were growing desperate for lack of resupply. Nick didn't believe General Westfield would initiate any sort of offensive action without his coffers being fully stocked with those prerequisite beans, bullets, and diesel fuel.

California was a mess according to all available sources. Phoenix had been abandoned, and the funeral pyres of Denver were said to be visible for miles. Resupply from the west or the north was unlikely. That left only the south, Mexico, and the east – right where he was standing.

Nick also knew the closest major point of resupply was Fort Hood, residing on the eastern border of his territory. He had stationed his scouts around the huge base's perimeter, hoping for an early warning if shipments were being prepared.

He had received just such a warning, early yesterday.

The Alliance's council had been stern and concise in its orders – the forces of West Texas could not initiate offensive action. That handicap had made his job all that more difficult, but he had to agree with the policy. The mouse is so overmatched, it never starts a fight with a cat. His people's odds probably weren't as optimistic as the rodent's.

They had worked quickly to prepare, throwing together a battle plan in record time. Diana and the council finally issued their approval.

Bishop seemed to be reading his friend's mind. "Good call on the pre-deployment of men. Maybe we can pull this off without loss of life."

"We'll see. They're getting close; you better head off to your squads."

"Stay safe, brother," Bishop replied, and then hustled off, zigzagging through the scattered rocks and boulders bordering the interstate, remaining hidden from the pavement below.

The convoy rolled out of the east, over 20 vehicles in length. The army had learned its lessons during the Second Gulf War, that conflict resulting in a change in how security was intermixed with the units carrying the precious cargo. Early in the war, the US had lost vital supplies to enemy action and had revamped procedures. Nick knew this… knew exactly where the armed escorts would be positioned. He had arranged his forces appropriately.

To the men in the lead Humvee, the scene they approached must have appeared surreal. There, blocking the westbound lanes of I-10 waited two police cars, each occupying a lane with flashing blue strobes for full effect. The toned figure that was Sheriff Watts appeared statuesque between the two cruisers and at his side a trusted deputy. Both men projected the epitome of authority - their crisp uniforms, hats and mirrored sunglasses adding to the effect.

The lead Humvee stopped over 100 yards short of the blockade, the driver and crew suspicious of an ambush. The belt-fed, 50-caliber machine gun mounted on the roof swiveled right and left, the barrel of the deadly weapon sweeping what appeared to be a completely empty desert and hillside.

The good sheriff bided his time, waiting with his shoulders squared and spine stiff. While the rest of the column hung back, the Humvee bravely inched forward. At 50 meters, it stopped again, the passenger door opening to discharge a frustrated master sergeant.

The man donned his cap and then proceeded to stride purposefully toward the pesky police officers. He stopped just shy of the two patrol cars.

"Move these cars out of the way, or I'll move them myself," the sergeant began, an air of obvious disdain for local law enforcement in his voice.

"I'll be happy to open this road, soldier… as soon as you present me with your hazardous materials permit," replied Watts.

"My what?"

"You heard me, son. It is my understanding those trucks behind you are hauling hazardous substances, and you are required to obtain a permit before transporting such items on a public road."

"Are you fucking crazy, old man?"

3

Watts looked the soldier up and down, shaking his head. "Sir, I don't know about where you're from, but around here I am addressed as 'Sheriff,' or 'Mr. Watts.' I'll ignore that lack of respect – once. The next time, I'll take it personally."

It was clear from Nick's perch that the sergeant didn't know what to do. After glancing back and forth between the deputy and Watts, the man spun on his heels and returned to his ride, mumbling all the way. There was little doubt he was radioing for his superior officer.

A minute later, another Humvee broke out of the middle of the truck pack, racing toward the front of the line. This time, an older man exited the passenger seat, Nick's binoculars indicating a rank of captain displayed on the man's lapel.

The officer was more cordial, approaching the local lawman with a smile and extending his hand. "Captain Harrison," he introduced.

Again, Watts repeated his demand for the required permits.

"Sheriff, I don't know what type of game you're playing, but I don't have any such permit, nor am I going to obtain one. We are federal troops operating under direct orders of the president of the United States. The federal government of a country, I might add, that is currently under martial law. Unless I wandered into Mexico by accident, you don't have any standing as far as my convoy is concerned."

Watts didn't hesitate, well coached by DA Gibson on how to act out his side of the debate. "Captain, this country, the land you see around you, is not under martial law. I am operating as a law enforcement officer, dutifully sworn by the elected officials of this territory."

Diplomacy quickly deserted the captain, his manner changing abruptly. "Sir, remove these two cars, or I'll push them aside and continue. I recognize neither your locally elected government, nor your need for any permits."

Watts took a step closer to the man, his 6'5" frame towering over the military officer. "If you want to start a war, son, go ahead. Touch either one of those cars and you'll be doing just that. We take our laws seriously out here."

For a brief moment, Nick thought Watts had actually pulled it off. For just a second, it looked like the captain was going to turn the convoy around. It was an unrealistic bout of optimism.

"Fine by me," Harrison replied, pivoting sharply and returning to his transport.

Nick watched as words were exchanged in the front seat of the command vehicle, and then the diesel engine revved

4

as the driver guided the heavy military unit forward.

Watts had been instructed not to risk his person. As the front bumper of the Humvee advanced, the sheriff and his man moved aside, stepping to the shoulder as the captain's driver pushed one, and then the other patrol car out of the way.

Nick sighed, disappointed he was required to execute the next act of the drama. Turning to Kevin who was waiting next to him, he whispered, "Blow it."

A red wire was connected to the car battery between Kevin's feet, the connection sending electrical current to the several pounds of detonation cord and explosives positioned around the overpass's support columns.

Despite being almost half a mile away, the explosion was tremendous. A wall of gray-colored debris burst forth from under the doomed structure, the blast wave sending boulder-sized chunks of the former bridge hundreds of feet into the air.

Time seemed to slow down, all eyes drawn as the crossing roadway wobbled, shuddered, and then collapsed onto the pavement below. Interstate 10 was now officially closed.

"Your move," whispered Nick, peering down at the command vehicle.

Captain Harrison's Humvee stopped, idling less that 100 yards past Sheriff Watt's now damaged patrol cars. Nick could only imagine the conversation inside, the machine gun's turret sweeping right and left. The officer's transport was quickly joined by two general-purpose trucks pulling out of the line, racing up to support their commander. Each disgorged a rifle squad, the infantry fanning out as if expecting an assault.

Once comfortable with his reinforcements, the captain again appeared, walking ahead to study the rubble blocking his path.

Bishop had been expecting this action. Raising a whistle to his lips, he inhaled deeply and then sounded a screeching signal.

Along both sides of the convoy, 400 men uncovered their spider holes. Each pit was just over a foot deep, strategically placed to address the entire length of the military column. Plywood, cardboard and burlap feed bags had been used to cover the fighting positions, the makeshift roofs then coated with a layer of sand. Each had been personally inspected by an experienced operator to ensure proper concealment.

There had been no shortage of nervous humor as the Alliance's men had taken to their hides, the exchange fueled by the fact that each dugout resembled a shallow grave.

Rifle barrels appeared from the exposed pits, all pointed toward the now wide-eyed troops piloting the convoy's assortment of trucks.

Sheriff Watts calmly trekked to his still tenable car, slowly turning the cruiser around and pulling even with a now very pissed convoy commander.

The old lawman's voice was firm, but reasonable. "Give it up, son. You're outnumbered, out-gunned, and we hold the high ground. Don't go down as another General Custer. Don't lead your command into a slaughterhouse."

Nick was on the balls of his feet. While he couldn't hear Sheriff Watt's words, he knew what the older lawman was saying. He prayed Harrison would have the common sense to surrender.

He didn't.

Mumbling "Fuck off," the officer walked back to his Humvee and began radioing orders for the convoy to turn around.

This too had been anticipated. Unbeknownst to the army commander, the Alliance had a convoy of its own - ten 18-wheeler tractor trailers now blocking the road behind the hemmed-in army column. The trucks had been used to transport the 500 men now surrounding the military units.

News of the trap reached the captain's ear before his driver could reverse course.

Nick watched as the officer exited his ride for the third time that afternoon. Approaching Sheriff Watts, the soldier asked, "Do I have your word my men will be well treated?"

"I can do better than that," the sheriff responded. "You have my word that your men are free to go. Use your troop haulers and return to Fort Hood with your men, Captain. I'm impounding the hazardous materials."

"Agreed," the commander replied, and turned to issue the appropriate orders.

"Oh, and Captain Harrison, please leave behind all of your small arms and ammunition. I don't want you changing your mind a few miles down the road."

Twenty minutes later, the remote countryside bordering I-10 erupted again. This time cheers of celebration rolled across the desert. The Alliance had prevailed in its first showdown with the government of the United States of America.

Bishop and Nick exchanged glances, neither man joining in the merriment. Both knew it would only become more difficult after today... both well aware that if war came to West Texas, there would be little to cheer about.

Chapter 1

The Davis Mountains
West Texas
June 7, 2016

Bishop watched the clear drop of perspiration fall from his nose, the bead landing on the side of his weapon. Accelerated by gravity, the small bubble trickled down the trigger guard, past the grip, and then hesitated at the cliff-edge of the carbine. *Don't do it*, he mentally warned the droplet, *it's suicide*.

Ignoring his plea, it fell to the sandy earth between his boots, joining several of its brethren already gathered there, a small circle of damp soil evidence of their collaborative journey.

Better sweat than blood, he thought, studying the miniature battle taking place between his feet. The liquid generated to cool his body was in a desperate struggle down there – a campaign to hold a tiny beachhead of discolored West Texas desert. The fluid was losing, evaporation overwhelming the invader, absorption mopping up the wounded.

There was just no way the sweat can win, he observed. The sun was too hot, the soil too vast and dry. Ever fighting for the underdog, he adjusted his exhausted body, covering the damp spot with his shadow, probably providing false hope for the soon to be routed forces below. It wouldn't make any difference in the long run.

Bored with the one-sided conflict, Bishop raised his gaze and studied the ragtag group of men scattered around him. He couldn't help but draw the analogy, likening his comrades to the perspiration, about to face an enormously superior force. *Don't do it*, he wanted to warn his friends, *it's suicide*.

War drums were sounding on the horizon, his tribe preparing for a conflict that they had little hope of winning. *It's suicide*, he wanted to scream at the top of his lungs. *Thousands are going to die on both sides, and in the end, we can't win*.

Knowing they wouldn't listen, Bishop held his consul.

The thirty men surrounding him had been hiking all morning, gradually gaining altitude as they progressed through the Davis Mountains of West Texas. The combination of thin air, a hot day, and the heavy, backbreaking loads carried in their packs was taking a toll.

Nick's booming voice interrupted Bishop's thoughts. "Two minutes, ladies," the big ex-operator warned. "We'll do another three miles and then break for chow. Wine *will not* be served."

7

Bishop watched as his dear friend, their instructor for the day, sauntered over and took a knee. "You doing okay, buddy?" Nick asked.

"Yeah. I'm holding my own," Bishop replied.

"It's only been five months since you died on the operating table, brother. That was one nasty-ass wound you took, and I don't want to see you overdo it. Besides, Terri will kick my butt if I carry you off this mountain suffering from a relapse."

Bishop ignored the reference to his overprotective wife, instead motioning to the other men with his head. "They're not soldiers, Nick. They're shopkeepers and farmers. They barely exercise proper muzzle discipline, much less realize the importance of things like noise control or bounding in an advance. I'm worried they will come out of this class thinking they can actually engage the military, and we both know that overconfidence can be deadly. In a way, that little episode with the convoy may come back and bite us."

Nodding his head and then lowering his voice, Nick replied, "I know, but what choice do we have? I ask myself every day if the Minutemen had the same doubts when they were facing the British during the Revolutionary War."

"If the US Army comes rolling out of Fort Bliss with 300 Abrams battle tanks, we'll be in a lot worse shape than those guys ever were. The British didn't have helicopter gunships and thermal imaging."

"No, but the Afghans held out against the Russians and us, despite all of our advanced weapons. It can be done," Nick countered.

"I know it can... but at what cost? The Mujahidin had 1600 years of warfare under their belts and were tough as iron spikes. They still fell by the tens of thousands, but their society was immune to the carnage and motivated by religion. I'm not sure our fledgling little community can or will pay such a price."

Nick nodded, familiar with the debate. Looking at his watch, he announced, "Let's continue this conversation later. Right now, I've got a class to finish up."

After patting Bishop on the shoulder, Nick rose and began motivating the troops. "All right, girls! Time to mount up. Straighten out your skirts, and let's get moving!"

The grumbling of tired, sore men rose from the group, sounds Bishop had heard a hundred times before. It didn't matter if it were the pine woods of Fort Bragg or the oil fields of Iraq, it was always the same. Men with sore feet and aching backs would bitch and gnash, creative curses forming in their throats. Just like always, they finally began moving, eventually forming up, and standing ready to accept more pain.

Bishop took his place at the rear of the column, watching as the single-file line of citizen-militia began to stretch out along the trail. Where it not for the task at hand, the vista would have been glorious. A sea of pinion pines covered the valley below, their dark green foliage in abstract to the blue sky and white, billowing clouds beyond. Had it been winter, they might have seen snow from this vantage. In the spring, fog would have blanketed the valley, the gray soup so thick that the single road traversing the area would have been impassable in the early morning. Not today, though. Today, the air was crisp and the sun hot. Today was the perfect day to train for an impending conflict that everyone prayed could be avoided.

As his gaze traveled up the mountainside, the scenery transformed drastically. Fields of limestone boulders competed with the pines, scattered gray outcroppings of rock and small strands of Navajo grass replacing the thinning trees as the altitude increased. Plant life finally gave up just above his position, replaced with towering, ominous walls of bare rock guarding the crest of the mountain.

Slowly the column snaked its way up... always up. Time seemed to creep slower than distance gained, a fog of mind-numbing fatigue and monotony falling over the men.

Bishop watched Nick, patiently moving up and down the line, coaching, encouraging and pushing with an energy no one else possessed. *He's done this so many times*, thought Bishop. *He knows what they absorb today might mean the difference between a battlefield grave and going home... if war comes.*

Nick's voice seemed to always be in the air. "Don't bunch up... Always scan for the likely avenue of approach! Where would you hide if you were on the other side and getting ready to hit us? Think people... damn it, think!"

Up ahead, Bishop saw the lead element approaching a narrow gap. Large rocks lurked above the trail, a scattering of foliage strewn below. Instinct slowed his footfalls, a warning forming in his throat. Nick saw it too, but for some reason didn't move to slow the column. Instead, he stood beside the trail and crossed his arms in annoyance.

A small, white paper bag arched through the air, a whiff of smoke trailing in its wake. Before it landed, two other similar objects joined it in flight. The three devices landed in the middle of the column, the closest man staring blankly, unsure of what to do.

A second later, the bags exploded.

Cries of battle rang down from the rocks, blood curdling screams of savage volume paralyzing the startled trainees. Clouds of choking, white smoke filled the air, burning already starved lungs and reducing visibility to a few feet.

The homemade flash-bang grenades were immediately followed by a hailstorm of paintballs raining down from the rocks above. At the same time, human figures rose from the vegetation below the trail, ghostly images appearing through the fog of battle smoke, shooting pointblank at the stumbling trainees.

Ambush, Bishop knew immediately, *and a damned good one.*

With instincts and reactions based on years of conflict, Bishop was moving before the detonations had finished echoing down the mountain. Screaming above the din, he rallied three of his closest comrades – issuing orders for the bewildered men to follow.

Up the side of the mountain he scrambled, loose gravel and a lack of handholds slowing his pace. Wide eyed with shock, his three trainees followed. Higher Bishop climbed, using piles of rocks, displaced boulders and natural undulations for cover. After they had managed to ascend 30 feet above the trail, he turned to his panting followers and instructed, "Form a line, and hit the enemy from the side. We are going to flank that ambush. Hit those sons of bitches hard and fast. Let's move!"

Without waiting to see if his small squad understood, Bishop starting moving toward the narrow gap, watching intently as the ambushing enemy maintained a steady rate of fire on the hapless trainees below.

It didn't take long to close the distance, silhouettes of the attackers popping up and firing from the hidden positions in front of Bishop's advancing line. He watched as one guy ignited a string of firecrackers, throwing noisemakers into the fray. Another man rose, spraying several shots into the stunned column and then disappearing behind a tree. There wasn't much return fire coming from his classmates.

Pausing to check the spacing of his men, he turned and hissed, "Let's go *now*! Your brothers are dying down there – roll into these bastards, and don't stop until they're all down!" And then he was moving.

The paintball guns didn't kick or simulate the noise of a real rifle, but it didn't matter. No one cared that blood wasn't really being spilled. Adrenaline and pride were providing plenty of motivation. Yelling at the top of his lungs, Bishop charged into the attackers, catching them completely by surprise. His men mimicked his actions and joined the counterattack, screaming bloody murder and firing their weapons at any target presented. It was all over in a matter of seconds.

Deke rolled over, grinning up at Bishop after an Academy Award-winning death fall. Glancing down at the two red splotches of paint staining his body armor, the operator flashed a thumbs up.

Offering his hand, Bishop helped the contractor to his feet and smiled. "That was one hell of an ambush, Deke. Nice spread on the kill zone. You would've had… what… half of us in the first barrage?"

Nodding while brushing the dirt off his pants, Deke replied, "Yeah. I saw you break off. I figured you'd try and flank us, but you got here quicker than I expected. Nice counter."

Their conversation was interrupted with shouting from below, Nick's voice booming up the mountainside. "Do you see now? Did this little skirmish make the picture crystal fucking clear? If I told you guys once, I told you a dozen times. Don't bunch up! Over half of you are dead or rolling around on the ground in agony and bleeding out right now. There wouldn't be enough of us left to carry off the wounded. You have to pay attention, damn it. The next time it won't be paintballs and firecrackers. It will be hot shrapnel and high velocity lead shredding your bunched up fucking bodies!"

On and on, the tyrant from below continued, the savvy teacher using a combination of embarrassment, military logic, and genuine concern with the shocked students to implant the message in their minds.

While Nick drilled home the lesson, Bishop and the ambushers meandered to the main gathering. Staying to the side, Deke's seven Darkwater contractors watched Nick's classroom antics, keeping their expressions stoic so as not to rub salt in any trainee wounds. Veterans of many campaigns, each of the professional warriors understood the purpose of the exercise. It wasn't ego, pride, or one-upmanship – it was survival. The ambush hadn't been a contest or game, but a tool used to teach a skill… an example hopefully taught with sham weapons now, rather than driven home with dead bodies later.

Besides, they had all been in the students' shoes. They all remembered what the men around them were feeling. It was necessary pain.

The troopers gathered in front of Nick looked sullen and beat. Many were covered with welts and splotches of color, the direct result of stinging paintballs. Others were coated in white, dusty powder – the residue of improvised flash-bang bombs constructed with extra chalk dust for effect. None of the victims looked very happy, a few were downright pissed.

Bishop lingered at the back of the group, showing Nick the respect of listening intently to instructions he had learned so many years ago. He had joined the class to get back in shape after the months-long convalescence required when he encountered a 9mm bullet and spent several hours on the operating table. Still, he worried about the trainees... worried that today's experience would pale to what they might face in the future.

While he listened to Nick reiterate the importance of awareness in the field, Bishop took a quick mental inventory of his performance and how his body was reacting. His legs seemed to ache more than normal, but other than that, he felt like his old self, at least physically. It was a good thing, with the storm clouds of war gathering on the horizon, and every man might be drawn into the looming conflict.

It was his mental outlook that was troubling. While he believed strongly in the cause, the thought of a large-scale conflict knotted his stomach. Had he lost his nerve? The thought was interrupted by the squawk of the radio on his shoulder.

"Bishop? Bishop? This is Diana. Do you read me?"

"Loud and clear, Diana. What's up?"

"It's time, Bishop. You better head back to town. I think Terri is going into labor."

It took the expectant father a moment to digest the news. He looked up to see everyone around him had paused, smiles plastered on their dirty faces. Shrugging with unfelt calm, Bishop pushed the talk button. "Okay, I'm on my way. Tell her not to get started without me."

Before anyone in the class could say a word, Bishop threw down his pack and paintball gun and then was running back down the mountain at full speed.

"It's his first one," noted Nick, addressing the now-chuckling circle of men.

It seemed like Bishop would never cover the three miles back to town, thoughts of Terri giving birth before he could return adding to his negative perception of what seemed like an ever-increasing distance.

After an initial burst of speed, he had to slow his pace. Despite countless hours of exercise and conditioning, he still wasn't up for such a sprint and eventually settled into a reasonable stride. While he ran, Terri's words that morning helped reduce his stress.

"I want you to go to the class, Bishop," she had stated without hesitation. "You're so sweet waiting on me hand and foot, but quite frankly I just want to sleep for a while and relax. Go play warrior games with your friends. I'll be just fine."

"But Terri, you're due any time now," he'd protested. "I feel like I need to be here."

She had hugged him close - well, as close as she could with her huge baby bump. "I want you to go. You're doting me to death, and besides Diana and I have a bunch of work to do this morning. We're running a government, ya know."

"I thought you wanted to sleep?"

Sighing, she'd stood on her tiptoes and kissed his cheek. "I do want a nap, but later. I've got to work a little. Go. Shoot. Blow the hell out of something or whatever the guys do. Recharge that wonderful testosterone. I'll not have a wimpy man about the house."

As he approached Alpha, signs of a growing civilization began to appear. A newly launched logging operation was felling pines in the distance, the humming of saws and other equipment interrupting the calm mountain morning. Wood was now in short supply, the first post-collapse home construction driving much of the demand. *I can't believe we've filled all the empty houses*, he thought. *It seems like only yesterday that half the homes in town were unoccupied.*

A mile outside of the city limits, he reached pavement, the smooth surface helping increase his stride. The second sign of Alpha's progress, the beeping of a car horn, interrupted his thoughts.

Glancing over his shoulder without breaking stride, he spied an older pickup slowing to pull alongside. The bed was full of cow manure and chicken cages. "Let me guess. Is Terri in labor?" A friendly voice called out.

"Yes, sir," Bishop responded between pants.

"Well, hop in, son. I'll cut a few minutes off your trip."

Bishop didn't know the man behind the wheel, but didn't hesitate to accept the ride. Jumping in the truck's cab, he grasped the offered hand. "Able Crenshaw," the older fellow introduced, "I thought I recognized you – you were hustling like a man on his way to have a baby."

Putting the truck back into gear, the driver continued, "I remember my first. I drove Jolene to the hospital at 3 a.m. in the morning. At least your child is being reasonable about the time of day for its arrival."

Chuckling, Bishop nodded. "I feel like the rookie with this father thing. Seems like everyone else has been through the experience already."

The older man grunted, "I remember that feeling too, thinking I was going to mess up or do something wrong. Let me give you a little advice. Relax and don't worry so much about it.

13

Human beings have been procreating for about 150,000 years. Little ones have survived being born in caves, buffalo hide tents and around campfires since we've walked the earth. Somehow they made it, surviving without all the fancy-smancy medical equipment and doctors. The dads made it through too, and most of them knew less than you do. You'll do just fine."

Bishop sized up his chauffeur, the mature, calming voice and common sense soothing his nerves. He estimated the fellow's age at close to 70. The faded overalls and weathered skin were indicative of a man who spent a lot of time outdoors. "By the way, how is it that you know Terri, sir?"

"I fought beside her during the battle of Alpha," he responded. "I was one of the lucky souls holed up at the church for all those months. When we faced conflict to survive, Nick assigned me to her team. I was a little unsure about her at the time, but she fought like a cornered wildcat," the older gent snickered, shaking his head. "That's one hell of a woman you got there, son."

"Oh, she's all that," Bishop responded. Wanting to change the subject, he glanced back at the odd assortment of cargo in the bed. "Hey, I sure appreciate the lift by the way. Did I catch you on your way to the market?"

"Yes, sir. I'm hoping to sell these chickens to be able to fill my gas tank. Then I'm planning to drive down to the river and sell the manure. I hear those farmers down that way are desperate for fertilizer. If I can get a fair price for my cow dung, then I'm going to drive to Meraton and purchase some stuff I've been lacking for a long time. Butter and salt are on top of my list. Toilet paper would be nice. If I could find a bottle of tabasco sauce, I'd be in hog heaven."

Smiling, Bishop said, "You never know what you're going to find at the market. I'm heading to Meraton myself, but not to shop this time. My wife wants to have the baby there."

Nodding wisely, the old rancher offered, "I hear that doctor there is a good sawbones. Talk is you have already given him a test drive or two son, so you ought to have had some opportunity to gauge the quality of his care. You give Miss Terri my best, although I'm sure she won't remember me."

Bishop thanked his benefactor again as he exited the truck, hustling immediately to the small bungalow he and Terri had been occupying. Diana met him at the door.

"Her contractions are still several minutes apart, so there's no need to be crazy rushed. Still, I would get on the road to Meraton sooner rather than later."

Bishop found Terri in the bedroom, surprised to find her reading a stack of papers with a laptop computer open nearby.

She looked up and smiled. "Sorry to interrupt the class," she offered. "I didn't want Diana to bother you, but I guess it's better to be safe than sorry."

Bishop sat on the edge of the bed, holding his bride's hand. Assessing the pile of paperwork, he gently chided, "You're in labor, you know. Are you planning to expand our irrigation system while you bring a new life into the world?"

"I could be in labor for days, Bishop. The pain comes and goes. The work helps take my mind off the contractions. Seriously though, you know how sensitive my nose is these days. You better go hop in the shower, or we'll be driving with the windows down all the way to Meraton. And I would rather not greet my child with bugs between my teeth. Don't worry, Bishop. I'm just fine."

Kissing her on the cheek, he made for the bathroom where he found a fresh set of clothes already laid out. During the quick rinse, his mind was engaged in check listing everything he needed to do for the upcoming event. The truck was already packed with their clothing and gear; its tank full of gasoline. He took a moment to reflect on how lucky they were to have fuel. If the baby had come just a few short months ago, he might not have been able to drive any distance at all. *If you think you're nervous now*, he reflected, *think about how jumpy you would be if you had to deliver the child by yourself out at the ranch.* Despite Terri's reassurances, it was a quick suds, rinse and dry, the pain and soreness he'd felt just minutes before seemingly washed down the drain.

A few last minute items laid beside the bed. As Bishop carried them out, Diana and Terri embraced. "Nick and I will drive down to Meraton as soon as he gets back," the mayor of Alpha promised.

And then they were driving out of town, Terri fussing with the passenger seat's controls. First, she moved the seat back to accommodate her extra girth, then readjusted it slightly forward to enable her to hear Bishop's words with more ease. Next, she tilted the seat back to position herself best for the contractions. Once she managed the more reclining position, she realized she would probably relax more if she were able to enjoy the distractions she could see outside the truck if her seat were raised. Her final undertaking involved finessing the ride through proper engagement of the vehicle's lumbar support in a last ditch effort to get comfortable. The expectant father rarely engaged his wife during the process, but quietly wondered how much more "adjusting" the seat's controls could take.

It was normally an hour's drive to Meraton, but Bishop couldn't keep his foot off the accelerator. Even before society's collapse, the two-lane Texas highway didn't see a lot of traffic. Post-SHTF, it had become even rarer to encounter another traveler. Now, with limited quantities of gas and diesel available, the nervous husband carefully passed the odd straggler now and then.

Terri's condition didn't encourage him to abide by the speed limit. Three times during the journey his bride groaned and arched her back, grimacing in pain. The first two occurrences caused Bishop to question if the child was coming out right there and then. In a way, his naivety helped the tense situation, Terri managing a chuckle despite the pain. He decided to keep his peace during the third contraction.

Twenty miles away from their destination, movement in the rearview mirror caught Bishop's eye. He glanced up to see a police car, lights flashing, rapidly catching up with his pickup. Despite living over a year with scarce traffic enforcement, his heart jumped at the sight, immediately wondering if he was about to receive a speeding ticket. The concern quickly passed, realizing that the few serving deputies had much, much more important things to do than set up speed traps.

The police cruiser passed Bishop, the deputy throwing a friendly wave as he went by. The lawman then pulled past, eventually settling in to provide an escort. "Jezzz, Terri. You'd think you were a VIP or something."

"That's Diana," his wife mused. "She must have called Sheriff Watts and told him we were on our way. How sweet."

"I dunno," the driver retorted. "Maybe he's just in a hurry to pick up some fresh produce at the market."

"Could be. Maybe he heard how I am eating for two and wanted to get in line first." Terri chortled nervously, shifting her weight again to get comfortable.

Before long, the outskirts of Meraton lined the horizon, the appearance providing the couple that warm feeling of returning home. The market seemed to be in full swing, dozens of trucks, horse-drawn wagons and saddled steeds lining the main road.

Bishop turned off Main Street and made for the rear entrance of The Manor, the town's only hotel and acting hospital. Much to the couple's surprise, a welcoming committee flanked the back gate.

Betty was the resort's manager and had bonded with Terri the first night of the couple's arrival after their harrowing bug-out from Houston. The older woman's expression made it clear she was concerned about the impending birth, her relationship with the expectant mom closer to mother-daughter than either of the girls would admit.

Pete, the town's mayor and bartender, was there as well, bookended with two stout-looking lads who obviously had been recruited for some heavy lifting.

As Bishop maneuvered to park the truck, he commented, "Do you think those two big guys with Pete are here to carry in our bags or you?"

"Neither one, my love. I think Diana has been on the shortwave again. She probably told Pete how nervous you've been acting, so he asked them to be here in case you faint," Terri teased.

Without missing a beat, Bishop replied, "Yeah, you're probably right. If they were here for you, they might need reinforcements."

Terri punched his arm in pretend anger, betraying the fact that she actually thought the comment was funny, but also recognizing her mate's tendency for cornball humor in times of high tension.

Bishop shut down the truck, hustling to the passenger side to help Terri safely maneuver her exit. Betty moved in close, anxious to put eyes on Terri and reassure herself that everything was okay. Just as Terri shifted her weight on the footboard to step down, a contraction racked her body.

Bishop scooped her up before she even began to fall, cradling her like a baby and pivoting directly for the hotel's gate. Terri, deciding it was useless to protest her ride, draped her arms around his neck and nuzzled his shoulder while she groaned and breathed through the painful cycle.

"Room number 114," Betty announced as she scrambled to keep pace.

As the couple passed through The Manor's famous gardens, Terri's contraction passed. Coming up for air, she whispered, "I'm glad we're here, my love. I'm glad our child will be born in one of the most beautiful places I've ever seen."

Bishop sensed what his wife was feeling and paused for her to look around. He had to admit, she was right. A full, mid-summer bloom was in effect, an array of color provided by flower and leaf washing over the one-acre enclave. Hummingbirds darted here and there, the tiny flyers enjoying a buffet unlike any other collection of plant life in the area. The perfectly manicured paths, fountains and walkways resonated with calm, projected relaxation.

"You can put me down, Bishop. I can walk now, my hero."

"You sure?"

Smiling, Terri nodded, not wanting to tell her husband that his cradle-carry was actually hurting her back more than helping her legs. She again kissed his cheek after he'd gently positioned her feet on the ground.

Terri took her time meandering toward the room, moving to smell a rare bud, pausing to enjoy the soft brush of a fern frond. Bishop, wary of the inevitable, pending contraction, never left her side.

Pete, after supervising the unloading of the couple's possessions, joined Betty on the porch to watch the young couple tour the gardens. "I adore both of those kids," he commented without taking his eyes away. "They're in love and so good for each other. It just seems to spill over and make you feel like a warm, spring day inside. You know, I miss having that kind of feeling in my own life. I guess that is what we all are looking for," he hinted. Standing alongside the innkeeper, he searched her body language after the comment for a flicker of recognition of his deeper meaning.

Betty reached for a watering can and tipped its contents into a nearby clay pot. "You see people like that every so often in life. What they have doesn't come along every day. You can tell; they're just made to be together."

"This entire town wouldn't be the same if they hadn't showed up," Pete observed, deftly steering the conversation to a more comfortable topic. "They both deserve for this baby to come into the world nice and easy. They've earned a break."

Betty looked up and nodded, her tone protective. "Don't you worry, Mr. Mayor. My girl Terri will do just fine. You go tend your bar and watch over the market. I've got this under control. I promise I will keep you posted as things develop."

Camp David, Maryland
June 7, 2016

The Colonel strolled into the conference room a few minutes early, hoping to review his report one last time before presenting it to his boss, the president of the United States.

Much to his chagrin, General Owens was already sitting at the table, his gaze focused at the large map presented across one wall of the large room. So much for having a few minutes alone.

Looking up, the hero of the Battle at Scott's Hill nodded and smiled at the Colonel. "I thought you might arrive early. How was your evening?"

The Colonel didn't answer immediately, proceeding to unload his briefcase on the table and using the time to compile his response. "It was informative to say the least, General."

The officer didn't respond at first, sizing up the older

man before speaking. Finally, "I wanted to fill you in on a recent event before you brief the Commander in Chief. There's been an incident at Fort Bliss that I thought you should be made aware of."

"In addition to our convoy being hijacked?"

"Yes," Owens replied. "When news of the ambush reached Bliss, General Westfield experienced a small rebellion. He put it down without resorting to arrests or violence, but the man is convinced he'll lose his command if we can't deliver food and other basic supplies soon."

"You've got to hand it to Bishop and Terri," he said. "They are creative, and there's definitely no lack of intestinal fortitude."

"I keep hearing and reading those names, but I've never had the pleasure," the general commented. "Must be one hell of a team."

"I worked with Bishop before the collapse. He's a stand-up guy with better than average skills in a fight. I also trust him. How our beloved army missed that one will always be a mystery, but he did his ROTC and then got out... maybe he was a late bloomer. Anyway, I tried to warn the president that it would be a mistake to underestimate what those people are capable of. They are months ahead of anyplace else in the country as far as recovering from the collapse. I know, over the last few weeks I've visited any place that even hinted at civilization. What I saw while I was out in West Texas actually warmed this old heart. There's a society, government, rule of law and growth. The boss isn't going to like this new turn of events at Bliss."

General Owens shuffled some papers on the table and then glanced toward the door to make sure the two men were still alone. In a low voice, he said, "He already knows, and you're right... he's not a happy camper."

A grimace crossed the Colonel's face. "And I suppose there is no shortage of advisors working overtime on his ear, telling him he needs to lay down the law with those rebels out west."

"Yes, that's exactly what he's thinking."

The Colonel stood and paced, finally settling near the map. After pretending to study it for a bit, he turned abruptly and whispered, "You and I both know the man is being pushed in that direction to cover up the failure of Operation Heartland. That whole thing is a fiasco, and West Texas is nothing more than a sideshow to divert his attention. Those people out there will fight. If anyone thinks for one heartbeat they won't, that would be a mistake."

Nodding, Owens agreed. "He knows that as well.

General Westfield has helped us convince the president of that fact. Still, I think most of the staff underestimates your friends. It seems like everyone around here is thinking of those folks out there as a bunch of country bumpkins."

"That would be a blunder... on so many levels. They just managed to move 300 tons of precious supplies from our side of the ledger to theirs. Is anyone else on our side? Is anyone else pushing for us to work with them, rather than against them?"

Before the general could answer, the door flew open and the executive staff began filing into the room. The line of department heads, military officers and assistants was closely followed by Secret Service Agent Powell, and then the president.

After everyone was seated, the chief executive called the meeting to order. "Colonel, I've read your preliminary report. Are you ready to submit the final version?"

"I am, sir."

And with that, the Colonel began passing around copies of the 15-page document. After everyone had received a copy and settled in, the president cleared his throat to continue.

"So our citizens in West Texas are producing electrical energy via a windmill farm. In addition, they have a refinery up and running, producing just at 500 barrels per day of product. They have expanded the irrigation system along the Rio Grande River, as well as initiated numerous small cultivation projects. Impressive... very impressive."

"I know a few members of their leadership, sir. They are doing an excellent job of integrating new people who relocate to the area, as well as expanding their infrastructure each week. In my opinion, they have recovered further than any other region of North America and are widening that gap every day."

Someone at the far end of the table snorted, mumbling, "By hook or crook."

The Secretary of Energy ignored the remark, "Amazing. I've been through that part of the country and there's nothing but sand and barren rock... maybe a few head of cattle. It's just stunning they've managed to put together what you claim in this report, Colonel."

The president looked around the table, noting most of the attendees were bent over their copies of the document, digesting the details. Addressing at the Secretary of the Interior, he asked, "Mike, have we run the numbers on what their output will do in meeting the goals of Operation Heartland?"

At the end of the table, a young man looked up and replied, "Yes, sir we computed the estimates. If we utilize all of their output, we can advance our timetable by a little over 12%. In addition, we estimate their agricultural production will save approximately 100,000 lives."

The Colonel couldn't keep the grimace off his face, addressing the secretary directly. "You're planning on taking all of their food?"

"No, no, no," interrupted the president. "No one is proposing any such thing. We would leave that region with the bare minimum caloric intake, just like most other Americans are surviving on. They won't eat as well as they are today, but no worse than the average American."

"Sir," the Colonel started, staring hard at President Moreland. "I must inform you that I strongly oppose anything other than a trade relationship with those people out there. I know them, and if this government tries to seize any of their resources, they will resist by any means available. They demonstrated that with the convoy."

The Commander in Chief actually snorted, glancing up from his report. "Yes, Colonel, they've made their intentions clear. Asking for the surrender of a US Army base sends a well-defined message, attacking the convoy was the exclamation point. Still, having the will to fight and the capability are two different matters. Regardless of the political situation out there, my position is based on the moral high ground, not on some need or desire for conquest."

General Owens joined the conversation, "I'm not sure I follow, sir. Moral high ground?"

It was the Secretary of Agriculture's turn. "We have millions of starving citizens. The death toll is rising every day. I believe it would be immoral to let part of the country grow fat while others die of malnutrition."

"I agree wholeheartedly, sir," Owens replied, his calm voice at odds with the obvious disdain behind his eyes. "But we can't just go in and take what people have worked so hard to create. That's not our way... that's not in the constitution I swore an oath to."

The president sat back, observing the interaction. "Gentlemen, must I remind everyone that we are still in a state of martial law? We have both the legal and moral right to do the best for *all* of our citizens. The people of West Texas may experience an outbreak of smallpox next month. Wouldn't everyone at this table agree to divert medical care to that region? Right now, they have more fuel and food than anywhere else in our land, and I for one believe we should utilize those resources in a way that provides the most benefit to the greatest number of people."

General Owens considered his commander's words carefully before responding. "Sir, I'm with the Colonel on this one.

Surely, we can come up with some method of barter or trade. Out military is stretched to the limit. Even a small scale fight would overtax our available resources and delay Operation Heartland even further."

"I agree," the Colonel supported, "Their leaders would welcome barter or fair payment of some sort."

The Secretary of Energy responded, "Even if we did have something of value to trade, they would only sell us a small percentage of what they are producing. I think it would be unwise to even attempt negotiations, especially given the number of people we are burying each day. Every pound of food is critical right now, and I won't support any plan that has part of the nation fat and happy while others starve."

And so the debate raged for over an hour.

It was General Owens who finally brought the issue to a head. "Mr. President, should I be drawing up plans to invade West Texas?"

Bedlam broke out around the table. Already frustrated men began to raise their voices and use foul language. The Commander in Chief finally slammed his palm on the table to call order.

"Gentlemen, this is getting out of hand!"

After the outburst, only the gentle hum of the ventilation system could be heard in the room. Most of the men seated around the table looked down or away, not wanting to make eye contact with their peers, or the president.

The general's question had brought the issue to a head, Moreland weighing his options. Sighing audibility, the chief executive finally reached his decision, "To answer your question General Owens, no, you should not draw up plans to move troops into our own territory. There will be no invasion, or large-scale military action. Our people have suffered enough already. I'm going to send in a team to negotiate with the people of West Texas, and you, general, are going to head up that effort. This meeting is adjourned."

Chapter 2

Meraton, Texas
June 7, 2016

"Give me my pistol, and I'll end your miserable existence right now!" Terri growled, her eyes piercing into Bishop, wild with fire and anger… and pain. "You lowlife, worthless pile of shit. I hate you!"

Bishop held her hand, squeezing it firmly, holding on. *Nick warned me*, he remembered. *What did he call it? "Transition."*

The expectant father still remembered how his friend's counsel had been tempered with humor, coupled with what Bishop hoped was a little hyperbole. "Now, it has been quite a few years since I was in your shoes. But in my birthing class, the nurse warned about a phase called transition. That bride of yours is going to hurt from her hair follicles to her tippy toes. She is going to be nauseous and have chills and half a minute later, she is going to be telling you to turn on the air conditioning because of the sweats. I'm telling you, man, it is like the pain causes some kind of chemical imbalance in the brain or something. She is going to struggle to manage these intense feelings her body is having, and your job is to ride it out as best you can. Anyway, be ready for her to spout some crazy shit, brother. My wife claimed I had shot her sister in cold blood. She begged the delivery room nurse to call the cops and have me arrested. Problem was my wife didn't have a sister. She was an only child. You gotta know this is coming and just roll with it."

"I love you, Terri," he said warmly, in line with Nick's advice. "Can I do anything to help?" his hand brushing her cheek to offer comfort. "You know I'd take the pain for you, if I could."

Her eyes changed, rage no longer contorting her face. "You know I love you, too."

She leaned back, still panting from the last contraction, the stack of high pillows against the headboard elevating her head, her torso partially upright. The doctor glanced at his watch. "They're three minutes apart. We're in the home stretch now."

Betty reached across the bed, brushing the hair from Terri's face and offering a cold washcloth. "You're doing great, sweetheart," she cooed. "You're doing just fine."

Bishop relaxed for a moment, appreciating the older woman's presence during the process. Terri's decision to have the baby in Meraton had been a point of contention. He had lobbied for Midland Station, the larger town equipped with a real hospital, more medical resources and skilled personnel. He wanted every option available, just in case something went wrong.

Terri had insisted on traveling to Meraton, her argument a belief that "People are more important than any ol' equipment." Now that they were here and actually experiencing childbirth, he understood her desire.

The Manor was an old friend in so many ways. Yes, there had been a gun battle here – a fight that Bishop was sure had ended his life. Despite that memory, the grand gardens and peaceful atmosphere of the landmark hotel held a special place in the couple's hearts.

As he watched Betty mothering his wife, Bishop realized his spouse's longing to return to Meraton ran much deeper than just the hotel. It was the town, its people, and energy that drew her. He had to agree.

Meraton had been an oasis after the collapse. The tiny berg had shrugged off society's downfall, banded together and carried on. The simpler life and slower pace of West Texas hadn't been so addicted to government, services and infrastructure. When everything extravagant went to hell, the self-sufficient population and surrounding ranches hadn't suffered nearly as much as most of the planet.

Terri and Bishop had resided in Houston when the US experienced financial devastation. They had tried to ride out the ever-increasing tide of anarchy, working hard to persist and keep their neighborhood safe. Over the weeks, it became clear that living next to a starving, desperate population center just wasn't a long-term survival option. They had bugged out, heading for the land of Bishop's childhood, an inherited hunting retreat nestled in the mountains of West Texas.

The journey across the Lone Star State had almost ended their lives. It seemed like every few miles offered a different challenge. It had taken weeks, expended all of their resources, and nearly destroyed their faith in mankind.

They had limped into Meraton out of gas, low of food, and desperate for reprieve from a world gone crazy. The 600-mile drive across Texas had left the couple feeling like life could never be normal again… that there was no future. Meraton changed all that, providing an optimism that was so critical. Hope was something they had needed badly. Could the birth of a little one solidify that hope?

Terri looked like hell. Her hair was stringy, drenched in perspiration, skin pale from exhaustion. Yet, despite the hours of agonizing pain, Bishop was proud of his bride. She had shown grit and determination, and that was all anyone could ask.

Bishop glanced at himself in the hotel room's mirror. *I don't look much better*, he admitted, noting the dark circles under his eyes, his face taunt from the rollercoaster of stress and worry, and then relief as the contractions passed.

"Terri, I'm seeing some really good dilation," the doctor commented. "That's a very positive sign. I don't think we're going to have to wait much longer."

The down time between her bouts of pain seemed to pass far too quickly. "Here we go again," she managed between her clenched teeth. Bishop moved to comfort, wishing he could do more as her head rolled back, and the howl of agony leapt from her throat. Panting. Deep inhalation. Screaming until her lungs were emptied.

And then it passed.

"On the next one, I need you to push," announced the doctor. "Do it just like we talked about. Bishop, keep reminding her to push. Your job is to be a cheerleader for Team Push."

The waves of hurt came much quicker, hardly a minute going by. "Push!" commanded the doc. Bishop squeezed Terri's hand, "Come on... push and breathe... push and breathe... that's it."

"The baby's coming, Terri. Keep pushing. Almost there. Just a little longer."

Then a new life arrived, a new person where there hadn't been one just a moment before. A new set of lungs inhaled for the first time – a new voice joined the choir of humanity. *A miracle*, he realized. *I've heard so many new parents use that word. I thought it was cliché. It truly is a miracle.*

Terri's position did not provide a good line of vision for the events now taking place, and she was craning to see. In a voice that betrayed her physical exhaustion, Terri prodded her husband for information. "How does the baby look? Is it healthy?"

Bishop took his eyes from Terri's for barely a moment to secure the update. There was blood – more blood than he expected, and it worried him. Beyond, he saw the doctor's hands moving in a blur, Betty standing nearby. It was the older woman's expression that told him everything was okay. Her eyes were filled with a mixture of confidence and joy.

"They're cleaning the baby up now," Bishop narrated for Terri. His eyes caught the movement of a swirling, pristine white towel, Betty's hands moving with both speed and grace. Moments later, she was standing beside Terri, offering a bundle. A tiny, wrinkly face was all Bishop could see. Crinkled, purple and bloody, that miniature image of humanity poking out from the white softness of its swaddle was the most wonderful sight he had ever experienced.

"Nine hours of labor," the doctor commented, writing in his journal. "I know it didn't seem like it at the time, but for a first child, that's not so bad. Mother and child are doing well. The APGAR score is good."

Bishop's head was spinning from it all. The long sessions of suffering endured by the woman who owned his heart and soul. The agony in his wife's screams. The sound of the baby breathing and its thin wail of life.

Betty was whispering to Terri, kissing her forehead after sharing the secret. For just a moment, Bishop felt a little left out, but it passed. He would never bear children – was excluded from the club. He understood that a connection had been forged between the two women that was not dissimilar to the bonding he had experienced in combat.

"Bishop," croaked Terri's hoarse voice. "Would you like to hold our son?"

"Yes... I would love to hold our.... Did you say... a boy?"

"Yes, it's a boy."

Death was a constant companion. Like a faint shadow on a gray day, the need to take life had stalked Bishop – always looming, a harbinger of what hid over the next hill of his life. So many times the Texan had pulled a trigger or wielded a blade. So many lives taken, each loss corroding a part of his soul.

The void wasn't filled with guilt or despair - just emptiness. Each death at his hand removed a spoonful of his inner being. He realized that if it continued, eventually he would end his days as a hollowed-out shell of a man, reliving nightmares and wondering what the afterlife would bring to a soul that had ended the existence of so many of his kind.

But not today.

As Terri handed him the tiny bundle, new life-energy filled his core. For the first time, he was on the opposite side of the equation - creating, not destroying.

And he liked it.

The new mother watched, beaming with pride as her mate accepted his son for the first time. Bishop could have easily held the tiny wrap in one hand, but didn't, instead cupping his palms together as if the infant weighed a hundred times its meager size.

It was the extreme of the dichotomy that filled her with bliss. Bishop's corded arms, so strong and capable, wrapping ever so gently around the helpless, fragile newborn. She hoped the child would feel the protection of those arms, the safety that laid within, just as she had experienced on so many occasions.

Bishop's expression flashed a carousel of emotions, like a revolving door of honesty opening to his inner heart. After pulling the baby close to his chest, he gazed at his mate, smiling but unsure if he were holding the fragile package correctly. The tentative moment quickly passed, replaced with his pure fascination at what he held in his arms.

"He's perfect," Bishop pronounced, again meeting his wife's eyes.

When the newborn found Bishop's finger and squeezed, the father's smile widened. "You're strong. Aren't ya, big fella?"

I'll teach you everything you need to know, thought Bishop. *Your mother and me, we'll fill you with honor and wisdom. You'll neither bully, nor run. We will teach you the value of integrity and make you aware of the treachery of men. You'll know right from wrong and won't be afraid to act upon that knowledge. We will give you the opportunity to improve our world – to make this a better place.*

It was a wonderful, silent moment for Terri and Bishop. He somewhat gingerly perched on the edge of the bed so as to share the precious treasure with her – the woman with whom he had created this new life.

Betty, not wanting to interrupt, padded to the door and exited as quietly as the old hinges would allow. Outside, one of Pete's helpers slumped on a bench, the lad clearly bored but unwilling to leave his assigned station.

"You can go tell Pete that Meraton has a new son. The baby is healthy, and the mother is doing just fine. Tell him I estimate it weighs somewhere around seven or seven and a half pounds. Ten fingers. Ten toes. Now repeat it back to me."

The young man did as he was instructed and in so doing was released by The Manor's caretaker, scampering off toward Pete's Place, excited to deliver the news.

When the door to the local watering hole burst open, Pete and several dozen customers all peered up with anticipation. Less than a minute later, glasses were being raised throughout the bar. Excited toasts of "It's a boy!" could be heard clear to the other end of Main Street.

The messenger's next stop was the town's ham radio operator. Moments later, his hands worked in a familiar blur across the knobs of the glowing transmitter, his voice informing listeners in all of the towns that made up the West Texas Alliance of the good news.

In Fort Stockdale, Midland Station, Alpha and other

communities scattered throughout the region, celebrations broke out. Someone launched a few bottle rockets in Fort Davidson. A police officer rolled through the streets of Odyssey, broadcasting the birth announcement on his patrol car's loudspeaker. Prayers were whispered at a small church, an excited usher passing the pastor a handwritten note, the news warranting an interruption of the carefully prepared sermon.

It wasn't that Bishop and Terri's baby was the first to be born after the apocalypse. There had been a handful of healthy children enter what was now a vastly changed world. No, the celebrations were due to an unspoken confidence... a reassurance demonstrated by one of the region's best known families. Terri was wildly popular among the people, her act validating that the world was indeed a good enough place to raise a child. Terri had faith – why shouldn't they?

Despite an unknown future that threatened war and a dozen other major problems, one of their leaders had brought a new life into existence. Like the pre-collapse birth of a royal in England, or the first child born of a new year, the news traveled fast, and for just a brief moment, the biggest concern on their collective minds was speculation over the newcomer's name.

Nick scrambled with one of his quick reaction forces, a dozen pairs of boots pounding along Alpha's sidewalks. The few citizens out at the early hour made way for the heavily armed men, unsure if it was another drill or the real thing.

Burdened with full combat loads, body armor and Kevlar helmets, the team rushed for the courthouse, separating into three groups as the landmark structure came into view. From the other side of the square, Nick spotted Deke and his contractors taking their predefined positions.

Word of a single Humvee entering Alliance territory had arrived a few hours ago, detected by the picket line of scouts watching the border. One of deputies had pulled the vehicle over shortly afterward, inquiring politely regarding the driver's intent.

"We are on our way to Alpha," had been the response from the four men inside. "Our job is to secure an agreement with the local authorities."

A wave of relief had flooded the fledgling organization's leaders. *Washington is finally acting logically*, they all thought. *We can avoid war.*

While Nick was as excited as anyone, he wasn't about

to be on the receiving end of a surprise like he'd just delivered to the convoy commander. "We'll let them approach without any hassle, but I want a show of strength when they arrive," he'd told Diana.

"Okay, but don't overdo it. Without Terri being here, I just want to buy us time and see what they're thinking. But... and this is a critical point... I don't want to scare them off."

And so the limited response to the diplomatic overture was deemed appropriate.

Ten minutes later, the Humvee rolled to a stop in front of the Alliance's main government building. Nick made sure his men were visible, but not intimidating. One of the visitors was an army general who seemed to take a strong interest in the placement of the security personnel.

Nick escorted the men into the courthouse after satisfying himself they weren't a threat. Diana met the four visitors in the conference room, smiling politely and offering refreshments.

After everyone was settled in and introductions were exchanged, General Owens began. "Miss Brown, we are here at the direct request of President Moreland. The president feels that a series of misunderstandings, combined with a lack of direct communication, are leading to a potentially hostile situation. This delegation's job is to address those issues."

Diana waxed diplomatic, her tone polite and smooth. "Thank you for clarifying that, General. Let me make it perfectly clear, right from the start – the last thing the people of our region want is conflict. We've all suffered enough violence and hardship. We only want to be left alone to improve our daily lives."

The man who had identified himself as an undersecretary of the Interior spoke up. "Do you have any interest in helping your fellow Americans?" The question drawing a harsh look from General Owens.

"We do, and we are, sir." Diana responded immediately. "We have welcomed and assisted thousands of refugees in the past few months, each individual provided with food, medical care and housing. Those multitudes, if not here, would be burdening your efforts in other parts of the country."

"That is a valid perspective," another of the visitors responded, "but there is the lingering issue of scale and equality. In addition to the reports we have received, I could see with my own eyes as we drove in - your people are living at a much higher standard than the rest of the country. Millions are hungry and existing without even basic services. We in Washington feel like a portion of your resources could assist tens of thousands more if properly distributed."

"We are not opposed to helping, as a matter of fact, we would welcome the opportunity. What would not be acceptable is an arbitrary seizure of our assets. All indications, both official and unofficial, have relayed Washington's intent as just that. This, no doubt, has led to your 'potentially hostile situation,' General."

The man from interior, despite General Owens's prior visual warning, couldn't hold his tongue. "We aren't here for crumbs and leftovers, Miss Brown," the man hissed. "It is ridiculous for you to assume that we would allow your people to thrive while the rest of the nation struggles."

Diana almost broke out laughing at the man, barely winning an internal struggle to remain nonplused. "I don't recall anyone offering crumbs and leftovers, sir. Our position is that a rising tide will lift all ships, and we would like nothing more than to be in the harbor. But let me be clear. We aren't just going to hand over our livelihood. Offer us fair value, and I'll wager you'll be pleasantly surprised at both our patriotic spirit as well as our sense of fair play."

"What is it you need, ma'am?" General Owens asked, finally getting to the crux of the matter.

The leaders of the Alliance had spent countless hours debating the answer to the officer's question. Even in such a small, newly formed community, there were already special interest groups vying for influence and attempting to steer the council along a course that benefited their constituents.

It had been Terri who had navigated the potential minefield, forcing every member of the ruling body to keep the long term needs of the Alliance at the forefront of their thoughts. "We're falling into the same trap that plagued Washington for years and eventually led to the downfall. We already have lobbyists. Let's learn from that lesson and not repeat the same mistakes," the pregnant woman had demanded.

Diana reached into her briefcase, producing a single, typewritten page. "We have complied a list of items, all having some value with our ongoing projects. Most of the list involves initiatives to increase our output of food and electricity. If you have access to these items, we hope to produce an even larger overage. That extra food could save thousands of lives. Provide us some of the tools, and we'll deliver the goods."

The four men from Washington huddled over the single copy provided. While they read, Diana watched their faces carefully, naturally looking for reactions to the document. She was entertained by a wide-ranging display of emotion, most of it negative.

The undersecretary dismissed the list with a wave of his hand. "Every community in the country is desperate for these same items, madam. If we had access to what you're asking for, we wouldn't be here right now."

Mayor Brown ignored the initial rejection, "Surely the government of the United States can come up with some of those items."

General Owens, again acting as the voice of reason, responded. Scanning the paper, he began reading a few of the entries out loud. "Valves, electrical wire, various chemical compounds... I'm afraid my colleague is right, Miss Brown, those assets are in high demand and short supply."

"And the rest of the list, sir? Are you telling me there is no fertilizer available? What about medical personnel and supplies – did all of the doctors and dentists die in the collapse? You are asking my people to sacrifice, and yet you appear to be unwilling to do so yourselves."

The undersecretary wasn't having any of it. "You are nothing more than greedy capitalists trying to extort from those who desperately need what resources are available. Even if we did have these items on hand, every single asset is being utilized to help the rest of the country."

Diana grunted, the smirk on her face condescending. "You mean like the 300 plus tons of supplies we just impounded... supplies that were being transported so that the army could move against us... come in and take whatever people like you believed we could do without."

There was no convincing the man from Interior. His expression was dismissive, throwing Diana a look as if to say, "You wouldn't understand."

General Owens, however, was the ultimate authority at the table. He smiled at the mayor of Alpha's point, conceding, "There may be some items on this list we can produce, if the value of exchange is fair. However, the first step is the return of the supply convoy your people seized."

Diana wondered if the two most verbal of her visitors were intentionally playing some sort of good-cop, bad-cop game that had been agreed upon before their visit. Dismissing that train of thought, she managed a smile at the general and replied, "Again, we are willing to sit and negotiate a mutually beneficial agreement, but I don't have the sole authority to commit to any bargain. I'll assemble our council tomorrow if you gentlemen would like to stay and see this through. More to your point, General, we would be willing to return the confiscated supplies once an agreement has been reached."

Owens was clearly disappointed in the response. "I will contact Washington and report on today's meeting. I was hoping additional escalations could be avoided, but now I'm not so sure.

We'll be back in touch, one way or the other."

The visiting delegation from Washington left to return to Fort Hood, their faces solemn.

After the Humvee was out of sight, Diana turned to Nick, "What do you make of that?"

The big man rubbed his chin, "At least they are willing to talk. I think that's a positive sign."

"It wasn't a good start, that's for sure."

"It's progress," Nick observed. "What's the phrase the politicians used? Cautiously optimistic? That's what I am… cautiously optimistic."

Chapter 3

Terri, true to her word, took the entire week off. The effort was forwarded in no small part by Bishop's feigned forgetfulness, sneaking his wife's laptop out of her overnight bag before leaving Alpha. The recovery period was necessary for the new mom, partly because she needed a break, but mostly because the news that Washington wanted to work something out gave her a little time. At minimum, there would be talk before war.

As word got around, all of the citizens of the Alliance exhaled, the burden of war lifted from their shoulders, at least for a while. Bishop wasn't so sure, but kept quiet, not wanting to spoil the bonus to what had already been their best time together.

The couple spent those heady days getting to know the newest member of their family, relaxing in the gardens and shopping in the market.

On the second day of their hiatus, the doctor stopped in to check on mother and child. After a quick examination of both, he commented, "Time to complete an official birth certificate, that is, as official as any paperwork is these days. Have you two decided what are you going to name the baby?"

It wasn't a new topic, but a subject both mom and dad had discussed numerous times before the infant made his debut. They had reached an agreement – if the baby were a girl, Terri would choose the name. Dad would choose if the child were a boy.

Despite that understanding, neither parent wanted to risk offending the other. Terri had helped Bishop narrow down the choices – two names she would willingly embrace.

"Hunter," replied Bishop, looking at his wife to judge her reaction. "I've always liked that name."

The doctor, wise to the intricacies of domestic relationships, didn't write it down until Terri had nodded her acceptance. Hunter it was.

The child didn't seem to care what he was called, as long as Terri provided timely meals.

"He's just like his father," she noted, cradling little Hunter while he nursed for the fourth time that day. "Fascinated with boobs."

"That's my boy."

On the third day, Terri announced she was suffering from cabin fever. "Walking the hotel halls allows me to stretch my legs a bit, but I need fresh air and a real walk. I'll be a little slow, but I'm going to get mean if I don't get out of this building."

Bishop wasn't sure Terri's strolling outside was such a good idea, having witnessed the amount of blood and pain involved in childbirth and mindful of the natural twists and turns to the paths in The Manor's gardens. Terri, as usual, prevailed. Betty served as babysitter while Bishop stayed close to his mate, still unsure of his wife's equilibrium.

The next day, she declared "retail therapy" was in order.

"Okay, I'll stay here with Hunter."

"Why?" the new mother had inquired.

Bishop was nervous about the step. "Don't you think it's a little early to be taking him outside?"

"He's got to go out eventually. He seems healthy enough. Go find a stroller if you don't want to carry him."

Shaking his head, Bishop replied, "He doesn't weigh anything. That's not my point. I worry about… about germs and such. You know, it is not like we can just head down to the corner drugstore if he gets sick these days."

Terri took her husband's hand and squeezed lovingly. "He'll be fine, Bishop. We'll keep the sun off of him, and he'll love it."

And so it was decided. The trio ventured forth on their first excursion as a family.

Hunter was an immediate celebrity. When the family exited the front doors of The Manor, a wave of silence swept the market, all heads pivoting to see what the fuss was about. Moments later, a single soul started clapping, and the applause spread up and down the busy street. Bishop turned to his wife and whispered, "I know it's been a while since they've seen me, but this is a little over the top."

Terri, despite having recently given birth, proved she could still punch with considerable force, her husband's arm receiving the impact.

Then there was what Bishop later coined, "The press of flesh." People, anxious to see the baby, began approaching from every direction, eventually forming a tight ring around the proud parents. Terri lost count of the hugs, cheek kisses and well wishes she received. Bishop must have shaken at least 50 hands. Hunter proved himself a charmer, opening his blue eyes and simply being cute.

Eventually, the bedlam subsided, and the couple started their tour of the market. They hadn't progressed more than 20 steps when Betty's scorn rang out above the hum of activity.

What are you two doing?"

Terri turned, smiling at her friend. "We decided to get out and about for a bit. Why? What's wrong?"

"Oh, I thought you were going shopping without looking at your gifts first."

"Gifts?" Terri asked, throwing Bishop a questioning look.

Betty nodded, "People have been delivering baby gifts for two days. I've got a lobby full of toys and clothes on one side. A stroller, car seat and playpen line the other side with barely room to navigate to the front desk. Sheriff Watts even dropped off two cases of disposable diapers."

Bishop was embarrassed by it all, every corner of The Manor's common room stacked with boxes, some even adorned with wrapping paper, bows, and ribbons.

"Oh my," Terri's reacted. "I wasn't expecting this."

"Well, you can leave it here for a while, but I'm going to need my lobby back eventually."

Bishop glanced down at Hunter, "You're only three days old, and already you have accumulated more stuff than I have. Way to go, kid."

After scanning the collection, the couple returned to the market, meandering here and there – simply enjoying the day. At one point, Terri engaged in a political conversation with a group of ladies selling handmade cloth, the product of a local loom. Bishop, bored with the topic, excused himself and decided Hunter was old enough to visit his first saloon.

Pete, as usual, was behind the bar. The smile that broke out across his face when Bishop and his son entered was brighter than the sunlight that flooded through the open door.

"Two beers," Bishop teased.

"Coming right up," Pete responded, never missing a beat.

"Actually, I'd love a cup of coffee if you have any. I think my friend here is fine."

There were few patrons at the early hour, most taking advantage of Pete's secret coffee stash. All of them abandoned their steaming mugs, moving to catch a view of the bundle Bishop protected in his arms.

After pouring Bishop's order, Pete demanded to hold the community's newest citizen. "After all, Terri said I was going to be the lad's godfather. We should get acquainted."

"Support his head," Bishop joked, finally handing Hunter over.

Pete grunted at the instructions. "I've held more infants than I can remember. Support his head, indeed."

The mayor of Meraton abandoned his duties behind the

bar, instead choosing to give his new godson a tour of the facilities. Bishop sipped his joe as Hunter made the circuit; each neon sign, window and table a point of interest and deserving a softly voiced explanation from the proprietor.

Pete was in a back corner when Terri came hustling inside. "Where's our son?" she inquired immediately.

"I don't know. I thought you had him?" Bishop teased, trying desperately to keep a straight face.

The effort failed, but Terri played along, responding in her best western twang. "I thought I'd find you here... you... you no good bum. Here I trust you with our firstborn child, and what do you do the first chance you get? You sneak off to a saloon. You go out drinking! Mr. Mayor, I believe we may have a case of 'contributing to the delinquency of an incredibly tiny minor.'"

Bishop's snort quickly turned into a full blown chuckle, his wife matching the laughter. Pete appeared, cooing at Hunter who seemed no worse the wear from his adventure.

"Hi, Mom," Pete greeted, happy to see Terri up and about.

Terri held out her arms, but Pete hesitated to return the swaddled bundle. "Now don't be in an all fired hurry there, missy. I'm bonding with the boy. Letting him know he's got friends in high places."

On a roll, Terri couldn't resist. "He already knows that, Pete. Betty has been smothering him with kisses for days."

Bishop, delighted not to be the butt of the joke for once, snorted out a mouthful of coffee and then tried to laugh and choke at the same time.

Good natured as always, Pete tried to pretend insult, but just couldn't pull it off.

The mayor cradled the babe in the crook of his arm, continuing the tour of the establishment until Hunter began to fuss. "He's probably hungry... again," Terri said, checking the diaper first. Finding no need for a change, Terri glanced around until she spied a dark corner. Retrieving an extra receiving blanket from the bag for modesty, she announced, "I'll be back in a minute, boys. I'm going to feed this bottomless pit."

The next day brought the arrival of Uncle Nick and Aunt Diana, as they introduced themselves. After Bishop's naming of Pete as the godfather, Terri had asked Diana if she would fill the corresponding maternal role. "I'd be honored," Diana replied, "as long as I get all the snuggling I can handle."

And so the couple spent their weeklong retreat showing off their new addition to countless visiting dignitaries and friends. Visitors came from all over the Alliance, including Mr. Beltran, DA Gibson and a host of others. Bishop was convinced the kid was

Senate bound, based purely on his early political connections.

"I'm more exhausted than before our little every-four-hours alarm clock arrived," Bishop noted as he packed up as many of the gifts as would fit in the truck.

"I know what you mean. I anticipated that having a baby would leave me a smidge tired. Hunter is easy compared to the demands of his social calendar. I look forward to a little private time," agreed Terri.

"I can't wait to get back to that punishment Nick calls a training class. The good Lord knows I need the rest," Bishop snickered as he piled a playpen on top of the mounting kiddie booty.

The drive back to Alpha was the most quiet the new parents had enjoyed since the birth. Even Hunter appeared to agree, the steady lull of the truck's movement encouraging his lids to fall before Meraton faded behind them.

Alpha proved only slightly more reserved than Meraton, the couple finding more gifts stacked inside their living room after entering the house. "I wish everyone hadn't spent their hard earned money on us," observed Terri. "We already had everything we really needed."

"They wanted to give something back, Terri."

"I know, I know… but still. You are going to have to enlarge the west wing of the ranch to accommodate all these goodies, my love. How are you with architectural drawings?"

"At least we know the mayor of Meraton personally. Should help us get a building permit without too much hassle," Bishop joked. "Seriously, Terri. All that work you have been doing with the Alliance is resurrecting the region's hope of a somewhat normal existence. I'll figure out something for little Hunter's mounting pile of stuff; you just keep rebuilding a future in West Texas for our son."

Alpha, Texas
June 18, 2016

The weight room at the university hadn't been looted, per say. Someone, no doubt starving, had ransacked the extensive facility probably looking for protein bars, but the equipment had been left intact. Once the content of the lockers and gym bags had been cleaned up, a few of the men had taken to visiting what had quickly become known as "Club Apocalypse."

Bishop was having a good day at the club.

His pre-collapse job in corporate security had demanded a high level of conditioning. Guarding oil company executives and equipment in some of the world's most dangerous places wasn't a career for the weak or slow. Because of this, he was well aware of what his body was capable of, as well as its limits. Before the terrorist attacks, he had considered himself the equal of any professional athlete as far as being fit. It was just part of his job… a part he enjoyed immensely.

Then everything went to hell, a general lack of caloric intake prohibiting exercise. Adjusting the weight-pin on a machine, Bishop recalled those lean days. After society fell, it was less than two months before he noticed how loosely his clothes were hanging from his frame. It wasn't long after that before his wardrobe became downright baggy. For both Terri and him, body fat became a thing of the past.

It wasn't just the volume of food available. For months, a well-balanced diet wasn't part of the equation. Filling your stomach didn't necessarily translate into eating healthy. Fresh fruits and green vegetables were often in short supply. Lifting weights for pleasure or training was absurd when there were barely enough calories for a body to survive. Energy was better invested in hunting and gathering more grub.

In the last few months, all of that had been reversed. Not only was Bishop eating well, but his convalescence had resulted in less physical activity. Hearty meals, combined with the fact that people weren't shooting at him every day, resulted in a gradual weight gain and lack of tone. Time to exercise his body.

And today was a good day.

Pushing hard against the weight-bar for the final set, he was happy with his progress. For some of the routines, he was back to pre-collapse performance. For a few of the endurance exercises, he had set new personal bests. Membership in Club Apocalypse was proving beneficial.

The sound of the doorknob interrupted Bishop's mental victory lap. Looking up, he nodded as Deke entered the room.

"I thought I might find you here, Slick," he greeted.

"What's up, operator?"

"How's the shoulder?"

"I'm back to 100%, at least on the weights and mobility. Damn, it's been a long, hard road."

Nodding, Deke seemed to drift off for a moment before replying. "Back when I was with the forces, I took a 7.62 slug in the hip. I remember the pain of getting back in the saddle. Just remember, pain is only weakness leaving your body."

Bishop laughed, "Save that bullshit for some recruit. Pain hurts, dude."

Deke chuckled, "Well, I had to say it… you know, for old time's sake."

As Bishop dried the perspiration off his face with a

towel, Deke shuffled his feet and looked down. Finally, he came out with it, sort of. "I came by to ask how Ms. Terri is doing."

"She's good, considering," Bishop began. His tone then became reflective. "How do women do that... I mean hump around a baby like that? I've carried a heavy ruck my fair share, but you eventually take it off. Until the baby was born, she was stuck with it 24-7. Then after all that, she suffers through hours of teeth grinding pain, loses about 10 gallons of fluid and half her blood during birth. But the fun's not over. Now, she has to get up every few hours to feed the lad."

Deke shook his head, "I hear ya. Amazing shit. They're stronger than we give them credit for, I think."

Bishop's visitor seemed to hesitate, almost as if he were summoning courage. Deke finally spilled what was on his mind. "I've got an issue building on my team, and I think it's getting serious. Grim's lost contact with his wife and daughter, and it's driving him crazy. He was getting the occasional message via Phil through the shortwave, but that stopped two weeks ago... just went cold-silent. Grim wants to mount a rescue. Half the team wants to go with him; the other half quietly thinks it's a suicide mission."

"Where do they live?"

"Middle Tennessee."

"Oh shit. That's like on the other side of the world these days."

"Yeah. We gave up hope of our employer retrieving us months ago. Mr. King had moved Darkwater's headquarters to Dubai a few years ago, and we've tried a hundred times to get through on the satellite phone. No one answers. Most of the guys are divorced, or like me and never married. A few left their wife and kids with family and are pretty confident they're safe. Grim, though, didn't have that luxury. He's a good man, but worrying about them is making him stupid. I caught him packing up to head out on his own two days ago. It took a lot of persuasion to cool his jets."

Bishop was familiar with the issue, and not just with Deke's man. The topic was part of daily conversation within the community as a whole.

Just like his exercise, contact with distant family and friends had taken a backseat to eating and security post-SHTF. Now that everyone's day wasn't completely preoccupied with day-to-day survival, people had the time to wonder about children, siblings and other pre-collapse relationships. Without phones, email or a post office, contact with relatives living far away was next to impossible. The few shortwave radio operators up and running did their best, but there just wasn't that many of them to form any sort of cohesive network.

"Anyway," Deke continued, "I was thinking of approaching your wife and asking if my team could acquire some gas, a vehicle and the other necessary supplies... should we decide to mount up and bring Grim's family back here."

Bishop shrugged his shoulders, "I don't see why not. You and your team have contributed as much as anyone since you've been here."

"Thanks for that, but... well... I didn't know what kind of reception I'd receive approaching her with hat-in-hand. After all, we did kidnap her, and some people hold a grudge over shit like that."

Laughing, Bishop recalled the incident that had brought Deke and his men into the community. Subconsciously rubbing his shoulder where the bullet had almost ended his life, he then shook his head to clear the cloudy, dark thoughts.

"Deke, that entire situation was fucked. You guys didn't know what was going on, and Terri and I didn't have a clue. I don't think she holds a grudge."

"We Tasered a pregnant woman, for God's sake. We didn't know she was with child, but still..."

Bishop interrupted, "And she shot one of you in the chest, didn't she?"

Nodding with a smile, Deke replied, "Yup. That was me. Thank the Lord for condoms and body armor."

"And I shot one of your men out at the ranch, right?"

Deke didn't reply, taking his turn to relive a troubled episode.

After a bit, Bishop continued. "Look, those were some crazy times. All of us did shit we regret. You also shot Nick's son, and I tried like hell to kill all of you out at the ranch. Before some measure of order was restored, it was just insane, and everyone knows that. Your team did the right thing once the truth came out, and that's all anyone can ask these days."

It took the operator a few moments to digest Bishop's words. Nodding, he said, "Any chance you'd tag along to echo some of that wisdom to your wife? Put in a good word for us?"

Bishop's brow wrinkled, "No, that I can't do. If I went with you, people might think I was lobbying on your behalf. We have hundreds of folks in the same spot, and I've got to remain impartial. I've had friends who had kids in college when everything fell apart, and they begged me to go retrieve their children. I couldn't. Almost every day someone approaches me with the same problem, and there's no way we can go retrieve every single citizen's loved one."

Deke frowned, not liking Bishop's answer.

Bishop sighed, clearly uncomfortable with delivering bad news. "Yesterday, Miss Emily approached me in tears. You know the lady I'm talking about – she works as a volunteer at the new clinic."

"Yeah, I know her... super sweet older lady who mothers everyone that comes in."

"Yup, that's the one. Anyway, she caught me walking down the street yesterday morning and asked... no begged me to go to Denver and bring back her sister. She's been having nightmares about her sibling being hungry and suffering badly. She confessed to feeling guilt with every bite of food she puts in her mouth. The sister would be 68 years old, if she's still alive. Given what we've heard about Denver, the trip alone might kill her – even if we had unlimited resources."

Deke replied, "I hadn't thought about it that way. Are you saying it's a bad idea to ask?"

"No, not at all. Your team is a little different than most folks. You guys have the skills to do it on your own. Most of the people who are missing a family member would need someone else to go out and bring them in, and there's not enough manpower to do that. Unless I'm missing something, all you need is material things, not manpower that we can't spare right now."

"No, we wouldn't need any people... just gas, food, maybe some ammo."

Bishop took a moment, trying to visualize Terri's reaction to Deke's request. Ammunition was a huge problem. Every guy with reloading equipment was being pressed into service, but there wasn't enough of the required powder and primers to last long. Some of the engineers were working on the problem, but so far no solution had been proposed.

Food wasn't an issue, at least not yet. Gasoline fell into the same category, the mini-refinery in Midland Station working 24 hours a day. Automobiles were in plentiful supply given that half the population was dead.

"How many miles is Tennessee?" Bishop asked.

"Almost 2,000 as the crow flies. In one of Grim's calmer moments, we pulled out a map and plotted a route. If you go around the larger cities, it ends up about 2,200 or so... round trip."

Bishop did the math in his head. The experience of his bug-out from Houston had taught him a lot of lessons, the most important of which was that gas mileage was terrible with the type of travel involved.

"Let's just say 2,500 miles round trip, given some margin of error. If you take a pickup, you're talking about 10 miles per gallon, so 250 gallons of fuel. That's five drums. No normal pickup can carry that much weight, even if you didn't take any food, gear or people."

Deke seemed to be checking Bishop's math, finally asking, "I was calculating about 15 miles per gallon. You think it would only be 10?"

Nodding, Bishop replied, "When Terri and I bugged out from Houston, that's about what we averaged, and I wasn't carrying that much weight. You start, stop, idle, reverse course and do all sorts of things that differ from normal driving. I wouldn't count on much more mileage than that. I also wouldn't count on being able to scavenge any fuel while on the trip."

The contractor's expression showed dismay. "I should probably double the amount of clock-time as well. That means twice the food and water."

"Carrying gasoline around in the bed of a truck when people might be shooting at you isn't a prime idea anyway. Let me think about the problem for a bit. In the meantime, you are on your own with Terri. Good luck, my man."

Chapter 4

Alpha, Texas
July 1, 2016

The chest was a little tight, but other than that, the suit Deke borrowed from Alpha's football coach fit. Not only was the lead operator dressed to the 9s, his entire team stood before the council, looking like a platoon of Secret Service agents out for a Saturday night on the town.

"Who is getting married?" whispered Nick to Bishop, both men sitting in the audience section of the council chambers.

"I think Deke and Grim have decided to tie the knot. Since the council legalized same sex marriages, you never know."

"I would have picked Moses. I hear he can cook."

Both men snickered, which drew a harsh glance from Diana. She flashed Nick a look that clearly read, "Don't make me come out there."

Deke finished his presentation, "In summary, my team wishes to thank this esteemed body for welcoming us into the community. We bring a unique set of skills to the Alliance and can continue to contribute for the betterment of our society. I believe there is no stronger proof of that statement than the fact that one of our members wishes to relocate his family here."

Terri, sitting in the middle of the elected officials, acknowledged the request. "Deke, on behalf of the council and me, I want to relay our sincerest appreciation for all you and your men have done for the Alliance. I have just a couple of questions regarding your proposal."

"Yes, ma'am," the contractor replied with a smooth tone, flashing his broadest smile.

"Smart man," Bishop whispered back to Nick. "New mothers love being charmed."

Terri adjusted Hunter's papoose-like carrier, and then focused her gaze on Grim. "My understanding is that you lost contact with your wife and child a few weeks back, is that correct?"

"Yes, ma'am," Grim replied, looking uncomfortable in the restrictive suit and tie, as well as being the center of attention.

"And how were they doing before this period of silence?"

"As best as could be expected. They weren't starving, but the pantry was bare most of the time. My land is out in the country, so security wasn't a primary concern."

"Thank you, sir. Is there anything else you would like to

add?"

Bishop leaned close to Nick's ear, "If he gets down on one knee and starts singing to Terri, I'm going to get up and kick his ass."

Grim took a step forward, briefly making eye contact with every single member of the council before returning back to Terri. "I miss my family. I worry night and day about my daughter. She's only 14 and would have been a freshman this year in high school. Surely you, as a new parent, can relate to what I'm feeling," the man stated with all sincerity. He then swept his hand to indicate all of the governing body, "All of you must be able to relate. Miss Brown, I understand you lost a son to this world gone insane. I'm told most of you have children. I beg you to put yourself in my position, to walk a mile in my shoes. How would you feel? Wouldn't each and every one of you move heaven and earth to reunite with your family? I am a capable man, benefactor of some of the world's finest training. I wouldn't ask anyone else to risk his wellbeing on my behalf. I only request a few small assets, and I'll do the work myself."

"His daughter is only a year younger than Kevin," Nick observed, his tone suddenly becoming serious. "I know I'd climb the gates of hell to get my boy back."

After a few hushed exchanges among the council members, Diana finally spoke. "Grim, we will inform you of our decision by tomorrow noon. Thank you all so much for such professional conduct, and thank you for your service to our community. This meeting is adjourned."

Hunter had been fussing, only his mother able to provide comfort. By the time the meeting had finished, he had fallen asleep in his carrier. It was getting to be a habit.

Bishop gently pulled the apparatus off Terri's shoulders, careful not to disturb the sleeping child. He wanted to give his wife a break.

She in turn helped Bishop become the load bearer, smiling at her husband's efforts. While the two parents adjusted the sling-like harness, Terri spoke in a low voice. "So, what do you think? Should the council approve the request?"

"I have mixed feelings about it. On one hand, the community's morale would get a boost if they pulled off the rescue. Some people would bitch a little about the use of resources, but 90% would understand, and it might give them hope."

Terri pondered her husband's view for a moment before responding. "We need those guys, Bishop. According to Nick, they are filling a badly needed role in the training and preparation of our defense forces. If these negotiations fail, we're going to rely on their skills and bravery."

"I agree."

"But on the other hand, we can't go sending a rescue team after every missing family member. It would break us in a matter of days. This is going to be a tough decision."

Hunter chose that moment to scowl, the infant's wrinkly face turning into a fussing cry. Terri smoothed the child's head, cooing with a soft voice. "You better give him back. I think he's more comfortable with me right now."

"It's okay," Bishop countered. "He has to get used to me at some point in time, even if I don't have boobs."

Terri laughed, nodding her head in agreement. But Hunter's protest continued to build, the infant clearly disgruntled with life at the moment.

Terri tried to fight it off, knowing it was best to let it play out. On and on, Hunter wailed, Bishop trying to sooth with a soft voice, even checking his son's diaper to verify that wasn't the issue. Regardless of Bishop's excellent care, Hunter's cries tore at Terri's core. She knew her child was not in danger, was fully aware that babies sometimes cry. It wasn't the first time, and it wouldn't be the last. She resisted the unbelievable urge to pick up the child to quiet it.

"Sometimes you just have to let them go," Bishop commented, seeming to sense his wife's mounting frustration.

The couple left the courthouse, walking to their nearby bungalow. Hunter paused briefly when they stepped outside, then continued to shriek as if in pain.

Halfway home, Terri couldn't handle it anymore. "Give him to me," she said, "I can't stand it. He's hurting over something, and its tearing me up inside."

Bishop lifted the papoose over his head, giving in to her wishes, not over concern for Hunter, but for his spouse.

As Terri accepted the baby, Bishop commented, "You're probably feeling the same thing Grim is. He can't hear his child's crying, but I'm sure he imagines it now and then. That has to be worse."

The moment wasn't lost on Terri. Despite the parent-switch, Hunter continued to let everyone in earshot know of his displeasure. He didn't stop his tirade until the couple was almost home. Suddenly, just as quickly as it had begun, the baby fell silent, apparently happy and calm.

"Gas," pronounced Bishop.

Terri's pulse and blood pressure returned to normal. She couldn't help but compare her feelings the past few minutes to the torture Grim must be feeling every day.

"I'm going to recommend that the council approve the

45

mission, Bishop."

Alpha, Texas
July 2, 2016

The candlelight waivered with any movement, the effect enhancing the melancholy expressions of the men congregated around the table. Empty coffee cups, calculators, maps and half-used pads of paper littered the surface, the debris evidence of both the meeting's duration and intensity. An assortment of chairs had been scavenged, pulled up by those who grew tired of standing while the seemingly endless debates ebbed and flowed.

Bishop scanned the faces of his comrades, taking a break from the frustrating exercise that fueled his throbbing head. Deke's team was there, eight elite fighting men with skills honed in some of the world's most violent places. Those who had witnessed the contractors in action had taken to calling them "ghosts," their abilities in battle almost mystical.

Nick sat across the table, his dossier of martial arts skills second to none. A recently retired Special Forces sergeant, he had taken the field on every continent and survived. More importantly, he held the respect of every man at the powwow. They had all seen him fight - they were all glad he was on their side.

What a brain trust, Bishop thought. *The potential for violence gathered in this one spot is amazing. What the hell am I doing here?*

The attendees weren't all elite warriors. Cory, the town's mechanic, was in attendance, his knowledge and contribution as critical as any trigger finger. The same could be said of Phil, the local ham radio operator. The skull session was rounded out with the community's resident pilot, Hugh Mills.

When the meeting first convened, Bishop had been concerned. In his experience, the presence of so many alpha type personalities often led to impasse and one-upmanship. These were motivated men, unaccustomed to failure, forever striving for the next higher level. Not only had they all achieved that level, they had thrived there.

This evening, testosterone hadn't been an issue. An air of competence and cooperation had dominated the discussions. Everyone's ideas were measured and considered equally, all concepts analyzed and given the same priority, regardless of the source. No, the attendees' conduct was nothing short of a testament to the professionalism of every man in attendance.

The problem was logistics.

Nick threw down his pencil, the effort inducing the

46

candle's glow to flicker, exposing the group's frustrated faces. Reaching for his mug, his brow wrinkled at finding it almost empty. Sighing, he grumbled, "It's the miles, and that's all there is to it. The math involved is simple – the supply line is too long. We can argue, debate, and discuss all we want, but until we overcome the limit of our range, nothing will work."

Tired heads nodded agreement, Nick's statement of the obvious serving to refocus everyone's attention on what seemed an unsolvable logistical situation.

Setting the cup back down, the big man continued. "We have to come up with a way to insert a rescue team 1,000 miles away and get them back. We need to do so with enough food, ammo, weapons and kit to give them a reasonable chance of success. Since we don't know the medical condition of Grim's wife and daughter, we have to assume they'll need assistance to get out and travel back here. There has to be a way."

"Maybe it can't be done," sounded Grim's voice from the corner, his tone showing just a hint of the distraught father and husband everyone knew was inside of the man. "Maybe it's just impossible."

"Stow that shit, mister," Deke scolded. "We've taken on bigger problems than this before and kicked ass. I'll not have anyone on my team throwing in the towel just yet."

Bishop admired Deke's leadership. The man neither bullied nor bribed, but led his team using a foundation of respect. Still, Grim's words weighed heavily on everyone's mind. They had analyzed practically every available method of transport known, and nothing passed muster.

Passenger cars and trucks couldn't haul enough fuel and supplies to make the trip.

The aircraft available suffered the same mathematical limitations.

There had even been suggestions of using a train, horse-drawn wagon, and large, semi-tractor trailer rig. While all of these solutions could handle the distances involved, each was dismissed for tactical reasons. What would the rescue team do if the train tracks were blocked? Was anyone comfortable driving a semi loaded with barrels of diesel fuel through desperate towns and cities along the route? Security was going to be enough of a challenge without carrying a bright, flashing neon sign that proclaimed, "I have a truckload of what you so desperately need!"

Phil's role as the town's radio operator had been to provide as much intelligence as possible, and the news from back east wasn't good.

The US government had basically forsaken most of the country in order to focus dwindling resources on the Mississippi

River Valley. The plan, widely known as Operation Heartland, involved jump-starting the crippled nation using the resources concentrated along the great waterway.

It made sense. The territory bordering the river had all of the essential ingredients to rebuild a nation. The multitude of navigable channels could provide transportation by barge and ship. Some of the nation's richest farmland was in the region – crops that were desperately needed to feed tens of millions starving along the eastern seaboard.

The southern end of the Great Muddy was populated with numerous refineries – fuel being a critical resource to move goods and power the economy.

Purely by circumstance, the river delta contained several nuclear power plants, the generated electricity desperately needed to make everything else work.

These days, ready availability of food, transportation, fuel and electricity within a relatively small geographic area was unique within the borders of the United States. In order to revive the crippled giant, the federal government began focusing all of its personnel and assets in the region, leaving several large cities to fend for themselves.

When the military was diverted to the delta area, many of the major metropolitan areas began to slide into absolute anarchy. Local government had completely disintegrated months ago. Without electricity, police, fire or any other semblance of society, there was no rule of law.

Lack of resources left the inhabitants poorly equipped to handle disease and starvation. The desperate population turned on itself. In Newark, the smell of a man cooking soup wafted out an accidently opened window. Over 150 people died in the ensuing riot, all fighting each other to steal their neighbor's food.

Central Park in New York was a barren field, every last bit of wood harvested by desperate residents trying to keep warm and cook any morsel of food they could find. Pigeons were practically extinct.

According to the limited amount of information available, ghoulish behavior had become commonplace, barbaric acts such as slavery, cannibalism and summary executions being reported by more than one source.

Boston had been practically wiped out by an epidemic of smallpox. Atlanta had survived its second burning only to endure a visit by Typhoid Mary.

It was into this environment that the gathering of brave men contemplated entering... all for the unselfish benefit of a friend in need.

Looking at the map for the hundredth time, Nick

announced, "The miles are the elephant. A big, mean, bull pachyderm dominating the room."

Nick's statement caused an idea to flash through Bishop's mind. He stood quickly, bumping the table and almost spilling his remaining coffee. Hovering over the map, he began to measure distances using his finger as a legend.

"What?" Nick inquired. "Tell me you've had an inspiration."

Bishop mumbled under his breath, "It might just work... maybe with a little luck..."

Several of the men huddled closer, peering over Bishop's shoulder in an effort to discover what he was doing. Grabbing a pencil and paper, he began jotting down numbers and scribbling. "I think..."

"Give him some room, damn it," Nick cautioned the others. "Let the guy think for Christ's sake."

After a few minutes, Bishop looked up at his friend and said, "How do you eat an elephant?"

"One bite at a time, of course."

"What I'm thinking is that we need to eat this elephant the same way – eat up the miles in little bits. We've all been trying to conquer the distance with a single solution, and that's not going to work. What if we established a forward base of operations, and then conducted the rescue from there? Kind of like a stepping stone approach, if you will."

Nick's expression showed puzzlement at first, and then the concept took hold. Shuffling through the myriad of assorted papers on the table, he eventually found what he was looking for.

"We could make two or three trips with the larger plane and supply the forward camp. We could stockpile food and fuel and then disembark from that point. It just might work."

One of the Darkwater men sounded off, "Are you talking about getting close enough to Grim's house to walk in?"

"No," responded Bishop. "We would have to find a functional vehicle in close proximity to the landing strip. Let's say Hugh took one of us up for a scouting mission. We would fly around until we found a small, abandoned airport about halfway between here and Tennessee. Chances are there would be a maintenance truck or nearby town where we could borrow a ride. We could then use that area as a staging point. Hugh would have to make a few more trips back and forth, bringing additional fuel and supplies on each lap. It just might work."

Deke was skeptical. "Do you really think you could find a functional truck? Sounds awful risky to me. Most folks, no matter how desperate, aren't going to take kindly to strangers dropping in from the sky and stealing from the locals."

"I know... there is risk involved. Anyone within visual range of the airport is probably going to wonder why, after months of zero activity, there is suddenly a lot of air traffic. They might gather up a few of their well-armed friends and come see what's going on. If we're discovered by the wrong crowd, the game is up."

And so it went. Point and counterpoint crossing through the air above the table. Almost everyone had questions, many offering answers as well. It was the first idea floated that evening that couldn't be dismissed offhand, and every single man was reinvigorated by the chance that Bishop's concept might just work.

Nick, busy with his calculator, announced, "The math works. Since we're cutting the distance in half, a pickup would have enough range. Hugh could fly in barrels of fuel, and we could carry enough gas and food in the bed to make it work."

"Sounds like President Kennedy's Berlin airlift to me," commented one of the contractors.

"Let's hope it works more like Berlin than the French Foreign Legion's mission at Dien Bien Phu," snorted another.

Despite everyone's smiling at the remark, all of them knew the meaning ran deeper - airlifting supplies wasn't always successful, and history was full of examples where the strategy had resulted in the deaths of brave men.

Nick glanced at his watch and announced, "Its late guys. I've got another class in the morning. I'd like everyone to think about Bishop's idea. Let's reconvene same time, same place tomorrow."

No one had the energy to protest, and the meeting adjourned. On the way out, Nick touched Bishop's arm, a clear signal for him to stay for a bit longer.

After everyone else had left, the retired operator said, "I'm assuming you know what the real issue is going to be, don't you?"

Exhaling, Bishop nodded. "Picking the team."

"That, my friend, is going to suck."

"That, my friend, is why you make the big dollars."

Alpha, Texas
July 3, 2016

Ultimately, the decision was Nick's, as he commanded the Alliance's defense forces. Today, he didn't like that responsibility.

Like any commander, he tried to execute his duties without personal feelings influencing his decisions. Like most of those who regularly issue orders that can lead to a man's death, it was extremely difficult for him to remain completely above the influence of personal relationships.

"If I'm the right man for the job," Bishop reassured his friend, "then I should go. I wouldn't be the first soldier who had to leave a newborn son. Don't worry about it."

Nick was still trying to sell the decision, as much to himself as Bishop. "I listed everyone's skills and experience. I prioritized what we've got going on here... who we could do without. You're the only guy who has driven significant distances in our post-collapse world. Hell, that trick with removing the fuses to stay dark was pure genius. No one else has done anything like that."

"Look, brother, you and I have been to hell and back together. Terri and I both trust your judgment. We have to think of the Alliance right now, not personal friendships."

Nick nodded, appreciating Bishop's acceptance of a difficult situation. "I sure hope Terri is as understanding."

"When are you going to tell her?"

Nick's face went pale. "What? Me? Ohhhh, no. I'm not going to say shit. That's your job, brother."

Bishop started to argue with his friend, but then reconsidered. "Let's let Diana do it! She's the diplomat. She can smooth it over."

"Now that's one hell of an idea. After all, she's on the council, and this is government business. Now you see why I want you on this mission? Deke and Grim are hellish fighters, but you... you've got brains. I have a feeling that mental firepower is going to be more important than anything else on this little sortie."

Bishop wasn't paying any attention to his friend's compliment; his mind clearly elsewhere. Finally snapping out of the trance, he grinned sheepishly and volunteered, "No. No, I'll tell her. It should come from me."

Bishop entered the hacienda like he was king of the castle. *A good offense is the best defense*, he told himself.

Finding Terri sitting in her favorite chair, surrounded as usual by paperwork, he bent and kissed her forehead. Hunter, lying on a blanket at her feet, received the same greeting.

Bishop rose from kissing his son and hiked up his pants. "Anything to eat?"

After a quick smile, Terri returned to the report in her

hands. "I don't know. I think there's some chicken out there. Warm up some of that rice from last night if you want."

Bishop wasn't really hungry and regretted the opening. He decided on a different tactic. Reaching down, he picked up Hunter and moved to sit on the couch. *She won't throw anything at me if I'm holding Hunter*, he thought. *She probably won't yell much either. My son – the shield.*

Despite his courage, mostly summoned while walking home after the talk with Nick, the new father had trouble forming the words now that he faced his wife in person. *You've taken on bank robbers, drug cartel kingpins and biker gangs*, he chided himself. *Get on with it. She doesn't weight 110 pounds soaking wet with a brick in each hand, and she's not wearing her pistol.*

"Terri, I need to talk to you about something important," he began.

Without looking up, she said, "Well, go ahead. I'm listening."

"I… uh… well, Nick needs me to do a job."

"So?"

"This job, well, it means going on the rescue mission for Grim's family. I'm really sorry, babe, but he's sure I'm the best guy for the role. I tried to talk him out of it, but he was insistent."

Bishop watched his wife closely, studying every inch of her face while waiting on a reaction. For a moment, he didn't think she was paying attention to him.

Terri shuffled a page, scanning the contents before commenting. "I know."

"You know?"

"Diana told me this afternoon. She said Nick was up half the night fussing over it, worried about asking the new father to leave his family on a risky trip."

Bishop couldn't read his spouse. *Was this the quiet before the storm? Was there a volcano building up for a massive eruption?*

He played with Hunter for a bit, unsure of any action other than waiting. Finally, he picked some words. "I don't want to go. You know that, don't you? I feel like my place is here with you and Hunter."

"I know," she replied calmly, never taking her eye from the document in her hands.

"So you're not upset?"

Terri sighed, finally making eye contact. "We went through this back when the Colonel's plane crashed. Remember? You didn't want to leave me then either, but we decided it was best. I had a baby, Bishop, not a paralyzing accident. I, like every other woman, am now a pioneer. A settler. My man has to go and

52

hunt, or fight, or journey afar to buy supplies for the cabin so we can survive the winter. It's all the same. I accepted that when you were in the hospital at Fort Bliss. It is our lot in life. So, to answer your question, I dread you having to leave, but I'm not upset. I will miss you terribly, think about you all the time, but I know it has to be done. I knew that when I recommended the council approve Grim's request."

Bishop nodded, and then rose to return Hunter to his blanket. He bent and kissed Terri on the forehead again, whispering, "I love you."

Before he could rise, she reached up and stopped his departure, pulling him close until their foreheads touched. "I love you, too."

After the touching embrace, Bishop stood and lingered for just a bit. "How about you go fix me something to eat, Ms. Pioneer," he asked in a low, manly tone of demand.

Despite the battle-tuned reflexes of a warrior, the physical prowess of a professional athlete, Bishop couldn't dodge the pillow. Terri's projectile flew true, inflicting a leg-crossing, bent at the waist groan as it nailed him right in the groin.

Hunter thought it was funny.

Chapter 5

The landscape below looked peaceful, untouched by the fall of society. The vantage provided by the small plane's altitude displayed the square patches of color and refinement, a visible sign that mankind had left his impact on the earth below. Bishop wondered how long it would take nature to reclaim its original randomness of shape.

Or maybe it wasn't that bad down there. They were 145 miles northeast of Midland Station, staying well north of Fort Worth. The area below was rural, land mostly used for livestock or crops. *Perhaps these country folk had fared better than their city counterparts*, he supposed.

Hugh's steady hand kept the small craft just above 6,000 feet, high enough for the plane to achieve good gas mileage, yet low enough to make out details below. While he hadn't said anything, the height had also relieved his concerns over some deranged individual shooting at them. He'd held his tongue when they had first taken off and stayed low, finding no need to worry the pilot. As they gradually climbed, he relaxed somewhat, feeling less and less like a target.

"You know for once, I hope we don't encounter any fireworks on Independence Day," Bishop commented, thinking about the danger involved in their sortie.

"I have to agree with you there. I used to dread retirement, worried I'd be bored out of my skin. Not so much anymore. I'm just fine with a nice quiet holiday," replied the pilot.

Their ultimate destination was Arkansas, more specifically the northwestern section of the Razorback State. Bishop had never visited the area, his knowledge limited to the reference guides salvaged from the university library.

He was surprised to find images of mountain ranges and emerald green forests that reminded him more of Appalachia than the Deep South. The change of scenery would be welcome. Being away from his wife and child would not.

Between Hugh's guidebooks and numerous travel references, the two men had settled on exploring three regional airports. All were listed as unmanned, all a considerable distance from any major town or city.

The plan was simple. Hugh would circle the airfield while Bishop studied the area with the best binoculars available in Alpha. If the landing strip looked clear and there weren't any people observed in the vicinity, they would circle again, scouting for suitable transportation.

Hugh had just enough fuel to check the three fields. If none met the requirements, they would have to return another day or change the plan.

The first airport was ruled out immediately, the debris of a wrecked aircraft blocking the runway. Perhaps it was the ill fate of one of his fellows, or simply the first reminder of how badly the world had gone to hell, but the crash site sparked muttered speculation from the normally stoic pilot.

"I wonder if he ran out of gas or had mechanical failure," offered Hugh. "No way to tell, I suppose," he continued, answering his own question.

The second airfield proved promising. As they approached, it was clear that the single concrete landing strip was void of wreckage. A metal building sat at the end of the runway. There were no cars present in the gravel parking lot.

As Hugh slowly circled, Bishop studied the area. He couldn't spy a single dwelling, and only one road passed beneath the plane.

"It is definitely isolated," Bishop reported. "For a bunch of guys trying to avoid people, it looks perfect. For a bunch of guys hoping to steal a good pickup, this doesn't look like a target rich environment."

"We had a strong tail wind all the way here," Hugh offered. "We've not used nearly as much fuel as I anticipated we would need. Want to circle around again?"

"Sure. Make a little wider loop if you can."

Ten minutes later, Bishop lowered the binoculars and shook his head. "There's nothing down there, which is good and bad. I love the landing strip, but I'm afraid we won't be able to find transportation."

"It's a state park called Petit Jean. That mountain over there is named the same."

"Petit Jean?"

"Yeah. Legend has it a French woman disguised herself as a boy to follow her lover as he explored this territory back in the 1700s. According to the tale, the lady fell ill and died, so they buried her on that mountain. I visited the park back years ago. Beautiful place."

Bishop pulled out a map, studying the area with an intense gaze. "Can you head north of here a little? There's an interstate up that way, and we might find abandoned cars."

Tapping the fuel gauge, Hugh nodded. "Sure thing."

A few minutes later, a solid dark line appeared ahead, growing into a four-lane highway stretching into the distance. As expected, a random sprinkling of vehicles lined the edges of the roadway here and there.

"Fly parallel with the asphalt if you can, I want to see if there's a salvageable ride," Bishop said.

"No problem. It looks kind of eerie down there, doesn't it? Do you suppose that people just walked away from their cars?"

Bishop sighed, the landscape below reminding him of those terrible days right after the collapse. "The aerial view brings back a lot of memories of Houston and when everything went downhill. People were desperately trying to get out of the big cities by the millions, probably thinking they could buy gasoline on the way to Uncle Joe's country home, or hoping a full tank would get them out of the metro area. The highway arteries couldn't handle that kind of traffic, and gridlock set in. Gas stations began to run out of fuel, and tankers couldn't get through to resupply. Folks drove as far as they could from the center of town, but eventually the mass exodus turned into a massive parking lot. People didn't just run out of fuel. They ran out of options."

Shaking his head, Hugh banked the aircraft and lined up to follow the road so Bishop could scout.

Unlike what he saw of I-10 during the Houston bug-out, the pavement wasn't solid, wall-to-wall vehicles. There was a semi here, a car there, randomly pulled to the shoulder where the tank had finally emptied. Many vehicles had their doors and hoods open; small pools of broken glass surrounded others, reflecting in the sunlight as the plane banked overhead.

"We're far enough away from Little Rock that the traffic had thinned out when everything fell apart. My guess is these cars belonged to the people who decided to bug out, but their tanks were only half full. It must have been quite a shock to find out that a pound of gold wouldn't buy a gallon of gas."

On cue, the plane passed over an area dense with cars and trucks, the glimmer of windshield glass showing vehicles packed tightly like sardines in a can. "What's that all about?" Hugh asked, pointing with a nod of his head.

"An exit with gas stations," Bishop answered. "I've seen that before. Everyone pulled off the interstate as the gauge approached empty, waiting in line for fuel trucks that never arrived. The potato chips and candy bars were no doubt devoured in hours. I'd wager violence started shortly afterward. Desperate, hungry people carrying weapons in the glove box were likely to have a short fuse."

After flying a few more minutes, Bishop said, "Let's turn around. I saw a few pickup trucks about two or three miles back that might work out. Can you land on the roadway?"

Shrugging his shoulders, Hugh said, "Don't see why not. The wind is calm, and it looks like there is plenty of space. I've only got the fuel to land and takeoff once though."

Eventually, Bishop spotted a section of road he'd noted on the first pass. "Set it down right there, as close to that truck as you can."

Five minutes later, the small craft achieved wheels-down, rolling to a stop next to a late-model pickup that was the same brand as Bishop's own 4-wheel drive back in Alpha.

"Keep your eyes open and the plane ready to go. If you see anybody, yell at me. I'm going to try and get that old girl started." And with that, Bishop opened the plane's door and jumped out.

After taking a moment to get the blood circulating through his legs, he moved to the plane's cargo hold and removed the "looter's bag," Cory had packed for him back home. Hefting the heavy duffle, he made for the red truck.

The first thing Bishop noticed was the driver's side glass had been busted out, but that didn't surprise him. Touring the roadways and scavenging anything useful out of abandoned cars had probably been a full time occupation for some of the locals. Bishop was counting on the inventory having been exhausted months ago, hoping the desperados had moved on to greener pastures.

Hustling over, his first task was to verify there weren't any human remains inside. While the driver's seat was beginning to rot from the window being open to the elements, no other issue presented itself on the interior.

His next priority was the fuel tank. Time and again, he'd seen people spiking gas tanks. A screwdriver or other sharp tool was used to poke a hole in the bottom of the tank in order to drain out any fuel. It was faster and easier than siphoning, but completely destructive, leaving behind a worthless hunk of sheet metal.

Setting down his rifle and bag, he rolled under the truck and smiled when he ascertained the tank was unharmed. *No sense in spiking an already empty truck*, he mused.

Rolling out from under the vehicle, Bishop pulled over his rifle and began an earnest inspection of the relic. A thick coating of dust and rain-grime covered the surface of what would have otherwise been a nice looking ride.

One tire was low, but still holding air. He smiled at Cory's insistence that a small hand-operated air pump be included in his heavy kit. Other than that, he couldn't find any problem on the exterior.

Opening the door, he noticed that the dome lights didn't shine – a dead battery. Again, this had been anticipated, most of the weight in his looter's bag being a fully charged spare battery. He popped the hood.

The engine compartment looked untouched. Using a pair of adjustable pliers, he switched to the new battery in a few minutes. Next came the fuel.

Rushing back to the plane, he pulled a five-gallon can from its tether in the small cargo area and then began pouring the gas into the tank. He only used a gallon – just in case he couldn't accomplish the next step.

Soon, it was time for the most difficult part of the salvage – hotwiring the ignition.

Cory had spent almost four hours working with Bishop on the issue. Modern cars had anti-theft computer chips built into their keys, locking steering columns and hardened ignition switches. It wasn't going to be easy.

The memory of the mechanic's words flooded Bishop's mind. "All the fancy doodads and anti-theft devices must eventually make a connection between the starter motor and the DC circuit. Computer chips, DNA testing or thumbprints, it doesn't matter. The battery starts the car – period. You need to find that connection and unlock the steering column, and then you're got a ride."

Pulling a thick, flathead screwdriver from the bag, Bishop inserted the tool into the keyhole and then gave it a good thwack with the hammer. It took a lot more force than he anticipated, but eventually the plastic and metal gave way.

Before long, he had practically dissembled the steering column in the process of locating the mechanisms to unlock the wheel.

Next, he began the search for the computer chip that controlled the ignition. Cory had shown him several examples of what to look for and where to find it. Four wires exited the black box, and before long, they were snipped.

Bishop looked back at Hugh, finding the pilot scanning the area and being a good sentry. "It's now or never," he whispered to himself and then touched the final two wires together.

The engine turned... crank, crank, crank... but didn't start. Cory had predicted it would take a while for the fuel to make it through the system and up to the engine. "Don't run the battery down, just crank it three or four turns until it catches."

Again, crank... crank... crank.

Hugh's warning broke Bishop's concentration on the obstinate machine, "We've got company!"

Movement drew the frustrated car thief's attention. Half a mile up the road, men were approaching. Bishop stepped on the truck's running board and raised his rifle. Using the optic to scan the newcomers, he didn't like what he saw.

Five or six figures were visible, each carrying a long gun. They were moving quickly and with some degree of caution. There was zero doubt regarding their intended destination.

Too many, judged Bishop. *They might be only curious... maybe even friendly... or maybe not.*

Keeping a constant visual on the approaching men, he returned to his brief criminal career. On the fifth try, the motor fired, but only for a moment. Still, the progress improved Bishop's outlook. With the seventh attempt, the engine started, ran for a few moments, and then died.

It kept running the next try. *Apparently, the eighth time is a charm*, Bishop thought.

After he was sure everything was working, Bishop put the truck in gear and did a quick 100-yard test drive. He spun the wheel hard, returning to pull up close to the plane.

Hustling, he threw his pack into the back and strapped on his chest-rig. An extra set of maps went flying into the cab.

"Okay, we've got transportation. I'm going to drive it to that airstrip and spend the night. I'll see you tomorrow for phase two of the operation. I'll turn on my radio around noon. Contact me before you try to land," he instructed Hugh. "Don't forget about me, and tell Terri and Hunter I love them. Now GO!"

"Good luck," Hugh replied as he throttled the propeller.

Bishop stepped back, keeping an eye on the approaching locals while the pilot turned the plane around in the median and then began gaining speed as he rolled down the pavement.

A minute later, the red truck followed, Bishop watching the men behind him growing smaller in the rearview mirror.

As he drove west in the eastbound lane, Bishop watched the plane fade until it was nothing but a small speck in the sky. The successful start to the plan, combined with his rebellious driving on the wrong side of the road, left him feeling pretty good about the day.

At one point, he considered moving over to the proper side of the highway, but dismissed it. *I may still get to make that trip with Terri to visit England, and this is good practice*, he mused.

After five minutes of putting distance between himself and the scene of his crime, he pulled to the shoulder and began to study the map.

As best he could tell, the airport they had flown over was 25 miles south of his current position, a casual Sunday afternoon drive before society had fallen. Now, he would have to navigate a cautious route through unfamiliar territory. The fact that the map wasn't detailed enough to show every county road was troubling. He was in unfamiliar territory, and unlike Tennessee Williams, he couldn't count on the kindness of strangers.

He knew to avoid the major roadways, as they would be the most likely points of congregation for any people in the area. Recalling Hugh's comment about the airfield being part of a state park, he decided to focus on getting in that general vicinity, hoping there might be directional signposts or other helpful landmarks.

Continuing west, he had covered three miles when an overpass appeared ahead. He again stopped, stepping out to scout the area with his rifle optic, but found nothing of consequence. It wasn't an exit, and he detected no movement.

Avoiding off ramps and their promised blockade of stranded relics was appealing, a hard lesson learned during the bug-out from Houston so many months ago. Images of those starving people, so desperate they used insects to thicken their soup, filled his mind. He shivered at the memory.

On the other hand, taking the truck off-road entailed certain risks. Busting an axle, getting stuck in the sand, or damaging a critical component of the drivetrain would put the mission at extreme risk.

Why is everything twice as difficult as before? he questioned, the query a reoccurring conceptual theme. A man had to be twice as cautious, take twice as much time and worry twice as much to accomplish even the most mundane tasks. When hunting in the mountains, progress was slow because a busted ankle meant death. When sharpening his knife, extra care was mandated – the smallest wound could mean death by infection in a world without antibiotics.

Forcing the melancholy from his mind, he pulled the truck to the shoulder again, dismounting with a rifle. Despite the discomfort of driving while wearing a full load vest, he decided to don it and his body armor – just in case. Sometimes safety overrode bulk and awkwardness.

He had selected a fighting load for this trip - lighter on food and water, heavy on ammo. If things went to plan, he'd only be without resupply for a day, so nourishment wasn't a primary concern. His chest-rig held eight full magazines of 5.56 NATO rounds, exactly 224 shots for the ACR rifle slung across his chest.

Night vision (or NVD), sidearm, knife, net and a few other essentials rounded out the heavy load. Everything else was in his pack, the risk of being separated from that critical cache always in the back of his mind.

The Arkansas highway department hadn't been mowing the borders of the interstate, and the weeds were thigh high. *I'm going to complain to my congressman*, Bishop mused as he stepped off the pavement and into the growth.

He slowly climbed up the embankment, making his way to the roadway crossing the interstate, stopping at the crest to scout both directions. Nothing. Weeds, woods and wilderness were all that filled his gaze.

The next step was to walk the once-grassy area between the interstate and the country road crossing above. He didn't want to hit a big rock or fall into a hidden ditch. The area was flat and smooth, no apparent truck-traps waiting to ruin his day.

Satisfied he could forge his own exit ramp without any issue, he returned to the idling truck and began gradually progressing across the uneven ground. A few minutes later, he pulled onto the county road and turned south.

While getting off the wide-open spaces of the federal highway provided some relief, the rural road was hardly a panacea of tactical security. He had simply swapped terrain suited for long-range engagements for surroundings that fostered close-in encounters.

Wooded land, dense with undergrowth, covered the rolling hills. Visibility was less than 100 feet in most directions. Compounding the issue were the curves and undulations of the road. Every pinnacle of a rise could deliver an unwanted surprise, every turn hiding what was around the bend.

There was also the uncertainty of the best driving speed for the truck. A slower pace gave him more time to evaluate his unfamiliar environment while haste made the truck a more difficult target. He settled on a deliberately cautious speed. The lack of traffic convinced him that the locals didn't expect intruders and thus would not be prepared with an ambush.

You're being silly, he chided himself. *You have no idea if these people would be hostile to you. Your imagination is running away to dark places without any cause.* Still, he proceeded with caution due to the unknown rather than any perceived threat.

"I need local information," he thought aloud. "It would sure help to understand the native mindset."

The road was working its way downward, a gradual slope that eventually revealed a bridge at the bottom. The ancient wood and iron structure wasn't aligned well with the pavement, and Bishop had to slow the truck even more for a smooth crossing. Glancing at the water below, he spied two youngsters with fishing poles along the bank of a large creek.

The two juvenile fishermen seemed as surprised to see Bishop as he was to see them. In a flash, they both threw down their poles and scampered into the cover of the bush.

Bishop stopped the truck, right in the middle of the bridge, unsure of his next move. He had progressed too far from the interstate to turn back, and there was no way to know if another route existed. The ten gallons of gas were by no means an infinite supply, and there was always the possibility of a chase or getting lost wasting his precious fuel.

The two boys reminded him of a scene from a Mark Twain novel. Minus any straw hats, both wore rolled up overalls and plaid shirts. He guessed the lads to be in their very early teens. Obviously, their parents had taught them not to talk to post-apocalyptic strangers.

They had run in the same direction he was headed, which meant depending on how far away their home was located, they might be issuing a warning of the approaching truck even now. Bishop had visions of a father, uncle, and older brothers rushing in a house, all of the men grabbing their shotguns to protect their family.

He had to continue; he had to take the chance.

Rolling across the bridge, he drove at a slightly faster pace. He saw the break in the forest up ahead, a mailbox announcing the homestead was close. He pushed down on the gas even further, intending to race by – praying no one was going to shoot at him.

The house was old, its faded clapboard in need of a good scraping and coat of paint. Two large elm trees, trunks so thick a man couldn't wrap his arms all the way around, provided shade for the front yard. The grass was short; the surroundings appeared well cared for. The two boys were there, standing next to an older woman wearing a gingham skirt covered by a pink and white checkered apron. A look of pure terror crossed all of their faces.

I need local knowledge, he thought. Hitting the brakes brought the truck to a complete stop in the middle of the road. As he glanced back, the woman drew the two lads close to her, wrapping her arms around them in a protective gesture.

"Mister, we don't have nothing worth stealing," she yelled.

Bishop thought about his response for a moment, shouting back, "I mean you no harm, ma'am. I'm just wanting some information."

There was no response.

Slowly, he stepped down from the truck and walked a few steps into the yard. Movement at the corner of the house caught his eye, and he snapped the rifle up in a fluid motion just as a small billy goat rounded the corner.

"Please don't shoot Gertrude!" shouted one of the boys, breaking away from the woman and rushing to hug the animal.

Bishop lowered the rifle, heart pounding like thunder in his chest. After a few breaths, he announced, "I'm not from around here, and I'm afraid of getting lost. I'm heading toward a town called Martinsville," he lied. "Is it close by? What's the town like?"

The questions, combined with the livestock's survival, seemed to relax the woman. Her hold on the remaining boy relaxed, her hands moving to wad the apron at her waist.

"Yes. It's not far."

At first, the short answer annoyed Bishop. Then he realized the lady was still terrified. So were the boys. He did his best to smile and relax his body posture. "Ma'am, I'm just as scared as you are. I'm a stranger in a dangerous world, and it's got me on edge. If you could provide me with some basic directions, I'll be on my way."

"These are troubling times, mister. You'll forgive my lack of manners and hospitality, but we've been robbed twice in the last three months. The last time they shot my man and almost hit one of my grandchildren. We're all out of trust and goodwill."

"I don't blame you... I've experienced the same, and it has me a little jumpy. Is your husband okay?"

He regretted the question immediately. Any villain would of course want to know if there was a man about. The woman's expression flashed with more fear, but then she relaxed.

"He's still alive, but I don't think he'll last long. We don't have any medicine, and there's no doctor here about. Even if I had the gasoline to run him to town, the clinic there closed down months ago."

Bishop nodded, the situation about what he expected. "Is there anything I can do? I'm not a doctor, mind you, but I've seen more than my share of gunshot wounds lately."

"The shot ran through his thigh. We got the bleeding stopped, but now he's running a fever, and there's pus. I don't think the wound would be fatal if not for the infection."

On his load vest was a medical kit containing a bottle of broad-spectrum antibiotics. They were more valuable than gold and ammunition combined.

"Ma'am, I've got some pills that might help your husband. I can't be sure, and as I said, I'm no doctor. I'm willing to trade them for some information."

She didn't know how to respond at first, almost as if she were already resigned to a death sentence for her mate and couldn't consider negotiating with the interloper. Her next words betrayed as much. "I've just been trying to keep him comfortable. It's all I can do."

Bishop reached into his blowout bag and retrieved the priceless bottle of tablets. He held them up and instructed, "These are like penicillin, or so I was told by a doctor. He said to take four the first day, and then three every day after. You're welcome to them."

The grandmother hesitated, Bishop's act of kindness seemingly so out of place from what she'd experienced the past few months. "What is it you want to know, stranger?"

"I want to know what to expect from the folks here about," Bishop explained, using the woman's colloquialism. "I plan on camping in this area for a few days and then continue on my way. What are the local towns like? Is everyone keeping to themselves? Has anyone organized any sort of government?"

"Do you have a map?"

"I do. I'll go and get it."

They unfolded the map right on the lawn. She pointed and declared, "You're right here. Our road isn't shown, but it heads mostly north and south. Eventually you'll come to county road 117. If you take a left, you'll run into Martinsville in fifteen minutes or so."

"What's the town like?" Bishop asked, looking for the reaction in her eyes.

"A few months ago, my husband ventured that way. We were getting desperate for some critical items, and he thought it was worth using the last of our gasoline. I stayed here with the boys. When he returned, he was shaken... almost scared. He said we wouldn't be going back there for a long time. That's all he said."

Her explanation wasn't much help. It could be anything, he thought. *Dead bodies, rogue gangs... could be anything.*

"Do you see much traffic on this road?"

"No. You're the first we've seen in weeks. I've saw someone riding a horse before that – didn't recognize him, though. Did you come in on that airplane that was flying around this morning?"

"Yes, I did."

"The boys were all excited at first... hoping the government was finally here to help. We hadn't heard engine noises for so long, we watched you fly around just for entertainment."

Her statement bothered Bishop, bringing up a point he hadn't thought much about. After digesting her observation, he realized the plane would have been an unusual sight for most of the country. Not good.

"Who robbed you and shot your husband?"

"I didn't recognize any of them, but we are guessing they came from Porter County. Always were a bunch on inbreeds up that way. Scum... pure scum. Anyway, they were after food. My man offered them a little, just to be neighborly, but they wanted everything we had. That's when the fight started."

Bishop pointed to the map again, "What's this area here?"

"That's the park. Petit Jean. I heard the rangers don't allow anyone on the grounds anymore. Rumor is that they're living like mountain men off the land. My husband tried to go deer hunting along the edge of the park some months back, and the rangers ran him off... warned him not to come back."

That makes sense, Bishop thought. The park rangers would know as well as anyone how to survive in the wild. He wondered if they considered the airfield as part of their territory.

"Does this road I'm on... does it go anywhere near the park?"

"Yes, it travels along the western edge, but I don't think you'll have any trouble as long as you don't enter the park's grounds." She looked down at the map and pointed to a spot. "There's a service road before you get to that turn. It's a gravel lane and is marked with no trespassing signs. Stay away from that road, and you'll be fine."

"Where does that road lead?"

"I don't know for sure. The park is huge, and I never drove down that way, never had any need. I've seen the rangers come and go, so I figured it was a service road or something to do with running the park."

Bishop didn't think he was going to get any more intel from the woman, so he handed her the bottle of pills and began folding the map. Smiling he said, "I'm grateful for your help. I hope this medicine helps your husband."

He drove away, waving back at a smiling grandmother and her two charges. After he was out of sight, he stopped, waiting to see if anyone pulled out to follow. *You just never know*, he considered. His solitude was uninterrupted.

While the price had been high, the exchange had been worth it. He knew the road he traveled was seldom, if ever, used. That was hugely important.

He had also discovered that the park rangers ruled their kingdom of green. They hadn't shot the trespassing hunter on sight, which in itself was an important fact. He also knew to avoid the town, but that wasn't any big surprise. In West Texas, the lightly populated rural areas had fared better than their city dwelling neighbors. There was no reason why rural Arkansas should be any different.

Pulling out a hunk of jerky, he sat in the middle of the road enjoying the snack while he pondered his next move. There was just no way to know if there would be the chance of getting a meal later.

He experienced a twinge of guilt, having lied to his informant about his destination. The deceit was harmless and probably unnecessary, but there was no way to be sure the airplane hadn't attracted the attention of more aggressive locals. They could show up at her home and ask some pointed questions. He was sure she'd tell a persuasive interrogator anything he wanted to know.

Shaking his head at the thought, he couldn't help but be saddened by the need to be so dishonest. Already this morning, he'd stolen another man's truck and lied to a grandmother. Living in a world without the rule of law sucked.

After pulling several swallows of water from his Camelbak, Bishop put the truck in gear and continued toward the park.

Chapter 6

Rural Arkansas
July 4, 2016

Granny's memory is still intact, Bishop decided as he eyed the lane. The narrow, unpaved path was adorned with an official looking signs identifying it as "Private Property, Official Personnel Only." Looking down at his hotwired truck, he decided he was about as unofficial as it got.

He pulled off the paved road, guiding the pickup through the densely wooded trail until he was no longer visible from the main drag – or at least as main of a drag as they had in this area.

He unhooked the two wires, not bothering to lock the doors because there wasn't any driver's side glass to begin with. *At least figuring out which wires start the thing will slow down any thief*, he mused.

Despite the isolated location, the one item he couldn't part with was his pack. Wearing body armor, a full load vest, and the heavy ruck would test his conditioning, but it was a small price to pay for keeping his possessions close.

He tried to put himself into the minds of the rangers. It wasn't *that* large of a park, so chances were the number of former state employees was low. A large swath of territory being held by a small number of sentries meant one thing – early warning systems.

"If I were holding this turf as my own," he whispered, "I would set up tripwires or some other device. Hell, the ranch isn't nearly this much land, and I did the same there, enabling Terri and me to hold the ground by ourselves."

The lane was what the military referred to as "a likely avenue of approach," or in other words, a good place to set a tripwire. He hadn't walked 200 yards before he found the first booby trap.

Someone had dug a trench across the road, about two feet deep and two feet wide. In the bottom of the ditch were sharpened spikes. Burlap feed bags had been stretched across the trough, supported by skinny sticks and covered with a thin layer of dirt and leaves. The contraption would stop a truck for sure, most likely disable a man.

Bishop's level of respect for the rangers moved up a notch as he began to step around the barrier, the color of rusty metal showing through the scattered floor of dried leaves. Picking up a stick, he gently uncovered a steel-jawed animal trap, just large enough to break a man's foot. *Beaver*, he guessed from the size of the apparatus.

The anti-personnel device slowed his progress even more. While nothing he had encountered so far was designed to take a man's life, having a spike through the bottom of your foot would ruin the afternoon, perhaps enabling a slow death from either starvation or infection. *Maybe I shouldn't have given Grandma my antibiotics*, he considered.

A hundred yards further, he encountered the next impediment. A large hardwood had fallen across the path, completely blocking the lane. After inspecting the trunk to make sure the tree had fallen from natural causes, he began looking for an alternate path around the blockage.

The canopy was dense here, turning the bright mid-afternoon into a dull, dusk-like setting that substantially reduced visibility. *I would put a tripwire here*, he thought. But there wasn't any.

He had walked a half mile away from the truck and decided to return and bring the all-important transportation closer. He'd scouted what was a clear path around the ditch, and would feel better having his ride close by where he could react in a reasonable time. If someone found the vehicle, it wouldn't take long to steal his gas… or the entire truck for that matter.

Twenty minutes later, he initiated the process all over again… scouting ahead on foot and then pulling the pickup forward. It took a lot of time, but it was the only safe way.

He almost missed the lane that lead to the airfield on the fifth iteration of his inchworm-like process. Overgrown with waist-high weeds and littered with fallen branches, it was the shape of the undergrowth that hinted at the cut. Two hundred yards further, he was peering from the woods at the concrete airstrip and blue metal outbuilding.

Relief surged through his mind, the concept of being lost forever in the woods of Arkansas having taken root in his subconscious. He lifted the rifle and scanned the area slowly, looking for any sign of human habitation.

While it was difficult to be sure from such a distance, the structure at the end of the runway appeared to have been completely unvisited for an extended length of time. The airstrip was surrounded by unkempt grass and weeds that had even begun to infiltrate the crevices of the asphalt on the tarmac. That unchecked growth appeared to be undisturbed, even where located in close proximity to the building itself.

Staying in the forest's cover, he worked his way around to the closest point of concealment, just behind the structure. *It's now or never*, he decided, and stepped from the protection of the woods. The rhythm of his breathing returned to normal when no one shot at him.

He made his way quickly to the building, the passage across the open grassland making him feel like a big, fat target. Right and left his head moved, always scanning for trouble. He remembered his instructor's harsh, shouted words, "Your head must be mounted on a swivel! Always move your head! Search for the threat!"

Reaching the parking lot without incident, he then proceeded to tour the perimeter of what was most likely a storage facility. Bishop kept his rifle up and ready, rounding every corner as if he expected the devil himself to attack at the turn. Isolated, out in the middle of nowhere, it felt childish at times, but healing from embarrassment took less time than recuperation from a gunshot wound.

Someone had already broken a pane of glass on the only door. No one had even bothered to relock it after the vandalism. Peering inside, he couldn't see more than a few feet, the complete darkness eliciting another surge of caution.

After removing his glove, he gently reached through the glass, feeling the edge of the doorframe. *I'd put a wire here*, he decided. *A good noisemaker would let me know if anyone were breaking and entering again.*

Feeling with his fingertips, he moved as far up and down as he could reach. There was nothing.

He turned the doorknob slowly, and then flung it open while throwing himself against the wall. Nothing happened. Realizing what he'd just done, he had to chide himself. *Did you really think the park rangers had hand grenades?*

He stepped inside, but only a few paces, quickly moving out of the doorway's silhouette. To his sunlight-adjusted eyes, the interior was coalmine black. *Blind men don't do well in close quarters battle*, he realized. *I'll just wait right here until my eyes adjust.*

Old instruction on urban combat cycled through his mind. Don't use the flashlight – it makes you a target. Bullets go right through most walls. The threat can be high or low.

While he waited for his vision to adjust, he tried to explore the building with his senses. Bishop consciously slowed his breathing, giving his ears every chance to hear that scrape of cloth or scuffle of a boot. When he did breathe, he did so with a focused effort to detect any sort of human odor... aftershave or unwashed body.

He reached into a pouch and removed a slight electronic earplug, inserting the device and then flicking the small switch. Used by hunters, the aid could enhance human hearing several fold, as well as protect his eardrum if gunshots did ring out inside the enclosed space. The building was dead silent and smelled of old engine oil with perhaps a hint of gasoline in the air.

Sensing nothing, he placed his palms against his eyeballs and pressed firmly. He waited until white lines formed in his vision and then released the pressure. The procedure seemed to help him see in the dark a little better.

Gradually, he began to make out the contents of the facility. The main entrance had opened into a small reception area, not much more than a countertop and a few visitors' chairs. There were two doors off the lobby, the first leading back to what he assumed was the manager's office. A desk was clearly visible, its surface cluttered with manila folders and a pencil holder.

The second entry lead to the main part of the building. Again, Bishop tested the door and found it unlocked. He repeated the same basic drill when opening the portal, taking cover against the wall, just in case.

The room he entered was an open, cavernous space, much darker than where he had just been standing. He could see enough to make out large pieces of machinery along one wall, dark shadows of wheels, sheet metal and robotic-like appendages.

The rifle was swung to his back, the .45 caliber pistol filling his hand. *If someone is in here, it's going to get close and very personal,* he thought.

When his vision had finally adjusted enough to move, Bishop encountered a problem. A path through the machinery appeared in front of him, but it was still too dark to see clearly. He considered his night vision, but it was difficult to hold the device and fire a pistol at the same time. The thought of tripwires stretched along the walkway froze his feet in place.

Again reaching into a pouch, he dug out a spool of ultra-thin fishing line. Tied to one end was a medium-sized lead weight. Digging in his maintenance kit, he pulled out the plastic cleaning brush and inserted the handle through the spool's center hole.

Bishop threw the lead weight like he was aiming a dart in a pub. As it flew through the air, the line unwound from the reel until the weight thumped onto the concrete floor. Bishop's thumb stopped the release of the line, the weight pulled it tight.

He then set the spool on the floor beside his boot and watched the line. If there were any angle at all, that could mean his cast had crossed a tripwire. If the line went flush against the floor, the coast was clear. There were no trip lines, and he exhaled.

Fifteen minutes later, he'd cleared the entire building evidently used for storage of the park department's lawnmowers.

Two tractors, each with attached bush hogs, plus an assortment of riding mowers, string trimmers, and other landscaping equipment filled the storage section. He noticed all of the gasoline cans were, unfortunately, empty.

On the way out the door, he found what the vandals had been after. A candy and soda vending machine lurked along the dark wall, partially hidden by a shelf of spare parts. The glass was broken out of the snack unit, every last morsel of potato chips, mints and peanuts cleaned out long ago.

The hinges had been pried on the drink machine, its interior as barren as its neighbor's.

Bishop moved back to the office, one last thing on his mind. Sitting on the desk was a telephone, and just as he expected, there was a plastic covered sheet nearby, listing phone numbers and extensions. Blowing the dust from the list, he counted twelve numbers, each corresponding to names like "Lodge Kitchen" and "Maintenance Shed."

There were also the home phone numbers for the rangers. He counted six in all. *Not good odds*, he thought. *I hope Smokey the Bear isn't on their side, too.*

Sleeping on the ground was never an attractive prospect to Bishop. Yes, there were times when that was the only option. But if it were at all possible to go horizontal above the earth's surface, he felt it was worth the effort.

It wasn't just the creepy-crawlers, slithering reptiles, or discomfort of temperature. There was a security aspect involved.

Tents restricted sensory input, added weight to a bug-out kit, and couldn't be repacked in a rush. They were great for camping or when bivouacking in large numbers, but not so good for a solo man trying to keep a low profile.

Years ago, an old Special Forces trooper had demonstrated how to use a survival net as a hammock, and Bishop had rarely slept on anything else since. Given his current desire to remain undiscovered, it only made sense to use the device and construct a nest.

After clearing the building at the airfield, he drove the truck to the edge of the woods bordering the facility. He had thoughts of camouflaging the vehicle with branches and foliage, but decided it wasn't worth the effort. He was running out of daylight and judged it a better use of his time to set up camp before darkness fell.

He wanted to be able to observe both the truck and the airfield beyond if at all possible, but those were not the only criteria. It took a bit of searching to find the right tree. Fifteen minutes of walking around in concentric circles led to the discovery of a stout oak with a suitable structure of branches. The appropriate placement and size of the limbs was critical. Long ago, he'd learned that picking the proper tree meant the difference between a good night's rest and the constant fear of falling out of the nest. *I'm a hatchling*, he mused. *I can't fly just yet.*

He stood looking up at two limbs protruding at just over a ninety-degree angle from the truck. Each was the size of his thigh, easily holding the weight of his body and kit. They were 12 feet above the forest floor, and there were no lower branches to climb. *Perfect*, he judged. *Not so high that I'll kill myself if I fall, but not so low that someone will walk right into me during a good REM cycle.*

He dropped his pack and scouted the area again, but found nothing out of the ordinary. Digging around in the heavy ruck, he finally withdrew a large, triple-pronged fish hook that most folks called a treble hook. This specific one was rated at 600 pounds. Attached were several feet of paracord, rated to hold 550 pounds.

The parachute cord was too thin to climb, even when knotted. Smaller in diameter than a normal lead pencil, there just wasn't enough girth to get a strong grip.

A youth spent hunting in the steep canyons of West Texas had resulted in Bishop's developing several different methods for ascending to high places. He'd used the traditional knotted rope, but that kit required a lot of space.

During jump school at Fort Benning, he'd been introduced to paracord, the line attaching the canopy to the chute's harness. It was amazingly strong for its size and was purposely designed to withstand shock.

He'd knotted zip-ties into the cord, spaced at useful intervals in order to provide foot and handholds. That method worked quite well, but it was difficult to untie the plastic strips once the weight of a man had pulled the cord tight.

A friend at HBR had introduced Bishop to a device called an "ascender," used by professional climbers. A molded hunk of aluminum slightly smaller than a man's fist, it would hold in place once the cord had been woven through. The ascenders provided excellent "steps" for his rope ladder.

Bishop estimated how many ascenders he would need and quickly configured his rig. Swinging the thin rope like a cowboy about to lasso a calf, he tossed the line over the branch.

The fishhook looped over and snagged the line on the second try. He then tied his pack onto the end of the line so he could pull it up after ascending to the perch.

Using the insoles of his boots and both gloved hands, Bishop pulled and pushed himself up the ultra-lightweight climbing rope, using the well-spaced ascenders for foot and handholds. He wouldn't trust it for great heights, but for single-story buildings and low tree limbs, it worked well.

In a few moments, he was pulling himself over the branch, careful to avoid the sharp hook. Shortly after achieving a solid roost, he pulled up his pack.

Stringing the net between the two limbs required patience and diligence. He wrapped the net completely around each branch, securing it with several stainless steel "S" hooks. Keeping his weight on solid wood, he tested the rigging with his pack.

As expected, the center of the net sagged under the ruck's weight. Tightening each side resulted in a taunt surface long enough for a man to lie comfortably and sleep. *If you're having one of those dreams where you're falling, you probably are*, he mused.

In reality, it would be almost impossible to roll off the net. Even with the strands of netting as tight as guitar strings, there was still some sag when he tested it with his full weight. The limb on each side of his body would act as a bedrail of sorts.

He finished a cold meal of beef jerky, pine nuts, and a muskmelon half he'd packed that morning. The tepid water from his Camelbak satisfied his thirst.

He decided to sleep without his vest and body armor, pulling off the uncomfortable units but keeping them close by. His rifle and night vision monocle stayed right at his side. He decided to keep his boots on, but loosened the laces for circulation.

Complete darkness filled the forest, the overhead canopy blocking any illumination by the stars or moon. The final birdcalls of dusk had faded by the time Bishop arranged his gear and body. An orchestra of insects serenaded his pre-sleep thoughts, raising their nocturnal choir with robust voices that actually helped calm his nerves. As long as the bugs were chirping, no one was around.

Tomorrow, around noon, Hugh would bring in another man and additional supplies. One more trip after that would be required, and then they would begin the journey across the country and hopefully retrieve Grim's wife and daughter. *It was a deed well worth the risk*, he reiterated for the hundredth time.

His final thoughts before sleep were of Terri and Hunter. He wondered if he'd be able to see any change in his son after being absent for a few days. *I love both of you*, he whispered, as he began to rest.

After a healthy dinner, Hunter let go with a robust burp that caused Terri to grin. "You'll fit right in at Pete's bar," she whispered, pulling the infant close in a loving embrace.

Terri laid the child next to her on the bed, leaning over to study the drowsy face peeking through its wrapper of soft blankets. He was eating well, and everyone seemed pleased with his overall development, but she couldn't help but worry. *I suppose that's the price of motherhood,* she reasoned. *I'll probably be studying this little guy until he's 40 years old, waiting and watching for something that needs fixing.*

Hunter, despite not seeing well just yet, seemed enthralled by his mother's face. Remembering Betty's advice, she turned off the light and hummed softly. "Adults are boring at night," the older woman had suggested. "If there's nothing exciting for Hunter to see, his internal clock can start matching yours. As much as you might want to, don't play with him after hours."

Lying in the dark next to her son, Terri's thoughts turned to Bishop. She'd received a report from the pilot a few hours ago, but didn't completely trust that people were telling her everything. She expected filtered reports from Deke's contractors. To those men, anything but a full-fledged war was boring.

Hugh's narrative outlining Bishop's little adventure into rural Arkansas had seemed a little too sterilized... a wee bit trite. *They're just trying to protect me*, she realized. *I wish there wasn't a need, but in a way I'm glad they show the courtesy. There's nothing I could do to help Bishop anyway.*

Bishop is the most capable man I've ever seen, she admitted. *He'll be fine. What we're doing is the right thing morally, both for Grim as an individual and the community as a whole. People are upbeat about the mission because it shows we take care of our own. Every citizen needs to know that we are all in this together, especially with trouble looming on the horizon.*

Making sure Hunter was asleep, she placed a ring of pillows around the baby, just in case he developed the capability to roll over during his nap. Unlikely, but the new mother wasn't taking any chances. She quietly left the room, heading back to the seemingly endless mounds of paperwork that accompanied her job. Thank goodness Betty had driven up from Meraton to stay with her for a while.

Two kitchen tables had been set up, their surface almost completely covered with accumulated reports, inventory sheets, requests and updates. She was keeping a promise to her husband – a pledge not to go into her office at the courthouse. She simply had the work delivered to her home.

"Can I get you something?" Betty asked, looking up from her book.

"No thank you, I'm just fine. Hunter is asleep after eating pretty well. I think he's starting to gain weight."

"That's good, Terri. Just watch what you eat because you're passing it through to him. Caffeine is definitely out. The sooner he sleeps through the night, the better you will feel."

Terri grimaced, "I hear ya... what I wouldn't give for a cup of coffee some mornings."

"You'll be weaning him before you know it. Then you can go on a coffee splurge until you're wired tight. Speaking of wired, you're not going to work, are you?"

Looking over at the stacks, Terri shrugged. "I was thinking of reading a little bit before turning in."

"Not too much, sweetie. You just gave birth a few weeks ago, and you're still supporting two people, one of which is growing like a weed. You still need to take it easy and get lots of rest, hun."

Terri glanced again at the piles of her nemesis, finally waving them off. "You're right. Besides, I'm not in the mood to read."

Betty set her book aside, patting the couch cushion. "Have a seat and take a load off. I'd love some good old fashioned conversation, if you're of a mind for a chit chat."

Terri accepted the offer, plopping down with a sigh.

"You seem to have so much on your mind lately. You're worried about the potential of a war, aren't you?" Betty began. "It's all anyone seems to want to talk about these days."

"I don't know why I had this naïve image of our people being able to rebuild without outside interference, but I did. It's hard enough making things work internally, without constantly looking over our shoulders because of a looming, external threat. What makes it worse is the justification for a war isn't crystal clear; it isn't black and white."

Nodding, Betty replied, "Is it ever?"

"I think it was with Pearl Harbor; that was pretty black and white. Going into Afghanistan after 9-11 seemed obvious enough. But right now, we're not even clear about our sovereignty even if someone did attack us. What bothers me the most is that if *I'm* this confused, I have to assume the typical person walking the streets of Alpha is just as troubled. My job is to make things better for people, not worse."

Betty nodded toward the bedroom where Hunter was sleeping. "You've added another responsibility as well. You have to make the world as safe and secure as possible for that child."

Grunting, Terri looked down. "I ask myself every day how much Hunter impacts my decision making. You know he tipped the scale that changed my mind with this rescue business. I sent my husband off on some dangerous adventure, and the emotions I felt over the birth of my son influenced my thinking."

"It's like anything else, Terri," the older woman responded, "becoming a parent is a life altering event. It changes you so much. In some ways, you will be stronger, in others, perhaps more cautious. Each individual adapts to parenthood differently. I have a feeling you and Bishop will be stronger, more rounded people for the experience."

An hour passed, the two women unwinding with pleasant conversation and shared experiences. When Terri began to yawn, Betty said her goodnights, stretching and then making for the spare bedroom.

Terri did the same, thankful Hunter appeared to be resting comfortably. Sleep came with Betty's words still echoing in her mind.

His still-groggy brain told him something was wrong. *Was that a dream?* he wondered. *Or was there actually a sound?*

Bishop opened his eyes to darkness, his first physical move an intentionally slow, slight reach of his hand to the rifle lying beside him. *There! There was the noise again – a voice.*

Someone was close. Bishop was reminded of the primary issue with using a treehouse as a bunk. *You can't get down quickly. If anyone finds you up in this tree, you are basically fucked.*

Again, the voice… a mere whisper… drifting across the otherwise silent forest. *Was it closer that time?*

Prudence advised his now adrenaline-charged body to remain absolutely still. As dark as it was, he didn't think the man owning the voice could see him. His imitation of a statue didn't last long. He couldn't stand the inaction, couldn't lie still. He gradually raised his head to peer over the edge of his bedrail-branches. *Nothing… can't see a damn thing.*

A parade of scenarios zipped through his mind, a

mental kaleidoscope covering every possibility, from a bullet slamming into his back from below, to staying put and hoping whoever was out there passed by. It was maddening.

"Go left or go right, just get the hell out of the way!" He remembered the words. The instructor was one of the feared "Black Hats," the cadre of elite men teaching Jump School at Fort Benning – educating mostly at the top of their lungs. *In other words, make up your mind.*

Bishop reached for the night vision. He justified the action by telling himself that it was too dark for his movement to draw the human eye. He powered up the unit and inched it to his face, bringing an alien world of greens and blacks into focus. A red light was blinking at the edge of the monocle's display. And then the picture went dark – a dead battery.

The anger at his carelessness barely overrode his fear of the threat. His inner voice spouted long strings of foul dialog, most of the tirade of vile vocabulary directed at his own stupidity. He had spare batteries in his pack, but there was no way he could swap to a fresh cell. In a tree. In the dark. With potential hostiles nearby.

Concern over discovery soon outweighed his self-directed anger. The sound of rustling leaves drew his attention. Then the murmurs... faint... the words almost intelligible.

Two men. Walking as quietly as possible. An occasional whisper between them.

Had he been discovered? Had they found the truck? Or its tire tracks?

Then the footfalls were close. Very close. A few steps and then a pause... more steps.

A twig snapped, no doubt from the weight of a footfall. The noise was so loud, it startled Bishop. They had to be practically underneath him. His grip on the rifle tightened, his muscles ready to spring.

"Why don't you try and make more noise?" a hushed voice hissed. "Why don't you just advertise to every deer in the county that we're here?"

"Oh great white hunter," came a sarcastic tone. "Please forgive me."

"Fuck you."

"If those rangers find us hunting on park property, they'll be some fucking going on, but it won't be you doing me."

"Fuck them, too."

Poachers. Bishop exhaled, relaxing his coiled frame. While discovery by the two hunters wouldn't be a good thing, it was a positive that they weren't looking for him. He remained quiet, waiting as their occasional footsteps and whispers faded into the distance.

As he started to rise, it occurred to him that the rangers might already be tailing the two trespassers. He'd give it five minutes before exposing himself – just to make sure no one was following the hunters.

No one showed, so he immediately changed the battery in the night vision and began preparations to follow the two trespassers. It wouldn't be good for Hugh and the resupply plane to land while there were prying eyes.

With body armor, load vest, laced boots and fully functioning monocle, Bishop lowered himself from a branch, suspended in the air until his arms were fully extended, and then dropped the remaining four feet to the ground. The impact was much louder than he anticipated.

And then he was off, tracking the two poachers, trying to make up ground.

Using the night vision, he could travel faster and with more stealth than the two men. As he moved to close the distance, a break in the canopy above allowed him to check the sky. There were no visible stars or moon. *Cloud cover*, he thought, *a potential issue for Hugh and the relief flight*.

Clearing his negative mindset, Bishop realized he couldn't do anything about the weather. *If I get socked in here for several days, I might need one of those deer myself*, he thought.

Bishop realized that a stalker has an advantage over prey. As long as the two men kept moving, their footfalls would mask any noise made by his approach. A single man can stop and listen, but a group of two or more must coordinate their pauses. Bishop wasn't worried about the two poachers – they just didn't impress as being that good.

What did put caution in the pace of his steps was the chance that the rangers were about. His only clue about their capabilities and resources were the anti-personnel devices rigged on the trail. While they were not bad setups, they weren't clever enough to merit anticipation of an extreme level of stalking skills.

He also knew that desert hunting was different than seeking game in a wooded area. Visibility was one obvious factor, the dense forest adding difficulty in spotting the target. For this and other reasons, he knew that most woodland hunters used a deer hide or stand, often elevated and commanding a wide angle of approaches. He slowed a bit, lest the hunters were already in their perch, lying in wait.

As he traveled, the forest took on a dull gray hue – the obvious result of the sun rising to a densely cloudy day. A few minutes later, the first raindrop smacked against a leaf, several more joining it within moments. The wind picked up shortly after, a clap of thunder rolling in the distance.

Great, he thought, pulling out his poncho. *This is just fucking great. At least I didn't run the truck through a carwash.*

The deluge built quickly, thunderclaps and flashes of lightening piercing the sky. The wind wasn't about to be outdone, adding its chorus to the storm. While his poncho would protect the majority of his body from the dampness, Bishop still sought refuge.

Unsure of exactly how dangerous bolts of lightning could be in a forest, Bishop started looking for some sort of shelter. The nearly constant flashes, combined with the horizontal blow of stinging rain, made him forget about the two men in front of him.

He identified a deluxe-sized tree that had fallen some time ago, its top landing on higher ground than the trunk. The resulting gap at the base of the hill provided a small space offering a little protection from the downpour and wind. It was the best safe haven he could find.

On and on, the storm raged. About every 20 minutes, the rain and wind would let up, and Bishop would think it had passed. He'd start to gather himself to move out, and it would all start all over again. Two hours passed before the mini-typhoon finally quit.

The sun remained hidden by a dense overcast of gray, and that meant no relief flight.

He moved out again, returning his focus to the two men he knew were just ahead of him. *They must be as frustrated as I am*, he mused. *All keyed up to go steal a meal, and the weather won't cooperate.*

He had advanced another 80 yards when he saw them, or more specifically, detected the movement of a bush where they had just passed. He cut hard right from his current direction, moving twenty steps to a large tree with more than enough girth to hide his frame.

As before, they were bickering with each other when they passed. While upset with the meteorological conditions and lack of meat for the dinner table, what really had rustled their feathers was being soaking wet.

"I thought you had packed the rain suits," accused one.

"Bullshit, you always carry those. Don't try and blame it on me."

Bishop grinned at the banter, thinking of his dead battery, happy in a way that he wasn't the only incompetent fuck walking the woods today. Apparently, around here they traveled in pairs.

After they had passed, Bishop cut in behind the two hunters, keeping them barely visible and making sure they didn't cause him any trouble. He moved from tree to thick bush, never leaving one position of cover before slinking to another. Every footfall was charted ahead of time, avoiding thickets of thorns and general entanglements as important as progressing silently.

Before long, the two poachers began following a path. Wider and better maintained than a game trail, Bishop was surprised when a sign announced they were progressing along one of the park's pre-marked hiking excursions.

How stupid, he thought. *Sure as shit, the rangers have this booby-trapped. I would.*

The terrain began to change as they passed, large rock formations appearing along the edges of the trail, glimpses of a steeply walled valley visible through the thinning vegetation. Another few hundred yards, and he began to understand why the state of Arkansas had put a park here – the view was postcard-esque.

The vista was ruined by two things, both happening at about the same moment.

Again, sheets of stinging rain began their soaking deluge without any warning, resulting in the already muddy trail becoming a puddle-ridden slop fest.

The second event was the abrupt halt of Bishop's quarry, both of the deer hunters moving off the path as if they had seen something ahead of them.

Taking cover behind a formation of truck-sized boulders, Bishop's little voice was warning that something was badly wrong up ahead. His premonition was proven correct by the report of a gunshot echoing across the valley. Then another… further off… then another… then several.

The safety came off Bishop's rifle, the ACR moving to his shoulder.

He almost killed the two hunters he'd been following. Both men came crashing through the underbrush, surprising Bishop with both their speed and position. They ran right past his hide, moving with the determined expressions of terrified men trying to stay alive.

Another round of gunshots rang out, making it clear what the two poachers were running from. Bullets cracked through the air, some passing directly past Bishop as he hugged the rocks for cover. He realized too late that he should be mimicking the fleeing men. Before he could even pick a direction, several men burst through the foliage and into the boulder field, shots ringing out from their weapons.

Fuck! I don't have a dog in this fight, he cursed. *Now*

what the hell am I going to do?

There were at least six men pursuing the retreating poachers. Spread out in a loose "V" formation, they clearly meant to kill someone, round after round zipping through the trees.

Bishop pulled off his poncho, the rain gear blocking access to his vest and ammo. As he peered around his rock fort, a bullet slammed into the stone surface not three inches from his face, the sharp splinters biting into Bishop's cheek like a swarm of stinging bees. It pissed him off.

Up came the red, illuminated dot of his optic, and he started dropping the hammer, firing intentionally low. The ACR was a 4th generation battle rifle, designed to pour hot lead at a threat, or in this case, multiple threats.

Bishop snapped four rounds left, pivoted right, and let six more fly. He then centered on the middle of the approaching formation and sprayed 10 more messages of his displeasure. Repeat in reverse, and then repeat again.

The empty magazines didn't hit the ground before a full box of pain-pills was jammed into the weapon. His movements were a blur, releasing the bolt, checking the ejection port for any problems, and then lead was flying at the approaching threats.

The ACR was like a comfortable pair of blue jeans in Bishop's hands. Smooth, flawless and rapid, his fire was controlled, well-spaced, and relentless. One man tried to advance, moving from behind the small pine he'd been using for cover. Like a magnet drawn to iron, his motion earned two rounds, geysers of muddy water erupting in the man's path. The fellow changed his mind and tried to reverse course, but the sloppy ground provided no traction, and he fell into the swill, both legs sticking into the air. Were it not for the deadly hailstorm of lead being exchanged, the routine would have been comical.

Bishop delivered a blistering 90 rounds in less than 30 seconds, shredding bark, snapping branches, and spraying mud. He wasn't sure if it was the cloudburst or the lead-burst, but he achieved the desired effect – the other guys stopped shooting. Their advance halted.

An eerie quiet fell over the forest, nothing but the falling rain daring to make a sound. Engaging in gunplay with a couple of guys with bolt action deer rifles was one thing; running into someone who knew how to spread suppressive fire with a high capacity weapon quite another. The momentum of the attackers stalled.

"Mark, you okay?" a voice called out.

"Yeah, I'm fine, but Jake's hurt," another responded.

"What the fuck is going on... who..." quipped another shaky voice.

Bishop analyzed the situation. He couldn't shoot low anymore. They were too close and most likely would regroup in a few moments. He could fade away into the forest behind, but they wouldn't give up trying to find him. If the truck were discovered, his plan would be jeopardized. If he were cornered, that would suck even more than losing his ride. A lucky shot into his head would really suck.

He didn't want to kill these men, even if he could manage that feat while being so badly outnumbered. They had been stupid and surprised this first time; he doubted if they would repeat the same mistake.

"I'm not one of the poachers," he called out. "I bumbled into your fight with them by accident. I've got no quarrel with you men. Let's talk."

For a moment, Bishop didn't think anyone was going to respond, but eventually they did.

"Who the hell are you?"

"My name's Bishop, and I'm from West Texas. I flew in on that airplane you probably saw buzzing around yesterday. I've got a job to do and ended up here by accident."

"Bullshit!" sounded from the right, the grunted response soon followed by a smattering of other mutterings that Bishop couldn't make out. He decided to push a little harder.

"I've been shooting low on purpose. Like I said, I've got no fight with you people, but if we don't reach an understanding, I'm going to raise my aim. There's no sense in anyone dying today. Let's not be stupid."

Again, the wind carried a variety of low voices through the rain, impossible for Bishop to judge the overall reaction from the other side. Finally, a clear shout reached through the storm.

"Okay, let's talk. I'm coming out," declared an older throat. Then a man appeared from the center of the attacker's spread, walking slowly to a clearing 40 yards in front of Bishop's hide. *There's the leader*, the Texan determined. *That took a pair of gonads to walk out like that. Gotta give him credit for guts.*

It could be a trap, he realized. *Could be a ploy to get me out from behind these rocks.*

Bishop hesitated a moment, deciding the risk involved in exposing himself was probably worth it. *These guys aren't all that sophisticated and, after all, talking was my idea.* He stood and moved from behind his stone shield, ready to dive back if shots filled the air. No bullets came.

He paced into the clearing, stopping 30 feet from an older-looking fellow sporting a full, but trimmed salt and pepper beard, and wearing a baseball hat with the park's name embroidered across the front. The man he faced was perhaps 60 years old, but it was difficult to tell with the bill of the cap and the rain jacket's hood. Muddy boots, filthy pants and a bolt-action 30-06 hunting rifle rounded out Bishop's first sight of the ranger.

To the men of the forest, Bishop was no doubt a spectacle. The desert colored vest, covering the bulge of body armor beneath, was bristling with magazines and pouches. The ACR was an unusually shaped weapon, its ferocity recently demonstrated. Fighting knife, radio, bush hat and bug-eyed combat glasses rounded out what must have been an intimidating sight to the host.

"My name is Frank Pearson," the man began. "I'm the head ranger... or at least I *was* the head ranger here at the park."

The man's voice was steady and low, and Bishop respected him instantly. Most people in Frank's situation, would show frayed nerves. Nodding, Bishop responded. "I was following the two poachers when they ran into your team. When they hightailed it back past me, I got stuck in the middle. I was trying to warn you off."

"What are you doing here? What do you want?"

Grunting, Bishop smiled and answered, "I know this is going to sound funny, but I'm on a rescue mission. My team and I are on our way east to retrieve the wife and child of a dear friend. The airfield at your park was picked to be our forward operating base. We had no way of knowing what the situation was here on the ground."

Looking around, Frank asked, "There's more of you?"

Shaking his head, Bishop decided to be honest with the man. "No, not yet. The rest of my team was supposed to fly in this morning, but I'm thinking the weather has delayed them. I came in first to scout and establish a position on the ground."

"Are you military? Work for the government?"

"No... well... it's a complex situation. I don't work for the US government, but it's a long story."

Frank studied Bishop, the man's gaze boring into the Texan's eyes. A decision was eventually reached, signaled by a slight nod and then an extended hand. "First, let's agree not to shoot at each other."

Bishop walked forward and accepted the handshake, smiling at his new acquaintance. "Fighting is never the right way if there's any other solution."

Frank turned to the woods, shouting, "Come on out boys; it's over."

Before long, Bishop was surrounded by a group of men who moments before had been trying to kill him. Despite the reassurance of their leader, all of them stayed behind Frank, eyeing the newcomer as if he carried the black plague.

One man was holding a rag against his head, blood soaking through the cloth. Bishop started to ask if the guy was badly hurt when one of the others commented, "He slipped in the mud and fell."

Relieved at not having wounded the gent, Bishop started to make a joke when another man's head snapped up, looking over Bishop's shoulder. A shot ripped through the air.

There is an instinct… a reflex of sorts, developed by those who have experienced combat. No amount of training can hone the reaction, no amount of practice can guarantee the skill. Bishop didn't consciously think about the whizzing bullet or its source. In his mind, a line appeared on a mental diagram, connecting the metaphysical dots between the sound of the discharge and his weapon.

As Bishop pivoted, the ACR was coming up, the motion smooth and practiced like a professional golfer's swing or the serve of a tennis pro. Fluid. Snap. To anyone watching, it was a blur.

His eyes registered the rifle first, then a second weapon came into focus. A thousandth of a second later, he knew one of the poachers was working his bolt, the other just taking aim. The empty chamber was ignored, the black hole of the soon to be fired barrel completely filling his vision.

The ACR's stock was against Bishop's cheek before anyone could inhale to shout a warning. The red crosshairs centered naturally, his eye and hand following the imaginary line already plotted and processed. He squeezed the trigger.

The empty shell casing was arching through the air, when the rifle barked again… and again… and then again.

The first target stood stunned, his eyes wide with shock as his knees began to buckle. The other man's head was looking at the sky, a round catching him directly in the chin. He simply fell onto his back.

"Fuck!" cursed Bishop, already rushing toward the two fallen men.

As he kicked away their rifles, his voice filled with pure anger. "Why? You ignorant fucks, why? Why did you come back, damn it! You were free and clear!"

A quick check told Bishop what he already knew – both men were dead. He stayed on his knee beside the second victim, waves of nausea racking his core. His anger flowed at the dead man lying beside him, "How fucking stupid! You idiots! What were you thinking?"

Of course, there was no answer.

Bishop felt a hand on his shoulder. He looked up to see Frank's eyes, filled with understanding of the moment.

"Why?" Bishop asked, the pain bleeding through with the single word.

"These two have been getting bolder and bolder over the last few weeks. I think they were becoming really desperate. Maybe all of us standing around, exposed and talking was just too good a target to pass up."

Shaking his head at the senseless act, Bishop finally stood and looked at the circle of men gathered around the bodies. No one would look him in the eye. "I didn't want this," he pleaded. "My God in heaven, I didn't want to kill today."

Despite the sympathetic postures surrounding him, Bishop's rage continued to build. He stomped off, heading back to his boulder-fort to pick up his empty magazines and poncho.

After giving Bishop some time to cool down, Frank approached and offered, "We're heading back to the lodge now. Why don't you come back with us and get dried out? We've even got a little food if you feel like eating."

The Texan's first reaction was to decline the invitation, his mood guiding him to sulk and isolate. A small inner voice reminded him of the mission, of how being on the right side of the locals would help things go smoothly. *Maybe establishing relations will avoid any more bullshit killing like just happened*, he reasoned.

"Thank you," Bishop responded. "It would be nice to get warm and dry. Building a fire today might be a bit of a challenge."

Men began building litters, chopping down saplings for the supports. An hour later, a column formed, two of its members being carried to their graves, a third wondering when the killing would stop.

Chapter 7

It was still a beautiful place. Despite the many months without funding, support or other benefits of society, the park's main lodge could only be described as stunning.

Sitting at the end of a valley with Petit Jean Mountain to the north, the placement of the main building was inspired. Bordering on a steep canyon wall, the vista stretched for miles down the gorge, beautiful hardwoods covering the gently sloping Arkansas hills for as far as the eye could see.

Bishop scanned the area as the column cleared the forest trail and entered the main grounds. The hotel, pool, main dining area, and parking lot appeared untouched – ready for the fall tourist season and those drawn by the changing colors of autumn foliage.

As he examined in more detail, a few things seemed out of place. Stacks of firewood were abundant, as were men with weapons – the lookout stationed on the hotel's roof probably not required before things went to hell.

Children ran here and there, childhood games of tag or hide-and-seek keeping the little ones occupied, the muddy ground making the games more interesting to some. Bishop spied another oddity, two women cooking over a campfire while a third carried more kindling to feed the flame.

"Most of the guests canceled their reservations after the terrorist attacks," Frank noted, hanging back to speak with Bishop. "Those that were already here, we offered to let stay after the news reports stopped, and the electricity didn't return. Most didn't, wanting to return to homes and family."

Bishop stopped walking, glad to give his back and feet a rest. The head ranger continued, "About three weeks after contact with the outside world ceased, one of our rangers came into the park and announced that the entire world had gone nuts. He kept calling it apocalyptic, and we all thought he was exaggerating. He said he had driven his family into town to get supplies, and they had been attacked. He described roving gangs, like you'd expect to see in LA or Chicago. They all had guns, and what few people remained were scared shitless of them. They tried to take the few gallons of gas he had left."

Nodding, Bishop said, "I understand. I've seen it before, and it doesn't even have to be a town or big city. It seems like anytime there is a group of people in trouble, the wolves start preying on the sheep. It's probably always been that way, probably always will."

Frank considered his guest, seemingly deep in thought. "It wasn't just one guy. The stories started mounting, and the electricity never came back on, no television or radio – nothing. It was like the whole country had gone dark and silent."

"In a way, it did – and not just because of the electricity. I was in Houston with my wife during that time. Even though we were living in a big city, we had no clue what was going on. We could see the fires, night after night on the horizon. It was spooky... real spooky." Bishop shuddered, thinking back about those times and then shook himself to clear the memories. "When the army finally rolled in, it split our little neighborhood apart. We were barely holding on as it was, and when half the people said they were leaving to go live under martial law, we decided to bug out."

Frank nodded, his expression showing familiarity with the situation. "We had meeting after meeting about doing the same. The problem was, no one could think of a better place than here at the park. Our job had been to protect the resources here, to preserve them for the future. You can imagine how difficult a decision it was to start consuming what we'd worked so long to foster."

Bishop's eyebrows rose, having never thought about that aspect before. "I bet it was a tough call," he agreed.

Frank motioned for Bishop to follow and then continued the discussion. "The next issue was the stragglers. At times, it seemed like the whole countryside was full of people wandering around aimlessly, eating anything they could find. Some groups were docile, almost lethargic; others were violent and aggressive. I remember driving down the road and finding a family with a fire and sleeping bags camped right in the middle of the pavement. They were living like wild animals."

As they talked, the men strolled toward the bodies of the two poachers. Bishop took a moment to study the men he'd just killed.

Both of the victims appeared traumatized beyond having been shot. The dead men were thin, their waistlines sunken narrower than their hips. Dirty, long fingernails, yellow teeth, and oily, uncut hair confirmed his suspicions. Bishop said, "You mean like these two guys? It looks like to me they were barely staying alive before they took a shot at us."

Frank put his hand on Bishop's shoulder. "I knew these two, ran into them a few times before everything went to hell. I had them arrested three years ago for poaching on park property. They were scum then, and the fall of society didn't help that one bit. We've been skirmishing with them for weeks. They were hard drinking, shiftless lowlife - without any family or foundation. Come on, let's go stand by the fire and dry out."

"I see you brought me another mouth to feed," sounded a female voice from behind. Both men turned to see a middle-aged woman approaching.

"Mary, this is Bishop. We ran into him on the 3-mile trail while we were hunting the trespassers. Bishop, meet Mary, the matriarch of our little community and my wife."

Mary sized Bishop up without offering her hand or any greeting. There was a stormy look in her eye, a suspicion no doubt enhanced by the two dead bodies lying at the men's feet. "How long is he staying?"

The woman's tone was clearly hostile, but Frank pretended not to notice. "I'm not sure, Mary. Why don't you ask him yourself?"

She glanced at Bishop, shook her head and then walked off without another word. After she had passed beyond earshot, Frank said, "I'm sorry. She hasn't been the same since everything fell apart. She has a son who lived outside Chicago, and we haven't heard from him in months. It eats at her every single day."

"I'm sorry to hear that," Bishop replied. "You two, of all people, should understand my mission. I'm on my way to retrieve loved ones and reunite a family."

Frank's eyes never left Mary, watching his wife as she approached another man and struck up a conversation. "That's a noble cause, for sure," he said to Bishop. "You're right. I do understand, down to my bones I understand. The world may have lost civilization, but I lost the sweetest girl this side of Little Rock."

Their discussion was interrupted by Bishop's watch alarm, signaling it was time to turn on his radio and monitor a specific frequency – the agreed upon procedure to make contact with the plane. Glancing up at the still overcast sky, he knew it was pointless, but followed the plan just in case. Nothing but static filled his earpiece.

Frank noticed the act, glancing up as well. "How many men is the plane bringing in?"

"There will be three of us on this little adventure. I hotwired an abandoned truck on the interstate and drove it down here. The plane is bringing enough gasoline and supplies for a pretty long drive."

Scratching his chin, a hint of slyness crept into Frank's voice. "I'm not trying to be nosey, but is there enough gasoline in Texas to support an endeavor like this? No offense, but you are better fed, equipped and organized than anything or anyone we've seen since it all fell apart."

Bishop chuckled at the observation, warming his hands by the fire, the heat slowly drying the mud on his pants. "It's a long story, but essentially several small towns in West Texas have banded together and formed a union of sorts. We've managed to get electrical power and limited refining of gas and diesel up and running."

"Are you going to retrieve everyone's family members?"

"No," Bishop shook his head in dismay. "I wish we could, but that would be impossible. The guy we're doing this with is a special case, and our ruling council approved the operation."

Frank seemed to take his time absorbing it all, turning his back to the flames and scanning his community. "I thought we were doing well here," he commented. "It sounds like we're behind the curve."

"You are doing very well here, at least from what I've seen in other parts of the country. I think we've gotten lucky, and circumstance put the right people in the right place. Your people are eating and secure, and that's a lot better than most folks I've encountered."

"Frank," a voice called out, "If you want some of this pork stew, you'd better get over here. It won't last long."

"Okay," the head ranger responded, "we'll be right over."

"Pork stew?" Bishop asked, a frown on his face. "You have hogs around here?"

"Wild hogs... they've saved our butt. We would have obliterated the local deer population in a matter of months were it not for Mary's feral pig cuisine. What was a major pest before the collapse is now keeping us alive."

Bishop had read news stories about the problem, the animals destroying millions of dollars of crops and property every year. Some of his co-workers at HBR had even gone on hog hunting excursions for fun. "Do you have bacon?" he asked with a bit of hope in his voice.

"No," Frank replied laughing. "There's no fat on' em, and thus no bacon. To be honest, they're not nearly as appetizing as domestic porkers, and that's why we make stew out of the more mature animals. The big ones taste like ass; the younger ones are more palatable, almost tasty."

Looking up at the still-gray sky, Bishop thought he should take advantage of a hot meal, even if it wasn't favored by the Maître d'hôtel. *I'll still tip well*, Bishop mused. *At least the dude was honest about it.*

Actually, Frank had undersold the stew. Wild onions, potatoes from a neighbor's legacy garden, and a few spices Bishop couldn't identify made the meal superior to anything he carried in his kit. Water was served from a metal bucket, a community dipper filling plastic cups covered with their handwritten names. Bishop stuck with his Camelbak, not having a cup and not seeing any spares. *Besides, you never drink the water*, he told himself.

Sitting apart from the main gathering, his host had been mostly quiet during the meal. After tipping his bowl and sipping the final bit of broth, Frank sat back and admired the view for a few moments. Bishop had the distinct impression the man was building up something important to say.

The lodge guest didn't have to wait long. Nodding at Bishop's load vest, Frank came out with it. "What caliber is your weapon?"

"It uses 5.56 NATO or .223 Remington. It was originally designed to replace the army's M4 platform, so it uses the same magazines and ammo."

Frank's eyebrows rose at Bishop's answer. "We've got two AR15 rifles, but we only had about 50 rounds, and that went quick after the trouble began. Now I'm relegated to a shotgun, a few rounds per deer rifle and a couple of handguns, and that won't last long. We used a lot of our ammo inventory today."

The hint was subtle, and Bishop decided not to take the bait. Frank was wanting some of Bishop's precious ammo, and he couldn't blame the man. He was doing exactly what Bishop would do if the roles were reversed. But, the concept of giving a man... a man he didn't know all that well... the tools that could hinder his operation didn't sit well with the visitor from Texas.

Bishop nodded, sympathetic to Frank's situation. "Ammo is the new currency in some places. A town near where I live had a marketplace where everyone bartered, and there was nothing more valuable than brass and powder."

Again Frank paused, Bishop assuming the fellow was working up the courage to ask for a gift - bullets. He was wrong.

"I know of something that might be of value to you and your team. It's a risk on my side, but if you'd consider bartering some of those rounds, I could offer a trade."

Bishop's eyebrows raised, now curious what Frank had up his sleeve. "Go on."

Frank chuckled, "I can see I'm sitting across from an

experienced horse trader." His voice then became serious. "I know of a man that lives about 15 miles from here, on the other side of town. He just recently returned home from the army. I'm not sure why, but he was involved in a big operation along the Mississippi river. He was a military policeman and might have valuable information, might be useful to you."

Bishop tried not to react, but inside his head was reeling. The weakest part of their plan was traveling through the Mississippi River Delta. They knew the military had a huge operation going on, an initiative called Operation Heartland. It was the government's big push to jumpstart the recovery. Other than that, the team from Alpha knew very little. Talking to someone who had worked in the area could be critical, especially an MP."

"Yes," Bishop replied, trying to keep his voice calm. "Such a person might provide some very useful input. How do you know about this man?"

Grinning widely, Frank responded, "He's my nephew. He hiked through the park on his way home. His wife and child were living with us while he was away. Despite my insistence that he stay here, he wanted to go back to his farm... was dead-set on doing so."

Remembering his determination to reach the ranch after the bug-out from Houston, Bishop could understand such an emotional drive. "How do you know he made it home?" the Texan asked.

"He's like you, Bishop. He's a capable man and left well-armed. We warned him about the situation in town, but it didn't seem to bother him much. He gathered up his family and set off about three weeks ago. I'm pretty sure he made it. He's always been a determined SOB."

"How long a trip do you think it would be?"

"Well, that all depends. Can we drive in your *rental*?"

Bishop considered the question, weighing the variables. The weather could keep Hugh socked in for days, which would allow for a trip on foot and keep the truck relatively safe where it was. On the other hand, a walking expedition would take longer and add additional peril.

"I'd prefer not to use the truck," Bishop decided. "It is more critical to our task than just about anything else."

Frank seemed to be working through the distances and pace. "Well, in that case, I would estimate we can accomplish the round trip in a day if we don't run into any trouble. Start off just before dawn, be back in the evening at dusk."

"What if we traveled at night?"

The head ranger snorted, "You do have a big pair of

nads, don't ya? I mean, I get it – traveling at night would be safer, but our progress would be slower."

"Not with one of these," Bishop replied, pulling out his night vision. "We can bust it cross country if we do it right."

The Texan passed Frank the monocle to examine. "My, my," was his only verbal response, the man intent upon fondling the device.

The quick-release optical mounting system was one of the finest inventions in the history of mankind, at least from Bishop's current perspective. Combined with a unified platform available on a huge variety of weapons, anyone could quickly swap optics, magnifiers, lasers, ranger finders and a variety of other rifle furniture between firearms in a matter of moments.

The technology also allowed for adaptation to environmental conditions, such as moving from the forest to open terrain, or as in Bishop's situation, the gray afternoon having faded into a starless night.

Without removing the zeroed-in optic, he could switch from daylight to lowlight by simply snapping on the night vision to his rifle. When he wanted to let Frank have a look, he quickly detached the palm-sized unit and handed it to his comrade.

And Frank wanted to have a look more often than not.

The two men had left the park two hours ago, following an old farm lane at first, then cutting across an open pasture as the light finally faded. Frank had drawn Bishop a map of the route with significant landmarks and approximate distances.

"We should mark rally points, in case we get separated," Bishop had persuaded. It really hadn't been a problem, as Frank wouldn't let more than a few feet of separation grow between them.

While the park ranger managed his noise discipline respectfully well, the man's insistence at staying up-tight and personal with the Texan was dangerous and annoying. If Bishop had believed the odds were strong that they were walking into trouble, he would have scolded Frank. After dropping a couple of strong hints that were basically ignored, Bishop decided to let it go. The chances of running into a problem in the woods at night were slim. *I don't know what he's been through*, Bishop reflected. *Maybe he has good reason to fear the night.*

Frank had retrieved one of the ranger's AR15s, for which Bishop had supplied two magazines – the negotiated price for the Intel-gathering soiree through the Arkansas countryside. Bishop hoped Frank wouldn't use up the ammo before the night was out... prayed he wouldn't have the need.

Their route required passing through the outskirts of Martinsville, bypassing the potential trouble spot deemed unreasonable due to the extra time that would be required for the journey. A series of impassable streams, swollen from the recent storms, eliminated any timely detour. Bishop wasn't overly concerned - given the hour and the small, hopefully unnoticeable, size of their party.

Stench was the first indication the community was ahead. A blend of wood smoke, sewage and a few other unidentifiable odors assaulted Bishop's sense of smell. It was unpleasant, to say the least.

As they approached the first few signs of what had once been a berg of almost 5,000 people, the town was quiet, given the hour of zero-dark thirty. Other than occasional whiffs of foulness drifting by, the first few businesses, homes and outbuildings all appeared normal.

Ordinarily when encroaching an urban area, staying in the shadows is a critical tactic. But not tonight. There were no streetlights, no moonlight, and no starlight. Even the high tech night vision struggled to paint a picture of anything more than basic shapes and outlines. Bishop felt like he was in a deep underground cave, so dark he wasn't sure where the walls ended and open space began. Twice he walked off the pavement they were trying to follow, the crunch of the gravel shoulder embarrassing, but otherwise harmless.

On the second misstep, Bishop halted abruptly and felt Frank bump into his pack a half second later. Shaking his head, he pulled the man down to take a knee and whispered, "I'm going to turn on the night vision's illuminator and my flashlight's infrared beam. The two of them combined will enhance the night vision enough to avoid trouble. As it stands right now, we could walk right into a pack of wild dogs, either canine or human, and not even know they were there until we felt teeth pierce flesh."

"Okay," replied the nervous man. "Whatever you think is best. Will it help me see?"

"No. The human eye can't recognize the infrared spectrum, but ..." Bishop pulled out a light stick from his vest, snapping and shaking the chemical device until a warm, green glow surrounded the two men. "I'm going to risk weaving this in the exterior webbing on my pack. Just follow it. It should show you where to step. If I stop or go to a knee, you do the same. Just follow the golden glow road, like Dorothy in that wizard movie."

The green light illuminated enough of Frank's face to show Bishop that the man didn't appreciate his humor. *Some people take things way too seriously,* thought Bishop. *What? You want to live forever.*

Bishop pulled his flashlight off the vest, using the glow of the chemical stick to make double sure he used the correct setting for the invisible infrared light. He still covered the lenses with his hand, before hitting the power button, knowing that even a small flashlight beam would be visible for miles on a night like tonight.

Bishop's torch clipped to the MOLLE ladders on his vest, and after adjusting the stream of light to the correct angle, he tested the effect.

Returning the monocle to his eye, he scanned the area and found he could see clearly out to 70 yards. *Much better,* he thought. *The only drawback is the battery usage - or if someone else has night vision.*

With his guiding light, Bishop could make out more of the town as they passed. It was creepy. Not a single light showed anywhere, not even a candle. Overgrown yards surrounded homes with dark windows, even the driveways succumbing to nature's relentless advance of unkempt foliage.

What had been piles of trash were scattered here and there, remnants of a time when humans bought their food in plastic and paper. Dogs, raccoons and other wildlife had visited the gathering heaps at some point, scattering contents that no human had the energy or initiative to clean up. *Nature was taking it all back anyway,* he thought. *Eventually it will take an archeologist to find any evidence of human habitation if this keeps up.*

The thought of dogs reminded Bishop of his primary concern before crossing through the town. Those four-legged early warning systems were a worry, but so far Frank and he hadn't heard a single bark or growl. *Had the animals learned to keep quiet - lest they be eaten? Had some desperate soul made a meal of them all to survive?* Bishop shook his head to dismiss the morbid thoughts.

His other fear of Martinsville proved unwarranted as well. There were no sentries. Remembering his trip across Texas, they had encountered roadblocks, fortified bridges and barricaded passages along the route. He mentally assumed this place would possess the same unwelcome obstacles, but it didn't.

How long had it taken before they realized it wasn't worth the effort, he pondered, stepping along a now weed-strewn sidewalk. How many weeks or months had it been before someone realized that the guys blocking the road in their pickups weren't encountering a single soul? No more drifters. Nothing left for anyone to loot. Who cares about security when there's nothing left to protect?

The concept saddened Bishop. Despite his desperate desire to avoid bumping heads with any locals, the degradation of the town to the point where there was nothing left to guard made a statement – a resolution of decay – an abandonment of hope.

In fact, the only barrier they encountered required nothing more than stepping just slightly higher than normal. A truck had slammed into a utility pole, causing the weakened support to fall into the middle of the street. No one had cleaned it up. No one had bothered. Bishop didn't check the rusted hull of the truck, but wouldn't have been shocked to see the bones of the driver still sitting behind the wheel. The bullet holes in the driver's door told him what had happened here over a year ago.

Before long, they were trekking across the countryside again, walking along the edge of a paved road once used by those folks who would venture into Martinsville to buy groceries, a new sprinkler head or perhaps a scoop of ice cream. To Bishop, the air grew cleaner, easier to breathe.

The spread between the homes bordering the roadway grew, the pavement narrowing after a while.

It was about then that Bishop noticed two shifts in their environment, both helping to lift the melancholy fog that descended on him in Martinsville. The first was the return of nature's orchestra of wildlife sounds. Tree frogs, crickets, and other creatures of the night raised their voices to an ever-increasing level as the two humans relinquished the concrete and asphalt of the town.

The second change was a break in the cloud cover. Bishop had just raised the night vision to scan ahead when the entire landscape illuminated like someone had turned on a giant spotlight. Really nothing more than a few stars poking through the cloud cover, the contrast was amazing. He turned off the battery-powered devices, exhaling in relief that the resupply plane would probably make it through tomorrow.

They hiked another handful of miles, the routine becoming second nature to the two travelers. Bishop would stop and scan with his nighttime helper, pivoting 360 degrees while scanning for any threat. After verifying their isolation, he'd plot 50 steps ahead and begin walking again.

Frank's whisper interrupted the process. "That's Mathew's driveway up ahead."

No sooner had the words registered, than a dog started

barking in the distance. "Just like you said," Bishop responded. "Let's stick with our plan."

Frank nodded and took the lead, stepping toward the mailbox. Bishop hung back, continuing to scan their surroundings, wary of the noise.

Frank's voice called out toward the house. "Matt! Matt! It's Frank. Matt, are you up?"

Bishop looked at his watch, doubting the man was awake three hours before sunrise. He was wrong. A voice sounded close by, causing both travelers to jump. "Frank," the tone low and mean, "who's that with you?"

"Matt, it's okay… that's Bishop, and I brought him here to talk with you. He's a white hat."

An outline appeared from the shadow of the property's fence line, the man's movement cautious and slow. Bishop remained still, not wanting to cause an incident. *I'd be a little jumpy too if I had unannounced visitors in the middle of the post-apocalyptic night*, he considered.

"The dogs started growling ten minutes ago," Matt stated. "I knew someone was fucking around. What the hell are you doing here, Frank?"

"I'm on a mission to rescue someone up in Tennessee," Bishop declared, taking a step closer to the two men. "Frank convinced me you might have information that could help us pull it off. Maybe save some lives."

"Well, hell's bells… this is just weird you two showing up like this… but all right. Come on in." And with that, the homeowner spun away and strode back up the drive without another comment. Bishop and Frank followed.

As the trio paced to the back of the house, Matt pointed toward the chained German shepherd that had sounded the alarm. "Fritz doesn't like the apocalypse. Before the shit hit the fan, he ran free, but now I have to keep him chained, or some damn fool will have him for lunch."

Before entering the screened back porch, Matt stopped, spinning to stare at Frank. "Are you sure this guy's okay, Uncle Frank? You know me. I never was much of a social butterfly, and I'm even less now. Before I invite him into my home, I gotta ask."

"I'll vouch for him, Matt. He's good people."

Again eyeing Bishop up and down, Matt made up his mind. "Come on in," he grunted.

After stepping through the door, the homeowner bent and retrieved a candle. Using a disposable lighter, he struck a flame to the wick. The entire porch was cast in a warm glow, revealing over a dozen bushel baskets full of food.

Bishop was amazed at the collection, spying apples,

walnuts, several different types of roots and two large bundles of what appeared to be cattails. Noticing his scrutinizing gaze, Matt commented, "When I bought this place years ago, old man Prichard kept a small orchard running. After he passed away in 2010, I kind of let it go. For a few years, I think most of the fruit rotted on the ground, but not anymore. The apples just ripened three days ago. I would guess there's another four or five bushel left."

Amazing, thought Bishop. *I never thought about orchards.*

"You've got enough here to start your own market. I've seen that done before. It's how my people back home initiated recovery," the Texan observed.

Matt digested the remark for a moment and then smiled. "I suppose it's been that way for thousands of years. When men with land harvested more than they could eat, they took their excess into town to sell. It's too bad that won't work here. If I loaded up a bunch of food, someone would try and take it from me. Someone would die."

Bishop grinned, now flattered over Frank's earlier comparison with his nephew. "In that case, the people in the town probably starved until they changed their ways. Without security, nothing happens."

Matt evidently decided not to delve into historical social development, especially three hours before dawn. "My Gloria knows how to can food, so I'm hoping by winter we'll have more than enough," Matt continued. "Last winter she and my kids about starved to death. Even Fritz was getting all 'ribby' and weak. I intend to make sure that doesn't happen again."

"I'm impressed," Bishop stated. "I sure hope you can keep a low profile. You're still pretty close to town."

Matt waved his hand in the air, the gesture pointing back at Martinsville. "Oh, hell no. Those scarecrows back in town ain't going to give me any shit. Hell, half of 'em don't have the strength to walk out here and carry a weapon at the same time. The other half is too damned stupid to worry about. I'm more uptight about random stragglers than that bunch of zombie-brains in Martinsville."

Bishop chuckled at the description, and then decided to get down to business. "Frank here tells me you were in the army, assigned to Operation Heartland."

Matt nodded, "I was an MP with the 377th. My stint was up a long time ago, but they weren't letting anyone out or issuing any leaves. I just left. Some might say deserted, but I had my discharge papers a week before everything fell apart. My CO knew I was headed home. He didn't lift a finger to stop me."

Bishop replied, "We want to drive across to Tennessee in a truck, extract a friend's family members and bring them back across. What can we expect?"

Matt snorted, "I expect you all would die. No one uses private vehicles in these parts. All civilians with gasoline were ordered to surrender their fuel months ago. Unless you're a farmer or an engineer with orders, only military units are on the ground."

The news confirmed Bishop's worst fears; they would stand out like sore thumbs. "That's not good news. I was afraid things might have degraded to that point." Nodding toward the baskets of food spread across the back porch, Bishop continued, "You mentioned farmers. How do they move their goods around?"

"I've seen horse-drawn wagons, families carrying baskets on poles across their shoulders... you name it. A few of the really big outfits have special permits for trucks, but it's rare to see one. The only cars on the road belong to the military or are government sedans."

"Shit," Bishop muttered, pacing a few steps in thought. "How would you do it? How would you get across the area they control? Could we fly over it?"

Matt motioned to a cluster of chairs at the end of the overhang. After the men were seated, he continued, "You can't fly; the airspace has an exclusion. While I never saw any fighters, the Air Force boys are pretty busy shuttling things around, so there must be radar and controllers."

"Trains, planes, and automobiles," Bishop grumbled, "there has to be a way."

"No trains either. Lots of boat traffic on the rivers, a lot of people walking."

"Could we fake orders somehow? What's the procedure?"

Matt gave Bishop's last idea a bit of consideration before answering. Finally, shaking his head, he replied, "I don't think that would work. You've got to understand things are clamped down pretty tight. Officers have full authority for field trials and summary executions. I bet I saw a hundred looters executed in the last four months. Same goes with deserters. Discipline is harsh – zero tolerance. If I were at a checkpoint, and you approached carrying men, supplies and guns, I'd verify your orders before letting you pass."

Frank broke his silence, "I've heard rumors it was bad. I bet there is quite a riff between the civilians and the army."

"Oh, the people hate the military and the government, despise them with a passion. It actually goes both ways. Most of

101

the guys in uniform aren't overly fond of their countrymen these days."

"Americans aren't accustomed to totalitarian rule. I bet the lack of food and freedom is going to cause tempers to boil over at some point," Bishop added.

Matt shook his head, "It varies from area to area and how well each commander is handling things. When the military first rolled into our town, people were so desperate, they bought into the government's story. The promise of food, electrical power and rule of law made a lot of folks toe the line. Starvation is a powerful motivator. But the process is taking too long. I was stationed outside of Memphis, and the general commanding our region promised electrical power would be restored in two months. The army lost a lot of credibility after four months had passed, and no juice flowed through the lines. The same bullshit predictions were made about food, too. The situation's a little better than it was when my family and I first came back, but not much. Let's just say Weight Watchers isn't doing a robust business in this market, that's for sure."

Bishop grinned at the bad joke, a little ashamed he found it humorous given they were talking about their fellow countrymen, family, friends and neighbors. "There has to be a way to get across," he finally observed.

Matt exhaled and leaned back in his chair, clearly deep in thought. "Maybe I'm painting too bleak a picture. You might be able to slide through, if you avoid the major cities. The army can't be everywhere at once. They're concentrated within the big towns and critical infrastructure projects, like the power plants and docks. If you avoided all of those, you might be able to make it. Crossing the Mississippi is still going to be a bitch, though. All of the bridges are tightly controlled."

"Every river is probably going to be an issue," Bishop worried. "We didn't think this was going to be a walk in the park, but it's sounding more and more like an impossibility."

Matt considered the dilemma for a bit, finally brightening with a thought. "Do any of your guys look like me?"

Bishop lifted the candle from the table's surface, holding the light to study Matt. "You know, now that you ask, you and Deke might be related. Why?"

"Hold on a second," Matt replied, rising from his chair and disappearing into the home's back door. A few moments later, he came out carrying a military ID card and a wallet containing an MP's badge and credentials. He passed the identification to Bishop.

Abandoning the candle for his flashlight, Bishop studied the pictures carefully. Looking up with a smile, he declared, "This just might work, especially given the date the cards were issued. Everybody looks different after what we've all been through. What would you want in exchange for a complete disguise?"

Matt rubbed his chin, thinking long and hard about the barter. Finally coming to a conclusion, he announced, "I want 1,000 rounds of 5.56 ammo, two pounds of canning paraffin, five pounds of salt, 100 broad-spectrum antibiotics, and the prettiest size seven dress you can find."

Bishop pulled a notepad from a zipper compartment on his vest. Without comment or emotion, he jotted down Matt's list and then looked up. "I think I can do this, but some of the items I'm not sure about. I'll do my best and be back here in two days. If you don't like what I bring, then the deal's off. In the meantime, I would like to leave you a map. If you can note units, deployments, strength… as complete a scouting report as possible, I might be able to throw in a bonus."

Looking around at the still dark backyard, Matt indicated his agreement with Bishop's request. "I can take out some time from harvesting in the orchard to complete the report. I'll see you in two days."

As the two visitors stood to leave, Bishop turned back to Matt and offered his hand. After the men exchanged the handshake, Bishop paused as if he'd forgotten something.

"I assume the dress is for your wife? I mean, you'd never fit in a size 7."

Laughing, Matt said, "Yes, it's for my wife. Her favorite color is blue."

Chapter 8

Bishop heard the plane's motor before his radio squawked. Before he could press to talk, the bird zoomed low over the runway, Deke's smiling face peering out the passenger side window as Bishop flipped his middle finger at the passing aircraft.

"We are good to go," Bishop responded, feeling a bit like a supporting character in a spy movie using the pre-agreed phrase. If he had said anything else, Hugh wouldn't land.

Walking off the center of the runway, he gave the pilot plenty of room… just in case. The ex-Air Force man put the wheels down gently and rolled to a stop a few minutes later following Bishop's waving arm to pull close to the airfield's sole building.

"What's up, Slick?" Deke greeted as he exited the plane. "Did you get us accommodations at the local Four Seasons?"

Bishop pretended to check his watch, managing to keep his voice deadpan, "Yes, I've got the presidential suite reserved, and I think you'll find it adequate, sir. We'd better hurry though; I have booked your massage appointment at the spa to begin in 30 minutes."

Deke laughed as he moved toward the cargo hold of the plane. "I hope she's one of those Asian back-walker types. They always give the best rub downs."

"I'm sorry, sir. I scheduled your session with Vito, the testosterone-charged, hairy ex-linebacker. I thought you preferred a more vigorous encounter."

And so it went, back and forth, while the men unloaded the plane's cargo. Hugh, wisely, remained above the exchange, obviously focused on getting his airplane back in the air as soon as possible.

Two 50-gallon drums of fuel came off first, quickly followed by cases of ammunition, food and other supplies. The entire load was rolled, carried or shoved to be stored in the small reception area.

"Okay, that's it," announced the pilot. "Terri sends her love. Your son is doing fine. Nick wants you to keep your head and your ass lower. That's all of the messages I was supposed to deliver."

Bishop dug in his pocket, producing a slip of paper with a neatly written list of items. "Hugh, get this list to Nick and Terri when you get back. There's been a slight modification to the plan, and we're going to need these objects. Please tell Terri I love her and that I'm doing just fine. It's safe here for the time being."

The pilot scanned the list, twice glancing up with a questioning look but never saying a word. "Will do," was his only response, and then he was climbing back into the aircraft.

Deke and Bishop watched him take off, both men experiencing a small pang in their guts as their lifeline to home and safety slowly disappeared into the distance.

"So what's the situation here?" Deke asked.

"I've made friends with the locals, gathered Intel on our destination and can even offer you a roof over your head tonight."

"Well, what the fuck have you been doing all this time, slacker? Lord in heaven, this ain't a pleasure cruise, ya know," Deke teased.

"Come on, I'll introduce you to the locals. If you're nice, they won't eat you. I'd put it at 50-50 you'll see tomorrow's dawn."

Deke grinned, "What more can a man ask for?"

Bishop wanted to show Deke the truck, now pulled close to the airfield. As the two men approached what would essentially be their home and base of operations for several days, Bishop produced his best used car salesman's voice, "Yes-sir-ee, she's low mileage, she is. Good rubber, runs smooth as a baby's butt. Only driven by a little old lady to church on Sundays. I bet this here pick'em up truck's never been over 40 mile per hour in its young life."

The newly arrived contractor played along, walking around the truck like he was seriously considering a purchase. He even kicked one of the tires. "But I was hoping for something a little brighter color."

Deke peered inside, spotting the bundle of hanging wires below the steering column. "Let me guess," he grinned. "It has a salvage title."

"I salvaged it all right," Bishop replied. "We can put it back with a note about the damage after we're through if it will make you feel better."

Deke's reply was interrupted, the operator's rifle snapping to his shoulder as he dropped into a crouching position, ready to engage. Bishop was a little slower, moving beside his partner and covering the opposite direction. A voice called out from the woods, "Bishop! Bishop, it's Frank. I saw the plane. Is everything all right?"

"It's cool," Bishop informed the now-alert contractor. "Remember, behave yourself or you might end up in the stew."

"Come on in, Frank," Bishop yelled toward the woods.

A few moments later, Frank appeared, paired with one of the other rangers. Bishop motioned for Deke to follow, immediately introducing the new arrival.

"Lunch is about ready," Frank announced. "I thought I would see if you gents needed any help storing your supplies, but I see we are too late."

As the four men headed for the lodge, Deke asked, "What's this change of plans you mentioned to Hugh, and how badly am I going to think it sucks?"

"Oh, you'll love it. Have you ever played a law enforcement officer on TV?"

Snorting, Deke replied, "No, but if I'm being sworn to uphold the law, you know my first act will be to arrest *you* for grand theft auto."

Alpha, Texas
July 6, 2016

"He wants what?" Terri exclaimed, a mixture of shock and anger in her voice.

"A dress," Hugh replied, nervous about being the messenger. "Size seven, blue, if possible. The nicest in town."

"Let me see that note," Terri replied, moving Hunter to the opposite arm. After reading down her husband's list, her gaze returned to the shuffling pilot as if asking for an expanded explanation. "A dress? Wax? Hand cuffs or nylon restraints? What? Is my husband on a rescue mission or attending an orgy?"

"I'm sure Bishop has a good reason for the request," Hugh offered, flushing red with embarrassment.

"He better. Anyway, go to the church and ask one of the volunteers there to help you find a dress. Don't make it too pretty. I have no idea where to find canning wax, but Diana might know. Nick can take care of the rest of it."

"Thank you, ma'am," Hugh responded, turning to leave. Before he could reach for the door, Terri stopped him.

Softly, almost in a whisper, she said, "Hugh... seriously... please tell me... did Bishop really seem alright?"

Smiling, the pilot turned to face her. "Yes, as far as I could tell. I didn't really talk to him much. He and Deke were insulting each other and joking most of the time... in a good-natured way... I think. He seemed a little high strung, but who wouldn't be?"

Terri took a step forward and put her hand on the older man's shoulder. "Thank you," she responded softly. "Thank you so much. Please let me know if you have any trouble rounding up the items on that list."

She watched the pilot leave her office, and then gazed down at the round, cherubic face of her child. "Let me tell you something about your father," she began. "He vents stress by spewing horrible puns and sometimes inappropriate innuendo. That's how he copes. Some of the people you encounter in life will become deadpan serious during an emergency, others simply fall apart. You, my sweet child, have been blessed with a dad who tells bad jokes. I'm sorry, but there's nothing I can do about it. He's old and set in his ways. I think you'll still love him. I do."

Terri smiled down at Hunter's lack of reaction, the infant seemingly happy to stare at his mother's adoring face. "You know what is even worse? I've started doing it too. It's contagious or something. You poor thing; you'll probably be cursed with the same terrible coping mechanism."

A light rap at the door drew her attention back to the portal, Diana's face peeking in. "Oh, good," she began, "I didn't want to interrupt Alpha's newest citizen during his lunch or nap time."

"He finished a little bit ago, come on in."

Diana set a stack of papers on Terri's already cluttered desk before walking over to smile at the baby. "Did you know we're producing wine now?"

"Huh?"

"Yeah, I had no idea Texas had wineries, but we do. They're just on the eastern edge of our territory, and joined our little coalition a few days ago."

Terri grinned, "I'll have to sample some local vino once young Hunter here is eating solid food. Until then, it's a no-go for me."

"Hey, I have a question that's probably going to sound a little weird. When Hunter is hungry, does it bother you at all... having to expose your chest in public?"

Terri grunted, "I've been exposing my boob in public for a long time... right now he's on a mission someplace in Arkansas."

Diana laughed and then waved a finger in the air, "No fair picking on Bishop when he's not here to defend himself. You're bothered by his request for a dress, aren't ya?"

"No," Terri replied, looking down at her post-partum figure. "I'm bothered by the size seven."

Both of the girls laughed at the remark, then moved toward Terri's desk. Diana's tone became serious, pointing at the stack of reports. "The latest attempt to get the natural gas electric plant up and running failed... again. Midland Station is complaining that they're not receiving their fair share of lumber.

Pete, as usual, wants to throw a party. Our treasurer is worried that the economy is growing so fast we're going to run out of currency soon. And the best news yet... the telephone guys think they'll have all of our towns connected via landline within two weeks. No word yet on the cell towers."

After finishing the data dump, Diana studied her friend. She could tell Terri's mind was elsewhere, and she couldn't blame her. "You're worried about Bishop, aren't you?"

"Yes, I am... again. It's okay though, he had to go do this. I just hope everything turns out as planned. I can't picture my future as a single mom. I want his influence on Hunter."

"I agree," Diana replied, a hint of a smile playing at her lips. "When you put the baby down, why don't we get one of the ladies to watch him, and I'll take you to lunch at Alpha's newest bistro. It's over on Walnut Street and is called 'The Garden of Eden.' I hear they have a chicken and pasta dish that's to die for."

"Sounds great. And thanks, Diana. Thanks for trying to cheer me up."

"He'll be fine, Terri. Bishop is just one of those guys you know is going to come back, no matter what."

Petit Jean State Park, Arkansas
July 7, 2016

Right on schedule, the static on Bishop's radio was again interrupted with Hugh's voice. This time Grim sat in the passenger seat as the plane flew low over the landing strip. This time Bishop and Deke mooned the plane.

"I hope no one from the lodge was watching that," Deke said as he buckled his belt. "They might wonder about your sexual practices."

"I think they already are as far as you're concerned," Bishop shot back.

Hugh's landing was a bit bumpy this time, but before long the aircraft rolled to a stop next to the hangar. Grim, smiling with relief at being back on solid ground, was greeted by his boss.

"Welcome to Hairy Ass, Arkansas. I'm Glute," he said and then pointed at Bishop, "and this is Max."

"I had to look twice before I realized you guys had your pants down. It was hard to tell the difference." replied the new arrival.

Bishop grunted, moving toward the cargo hold. "If you two are done with your juvenile shenanigans, we need to get this

109

aircraft unloaded."

Laughing at Bishop's sudden highbrow demeanor, Deke observed, "You had your pants down, too, brother."

"I thought it was some secret signal between you elite operators… like a cloak and dagger handshake or something."

Hugh joined in, helping carry a box into the storage area. "I got everything on your list, Bishop. A lady who owns a candle shop in Meraton provided the wax. The rest was easy. Nick raised hell over the extra 1,000 rounds of ammo, but other than that…"

"And Terri found a little blue dress?"

A pained looked flashed across the pilot's face, his expression a mixture of not knowing how to respond and not wanting to. "Well… she did send something."

Bishop laughed, patting Hugh on the back. "Never mind. Don't answer that. Here's what you can tell her." And then Bishop explained to Hugh and the rest of the team what the plan was.

After he'd finished, Deke whistled. "Man. It sounds like the world has really gone to hell. But I like the plan. That might just work."

"We need to get my wife and kid out of that shit," added Grim, his determination now stronger than ever.

"We will, brother," Deke reassured. "We will."

Hugh wished everyone good luck and a round of "See you back in Alpha soon," and "Tell everyone we'll be fine," followed. The three contractors watched the pilot enter the plane, standing motionless until the craft was nothing but a speck in the western sky.

"Let's get at it," Deke said. "We've got a lot of work to do."

A series of debates ensued as the men prepared for the trip to Matt's house. After Bishop had briefed Deke and Grim on what he had both seen and heard about Martinsville, everyone had a different opinion on what should be loaded in the truck and what should be left at the airfield to be retrieved later.

The disagreement had centered on how much they could trust the park rangers and other residents of the area not to pilfer their stash while they were gone. One man argued they should pack heavy on firepower. Another maintained that in doing so a stray bullet from a hostile along the trip might mean the end of the mission – and their lives.

"It's a fucking time bomb," Grim commented, looking at the collection of gasoline and ammunition. If somebody gets off a lucky shot and hits that load in the back of the truck, we could all become Airborne Rangers, blown sky high without a chute."

"But everyone at the lodge knows what we're up to and why the plane kept coming back," Bishop argued. "I'm normally a pretty trusting guy, but those folks are desperate. If we leave our supplies here, it might grow legs and walk off while we're gone."

It was finally decided to load the truck, stacking the dangerous supplies in the middle and surrounding them with food, clothing and other essentials that would hopefully provide a shield.

It was approaching dusk by the time the men had fueled the pickup and wedged in all of the supplies. A tarp covered the cargo, an effort to prevent prying eyes from viewing what essentially amounted to a king's treasure to many of the people they would be passing by.

Bishop, having the most experience operating a vehicle via night vision, was the designated driver, Deke and Grim riding in the back behind the cab. The truck was heavy in the rear, down on her shocks from the weight of the cargo. All of the men knew that wouldn't be the case for long as consuming fuel and food would lighten the load as they progressed. They all hoped that the usage of ammunition wouldn't contribute to the loss of weight.

Dusk was painting the early evening sky as they approached the outskirts of town. During his earlier scouting trip, Bishop discovered a slightly different route that better accommodated a vehicle. Still, things appeared the same to Bishop until they entered what was essentially the main business district.

The fire and smoke spitting from several trash barrels was the first hint of human occupation, the flickering light evident from a considerable distance through the NVD monocle. Deke, standing in the bed and scanning with his thermal unit reported at least three hotspots ahead. Noticing the aroma of burning wood when the breeze changed, and trio spotted the people congregated around the fires.

Bishop could tell they were thin, even with the limited depth perception provided by the night vision. There was something about the way their clothes hung from their shoulders that gave a hobo-like impression, long before he could make out any details.

Always thinking of security, his attention was drawn to the fact that none of the small groups of people carried any weapons – at least not long guns.

"Stop here," hissed Deke through the open window. "Grim and I will dismount and investigate. There's a bunch of debris and shit up in the roadway up there, so we can't just blow through at high speed anyway."

"Losing a tire wouldn't be good," Bishop reiterated.

Before he could let the truck roll to a stop, the two contractors hopped out of the bed, the boots making a solid thud on the pavement. Carrying weapons at low ready, they proceeded to walk in front of the truck, heads scanning right and left.

The first group of residents were so stunned by the appearance of the men and truck, they didn't move or say anything. Men with long beards, ragtag clothing and hollow eyes stood and stared as Bishop passed. He didn't hear anyone utter a single word, just blank expressions and the slight movement of their heads as the truck passed.

The second group of locals, having a longer field of view, had the time to gather their wits and react. One man took a step forward, raising his hand as if he wanted Bishop to stop. A small child scurried away as if instructed to hide by some guardian. *Or to alert others*, thought Bishop. *I know drug dealers in the big cities use children as early warning devices... I wonder...*

Grim must have had the same thought. Bishop heard him hiss at Deke, "I think the advantage of surprise is no longer with us."

They traveled another block, two abandoned, burned out vehicles blocking portions of the road. At one point, Bishop had to drive up on the sidewalk to pass. Broken glass was strewn everywhere, some from windshields, some from store fronts. Trash, busted pieces of furniture and even a toilet seat littered the roadway. Travel was slow going.

At first, Bishop thought the arrow was simply a stick someone had thrown at Grim. Bouncing harmlessly off the plates of his body armor, the operator froze momentarily, puzzled by what had just struck his chest. It wasn't until he looked down at his feet that he realized someone had just shot at them.

"Move!" Deke ordered, advancing in front of the truck at a trot. A moment later, Grim had caught up. Another arrow bounced off the truck, missing Bishop's empty driver's side window by less than a foot.

The operators were so distracted by the random shots, they didn't see the crowd gathering up ahead, blocking the only passage out of town.

Deke spied the massed throng first, immediately holding up a fist in the air to signal a stop. The two scouts took a knee, weapons shouldered and ready to engage.

There looked to be about 30 souls trying to block the rescuers' escape. Shovels, axes, baseball bats and long pipes filled their hands. *A human roadblock*, thought Bishop. *Now what are we going to do with this?*

"No one is shooting," observed Grim, surprise in his voice.

"I guess they're out of ammo," Deke replied.

"Completely? Not a single bullet among them?"

Bishop didn't care and definitely didn't want to hang around and ask questions. "Get back in the truck," he said. "I'm going through, one way or the other."

Grim took his cue from Deke, waiting until his boss had nodded and then moving with haste to the bed. Bishop could hear his rifle thump the cab's roof, a sure sign Grim was ready to cover his boss.

Deke cupped his hand and yelled, "You in the road! You people get the fuck out of the way, or we will run you over. We're just passing through."

The throng ignored the warning.

Movement in the mirror caught Bishop's eye, a quick glance confirming the worst. Another cluster of ten men were moving up behind them. "Movement on our six!" Bishop yelled at his team. An arrow whizzed past Deke's head, clattering across the pavement.

"C'mon, Deke! Let's blow this pop stand before this shit gets out of hand!" Bishop yelled.

Deke rose, backed up two steps and then rushed for the truck. As soon as Bishop heard the boots hit the bed, he pushed down the gas, hit the horn, flipped on the lights, and steered the grill right at the center of the approaching mass of people.

At 150 feet, he didn't think they were going to move, visions of bodies flying like bowling pins as the truck plowed through.

At 100 feet, a few legs began to scurry, uncomfortable at the game of chicken they were playing with a quickly approaching bumper and grill.

At 50 feet, people were seriously trying to get out of the way.

Bishop hit the brakes. Despite the heavily laden truck having only achieved about 30 mph in the short distance, it must have seemed much faster to the pedestrians. He controlled the speed just enough to pass through at almost the same instant that the last person managed to get out of the way.

Someone swung a shovel handle or similar stick at the windshield as they passed, the wood breaking harmlessly against the roof-support above the driver's side mirror. A few others threw rocks that might have scratched paint, but never threatened to stop the pickup's progress.

And then they were in the clear.

Almost as suddenly as it had appeared, Martinsville disappeared. Before anyone could comment, open fields and dense forest began to border the pavement, only the occasional home or structure visible from the road.

Bishop, waiting until they were over a mile outside of town, slowed the truck. He eventually stopped in the middle of the road, not really concerned about annoying another driver. *That's a bad habit*, he thought. *A traffic ticket would cause my insurance premiums to go up.*

"You guys all right back there?" he called from the cab.

"We're good. That was just fucking bizarre, dude. It was zombie-like weird," replied Deke.

Grim was shaken. "I want a shower. Even though I didn't touch any of them, I feel the need to bathe. I actually think they would have eaten us if we hadn't busted through."

The three men took a few moments to chill out, all of them casting casual glances back at the town as if the hordes of man-eaters might be in hot pursuit.

The remainder of the drive to Matt's house was uneventful, and all of the men from Texas were just fine with the monotony. Their host for the evening greeted them at the driveway, claiming to have heard their truck engine over two miles away.

"It just goes to show you how bad things have gotten," Matt declared. "When a man can hear a truck engine so far away, well, that makes a statement."

After everyone was settled on the back porch, Matt asked, "Did you secure the goods?"

"I've got everything you asked for," replied Bishop.

"Even the dress?"

"Even the dress."

Matt cast a glance toward the house, kitchen noises drifting through the screen door. He whispered, "That girl deserves a new dress. She's been through hell."

The host then turned his attention to the men surrounding him, apparently sizing them up for the first time. "You guys look like a bunch of hard cases. You might just have big enough nads to pull this off. I'll be right back."

Returning with a box, Matt stared at Deke and then Bishop. "Is this the guy you thought looked like me?"

"He's close enough," replied Bishop with a grin. "You're both ugly fucks."

"That ain't no shit," laughed Matt, winking at Deke.

A uniform, papers, notebook and Bishop's map came out of the box. Matt held up the army fatigues, and again checked Deke over. "This will probably be a little loose on you, but a lot of guys have lost weight. I left my patches and insignias in place. I ain't got no use for 'em anymore."

The powwow on the back porch continued for another five hours, the men studying maps, procedures and other information Matt thought the rescuers needed know. At times, it was difficult to absorb the core dump, but everyone took notes and paid rapt attention. All were professionals, accustomed to being avalanched by massive quantities of data reviewed in short order by commanders and supervisors.

Finally, everyone agreed the exercise was becoming redundant. The mentally exhausted men stood and stretched, working away the stiffness resulting from Matt's extended tutelage. Everyone felt they knew their role.

Bishop led Matt to the truck and lifted the tarp covering the payment. Ignoring the ammo, salt and wax, he immediately reached for the frock, kept secure in a heavy plastic garment bag. Even in the dim moonlight, Bishop could see the smile engulf the fellow's face. "She'll love it!" Matt declared.

"Good," replied Bishop. "Now I've got one more deal I want to make. I'll throw in an extra pound of salt, and 10 shotguns shells in exchange for a bushel of those apples."

Matt didn't hesitate, nodding his agreement.

With Grim and Deke hefting their share, the bartered goods were quickly unloaded, the empty spot in the truck refilled with the box Matt had provided and a large basket of apples. The men all voiced mutual "Good lucks," and "Take cares," and then the trio of Texans was headed back toward Martinsville.

"I'm not sure I'm ready for this shit again," announced Deke, leaning around the edge of the cab so Bishop could hear him clearly.

"Maybe they're all out of arrows," Grim chimed in.

"Throw the apples at them," Bishop barked out the cab window. "Throw a bunch of them... toss them all if anyone's awake."

Grim was upset. "What the hell is he talking about, Deke? Has he lost it? Throw apples at the zombies?"

Deke's expression changed from a look of pure puzzlement to a smiling nod. "You know, that's not a bad idea. As a matter of fact, that's one hell of an idea. C'mon Grim, let's see if you can make the Yankee's spring training this year."

Slinging his rifle, Grim bent to pick up a handful of the orchard projectiles. "I think you've both gone over the edge, but what the hell. Maybe that archer will do the William Tell trick," the operator grumbled.

The crowd in Martinsville had thinned somewhat, but they weren't nearly as surprised by the appearance of the truck this time. They had also improved the roadblock – a little.

As Bishop approached the center of town, men scrambled to form up in the street, many standing behind the makeshift barrier made of a picnic table turned on its side and a knee-high stack of old tires and rubbish. Bishop considered both the men and their fortification pathetic. The truck could easily push through with little chance of damage.

"Whatever you do, don't throw any apples in our path. Throw them off to the side, so I don't have to run over anyone," he instructed from the cab.

Deke's voice answered, "Fire away!"

Bishop turned on the headlights in time to see the first apples arching through the air, one of them pelting a man with a tangled gray beard right in the chest. It took the two throwers a few tosses to get the range, but in a matter of seconds, a virtual blizzard of fruit was flying toward the men at the roadblock.

At first, Bishop didn't think his idea was going to work. He was just about ready to plow into the throng when someone shouted, "They're throwing apples! Apples everybody, apples!"

A few of the defenders looked around, one man finally spotting the missile that had just struck his shoulder. Bending, he held the prize in the air like it was a hard-earned trophy, his voice joining the growing chorus. "Apples!"

Meanwhile, Deke and Grim were playing baseball from the bed of the truck, their arms looking like windmills as they threw as fast as they could. Regardless of the threat, obstacle course and overall danger, Bishop had to smile at the commentary coming from the pickup's bed.

"Two down, bottom of the ninth," Deke's voice rang out. "Strike three!" he yelled, doing his best imitation of a baseball commentator.

In less than 20 seconds, the citizenry of Martinsville changed their focus from stopping the truck to collecting food. In 45 seconds, they were scrambling, clawing and fighting with each other over the small, round prizes. One man stood calmly chewing his catch – an island of tranquility surrounded by hailstorm and riot.

Bishop hit the gas just as Deke and Grim exhausted their ammunition, the battery of fruit-projectiles abruptly stopping. As Bishop slowed to push aside the hastily erected barricade, he noted men scampering around, using their pockets, shirttails and even armpits to hold apples. Three other residents were fighting over who had first spotted a particularly well-thrown example.

The diversion worked.

In a matter of minutes, Martinsville was in their rear view mirror, and Bishop was again driving in the open countryside, Deke and Grim both bragging on their battlefield performance.

"Did you see that dude I nailed in the nuts with my curve ball?"

"Yeah, but that was nothing compared to the guy who tried to catch my high heater - he took it right on the nose."

Bishop smiled at the competitive banter, glad they had absconded without having to seriously harm any unarmed people... people whose only sin was their desperation and hunger. *That could have been Terri and me back there*, he considered, the thought burning off layers of his escape euphoria.

He drove the rest of the way back to the park in silence, visions of a thin, haggard Terri holding a starving child in her arms.

Hunter announced the end of his nap with a half-hearted cry that interrupted Terri's attempt to catch a short snooze for herself. She didn't mind, having been unable to nod off. Sleep was going to be a rare commodity for the next few days.

It wasn't the infant's need for feeding and changing that kept her from resting, but rather the upcoming meetings with the representatives of the federal government that consumed her thoughts.

Diana, Nick and she planned to extend every courtesy, despite the initial holier than thou attitude and demeanor displayed by some of the participants. At one point, Terri thought Nick was going to put one of the men on his ass, and she would have applauded the event.

Hunter didn't seem to care about the upcoming powwows. His fussiness ceased the moment his mother's face appeared over the rails of the crib, his small mouth moving in what she decided was an attempt to return her smile.

"You need a clean diaper," she sniffed, and lifted the tiny body onto her shoulder.

As she gently laid the baby on the changing table, she tried to pull herself up to a better mood. *After all*, she thought, *I still have disposable diapers. Using cloth would be a huge hassle.*

Lifting Hunter's backside, she slid a clean one underneath and then pulled the sticky tabs tight around his midsection. *I need to send Sheriff Watts a note, thanking him for this wonderful shower gift*, she remembered.

Hunter, as usual, was hungry. Grabbing a burp rag and landing in one of her more comfortable chairs, Terri began nursing the seemingly insatiable child. "It's a good thing you don't have a twin. You wouldn't want to share," she whispered, rubbing his cheek. "I would have to ration both of you, which would make you both mad."

And that was the crux of the problem – distribution of limited resources.

Terri completely understood President Moreland's predicament. On one hand, a portion of what he still considered his people, were eating well. On the other hand, thousands were dying every day from starvation. Wouldn't everyone be better off if the resources of one region were shared with the other?

"But we earned it," she said to Hunter, with only a half-hearted conviction. "Okay, maybe we inherited part of it and earned the rest. But still, we could have ended up like the rest of the country if we hadn't...."

Terri had to reprocess the concept. "If we hadn't what? Killed people? Been better shots? Been more aggressive, or kind hearted? What did we do to earn this blessing?"

Hunter didn't answer, but that was okay with his mother. Debate had raged in the council chambers for hours over this very subject, and there had been no resolution. As a matter of fact, the topic had divided the citizens of the Alliance like no other.

Currently, anyone who could make it into Alliance territory was welcomed, fed, given shelter and then employment if at all possible. Many of the newcomers were near starvation, more than a few suffering from dysentery, bronchitis and phenomena. Those who were too sick to work were taken care of by government resources and volunteers. It wasn't unusual to see shock or other mental issues among the immigrants.

"See, Hunter, we're not stingy, greedy people like some say. We help those who need it."

But all of the previously empty, existing homes were at close to 100% occupancy, a shortage projected the following month. This fact, combined with the rumored outbreak of plague back east, had led to groups of Alliance citizens asking their elected officials to stop the open door policy.

"We'll eventually be overrun," several had commented. "There's just not enough to go around," others had argued.

118

The entire mess was complicated by the behavior of the US government, and their anticipated demand that the Alliance share their bounty. Share? "More like give," Terri said to the child in her arms. "They want us to just surrender our resources so they can distribute them to someone else."

Despite the concept rubbing her the wrong way, honesty demanded that she give the idea merit. Would the nation, as a whole, recover quicker if the people of West Texas did without?

Was it worth war?

Another segment of the local population had taken the tried and true approach of capitalism. "We'll just figure out a way to make more," some had ventured. "Give the assholes back in Washington what they ask for. We'll just increase our production somehow."

Terri knew that answer was wrong. Her instinct told her that if the Alliance did manage to increase their output, Washington would only come back and want more. After a while, what would be the point of working harder if someone was just going to come and take it away?

Hunter signaled his full tummy, pulling away and gazing at his mother. Terri rearranged her blouse and then lifted him to her shoulder, tapping lightly on his back to stimulate the air bubbles in his system. The technique produced a robust noise, so loud Terri had to laugh.

"You remind me more and more of your father every day," she joked.

Hunter responded by spitting up all over her clean blouse.

Growling, Terri set the child down on a blanket and went to fetch a clean top. As she changed, she smiled, pretending to scold the youth despite the cheery voice.

"You won't have me around to throw up on forever, young man," she teased. "One of these days you'll have to fend for yourself."

Hunter kicked and flung his little arms and legs, enjoying his mom's antics and attention.

The incident immediately produced an analogy. She knew that one day soon, Hunter would be weaned, and after that, would feed himself. Eventually, as an adult, he would have to be self-sufficient, even producing his own food. Hunter would be motivated to do so by a variety of reasons, not the least of which was the fact that her breasts couldn't provide the nutrition his maturing body would require.

"That's the problem," she said to the child at her feet. "When and how do we wean the US government? At what point do they become self-sufficient? What size breasts do we need in order to keep feeding the rest of the country?"

Chapter 9

Rural Arkansas
July 8, 2016

No specific borders had been defined as far as Operation Heartland was concerned. The general orders, issued by the Pentagon to field commanders, stated that the "primary concentration of assets" was to be 150 miles east and west of the Mississippi River.

According to Matt, it was left up to individual commanders where they exerted their influence and control. The ex-MP also divulged that some regions had more turf than they could handle given current levels of manpower and mobility. The Memphis region was one such example, with the 150-mile western line of demarcation including Little Rock, the capital city of Arkansas.

"There's no federal government presence in Little Rock," Matt had described. "As a matter of fact, it's off limits for some reason. Rumors speculating why abound, but you won't encounter any military forces before West Memphis, and probably not before you reach the bridge crossing the Big Muddy."

The rescue plan called for traveling at night, a tactic Matt had encouraged. "With no electrical lights and candles in short supply, there are very few people up and about after dark. Even if there are functioning local cops, their numbers are few, and half of them are as desperate as the civilians. Survivors, for the most part, hide behind locked doors at night."

The sun was just rising above the Arkansas hills when the trio made it back to the park, Deke and Grim teasing Bishop, calling their chauffeur Mr. Johnny Appleseed and christening the truck the Red Delicious Express.

After identifying a safe place to park, the plan was to sleep during the day, the men taking shifts for sentry duty.

Bishop had the final watch, his thoughts consumed with Terri and Hunter. His son was only a few weeks old, barely a presence in his life, and yet he felt a strong urge to hold the child. *He can't walk or talk or do much else, yet I miss him*, he thought.

Deciding a cup of coffee would help him make it through

121

the long night of travel ahead, Bishop sat around the campfire heating water. After scanning the perimeter, he settled in to wait for the liquid to boil. He wondered how many soldiers had toyed with the embers at the edge of just such a fire, missing their families on the eve before the dawn's battle.

I'm only going to be gone a few weeks at most, he realized. *A lot of men have had to leave their homes for months or years. How did they cope with that? How did they make it through?*

Bishop thought about ancient warriors, legionaries from Roman times and Royal Marines serving aboard slow-moving ships at sea under the flag of the worldwide British Empire. *Those men had to leave for years at a time. Was it a job only suited for men who didn't feel the pain of separation?*

Technology had probably improved things a little, he decided. American troops in Iraq and Afghanistan deployed for a year or more, but they usually had access to email, limited phone time and sometimes even video calls. *That would take the edge off the hurt*, he realized, *but the longing would nag and persist.* Still, he'd give anything to hear Terri's voice on command.

The occasional news story, covering a soldier's return home to meet a child born while he was at war, popped into Bishop's head. *How did the wife deal with that? What was it like to sit in some foreign country and wonder if your new child had ten fingers and ten toes?*

I'm just being a wimp, he decided. *A lot of guys suffered much worse than I have. Suck it up. Get on with it.*

Movement from the hangar distracted Bishop's thoughts, the figure of a sleepy-looking Grim darkening the doorway, stretching his arms high above his head. The timing of the contractor's appearance reinforced Bishop's determination to complete the mission.

If I'm feeling these emotions over a wife and child that I know are safe and among friends, imagine what Grim is feeling given his family's situation, Bishop admitted. *I don't know if I would hold it together as well as he has.*

"I'm heating up coffee water," Bishop informed the new arrival.

Before Grim could muster an answer, Deke's voice sounded from the doorway, "Anybody made coffee yet?"

After the java was poured, the three men studied the most detailed map they possessed. Traveling on the interstate was strictly nonstarter after Bishop had relayed the story of what he had discovered on I-10 heading out of Houston.

Choke points, such as bridge crossings were discussed at length, procedures established to ensure safe passage. The overriding principle was always the same. People, all of them agreed, were to be avoided at all costs. Nothing else could endanger their quest as much as other human beings.

The resulting route, highlighted on the folds of the map, was a zigzag affair across the Arkansas countryside, with Memphis as the final destination. All three of the travelers dreaded that final leg of the journey, but no other solution for crossing the Mississippi had been found. They would simply do their best to arrive at the Tennessee border without trouble and trust in the plan established on Matt's back porch.

An hour later, they set off, Bishop driving without lights while using his night vision. Grim and Deke rode in the bed, boxes of supplies arranged to provide semi-comfortable seats while at the same time protecting the two 50-gallon drums of fuel stored there. They all knew the arrangement wasn't bulletproof, that one stray round igniting all that gasoline on everyone's mind.

Bishop had decided not to remove the fuses that would disable the pickup's lights. He'd implemented that tactic on the bug-out from Houston so his brake and dome lights wouldn't illuminate their position by accident. This was a different trip through less populated territory, and it had been decided that the truck's high beams might be useful in some situations. There were also three rifles aboard – more firepower and better odds of surviving an encounter than Terri and he had possessed on their excursion.

Their chosen route would crisscross through the mountains and hills, eventually snaking through expansive, flat farmlands.

For the first few hours, they observed no one, and only occasionally did the glow of a candle or fire show on the horizon. It was as if the people of the Razorback State had simply disappeared.

The black is cold, white is hot landscape displaying on Deke's thermal imager presented a picture of geometric equality and uniform shape. Without depth perception or previous knowledge, he wouldn't have had a clue what he was viewing. It could have been a modern art sculpture, a Euro-style housing complex, or its true composition – a dam over the Arkansas River.

"What's the name of this place again?" Grim whispered, resting on one knee slightly behind Deke.

"Toad Suck Dam," replied his boss, having trouble keeping a straight face even after repeating the location's name several times.

"And how did it earn that lofty mantle?"

"No fucking clue. Now shut that pie hole of yours and open those eyes."

For the third time, Deke swept the area, detecting nothing but the river meandering its way slowly southward and the unusual structure of the combination dam and bridge.

The weir's flood gates rested between the oddly shaped pillars of the bridge, those supports resembling upside down pyramids with a rectangular base. From Deke's angle, the structure looked odd, out of place, given the background of the rural surroundings.

Shaking his head at the design, he turned to Grim and instructed, "Let's go across. I don't see a soul on this side of the river. Let's make sure there's no one waiting with a surprise on the other side."

"How would they be waiting with a surprise? We haven't seen a single car or truck all night. It's 2 a.m. How would they know we're coming?"

Deke shook his head at the stubborn co-worker. "You know the procedure. Getting hit by hostile fire halfway across a bridge doesn't make for a lovely evening. We're going to follow the rules, Grim, even if we never see another human being again."

"You're right. My bad. I'm just anxious to see my kid and my wife. Don't pay me no mind."

Each man took a side of the narrow, single-lane road that topped the dam. The river was about 300 yards wide at this spot. The bridge, with its adjoining abutments, was almost twice that length.

The two men had worked together for years. Having been taught in the same schools and serving in the same units, they functioned as if controlled by a single mind. Each would take turns bounding, or leap-frogging the other, one always scanning forward while the other covered the rear.

They were one-quarter of the way across when Deke held up his fist, signaling an immediate halt. He could see a heat source in the thermal, but at this distance, it was nothing but a blob.

The water, streaming over the dam's spillway, eliminated noise as a sensory input. It was too dark for the human eye to detect anything of value on the far side of the river. They were completely dependent on the electronic device.

Deke moved to Grim, hoping his side of the bridge

would provide a better angle.

"What's up?" his partner asked.

"I've got a heat source in the scope," Deke replied. "Could be human, could be deer... hell, might even be a cow."

"After seeing those shuffling skeletons back in Martinsville, why am I skeptical that beef is walking around fresh on the hoof?"

"Agreed. Let's go check it out."

"After you, fearless leader."

The two men continued another hundred yards, the image slowly revealing the clear outline of a human shape. Again, Deke signaled a stop, moving to Grim's side.

"I've got one man, armed. There are two campers, a fire that's just about burned out, and a big stack of fishing poles leaning against a tree. There's junk spread all over the place. They've been here for a while."

"What's the call?"

"He's not aware of us yet. Appears to be sleeping in a hammock. I suggest we go see what the deal is."

Grim considered the idea for a minute, finally turning toward his boss and asking, "Should we call up Bishop?"

"Yeah... we'll have him bring the truck up a bit. He can be our reserve. If we get into trouble, we might need the help."

Turning his face away from the potential threat, Deke keyed the radio's microphone. "We've got what appears to be campers up here on the east side of the bridge. You're clear up until that point. Come on just in case we get in trouble. Stay dark."

"Affirmative on no lights. I'm mobile," Bishop's voice responded through Deke's earpiece.

Turning back to Grim, Deke said, "Look at the color of the concrete they used on this bridge. It's a light gray. They'll see our dark shapes against this background as we approach, even in this low light."

Grim checked it out, nodding his agreement.

Deke finished with, "Well, I guess we should just use that as part of our cover story. Let's just walk up, like two lost travelers, out for an evening stroll... stopping by to see what's up."

The two men made it to within 80 yards of the campers before a gentle tug pulled at Deke's pants. Before the operator could react, a thin strand of fishing line pulled taunt, immediately followed by a can of rocks hitting the pavement on the far side. The man in the hammock bolted upright, reaching for his rifle.

"Shit! A tripwire," Deke's voice rang out, much louder than he intended.

It was only a few seconds later that a voice called from the end of the span. "You on the bridge, halt! Stay right where you are."

Looking at each other, the two contractors shrugged and stopped walking. Deke could barely make out Grim's utterance. "What amateur bullshit. Clearly these guys don't have a clue." The statement was followed by the audible clicking of the safety on Grim's rifle.

"I fell for it. Don't go getting cocky. I've now got three people over there. I've kicked the ant mound. Make that four people," the embarrassed operator responded.

Deke moved the small radio to his palm, thumb resting on the press to talk button so Bishop could listen in on any conversation.

Two shadows approached, eventually materializing as men carrying weapons. "You're on private property," began the first guy, his voice harsh and intimidating. "What the hell are you doing here?"

"We were up river, hunting deer. We crossed in a boat, and it must have pulled loose in the current. This bridge was the closest way back across."

A grunt sounded, quickly followed by, "Sounds like you're up shit-creek without a paddle." Both of the bridge tenders thought the remark was funny.

When neither Deke nor Grim offered any reply, one of the shadows continued. "This is now a toll road. You can't pass without paying up."

"What's the toll?"

"That depends on what you've got. I see rifles, and if you were hunting, you've got ammo," came the terse response.

"You'd take a man's only source of meat? If we don't hunt, we don't eat," replied Deke.

The question was met with chuckling, the two locals evidently finding Deke's argument humorous. Grim didn't appreciate the response. "I only see two of you. Maybe you've got a man behind you. No big deal. How about I just shoot both of your sorry asses and cross the bridge for free?"

They thought Grim's proposal was funny as well, the laughter continuing for a bit. Then one of the highwaymen's voice sounded, his tone low and mean. "Tough guy, huh? Well listen up, Mr. Bad Ass. You see that stick right beside you? That's exactly 100 yards from my best shot, who happens to have your chest dead center in the crosshairs of his 30-06. Your partner over there, well, he's only got a 7mm Mouser pointed at his head. My guys don't miss. Every 25 yards is marked on this bridge. You'll never make it back across, even if you do kill me. They'll shoot you down, and then roll your bodies into the river."

Before the contractors could respond, Bishop's voice hissed in Deke's ear. "Stall them. Give me two minutes."

Despite being puzzled at the request, Deke did as he was asked. "So how much ammo do you want for passage?"

"Half of what you're carrying. That's the toll."

Before either of the operators could respond, the other bridge keeper added, "And 50% of anything else you might be carrying that we might want."

Deke acted like he was thinking over the offer, wondering if it was a bluff. Probably not, he determined. "I'll give you 10 rounds, and that's that. If that's not acceptable, then we can just reenact the OK Corral right here and now. I promise neither of *you* will make it home before your snipers kill us."

The offer wasn't rejected outright, whispers of a hushed conversation floating across to Deke's ears.

"No deal," came the response. "This is our bridge. Now set those guns down."

"How about we just find another place to cross," suggested Grim, having picked up on Deke's stall tactic. "Fuck this. I'll walk until we can find another way across the river."

Again, laughter sounded from the two locals. "You two aren't the sharpest tools in the shed, are ya? You're going to pay up, come hell or high water. If you turn and walk away, we'll drop your asses and then take *all* your shit. The crocodiles downstream appreciate the occasional meal we send their way."

Deke was trying to think up something to say when Bishop's voice again sounded in his ear. "I've got both of the snipers on the far bank in my sights. When you hear my first shot, drop those two fuckers where they stand."

"Grim, do you remember that roadblock in Bosnia?"

A moment later, the operator acknowledged, "Yeah, sure do."

"Same deal here, buddy."

"Gotcha."

For a moment, the four men stood staring at each other, the constant drone of the water below overriding any other sound, until Bishop's shot.

As the report echoed across the open spaces, the contractor's rifles snapped to their shoulders. The distance to their targets was only 30 yards - the two locals didn't have a chance.

In the bedlam that followed, Deke had no idea if Bishop had gotten off a second shot. He fired two rounds into the chest of the closest man and then rolled across the pavement, ending in a prone position with his weapon ready to address any remaining threat.

Bishop's voice came across the radio again, "I dropped one; the other I think I only wounded. He ran off, and I can't see him anymore."

"Fuck!" Deke shouted, looking over at Grim. "One of the snipers is still moving over there. We gotta go clear it out."

"He missed?"

"Yeah, he missed one. Come on, let's get this over with."

Running the remaining 80 yards to the end of the bridge was risky. Silhouetted by the white background of the structure's concrete, Deke and Grim tried to weave back and forth, a weak attempt to make any shooter's aim more difficult.

They didn't detect any incoming fire during the sprint, and both men finally exhaled as they found cover on the far bank. Deke keyed his radio. "Any idea where he went?"

"They were both behind that picnic table to your right. I couldn't see his retreat."

Deke braced his legs for the next rush, he and Grim moving together. They made the table in ten steps, both men going prone next to the heavy wooden piece. They could see the body of one sniper, his arms spread eagle on the ground.

Deke was just raising the thermal when a noise reached his ears. A low-pitched moan sounded from behind a pile of trash next to the camper. He couldn't see any heat signature, but it was obvious someone was over there.

Nodding at Grim, both men sprang up and rushed the refuse heap, each approaching from a different vector. They found a man braced against a stack of old tires, both hands holding his stomach. Grim immediately kicked away the wounded fellow's rifle and began scanning the area in case he was bait or some of his comrades were coming to help.

When Deke knelt next to him, the man moaned again, and then made eye contact. A growing pool of damp earth between the guy's legs told Deke all he needed to know. Bishop hadn't missed his second shot.

"It burns like fire," the injured man managed with great effort. "It feels like I'm burning up inside."

There wasn't anything Deke could do. Bishop's round had caught the victim two inches below the sternum, the hollow point bullet expanding to create a quarter-sized tunnel of destruction through the man's middle.

Before he could think of anything to say, the wounded man shuddered, coughed and then again made eye contact with Deke. "Live by the gun, die by the…" And then he was gone.

Grim's warning interrupted the moment, "I've got

movement at the camper."

Deke spun and stood in the same movement, his weapon ready to engage. A figure was running toward them, its appearance ghost-like as willows of cloth floated in the dim light. He almost fired, but something told him to hold, and he was glad he did.

A woman, wearing a loose fitting nightgown ran toward them, bending immediately to check the dead man. "No! No, Jack! Oh, my gawd!"

Deke wanted out of there. He keyed his mic and broadcast, "All clear over here, Bishop. Get that damn truck across right now."

"On my way," came the immediate answer.

"You son of a bitch!" The woman's voice rang out. "You've killed them all."

"Lady," Grim answered, "It was us or them. What the hell did you expect us to do?"

Before the woman could respond, Deke grabbed Grim's arm and pulled him away. "Come on, man. Let's go meet Bishop and the truck."

As the two contractors trekked toward the road, two more women and a single child came rushing up to join the grieving widow. Everyone was crying, whiffs of angry words mixed with the remorse.

"Should we take the weapons?" Grim asked.

"No, I'm not going to leave a bunch of women and children out here without firearms. We probably just issued their death warrants anyway."

It was a couple of minutes before the pickup's motor sounded across the river, the event quickly followed by the appearance of a dark shape moving across the gray concrete background.

"You guys okay?" Bishop greeted as he pulled to a stop.

"Yeah, we're all right," Deke responded. "Let's get the fuck out of here."

Bishop waited until the two passengers climbed into the bed. He was just reaching for the gearshift, when sparks flew from the hood. Three more shots sounded, one of the rounds cracking inches away from the open driver's window. A glance showed one of the women holding a rifle, firing haphazardly at the truck. Grim's voice shouted, "Go! Go! Go!"

Before he could react to the warning, the passenger side mirror exploded in a cloud of glass.

He floored the truck, barely keeping on the narrow road until he could raise the night vision to guide his steering.

"I thought we should've gathered up those rifles," an

angry Grim shouted. "Those poor, helpless widows you left back there just decided to shoot at us. We'd all be crispy critters if she'd hit one of these gas cans."

Deke didn't respond.

The trouble with the truck started on a gradual uphill grade. Bishop noticed a hesitation, almost as if the transmission was having trouble shifting gears. Another two miles passed before the first jerky pause and then another. Five minutes later, the truck wouldn't shift out of first gear.

The road they were traveling had once been a popular highway, the now dark traffic signals, center turning lane and no stop entrance and exit ramps an indication of engineering designed to handle heavy traffic loads. They had been making every effort to stay on country lanes, but this section of northern Arkansas left them no choice but to use this route.

Of course, the truck had chosen this leg of the journey to act up. The "check engine" light illuminated on the dash.

Bishop spotted a sign for a rest area up ahead and a few minutes later, they limped off the main road.

"What's going on?" questioned Grim from the bed.

"Truck's broke. It won't shift."

"Fuck."

Bishop exited the cab after popping open the hood. Deke and Grim jumped down, scanning their surroundings and then moving off to check the two cars parked in the lot. In moments, they returned, joining Bishop at the front of the truck.

The driver was shining a red flashlight around the engine compartment, the dark, greasy engine looking almost evil in the crimson glow, like some demon machinery designed with ill intent.

"See anything?" Deke asked.

"Looks fine to me," Bishop responded, moving his head to examine both sides of the V8. "But then again, I'm not a wrench jockey by any means."

Grim was impatient, his head pivoting around the area as if he expected an ambush at any moment. "If it looks okay, then let's go. It'll still run, won't it?"

"It will run, but only about 5 miles per hour. We'll eat through our gas like crazy with it like this. Besides, what if we need a quick getaway?"

Bishop closed the hood, moving to the side and shining

his light under the truck. "Something's leaking," he announced before lying on his back and sliding underneath the pickup. A few moments later, a resounding "Shit!" sounded from beneath the wounded vehicle.

He reappeared, rolling out and shaking his head. "Those women hit something critical. I can't tell exactly what, but there is a hole in the transmission. We're leaking fluid like crazy, and have probably already done some permanent damage. It's too hot to touch."

Deke calmly studied the area, "It's going to be light soon. If you can pull it over there behind the bathrooms, it won't be visible from the road. This is as good a place as any to hole up and decide what to do. Besides, I'm getting hungry."

"Sounds like a plan," Bishop agreed.

Ten minutes later, the truck was hidden behind a single-story block building that had once been the rest area's primary attraction for travelers. Small signs announced facilities for both sexes. Bishop, taking on the task of clearing the building, grunted when he hesitated at the ladies' doorway. *Old habits die hard*, he thought. There were no occupants of any stall, male or female.

The three men busied themselves making camp. They had just finished when the warm glow of the pre-dawn illuminated the countryside surrounding their temporary bivouac. Deke stood for a moment, taking it all in.

"This would have been a good spot to stop on a long car trip," he noted, nodding toward the mature hardwoods scattered around the grounds. "A nice, shady spot to let the kiddos burn off some backseat energy and for the missus to use the facilities."

Bishop nodded, smiling at the seldom seen soft side on the operator. Noticing his friend's expression, Deke added, "What? I have a mom and dad. I have brothers and sisters. I dated girls. I wasn't created in a back room at Fort Bragg and turned loose on the world, ya know."

"I'm glad," was all Bishop said before moving off to start a fire.

After the men had eaten and determined their order of sentry duty, there wasn't anything else to discuss except the topic they all dreaded. What to do about their transportation.

"We need a new truck," Bishop offered, hating to broach the subject.

"And where might we find one of those?" Grim replied.

Without answering, Bishop fetched the map from the cab, spreading the folds open on a nearby picnic table. He was soon joined by his two mates.

"We're about here," he began, tapping a spot on the paper with his index finger. "We've been running parallel with this

131

interstate... I-40... all night. I'm thinking we hole-up here, and then one or two of us can hoof it down to that road... see if we can retrieve another truck."

Deke considered the option, scratching his chin while thinking. "How would we carry gas? A battery? All the stuff you would need to get a relic started?"

"That's why I'm thinking two of us should go. One guy can't carry all that. We would need a couple gallons of gas, this truck's battery and a few tools. It's just over 25 miles to I-40. Let's say we'd have to walk another five miles before we found a suitable truck. It could be done."

Deke's gaze darted toward the horizon, obviously working through the problem. "So two guys carrying a very heavy load, humping 30-40 miles through what could be very dangerous territory. That doesn't fit with my vacation plans. Any Plan B?"

Bishop countered, "The only part I think would be dangerous would be the walking along the interstate. Since we're on foot, we should be able to circumvent any trouble spots, like exits. There are no towns along that stretch, and we're far enough east of Little Rock that the population should be pretty thin."

Grim cleared his throat, nodding toward the two cars in the parking lot. "We can't salvage a part or something from those cars and keep the same truck?"

"The bullet struck part of the transmission and what I think is the crankcase. Even if we could find a fit, there's no way we can do serious repairs without tools and knowledge. I think we've burned up some gears or something, so patching the leak and topping off the fluid probably wouldn't do us much good. We might get stranded out in the open someplace, and that would suck."

Grim had to agree with the assessment, even though he didn't like it. "How about we catch some shut-eye and mull it over? I'm beat and not thinking clearly. You two can't be far behind."

"Now there's the best idea I've heard in a while," added Deke. "I want to keep our after dark schedule, regardless of what we do. My eyes are burning, and my legs ache. Let's crash and then make a decision."

Yawning, Bishop nodded and said, "Stop talking about it, damn it. You two are like a mother singing a lullaby, and I've got the first watch."

The merging aromas of coffee and smoldering hickory chips lured Bishop from his dream. He had decided to sleep in the fully reclined driver's seat rather than risk rolling off a picnic table, like the accommodations chosen by his partners.

The sun was low in the west, probably two hours from slipping over the horizon. Peering at his watch, he noted the four hours of rest he'd achieved.

"Well good morning, sunshine," Deke greeted, observing movement in the truck's cab. "Room service should deliver the eggs and bacon to the door any minute now."

Rubbing his eyes, Bishop managed a weak, "Hope you ordered mine scrambled with cheese."

Bishop's frame was stiff, a symptom of never having fully relaxed or been comfortable in the driver's seat. After a stretch and yawn, he wandered off to find a tree to stand behind.

A mouthful of water combined with a short squeeze of toothpaste satisfied his bare minimum hygiene requirements. The first sip of coffee made him feel somewhat human. "I'm getting too old for this shit," he mumbled.

Grim was setting up a wire grill over the campfire, a cooler of food nearby. "I want to fix the last of this beef we brought from Alpha. The ice in the cooler is gone, and these steaks will spoil before too much longer. How do you like yours cooked?"

After eating the thick slices of well-cooked meat, topped off with canned corn and fresh green beans, the men sat in silence, again trying to avoid the difficult decision that could make or break the mission.

"I can't come up with any alternative to Bishop's idea," Grim finally said. "How 'bout you, Deke?"

"Nothing comes to mind. One thing's for sure, we can't just stay here and hope a better option presents itself. I didn't see or hear another soul during my entire watch."

And so they began talking through the plan, covering as much detail as possible. At one point, Grim rose from his haunches and said, "I found something that might help. I got bored during my watch and jimmied the trunk lids of those cars... just curious. Check this out."

The operator walked toward the parking lot, returning a minute later pulling a bag of golf clubs on a two-wheel cart. "I think this might help with the weight."

Bishop smiled, the small bit of good fortune helping

cheer him up. "That's one hell of a find, Grim. Nice. Very nice."

Deke glanced at the sun and then announced, "We've got a hell of a lot of work to do if we're going to leave tonight. Most of it will be easier with daylight. Let's get moving."

"Well, crap! How is a guy supposed to practice his putting on this little vacation, gentlemen?" Bishop quipped as he removed the bag of clubs from the cart.

It had been decided that Grim would remain behind to guard the truck. Given that responsibility, the contractor began setting up his security, running tripwires in key locations around the rest area.

Bishop set about removing the battery from the truck and filling two plastic milk jugs with gasoline from the barrels. "The gas will melt this plastic in a day or two," he commented. "We've got to find something quick."

Deke busied himself packing supplies for the trip. Besides the truck rescue gear, water was the heaviest commodity. After the basic necessities had been gathered, he and Bishop exchanged a quick inventory of the personal kit each would bring.

"We don't need two blow-out bags," Deke noted, setting aside his medical kit in order to make room for other weighty items.

"I'm going to leave my big rifle behind," added Bishop. "That way we can share common ammo and mags."

As dusk fell, they completed the hurried preparations, all three men announcing they were ready by the time the moon appeared in the sky above.

"See ya in a day or two," was the only exchange between Grim and the two-man raiding party.

"You fucking better," the lone sentry replied.

As Bishop and Deke headed off into the night, all three men were analyzing the dangers that lie ahead. If the raiders didn't return, Grim was in a bad spot. If anyone got hurt, the chances of survival were low. If the truck were discovered by locals, how long could the lone sentry hold out against a motivated attack?

Just like life, Bishop thought as he pulled the supply-heavy cart along the pavement. *There are always about a hundred things that can mess you up. It's a wonder we've made it this far.*

Chapter 10

Central Arkansas
July 9, 2016

They were hugging the tree line, trying to straddle the border between the dense woods and the untilled field, trying to negotiate a compromise between walking fully exposed in the open and slugging it through thick briars and brush. Trying to circumvent the tangling, pricking foliage at night was undoable, so Bishop and Deke decided to chance for lighter cover along the edges of the woods.

Bishop had no way of seeing the game camera. Mounted 15 feet on the side of a tree and angled downward, the battery-powered device sensed the Texan's passage via its motion detector. Had Deke been using his thermal imager, or Bishop scanning with his night vision, either man would have seen the infrared flash emitted by the unit. Timing was against them, both men using only their eyes at the time of the passing.

Deke passed through the beam next, his picture snapped with surprising clarity. The images of the two men were transmitted via wireless radio to a computer server residing just over a mile away.

The never-sleeping machine detected the incoming message instantly, initiating a stored program to scan the images attached to the camera's broadcast. As the binary processor read each pixel, the stored algorithms made a decision in less than a second. There were human shapes in the photographs.

A second computer program was loaded, this one following pre-configured instructions directing it to sound an alarm. A constant "beep beep beep" immediately began ringing from the machine.

C. J. Ledbetter hadn't heard the alert in so long, his sleepy brain had trouble identifying the sound. The first thing that his groggy mind determined was the solar inverters must be complaining of low batteries. He quickly realized this was a different tone.

Pulling back the covers, he rose gingerly from the bed, the flashing monitor of the nearby computer system answering his question.

Padding quietly across the bedroom floor, he gazed at the screen and didn't believe what the machine was telling him. There, displayed on the large monitor, were the images of two men – one pulling a cart of some sort. Both were armed, rifle barrels and magazine pouches clearly visible.

C. J. couldn't comprehend it for a moment, his barely awake fingers stumbling across the keyboard to verify the date and time of the pictures. Reality struggled to set in.

His next action was to identify which camera had snapped the photos. Again, the keys clicked, and the display refreshed. He stared at the photograph's audit trail with wide eyes. The two strangers were just over a mile away.

Ledbetter paced to the window, staring over the nighttime landscape as if the two intruders might be stalking around his yard. Realizing there was no way the two travelers could have covered the distance in such a short time, he tried to recall his checklist. He had to raise the alarm with the other members of his group.

A man can walk a mile in 12 minutes, he thought. *I've got 20 minutes, tops, to get everyone up.* A rustling of cloth told him one person no longer needed to be rousted. Judy was already awake.

"What's the matter, C. J.?" his wife's soft voice asked.

"We've got intruders. Go look at the computer screen. I've got to get dressed and wake everybody up."

Shirt, pants and boots, in that order. He was so nervous he tried to put on his boots first. Rifle by the door. The AR felt reassuring. He turned on the night vision, pleased the battery still held life. The extra magazine in each back pocket helped as well. Out the door.

He moved at a brisk pace toward the guesthouse, the sound of gravel crunching under his boots causing him to flinch.

Thump! Thump! C. J. was slamming his tight fist against the door over and over again. "We've got intruders coming in from the north. Two men, heavily armed. Are you up?"

Thump, thump, thump again. "Are you up?"

"Yeah. Yeah, I'm up, C. J. Did you say two men?" replied the hoarse voice of his oldest son-in-law. The younger one was dead – killed a year ago by intruders, just like the ones captured by the game camera.

"Yup. Grab your rifle, and meet me by the mailbox," he replied, trying to sound casual and confident.

He didn't wait for an answer, moving on to the 5th wheel camper parked nearby. He knocked loudly on the aluminum door. Again, he relayed the message to his two sons. A horrible vision passed through his mind. Would tonight be the night they lost somebody? *My God*, he thought. *I couldn't stand to lose one of them. Please Lord, not tonight. They're too young.*

He then moved to the second camper, his brother already stirring from the noise. "How many?" his sibling asked at the door.

"Two. Military rifles, chest rigs, big packs. They ain't deer hunting. We've got 10 minutes."

"I'll be right out."

He headed back toward the main house where Judy met him at the door. "Get the girls together; stay in here with your pistols and the shotgun. It's probably nothing, but we can't take the chance."

The tone of his voice left no room for question or protest, not that she would've voiced any objection. His bride of 29 years simply nodded and then mouthed the words, "I love you."

Ledbetter strode purposefully toward the mailbox, keeping on the grassy edge of the driveway. After arriving at the rally point, he turned to survey his spread.

Everyone called it the Alamo to his face. He also was aware they called it Ledbetter's Boondoggle behind his back – at least they did until the world went to hell. Now, he doubted anyone used that term anymore.

With four years of shop class at William Jefferson Clinton High School under his belt, C. J. had taken a brand new set of tools, loaded them in the trunk of his old, but well-tuned Chevy, and gone looking for work as a mechanic in Little Rock.

Three years later, he was the shop foreman at a large auto dealership. Five years after graduation, he opened his own business. Ten years to the day after leaving high school, he opened his fifth auto repair store.

Life was good for C. J. and his hometown sweetheart. Their first baby came less than two years after leaving school. The stork delivered the fourth child seven years later.

As he waited at the end of the driveway, he grunted at an old memory. "I found a girl who doesn't mind a man who can fix things and has a little dirt under his fingernails when he gets home." He hoped he could fix this thing tonight without any of his family getting killed.

After the second shop had opened, the only dirt under the proprietor's fingernails was from counting money. A nagging recession meant people kept their cars longer. Older transportation meant more repairs, and his business boomed.

Seeming to ride above the economic agony plaguing the rest of the country, C. J. traveled through life with few concerns, enjoying the fruits of his hard labor and wise management. Even the Second Great Depression didn't impact his livelihood – at least not at first.

As the hard times continued, he began to develop a nagging feeling that something just wasn't right. A storm was building, just over the horizon... a troublesome sense that something bad was coming down the road.

He began to research on the internet, finding other like-minded people who felt the same way. He learned an entirely new vocabulary and acronyms, terms like bug-out, prepper, and SHTF.

The purchase of 30 acres two hours north of Little Rock met with raised eyebrows from his wife, Judy eventually agreeing with the investment despite not believing his excuse for one second. "Go ahead and buy that country place if you want C. J., but I don't buy this story of yours. Why would a man your age all of a sudden want to take up hunting?"

He justified the solar power system since it was a remote area, using the logic that, "It takes the utility company forever to restore power after a thunderstorm out here." She didn't even comment on the 300 pounds of freeze-dried food she found stored in the cupboard one weekend. The two sealed boxes of seeds remained unnoticed, artfully hidden under some junk in the barn.

It was the purchase of the AR15 that caused a domestic disturbance. "Why do you need that?" she had tested. "What is going on? You're scaring me."

"Look, hun, I'm concerned, not crazy. There's just so much going on that's bad right now. It makes me feel better to do these things. You know me, I've always provided for our family. This is the same thing – I'm just providing for what I think the future may hold, the worst case scenario."

Judy and the kids had accepted his activities, only the occasional joke accidently reaching his ears. He didn't care. It just felt better to prepare, to be self-reliant.

His redemption came after the terrorist attacks pushed the already crippled nation over the edge. When the power went out in their suburban Little Rock home, C. J. started gathering up their belongings. When the first food riot broke out downtown, he started packing the car. He barely managed to get through calls to his family members before the cell towers went down. No one laughed at him anymore.

The sound of footfalls pulled C. J.'s attention back to the present, his two sons approaching. "Dad, why would anybody be out in the middle of the night like this?"

"I don't know, Junior, but it can't be good. Maybe somebody got word about what we've got here... the food and fuel and stuff. Maybe these men are only passing through. After what happened the last time, we can't take any chances."

Two years ago, the nineteen-year-old boy would have argued with him. Not now. *He's grown up. Dad's not so crazy dumb anymore*, C. J. thought. *I guess it helps that dad ended up not being such a nut job*. Both boys were strong and proud – just the way he wanted them - independent, not uppity.

Movement at the edge of his vision distracted the father, but it was only Judy herding the girls into the safety of the main house, the females moving calmly and silently. *Good.*

His brother arrived a few moments later, a rifle slung across his chest. "What's the plan?"

"They're coming in past the big deer hide. If we hurry, we can cut them off there – before they catch sight of the house. The pond on one side and that heavy thicket on the other will force them to walk right through the gap, just like the deer. You and Junior will use the hide; we'll go over where you got that deer last week. We'll be there waiting on them."

Rubbing his chin, the older Ledbetter asked, "And what? Are you just going to open fire? Are we going to try and talk? Fire warning shots? I gotta ask again, what's the plan?"

The dilemma had been discussed a hundred times, the conversations always ending with C. J. believing he would know what to do when the time came, if it ever did. "It will be just like any business deal or encounter with an angry customer; we'll know what to do," he had always concluded. "We'll play it by ear."

Now, in the middle of the night with a real threat approaching, he wasn't so sure.

"Just follow my lead," he told his brother. "If I start shooting, you guys join in. If I talk, then hold your fire. I can't be sure until I see them with my own eyes."

C. J. could tell his sibling didn't like the answer, but there wasn't time to argue. They headed out, moving at a brisk pace.

Deke pushed aside the bush and froze, surprised by the open space he encountered. The pond wasn't large, not even a small lake. He judged it to be half an acre at most, but still a surprise.

The rustle of pine needles told him Bishop was beside him, evaluating the same obstacle. "Guess we go around, unless you're wanting a swim." the Texan whispered.

"Guess so. You could use a bath though. But I didn't bring any soap."

"Men perspire, women glisten," came the retort.

Deke waited on Bishop to scan right and left. His light amplification device provided a slightly better picture than his own thermal, when heat wasn't involved.

"Looks like the woods are a little thinner to the west. Let's go around that way."

"Gotcha."

Waiting on Deke to move out, Bishop pushed the button to light his watch dial, curious how much longer it would be before his partner took a turn pulling the golf cart. While still better than humping the 90 pounds on his back, pulling the little bastard cross-country was exhausting. He still had another 30 minutes before he could hand it off and walk like a normal man.

Not only was the cart heavy, it was noisy. Despite stopping and readjusting the load several times, the gasoline occasionally sloshed while the box and battery creaked. It was just a little more than annoying, especially to men who took such pain to move silently. Deke had taken to calling the wheeled device, "Bishop's little red wagon."

The pause allowed Deke to achieve a 15-foot head start, a reasonable separation by Bishop's way of thinking. He turned the buggy's wheels in the soft soil and began his best imitation of a draft mule.

It had quickly become evident that pulling the wagon with one hand didn't bode well for Bishop's spine. Besides making it difficult to keep his balance, walking while half-twisted at the waist was a prescription for pain in his lumbar region. After the first few miles, he'd arrived at a solution – cutting a small length of paracord from his kit and making a quick harness around his middle and over his shoulders. He could unhook his load with the flick of the wrist if need be, and other than trekking slightly hunched over, his movements were otherwise less restricted.

Still, the cart occasionally tipped over on uneven ground. That fact, combined with constant entanglement in low vegetation had put Bishop in a foul humor. Deke showed no sympathy for his buddy's oxen-like plight, never deviating to travel a smoother path or avoid undulations.

Bishop amused himself by toying with ideas of revenge when Deke took his turn.

So it was a relief when they arrived at the edge of the pond and found the game trail. Taking a knee, Deke waited until Bishop caught up. "I've pulled you through some nasty shit, brother. I'll take my turn early," the contractor whispered.

Grunting, Bishop said, "Ohhh... now you're willing to take a turn... right when the going gets easy. What a buddy."

"Take the offer or wait, Slick. Your call," Deke replied, his smile showing in the dim light.

"I'll take it."

Bishop began unhooking his apparatus, intending to show mercy by letting the other man use the makeshift harness. The process was a little problematic in such low light.

"You okay with a little light? I can get you into this thing easier that way."

Deke scanned the perimeter with the thermal, seeing nothing that resembled human temperature. "Sure."

Bishop made sure his torch was set to red, and then flicked on the light. He quickly set about draping the harness around Deke's shoulders, when something shiny on the ground caught his eye.

Holding up a finger, Bishop took a step and bent, lifting a rifle cartridge for his partner to see. It was a 30-06, a popular hunting round – and it was fresh, only a thin veneer of tarnish on the brass case.

In a blur of movement, the light was extinguished, both operators facing outward in a low crouch – both sweeping the area with their monocles.

Deke whispered, "I don't like this. I don't like it at all. Somebody took a deer or hog here. Could have been last week, could have been a couple of hours ago. With that pond on one side and that dense growth on the other, this is where I'd set up to hunt animals… with four legs, or two."

Bishop wanted to groan at the concept of reversing course, the thought of doubling back with the cart making his legs hurt. Still, Deke was right. Someone was clearly in the area – someone with a rifle.

While the Texan covered, Deke cautiously reached for the cart and began backing out of the gap. Bishop gave him a few minutes, enough of a lead to reach good cover, and then he slowly withdrew, sweeping left and right with both eye and barrel.

Fifty yards away, C. J. lowered his night vision and grunted. Turning to his son, he pulled the boy close and announced, "They're backing out. They must have seen us, or some sign of us. I saw one guy pick something up off the ground just before they opted to retreat."

The lad only nodded, not daring to make any noise.

"You go tell the others to stay put. I'm going to follow the two out, make sure they don't circle back on us."

Again, a quick nod acknowledged the order. C. J. stayed put behind the mound that had hidden them from Deke's

141

thermal scans, watching as his son moved toward the deer hide.

After allowing for what he considered enough time, C. J. slowly rose and began moving toward the deer trail, careful with his footfalls and trying desperately not to give off a warning to the men he intended to pursue.

He believed the intruders also had night vision, but couldn't be sure. At one point, he thought for sure they were sweeping the area with something, but it was difficult to tell.

He also knew that whatever was on the cart being pulled by the two men was heavy. When he reached the spot where they'd paused, he could see the tracks left behind by the wheels. That would make them easier to follow.

He'd trail them to the border of his property and if they continued away, he'd leave them alone.

Their sign was easy to follow, even without the light-amplifying device. Weeds were flattened, and the trough created by their cart obvious in the patches of bare earth. He stopped suddenly, listening intently, sure he heard a noise ahead... a sound foreign to the woods.

He didn't want to get too close. Now outnumbered, his only intent was to make sure they weren't headed for his homestead and family. Other than that, he could care less about the strangers' intent.

The trail took him into a clearing, a space where some combination of sun, soil and moisture prohibited the foliage from growing thick. He stopped again, studying the open area with intensity, hoping to get a glimpse of the men he was following.

There! Almost to the point where the woods grew dark again. There was the man pulling the cart, clearly visible as he bent over to adjust the cargo.

C. J. felt something cold on his ear, at first believing some liquid had dripped from the canopy above. A voice, harsh and low commanded from behind, "On your knees... nice and slow." The cold barrel pressed harder into the cartilage, an obvious signal meant to communicate the seriousness of the demand.

The ex-mechanic had never felt anything like the terror that now surged through his body. He couldn't command his legs to kneel, couldn't make his lungs breathe or his voice function. He just stood there – frozen like a statue.

"Don't be stupid," the voice hissed again. "You're not that good, and I am. On your knees or die."

Finally nodding, C. J. managed to fold his joints and drop down. He had just settled his weight when a hand grabbed his shoulder and pulled him back on his haunches, his knees screaming in pain. Before he could even inhale to moan, his rifle sling was sliced, and then the AR gone.

Another hard shove, and his face was in the leaves on the forest floor, a heavy weight on his back. Hands began roaming his person. He felt the magazines pulled from his back pockets. *They're going to kill me*, raced through the prisoner's mind. *They're going to shoot me right here on my own land. Oh, Judy. What will become of my Judy?*

Again the same voice, softer, "Go check to make sure no one is following him," and then the slightest of footfalls fading into the distance.

"What's your name?" began the whisperer.

When he didn't answer, a boot nudged his leg. "What's your name?"

"C. J. Ledbetter," he managed, his voice sounding weak and distant.

"Well, Mr. Ledbetter, why are you following us?"

For some reason, the question seemed odd... difficult to answer. "I... I... you're on my land. We had trouble... I wanted to protect..." and then he gave up, embarrassed at the fear that controlled his throat.

"We?" the voice sounded. "There are more than one of you?"

Damn it! Thought the man on the ground. *I can't believe I just told him about my sons.*

Again a slight rustle and then a low voice, "I don't see anybody else."

C. J. saw a knee next to his head, felt a presence close to his ear, the man's breath hot against his skin. "Start talking right now, Mr. Ledbetter. My partner and I are only trying to pass through. We didn't even know you were here. Start working those vocal cords before I lose my temper."

There was something about the voice in his ear – something in the tone that allowed hope to flow through his veins. "They're not following you. Only me. I'm alone. I told them to stay put until I made sure you were headed off my land," sputtered C. J.

"How many?"

"My sons and brother... uh... four of us altogether."

"Stand up."

The command was so unexpected, he wasn't sure he'd heard it right. "Go on, stand up."

He was shaky, his limbs tingling as if they were asleep from lack of circulation. Somehow, he managed to rise. He looked up to see the outline of the man who had taken him so easily – turned him into a helpless blob of boneless flesh.

"Now I'm only going to say this once, so clear your ears.

You go back and tell your kin to stay put. Don't follow us, and we'll leave you alone. Come after us, and blood will flow... Ledbetter blood. How far east do we have to travel to get off your property?"

"A half mile... maybe a bit more."

"Okay. We'll stay off your place, if you don't stalk us. Do we have a deal?"

"Yes," C. J. answered, a glimmer of hope clear in his voice.

"Good."

The stranger held up the captured weapon, ejected the magazine and cleared the round in the chamber, catching the errant shell with a deft motion of his hand. "I'll leave this ammo and the two mags I took from your pockets about a hundred yards up this trail. You can find them in the daylight. Your night vision will be there, too. Don't be stupid, Mr. Ledbetter. Go home to your family, and don't let your ego get the best of you. Don't start thinking about the son of a bitch who got lucky and bested you out in the woods."

The man stepped closer then, his presence forcing C. J. to look up into his eyes. They were dark, reptilian-like and unblinking. The voice dripped with violence, despite the hushed volume. "Listen carefully, my friend. I will kill you and your clan without remorse. I'm going to spare you just this once. Now go back and tell the others any story you want, and then go home. Pray you never see me again."

And with that, the stranger shoved the empty rifle into C. J.'s chest, and then the two intruders were moving, walking briskly back to their cart. The landowner stood in shock, watching the interlopers disappear into the tree line, like two ghosts passing through a wall.

Waves of relief and joy swept through his soul. He felt a sudden urge to hug the nearest tree, kiss the ground and bless the forest. "Thank you, God," he kept repeating to himself.

Eventually the euphoria wore off, resulting in a hard crash from the emotional high he'd been riding. In a short time, he went from boundless energy and goodwill to bone-weary exhaustion. Turning, he headed back to his sons and brother, not embarrassed at all to tell the truth of what had happened. *Besides*, he realized, *I would be violating God's law if I were dishonest about this wonderful gift, this prayer he has answered.*

Bishop scanned I-40 with his optic, dawn threatening to bathe the interstate in light at any moment. It was as he'd anticipated being this far east of Little Rock, completely void of any traffic, motorized or human.

While that was a positive development, it was offset with bad news. There wasn't a single abandoned car or truck in sight.

"How far do you estimate we can see?" Deke asked, resting his sore back and legs on the knoll they had selected for cover.

"I'd guess three quarters of a mile in each direction," Bishop replied. "It's just our luck to vector in on a completely barren stretch of road."

Deke sighed, unlacing his boot and pulling it off. "I suppose that beats the hell out of cresting the rise and bumping into a thousand starving zombies."

"I suppose."

After removing both boots, Deke began rubbing his feet. "I don't know if I feel any worse pulling that fucking red wagon of yours than I would have humping that load on my back."

"Both would suck, and clearly, we're not done walking yet."

Bishop pulled a drink from his Camelback, the tepid water doing little to make him feel better. "Which way – east or west?"

"Flip a fucking coin for all I care. My dogs are barking, my spine is compressed, and I can't feel my right knee anymore."

"Wimp. That was just a stroll in the park. At least it's not 110 in the shade with sand blowing in your face."

Deke grunted, "You Texans... always think you're so damn rugged. Fuck that shit. You're hurting as badly as I am, you just won't admit it."

Bishop laughed, but wasn't ready for a confessional. He liked Deke, respected him enormously, and enjoyed the man's competitive spirit. No way he was going to admit how badly he felt. "I don't have a coin to flip. Do you?"

"No, I thought I would use my American Express card on this trip. They have a great rewards program, you know."

Bishop chuckled, still studying the roadway below, as if he expected something to change.

"Tell you what," he began, "Let's head east, away from Little Rock. I'm also game for walking along the road for a bit. It will make it easier going."

"Now there's an idea," replied Deke, pulling on his boots.

The two men reached the flat surface of the highway a few minutes later, the open expanses making them feel somewhat exposed. It was Bishop's turn to tow the cart, a task he managed while studying the map.

"Far as I can tell, the nearest town is 11 miles ahead. It's just a speck on this map, but if we don't find a truck to hijack in the next seven or eight miles, I'm going to start lobbying to turn around and head back east."

Visions of Martinsville and busting the roadblock with apples filled Deke's mind. "I'm good with that."

While the walking was easier, their pace remained slow. Bishop estimated he was carrying 35-40 pounds on his back, another 15-20 with weapon and kit. Deke was equipped with about the same load. Despite both men being in excellent physical condition, their quest was taking a toll on their bodies and minds.

They spied the first relic at just over a mile. An 18-wheeler was pulled to the side of the road, the contents of its trailer scattered all over the pavement. Bishop had seen this kind of thing before, looters ransacking any building, vehicle or storage area, desperately looking for sustenance.

This specific example involved PVC pipe with an assortment of sizes, lengths and fittings strewn for several yards. Deke grunted, "If I pried open a trailer and found the first ten feet were loaded with something I couldn't eat, burn, or trade, I don't think I'd waste the time or energy clearing the whole thing."

"Desperate people aren't always logical. Malnutrition does crazy shit to the brain. Nothing shocks me anymore."

The duo kept walking, the next mile markers becoming both their goal and a torturous reminder of their slow progress.

"I ran out of gas once, a long time ago, out past Bumfuck, North Carolina. I had to walk 15 miles to find gas. It didn't seem so bad at the time," Deke reminisced.

The next vehicle they spotted was a high-dollar German sports sedan. Someone had smashed the dashboard and removed the stereo, as well as pried open the trunk and hood. "Can you eat radios?" Deke questioned, not really expecting an answer.

The pastoral view over the next rise actually improved Bishop's spirits. A long valley stretching off into the distance greeted the two. The outline of several vehicles was evident despite the morning sun obstructing their line of sight. Shading his eyes with his hand, Bishop looked at Deke and grinned. "A target rich environment."

And it was.

Two miles and four relics later, they spotted the pickup. It wasn't as new as Bishop's first theft, but appeared to be a sturdy ride. One tire was completely flat, the others low. The key was the gas tank.

Bishop scooted under the rear bumper, praying no one had damaged the goods. The tank appeared untouched.

"Let's see if we can get this baby started. I'm sick of walking."

The cab was unlocked, all glass intact. Bishop found a piece of paper lying on the driver's seat, a handwritten note. It read:

To anyone who finds my truck, my name is Steve Kitchener. I thought I had enough gas to make it to my sister's house in Memphis. I did not. I'm going to walk the rest of the way. You can reach me at any of the following telephone numbers, if the phones ever start working again. God help us all.

"I hope you made it, Steve," Bishop mumbled, handing the yellowed paper to Deke.

Their second break of the day was due to the owner's hope of someone recovering his ride. A single key was left in the ignition.

"Only use half a gallon of the gas. If we can't get it started, we'll have to try another one," Bishop directed.

The battery change went off without issue, as did the refueling. Holding up crossed fingers in the air for good luck, Bishop hit the key.

Like before, a lot of hard cranking and sputtering filled the air along I-40. On the fifth attempt, the engine fired and then died. A few moments later, the motor caught and kept running, a large cloud of black smoke signaling the unused machine's protest at being disturbed.

"Go ahead and fill 'er up," Bishop said with a huge grin on his face. "Check the oil and do the windshield while you're at it."

Flipping his mate the finger, Deke set about pouring the rest of their precious gasoline into the tank.

And then they were driving, Bishop again using the wrong side of the road after a quick U-turn.

"Beats the hell out of hoofing it," Deke commented, his attitude now much improved.

"I hope Grim likes the color. He's so sensitive about such things."

It took the truck thieves almost an hour to find their way back to the rest area. An unmarked intersection, wrong turn and Bishop's keeping the speed low to conserve their limited gas resulted in a much longer drive than either had anticipated.

Grim was nowhere to be found when they first pulled into the parking area, only showing himself after his two partners exited the cab.

"I was thinking about shooting up that truck on the spot, but then decided to wait and see if it was anybody I knew," he teased. "What took you guys so long?"

"We ran into a busload of strippers, and they needed our help," replied Deke. "We were going to come back and get you, but Bishop and I decided we could handle it ourselves."

"Ha. Ha. Ha," came the much-anticipated rebuttal. "You two were most likely chased off course by two little old ladies with umbrellas. Then you probably got lost."

Deke ignored the counter, looking back at the direction Grim had come. "Why were you hiding, Grim? Did a raccoon wander through the rest area and freak you out?"

And so it went, back and forth. The three men sat about unloading the disabled clunker, transferring their goods to the new chariot, each complaining that the other two weren't carrying their share of the load.

"I'm going to miss this old girl," Bishop mused as the last of the cargo was lifted. "She carried us through a lot."

Grim grunted, his expression making it clear he harbored no emotional attachment to a machine.

After everything was loaded, the men decided to catch some sleep, Bishop and Deke suffering due to their extended stroll. Showing a rare bit of sympathy, Grim offered to take a double watch so the two walkers could get some extra shut-eye.

"I need you guys on top of your game," he observed. "That way you won't slow me down."

Wolfing down a quick meal, Bishop reached a speedy decision regarding his temporary sleeping quarters. The driver's seat was substituted for a picnic table, his poncho used as a sheet and his pack as a pillow. He dozed off, half-listening to Grim tease his boss about being out of shape and getting old.

148

Chapter 11

Eastern Arkansas
July 10, 2016

As the trio of rescuers progressed across northern Arkansas, the landscape quickly changed from rolling hills to flat, featureless prairie. Miles and miles of endless fields stretched across the horizon, the domination of agriculture only occasionally interrupted by a small patch of woods or towering grain silo.

Bishop's predisposition to avoid both areas of population and traveling via the more popular thoroughfares was based on experience gained over a year ago - when anarchy was young and full of vim and vigor.

It soon became obvious to the team from Texas that lawlessness hadn't aged well – a toothless old beast whose look was far worse than any bite.

Other than the chance encounter at the Toad Suck Dam, it appeared as though society had neither the energy, nor the will to do much more than to bleed out from her injuries.

The few people the travelers did encounter barely acknowledged their presence, once it was determined the three strangers riding in the truck weren't a threat... not that the statistical sampling of the area's residents was overly large.

After leaving the rest area, the first locals they encountered were a family riding in a horse-drawn wagon. When the father had recognized the truck's now-rare engine noise, he had reached immediately for the weapon at his side, relaxing as soon as he was satisfied he wasn't the target.

Another couple, working a garden plot near a small farmhouse was only briefly visible, the truck zipping past in the fading light of dusk. Still, there had been zero sign of aggression.

Bishop decided it all made sense - things had changed. Months without gasoline, electricity or plentiful nourishment had no doubt served to modify the behavior of the local population. The few folks they did encounter barely acknowledged the team's passage. No one tried to raise any barriers to their progress.

They made good time, despite keeping the pickup truck at 40 miles an hour or less. Regardless of the lack of threat, they proceeded cautiously, scouting every intersection and bridge, avoiding towns wherever possible, always wary of meeting their fellow human beings.

Rivers were still an issue. Having been raised in West Texas and living in the Lone Star State most of his life, Bishop wasn't accustomed to the sheer volume of streams and large waterways they encountered. To him, it seemed like every few miles brought another bridge that had to be properly cleared, each crossing a chokepoint offering those with nefarious intentions a prime spot for ambush or other mayhem. Still, no bushwhackers were found.

And then the map, terrain and landscape all combined to inform the trio that they had arrived at the mighty Mississippi River.

As Bishop stood gazing at the distant landmark, he couldn't help but feel a sense of awe. Mankind had sought to enslave the river, to restrain her freedom with shackles of dams, levees and dikes. Men wanted a servant, a beast of burden controlled and demur. Despite a seemingly endless number of projects, billions of dollars, and some of the finest minds available in the Army Corps of Engineers, the great river would have none of it. Every so often, she would shake off the chains of slavery, humbling those who sought to be her masters, running free and making all lesser creatures flee before her might.

Perched on the hood of the truck, his vantage allowed for a panoramic visual of the moonlight reflecting across the surface of the distant waterway. He couldn't help but feel a kindred spirit with the river, his mind comparing the similarities between the waterway's plight and that of human liberty.

How often had governments attempted to restrain their subjects with the yokes of law, tax and subordination, all with the intent of creating a beast of burden – controlled and demur? Weren't those restrictions and regulations the same as the works of earth and concrete that sought to force the river into captivity? Was the collapse as inevitable as the rising waters sure to devastate with the flood of anarchy?

The Texan snorted, carrying the analogy further. Like the river beyond, men had overcome the restraints erected to confine them. Throughout history, rule of law had been overwhelmed, as easily breached as the levees below, the resulting destruction just as poignant. Was he now living in such a period? Wasn't this recent upheaval of society like the floodwaters unleashed by the river? Wasn't lawlessness just as inescapable? When rule of law was eventually reestablished, would man have learned his lesson this time and not crowd the river of freedom that energized men's souls?

Bishop shook his head, deciding his species probably would not mend its ways. *We might be smart enough not to rebuild along a river, but the wisdom to ensure true freedom still eludes us.*

He then reconsidered the verdict, the harsh sentencing

to eternal conflict and struggle pronounced by a one-man cynical jury. Here, today, there was evidence to the contrary, the undeveloped land Exhibit-A in the trial playing out in his thoughts.

Where he stood, there was nothing but sandy soil, trees and low grasses – a reserve left to Mother Earth out of respect for the waters beyond. *Evidently*, Bishop decided, *Man is capable of learning, eventually showing respect, and keeping his distance from the waterway*. With only a few exceptions, like the concrete bastions fortifying the major cities, there were no homes, businesses, or roadways immediately next to all-powerful flowing water.

Although pre-collapse news reports often showed video of small towns, neighborhoods and farms being inundated with rising water, for the most part, mankind did not rebuild after these great floods.

It was along this unclaimed border that the rescuers approached the crossing at Memphis, vectoring from the north so as to avoid the population directly to the west of the Tennessee metropolis.

To the south, Bishop could see the dark skyscrapers of Memphis. The wall of tall buildings provided an eerie backdrop to the rollercoaster-like arches of the I-40 bridge, a passage for their river crossing – if the trio made it that far.

Just as Matt had said, military vehicles blocked the 3-lane interstate roadway heading eastbound into the city known for its blues music, prize-winning barbecue, and southern hospitality. Bishop had expected to encounter lines of vehicles waiting to enter the metropolis. What they actually found were a few pedestrians milling about, exchanging glances with a bored-looking group of sentries screening those who were attempting to head east.

"It looks like time to become thespians, boys," Grim announced, lowering the optic, he'd been using to study the troopers beyond.

"The West Texas traveling road show presents, 'How to Succeed with Infiltration Without Really Trying,' starring yours truly, the one and only William Deke-speare."

Bishop nodded without comment, his reaction to the humor dulled by a tingling network of nerves creeping toward his core – a symptom commonly felt when he was preparing to do something dangerous. "If we keep cool heads, everything will go just fine," he said, more to reassure himself.

"It'll be okay, Slick," Deke said, patting Bishop on the shoulder. "We have pulled off better impersonations than this before. You should see our friend Grim in a dress, playing the part of a Muslim woman. Academy Award material it was. I swear it."

Grim, not recognizing Deke's attempt to bolster the team's confidence, looked up and frowned, obviously deep in thought. "That was the mission we lost that kid from Florida, wasn't it? What was his name again?"

Deke's eye roll was clear, even with only moonlight. He waved Grim off, mumbling, "When we get back, I'm going to enroll your grumpy ass in sensitivity training or some shit."

With their scouting completed, the three men sat about preparing for the next step. Grim and Deke immediately began donning the uniforms and other critical items necessary for their roles, most of the costumes provided by Matt.

Deke set about changing into the MP uniform. Just as Matt had predicted, the fatigues hung loosely off his shoulders, the pants baggy around his waist. By the time the contractor was finished, Bishop believed that if he had met the man randomly, he would have believed he was a military policeman.

The play's script, created on Matt's back porch, was simple. Deke, posing as an MP, would tell the soldiers at the checkpoint that he had been pursuing Grim, now his prisoner. According to the real MP, the black market exchange of rationed items such as food, gasoline, ammunition and medical supplies was a common problem within the territories controlled by the military.

Furthermore, the ex-soldier had stated that things occasionally got so out of hand, the military would pursue those involved. Often, the smugglers had a wide-ranging market, which meant law enforcement would have to travel great distances in order to catch those profiting from the underground economy.

"They should let you through," Matt had predicted. "While I never personally was assigned such a mission, I did know other officers who were."

While they had tried to anticipate every possibility, Bishop was still concerned. Their story and disguise was thin and could be easily penetrated by any of the soldiers manning the checkpoint. Arriving at such an early hour, they were depending on tired eyes that weren't paying close attention. Deke's ill-fitting uniform, was just one example. While it was reasonable to believe that most of the soldiers working in the area had lost weight and thus their uniforms would be baggy, Deke was well fed, healthy, and showed no signs of protracted periods without proper nourishment. *He doesn't exactly look like he's missed any meals*, Bishop thought.

They waited until almost midnight, the bewitching hour. Given their approach through the backwoods, they had to backtrack a few miles in order to drive the truck up to the roadblock as if it had arrived from the wilderness of the West. There were six or seven soldiers milling around, their posture and body language relaying calm demeanors.

Bishop's eyes darted here and there, taking in more details as they closed the distance to what they believed was the most dangerous leg of their journey. He immediately noticed one of the Humvees. Parked sideways on the pavement was the model that had been mounted with the 50-caliber machine gun on its roof. The mere presence of this most feared of weapons caused his heart to race, only to relax slightly when he determined the belt-fed blaster was unmanned.

"It doesn't look like they're expecting much trouble," Bishop said to Deke while they were still too far away to be heard.

"Hungry people probably don't put up much of a fuss," replied Deke.

"Neither do civilians against that Ma Duce mounted on top of that Humvee," noted Bishop, referring to the M2, 50-caliber machine gun.

"I was trying to ignore that; thanks a lot," grunted the voice from the bed.

In their planning, they had hoped that there would be a queue. The best-case scenario would have been dozens of people desperately waiting to pass through the checkpoint. Bishop wondered if they had made a mistake, the tactic of waiting until such a late hour now not seeming so crafty.

Closer to the checkpoint, the headlights illuminated a white line painted across the pavement. Someone had neatly lettered "STOP" in large, white letters. Bishop applied the brakes, the front tires resting on the demarcation.

Just as he had feared, the appearance of a motorized vehicle drew the attention of the sentries. A younger soldier started to advance toward the truck, evidently taking his turn to investigate new arrivals. He was called back, an older man, probably a sergeant, deciding that he would "Take this one."

Hitching up his pants and straightening his blouse, the NCO approached with his weapon at low ready, passing by the driver's window to inspect the bed of the truck where Deke sat guarding the captive Grim. Their supplies were covered by the tarp, several crisscrossing strands of paracord securing the cover.

After satisfying himself that there was nothing overtly dangerous in the bed of the truck, the guard approached Bishop's window, keeping his distance and stopping a few feet away.

"State your business," the man barked, the volume an

obvious attempt to broadcast authority.

"You need to talk to the guy in the back," Bishop calmly answered, jerking his thumb toward the rear of the bed and defusing the sergeant's bluster. "I'm not in charge."

Tilting his head as if considering the answer, the soldier shrugged his shoulders and then proceeded to take a step back and look up at Deke. Again, he spouted the same challenge.

"Sergeant, I am with the 377th MPs. I am returning to complete an operational order issued by the Memphis Regional JAG. This man," he stated, pointing at a handcuffed Grim, "is my prisoner." Deke then handed the man his ID card.

Bishop's pulse jumped when a flashlight was produced to check the offered identification. The beam shimmered on the fake ID, then swept to Deke's chest. Bishop thought it was a positive sign that the sentry didn't blast the light directly into the supposed-MP's face, an indication that the sergeant was at least considering the accuracy of their story.

"So, this man is your prisoner," the sergeant said, nodding towards Grim.

"Yes, Sergeant. I've been chasing him for nine days."

Taking a step back toward the front of the truck, the soldier illuminated Bishop's face through the opening, "And who the fuck might you be?" came the demand.

Deke didn't give Bishop time to answer, raising his voice just a tone, "That man is a civilian bounty hunter," he responded. "I enlisted his services as he was familiar with this criminal's modus operandi. He has a reward coming."

The sergeant spit on the ground while giving Bishop a harsh look. Under his breath, the guard mumbled, "Fucking bounty hunters."

The man was clearly lost in thought for a few moments, the unusual situation bristling his instincts. Finally, he directed his attention to the bed, sweeping the light over the tarp. "And what do we have underneath there?"

Deke's answer was dripping with annoyance, "There is food, fuel, ammunition and other supplies that this fugitive absconded with. I need to return these to my unit as their sudden disappearance has caused my CO to land on the Colonel's shit list."

"I need to take a look," the sergeant proclaimed.

Deke grunted, a look of disgust filling his face. "Look, pal, I've been chasing this man through half of hell's sewer pit. I'm tired, dirty, and behind schedule. I just want to get back to my unit, take a hot shower and sleep in my own rack."

The exchange made Bishop cringe as he tried to remain calm behind the wheel. His mind began racing through their options, mainly seeking any way to get out if Deke's gamble failed. Shooting their way through the roadblock was impossible, even if they could surprise the troops manning the checkpoint. The civilian pickup had zero chance of pushing aside the heavier military vehicles blocking the way. Besides, he was sure there would be hundreds, if not thousands more soldiers, waiting on them by the time they could cross the bridge.

About the only option he could figure, if things went horribly wrong, was to back out. Even though there was no one behind them in line, Bishop didn't think the truck could outrun the 50-caliber machine gun mounted on top of the nearby Humvee. Its heavy bullets would shred the thin sheet metal of the civilian transport with just a short burst. He didn't like that option.

While Bishop desperately sought an escape route, it became clear that the sentry didn't know what to do. Civilian vehicles were a rarity these days, especially ones occupied by a military policeman, a bounty hunter and a prisoner. It almost sounded like a bad joke. "Did you hear the one about the…"

The hour was late, another fact not lost upon the guard. For a moment it looked as though he were going to pivot and return to the nearby vehicles where he could radio in and ask for advice or permission. But then the man's posture changed, his feet taking him back to the bed of the pickup where Bishop thought he was going to demand the tarp be removed.

While that wouldn't have necessarily been a story–killer, Bishop was sure an inspection would discover weapons and other equipment that didn't correspond with Deke's tall tale.

Finally, the man reached a decision. Without another word from the members of the rescue party, he cupped his hand to his mouth and yelled to the troopers manning the barrier, "Let them pass!"

Relieved and somewhat giddy at their success, Bishop's only thought was, "I hope they haven't lost the keys to those Humvees, it would probably take AAA an hour to get out here."

The truck was almost to the pinnacle of the bridge before Bishop's heart slowed to a normal pace. There was enough moonlight and surface reflection to clearly see details of the skyscrapers that made up the Memphis skyline just south of their crossing. While he had only passed through the city while on vacation long ago, Bishop knew that a significant number of high-rise buildings had been built in the metropolis. The sight of every single window now cold and dark was like a demoralizing veil of doom had descended over the once vibrant community.

Adding to the depressing landscape was the number of abandoned vehicles on the outbound side of the bridge. It was clear the military had removed enough of the relics to enable passing of the required government traffic. The remaining evidence of the mass exodus from the city center was left to sit and rust. Bright, shiny paint jobs and clear glass windshields were now covered with more than 12 months of dusty road grime, pollen, and other airborne filth. The entire scene was disheartening.

After reaching the highest point of the broad span, the gradual downward slope led directly into the city center. An almost identical twin to the roadblock they had just passed was set up on the outbound side of the bridge. It too looked to have very few customers at the moment.

Bishop had to drive slowly as they progressed through downtown Memphis. Despite being on an eight- lane interstate that had been designed to handle massive amounts of rush-hour traffic, there were places where passage between abandoned vehicles required a careful speed.

Deke, satisfied that they had passed muster with the local authorities, quickly removed Grim's restraints with a key from his pocket. The now–free operator rubbed his wrists in mock protest, grinning at the pretend lawman.

Despite the hour, they began to notice more and more people as Bishop inched the truck through the narrow pathways cleared along the interstate. Long lines of citizens stood, sat and mulled around the sidewalks for several blocks in one section, blankets, lawn chairs and low stools scattered about. The scene reminded Bishop of pre-collapse video depicting shoppers camping out in front of stores in order to be the first to purchase some new item with a low-price guarantee.

These people, however, weren't waiting in line to buy the newest flat screen television. One such queue was obviously for medical treatment. A hand-painted sign, leaning against the overturned trailer of an 18-wheeler, announced "Carson Medical Center – Next Exit." Shortly afterward, tents, set up in the grass of a high school football stadium, sported large red crosses and white circles that could clearly be identified as the rescuers passed. Hundreds of people were lined up along the sidewalk next to a hastily erected fence that was guarded by sleepy-looking soldiers with M-16 rifles. Many of the waiting patients looked as though they had been camped out for days. Bishop wondered how they received water, or if anyone really cared.

"Why didn't they set up in one of the hospitals?" Grim asked from the bed, his attention obviously drawn by the scene.

Before anyone could respond, the burned out skeleton of a large building came into view, its placard declaring "St. Martin's Hospital," and answering Grim's query.

Additional hand-painted signs, lettered in traditional

military stencils could be seen here and there. Some gave directions to be used by soldiers, acronyms that probably wouldn't have been understood by the average person walking the streets. The letters "HQ," probably a battalion headquarters, with a red arrow pointing down a side street was one such example.

Other instances were clearly spelled out as if intended to be utilized by the local citizenry. "Distribution," left little mystery regarding the intent of one area. Again, long lines of people lying asleep on the ground, leaning against walls, sitting in lawn chairs, waited in line for their government handouts.

"I wonder what type of food they distribute," Deke commented, his gaze focused on the waiting multitude.

"I hope it's better than MREs," Grim responded. "But then that makes me wonder how many millions of those delicious cardboard buffets the government had in stock?"

At night, the signage wasn't really necessary. The army had erected portable banks of floodlights around its major facilities, the towers illuminating the cityscape here and there. The generator-driven pools of bright, white light cast spooky shadows and grotesque outlines across an otherwise dark background.

Bishop noticed most of the people stayed in the light - but not everyone. Occasionally his eye would catch scampering images of movement in the dark corridors of side streets and alleys. *The predators*, he thought. *They would stick to the shadows, culling off the occasional prey that wandered too close. What would I be if I lived here… hunter or hunted?*

Shaking off the lurking, foul depths fostered by the mind movie, Bishop returned his focus to driving. It wasn't easy. Evidently, the army had grown tired of towing vehicles and creating a clear route in a straight line. Every so often, the blockage would force him to exit off of the main road and travel some distance on the surface streets. Losing the barrier of elevation provided by the interstate was stressful, and all of the operators ceased any banter, focusing on the humanity that was suddenly closer – dangerously close from Bishop's perspective.

The haphazard pathway also caused another type of stress – staying on course.

Grim had drawn on the map depicting the shortest route to the location his home. It was a small town 25 miles northeast of the center of Memphis, and only one direct route was feasible during normal times, let alone when tens of thousands of abandoned relics littered the streets.

"I'm lost," Bishop declared at one point. "I couldn't take that exit back there, and the next one doesn't match the map."

"Look for someplace to stop," replied Deke's voice from the back. "We need to eat, fuel up and take a break. This is creeping me out, making me jumpy."

"No shit," added Grim.

But simply pulling over with a truck full of goods, supplies that would no doubt cause a riot if discovered, wasn't easy. They needed someplace slightly hidden - and defendable.

After a few blocks, Bishop hadn't found an acceptable hideout. Without streetlights, his vision was limited to the narrow range afforded by the truck's headlights, and that added to the difficulty.

"I think we should continue out into the countryside," he observed. "We might pull off into a dead end or find ourselves in an untenable position. There are too damn many people around."

"Okay by me," Deke responded. "One thing for sure, we can't get into a fight with all the military around. I'm sure they hone right in on gunshots."

"I remember Matt saying that personal firearms were forbidden inside certain zones. Shooting would definitely draw attention," Grim added.

And so they kept on driving, Bishop doing his best to maintain their course to the north and east.

After an hour of twisting detours, reversing course to avoid blocked streets, and a few debates at intersections, their surroundings began to change. Fewer and fewer businesses lined the streets and stop signs replaced now-dead traffic lights. Even the residences began to thin out, larger lots eventually turning into walled subdivisions and apartment complexes. They also observed only the occasional person up and about.

"Turn in there," Deke shouted from the back. "I bet that's a great place to hide."

Bishop had the same thought, his hand naturally reaching for a turn signal that wouldn't be seen by any other drivers.

The sign proclaimed the driveway as belonging to "Shady Lawns Cemetery." As the truck turned into the lane, the high beams illuminated an undulating landscape of evenly spaced monuments and tombstones. The property was also populated with numerous large trees, no doubt contributing to the establishment's name.

"You guys are fucking nuts," proclaimed Grim. "I vote we stay on the road and deal with the zombies out there rather than the ghouls in here. This place is Creep Central."

Deke laughed, no doubt enjoying the big, bad operator's dislike of boneyards. "Oh, come on now Grim... with a name like yours, I thought you'd be right at home here amongst the spirits."

158

Bishop continued driving, the unkempt grounds making it difficult to see the myriad of cut-offs, lanes and access points that divided the large cemetery into sections. Eventually they rolled into an area dominated by colossal monuments, some as large as a small shed. Many of the mausoleums were ornately carved with images of angels and other deity-based icons, most of which were distorted into less-than-holy images by the light playing off the passing truck. *I'll have to remember this drive for Hunter after he's older. What a great Halloween tour this would be*, Bishop thought.

Finding a spot hidden from the road by a small hill and dominated by huge concrete markers, Bishop stopped the truck. "Here we are boys, the Memphis Four Seasons North."

"I'll say it again," stated a nervous-sounding Grim. "You guys are fucking wacko."

Deke, trying desperately to keep command in his voice, instructed, "Grim, scout the area. Bishop and I will set up here."

"Thanks," came the mumbled response.

As soon as the operator begrudgingly moved off into the night, Deke elbowed Bishop and whispered, "I know we've got more important shit to do, but I can't help myself. I never thought I'd see the day when Grim was put off by anything, so I can't pass this up."

Bishop watched as Deke dug around in his chest-rig, eventually producing a small, black device that resembled a flashlight. He set the unit on the bed of the truck, carefully aiming at a distant tombstone of particularly dubious outline.

"Now watch this," Deke announced, the glee obvious in his voice. He flicked a switch on the box, and the small green dot of an aiming laser appeared on the monument. He then raised his rifle and turned on a similar piece of equipment that emitted its own green circle.

Carefully aiming his rifle, Deke lined up the two projections and Bishop broke out chuckling. There, on the distant stone, shown two ghostly green eyes shimmered in night.

"He'll start shooting," predicted Bishop. "He's on edge so much that he'll raise his blaster and saw that stone in half."

"That's where you come in. You've got to stop him right before he pulls the trigger and alerts the authorities," Deke explained.

"Oh, yeah, right! What do you want me to do? Strip the rifle from his hands?"

"Think of something... Here he comes."

Grim whistled twice, the given signal the team had agreed upon some days ago. As he walked around the side of the truck, Deke hissed, "What the fuck is that?" and shouldered his rifle to make the pair of eyes.

Grim's head snapped up, his lips parting as if to shout something, his rifle flying to his shoulder. Bishop grabbed the barrel and pulled it down, the effort taking a considerable amount of strength. "You can't shoot, dude. Besides, bullets don't bother ghosts."

"But... but... but what the hell is that?" Grim's voice stuttered with genuine fright.

Deke couldn't hold it any longer and started laughing, slowly lowering his weapon to betray the laser's source.

"Oh, very fucking funny, Deke. What a couple of ass-clowns. Besides, I wasn't scared."

"You should be," a very close, strange voice sounded.

And then complete bedlam exploded around the truck.

They appeared out of nowhere, wisps of brushing cloth, the random sound of a footstep nearby. How they had managed to get so close was beyond Bishop, but he really didn't have a lot of time to ponder the issue. Almost instantly, they were among the rescuers.

An outline appeared in front of Bishop, just enough light for him to see a movement that reminded of a baseball player swinging a bat. Instinct saved his life as he barely ducked under an axe blade whizzing so close it brushed his hat.

There is nothing worse in a fight than being surprised, and the team from Texas had been taken completely cold and unaware.

Bishop moved right half a step and then at his foe, using the gap created as the momentum of the attacker's weapon twisted his body at the waist with the follow-through of his homerun swing. Now inside the fellow's wheelhouse, the Texan raised his left leg high and kicked down with all his strength. The blow landed with a sickening crunch, just above the axe-wielder's kneecap. A howl of pain filled the air.

They were so close and it was so dark - an all-out fur ball of hand-to-hand combat erupted.

The grip of his fighting knife filled Bishop's hand, the blade clearing the sheath as brief memories of another time in South America filled his mind. His thrust came up and into the center mass of the opponent, every cord and muscle of the Texan's arm straining with the force behind the blow. The point of the weapon found flesh and then bone, the forward motion stopped only by the knife's guard.

Bishop's entire focus was on bringing the threat down – taking the man impaled on the end of his knife out of the fight. Making sure. Lifting with the significant strength of his right arm, he attempted to carve flesh inside his foe's torso. The blade moved very little, no doubt hindered by ribs. He pulled back, readying to thrust again, but never managed the strike.

Another attacker lunged at him, stepping in from his left, grunting and swinging. The air hissed as the Texan sidestepped, this time the rear fender of the pickup reverberating with a loud thud from the impact of a blunt instrument. Before he could counter, a third man attacked, light reflecting from a machete as it sliced through the air. The long-blade slammed into Bishop's armored midsection, the force of the blow painful but unable to reach his flesh due to the Kevlar plates.

Bishop's knife found work, first dispatching the machete-wielding attacker with a brutal blow to the face with the hilt, then addressing others as they leapt into the fray. The sheer number of adversaries, when combined with the darkness, resulted in a blur of absolute chaos.

Bishop's right arm was a frantic piston of killing steel, stabbing and slashing like a boxer working a speed bag. The torsos, necks and limbs of his antagonists suffered badly.

Sounds of desperate combat filled the graveyard, grunts, moans and the gasping for breath competing with the grotesque reports of breaking bones and blows crushing human flesh.

The bodies piling up at Bishop's feet began to impede the assailants, the barrier of dead and dying men slowing their advance. As the fight continued, the pavement became like an ice rink, coated with a slick layer of blood, entrails, urine, and sweat – the lack of sure footing adding to the mayhem.

During one brief reprise, Bishop saw Grim go down, a dog pile of entangled arms and legs, bowled over and withering on the ground. Checking on Deke, he looked back just as the operator delivered a savage butt-stroke, the stock of his rifle nearly splitting the victim's skull. Deke was holding his own; Grim was in trouble.

Bishop tried to move toward Grim, but his foot slipped on the blood-slick pavement, and he went down. The loss of balance actually saved his life, a crowbar impacting right where his head had been.

While Bishop tried to regain his feet, another aggressor managed to step in close. The Texan slashed from the ground at the unfortunate fellow's leg, his blade slicing into the Achilles tendon. The man fell in a heap, landing on top of Bishop and immediately grappling for the Texan's throat. Bishop let him.

He knew a man didn't choke to death in mere seconds, didn't think the guy on top of him was strong enough to crush his windpipe. Bishop tucked his chin to his chest, feeling the pair of hands struggle to tighten their grip around his neck.

Bishop's hand, in the meantime, was tightening around the grip of his pistol. *Fuck it! I don't care if the army hears gunshots. We're dying,* Bishop thought as the .45 cleared the holster. And then its barrel was pointing up, into the center mass of his foe. Bishop's thumb found the safety, his finger on the trigger. He pulled… and then pulled again.

The man on top of him shuddered, bolts of pain and surprise racking his frame. To Bishop, it seemed like an eternity before the pressure on his throat began to lapse.

Pushing off the limp corpse, Bishop struggled to regain his feet. He rose, gasping for breath and using the truck for balance. Finally standing, his attention was drawn to a man on the opposite side of the bed, cutting through the cords that secured the tarp. The grave robbers were moments away from having access to their supplies.

Enough! We are going to lose everything - even if we do survive, raced through his mind. The thought was accented by a numbing blow to his left arm.

Firing from the hip, Bishop put two rounds into the closest shadow. Another two hollow points struck the next man as the attacker charged, a shovel wielded high above his head, ready to cleave downward.

Three steps to the front of the truck revealed a mound of struggling flesh, one man raining down blows with his fist as Grim held the attacker's knife at bay. Two others were trying to pin the struggling operator so their friend could deliver a deadly strike with the blade.

Bishop's kick would have made a football punter proud, landing square in the midsection of the man straddling his partner. Another shot rang out, quickly followed by a pistol whip to the back of a neck. Bishop's sidearm was empty.

The handgun's roar signaled an escalation, a new level of violence now declared by the defenders. The occupants of the cemetery paused, their aggression and determination wavering.

Bishop managed to help Grim climb over the edge of the bed, the effort handicapped by the unsure footing and the Texan's numb left side. After making sure Grim was safe, Bishop spun towards the rear of the truck as he reloaded the pistol. Rounding the bumper, he found a heap of bodies lying on the ground. There was no sign of Deke.

It took him a moment to scan the casualties, five bodies haphazardly strewn on the pavement. None of them were his partner. When he was satisfied Deke hadn't fallen there, Bishop determined that more light might help his search. Besides, he wanted his rifle out of the cab of the truck.

Words heard long ago echoed through his mind, "A

pistol is what you use to fight your way back to the rifle you should have never set down in the first place." Bishop now had a full appreciation of that wisdom.

He fired three more random shots at dark images as he moved to the door, the effort intended to keep the hoodlums at bay rather than reduce their number.

The headlights illuminated a gory scene. Fighting with edged weapons and blunt instruments always resulting in horrendous injuries. The men engaged with the rescuers had suffered badly at the danger-close combat. Blood ran in rivulets towards the low side of the pavement, the butchery of raw flesh and exposed fractures all contributing to the nightmarish scene capped by the background of the gravestones.

Taking his eyes away from the horror, Bishop spun and moved again for the back of the truck, thinking that he had mistakenly missed Deke's body amongst those scattered at the rear of the vehicle. There was just enough light from the red lenses for Bishop to determine the outline of two men dragging away another body. It took a moment for his mind to absorb the image, to realize that it was Deke being towed off by two thugs.

As he pivoted back to enter the truck, three dark outlines rose up and charged from a nearby row of headstones. The 230-grain hollow point slugs slammed into the line of men. Again and again, the pistol barked, the range too close to miss. His last target fell, dropping to his knees while grasping his throat where a bullet had ripped a significant portion of his windpipe to shreds. His head landed on Bishop's boot with a foul thud. Another magazine of pain pills filled the empty pistol.

And then he was in the driver's seat. The reverse lights and rearview mirror confirmed that Deke was being dragged by two assailants. Bishop immediately gave the truck gas, backing it quickly towards the two ghouls making off with his friend's body, their progress burdened by the weight of the unconscious man and his load gear.

A series of thumps and bumps signaled the truck's rolling over the bodies lying on the pavement, Bishop in such a rage that he didn't even care if they were already dead or not.

The two body snatchers glanced up as the reverse lights grew closer, a look of fear filling their faces. They dropped Deke, scampering off to disappear into the pools of shadow created by the monuments. Bishop slammed the truck into park, flinging open the door and racing back to retrieve his injured comrade, this time carrying his rifle.

Deke was unresponsive.

Despite the adrenaline racing through his veins, Bishop struggled for a moment, having difficulty lifting his buddy onto a shoulder, the throbbing pain in his arm hindering the effort.

It was without remorse that Bishop unceremoniously dumped his friend into the bed of the truck, hardly noticing Grim's growl as most of Deke's weight landed on the injured man. There just wasn't the time to be gentle.

Whoever the assailants were, they possessed large numbers and were willing to assume extreme causalities. Bishop had little doubt they were probably regrouping - only temporarily halted by the usage of firearms. He managed the driver's seat, his numb arm causing a fumble as he reached to close the door. He was just clutching the gearshift when the passenger side window exploded inward, the dark head of a spade in the opening. Shards of glass sprayed across the interior of the cab, the blizzard of crystalline splinters only serving to accelerate Bishop's movements.

Finally, the truck was rolling, a small sense of security delivered by the motion. The refuge was both false and short-lived.

As he gained speed, a hailstorm of rocks, chunks of tombstone and miscellaneous tools began impacting the hood and windshield. Bishop saw a claw hammer rattle off the fender, quickly followed by a pickaxe flying through the tunnel of brightness created by the headlights.

And then it was quiet, nothing but the rush of air and the growl of the V8 under the hood.

He would never be able to recount how he found his way out of the graveyard, which direction he'd turned, or how far he had driven in the blind terror. He had forgotten all about his two comrades in the bed, his brain completely focused on escaping the never-ending waves of ghoulish attackers.

Once they were clear, concern for his passengers returned. He drove on, knowing the two men in the bed were doing their best to issue medical care and treat each other's wounds.

Chapter 12

Memphis, Tenseness
July 11, 2016

When Grim first called out, Bishop didn't recognize the tone of the man's voice. It was weak, barely audible and yet there was an underlying layer of urgency that carried through his message.

"Bishop, you need to stop the truck. We're losing Deke."

The timing of the request, at least, was fortunate. Bishop spotted the strip mall within moments. He turned in, the truck's lamps showing signs of the retail outlet already having been looted, weeds and mounds of litter and leaves scattered around the vacant parking lot. It was obvious the facility was abandoned. Bishop guided the truck-now-ambulance behind the single-story building, discovering two delivery vans backed against a loading dock. Both the vehicles and the warehouse showed signs of forced entry from long ago. He pulled between them, hoping the cave-like shelter provided by the two large trucks would provide some level of concealment.

Bishop jumped out, rushing to help the men in the back. He switched on his flashlight, hoping to assist and assess at the same time.

The beam of light confirmed his worst fears. The first thing that caught his eye was the large pool of purplish liquid spreading across the bed's floor. Grim, doing the best he could with the use of only one arm, was desperately trying to stem the bleeding. Empty packages of gauze and red-stained medical wraps littered the area.

Deke was lying prone, unmoving, his skin shrouded by a grey pallor that Bishop had seen before... far too many times on the battlefield. While the wounded man's eyes were open, they didn't move, fixed on an empty spot in space somewhere above Grim's shoulder as he hovered over his friend. Bishop leaped over the sidewall, trying to gain a better angle to assess the victim's injuries. What he found caused a wave of nausea to sweep his core.

It wasn't the purplish slashes on Deke's chest and shoulders, the lacerations serious, but not life-threatening. Nor was the series of blue and red welts a primary concern. Bishop's attention was drawn to the inch-long puncture wounds that were gushing life. He had to stop counting the deep wounds after the first four, knowing, even as he reached for his own limited supplies of bandages, that the effort was hopeless.

He couldn't accept the prognosis – digging in his blow-out bag with the intent of adding his own aid to that already being applied by Grim.

Grim seemed to realize the futility of it all at the same moment, his one functional hand slowing the desperate application of pressure and cloth to the wounds. He looked up at Bishop, a storm of emotion brewing behind the warrior's eyes.

A wet, racking cough came from Deke's chest, his entire body shuddering from the effort.

"I know," the weak, hoarse voice croaked from the wounded man's throat. "Don't waste your medical kit. You might need those supplies later."

Bishop was in shock. A flood of anger surged through his system, at the same time his throat tightening. He wanted to do something – anything - to save his friend. The only idea his utterly exhausted mind could settle on was to make the man comfortable. There just was nothing else.

Dropping to his knees and squeezing further into the confined space, Bishop worked to roll up an edge of the tarp, sliding the makeshift pillow under the injured man's head. The effort didn't go unnoticed, the dark pools of Deke's eyes focusing on Bishop.

"Thanks," his raspy voice managed.

"Don't you fucking die on me," Grim pleaded. "You son of a bitch, you hang on; you're not going anywhere."

Another severe bout of coughing shook the wounded man's frame, blood appearing under his nose and at the corners of his mouth. While his movements were slow, Deke managed to flip a middle finger at Grim and then smile. "Like I said, brother, I know... I know it's over, and it's okay."

Again, those eyes haunted the medics, so deep and dark against the background of Deke's pale skin and the artificial glow of the flashlight. He managed to focus on Bishop, the smile still showing at the corners of his blood-speckled mouth. "Get Grim's family out, operator. Make it worth this. Promise me you will, and I'll go feeling like I've made a good trade."

Bishop tried to find the words, struggled to make his vocal cords function in a throat tight with emotion. He finally managed a nod and then a weakly uttered, "I promise."

A nod from the dying man acknowledged the acceptance of Bishop's commitment, and then his gaze swept skyward. Neither Grim nor Bishop needed to check for a pulse or listen for breathing. It was obvious when the light behind those eyes dimmed for the final time.

Bishops slowly reached forward, his hand gently closing the lids of the now lifeless eyes. "Rest well, brother. Your hardships and campaigns are over. Go softly... go to peace."

Grim shifted his weight, leaning over to kiss the forehead of the man with whom he had suffered so much hardship, and celebrated countless victories. As Bishop watched, silent, deep sobs racked Grim's body.

A dragon named *Revenge* began to breathe fire into Bishop's soul.

Boiling hot, sulfuric rage raced through the Texan's veins, fueled as the great monster spread its all-powerful wings and commanded payback. Bishop's knuckles grew white as he squeezed his rifle, an irresistible desire pounding in his temples. He would return to the graveyard and fill hell with the souls of those who had murdered his friend. He would spray lead until the last empty magazine rattled to the ground, and then wield a blade until his hand could no longer maintain a grip. His would then render their limbs with his bare hands, and after his muscles played out, he would eat them alive, bathing in the glorious bloodbath that was *Revenge*.

Vengeance against whom? Some small voice battled the dragon. *Against Grim because he didn't sweep the area well? Is my lust for blood only to avoid blaming myself for clowning around with Deke? Was it all the dead man's fault for picking the location in the first place? Who deserves my ire?*

Then Deke's final words came rushing back. "Get Grim's family out, operator." There was that word – *operator*. A label only earned – a reward for those who obtain a level of skill and professionalism above and beyond.

What would an operator do? Bishop asked himself. Would a professional turn this truck around and unleash pure hell on those unarmed men? No. The professional would continue with the mission and honor the fallen when time allowed. That's what an *operator* would do.

The thought broke the dragon's spell, the mental monster retreating into a remote cave in the back of Bishop's soul. He moved to check Grim's arm.

"How bad is it?"

"I think the arm's busted," Grim replied. "I'll be okay. I'm not bleeding."

After covering Deke's body with part of the tarp, Bishop maneuvered to check Grim's limb. Rolling up the operator's sleeve, he revealed the swollen red and purple area, a bone between his wrist and elbow obviously fractured.

"It's busted, that's for sure," Bishop said. "I don't know how long it will be before we can get you proper medical attention. Do you want me to try and put on a splint?"

Grim nodded, his gaze remaining fixed in the direction

of the body lying at his feet. Bishop had to wonder if the man wasn't going into shock from either the physical pain or the loss of his longtime friend.

Each of the operators carried a flexible aluminum splint that when rolled up required little space in the always crowded medical kits carried on their persons. Bishop found Deke's, rightfully believing it would be easier than digging through his kit to find the rarely used item. While he had never set a broken limb, the training received at HBR kicked in, the procedure coming back as if he had been taught only yesterday.

After warning the patient, Bishop grasped the broken limb just below the elbow and just above the wrist gently pulling until he felt movement, Bishop aligned to two ends of the bone as best he could. Grim, other than a sharp inhalation of air and a slight grunt, remained silent.

A few moments later, Bishop's hands moved in a blur as he secured the temporary splint with the roll of tape.

"Thanks," was the patient's only comment.

"Do you have anything else I need to take a look at? I think we need to get out of here as soon as possible."

Grim managed his knees and then rose to his feet in response. Pulling his carbine up with his good hand, he rested the weapon on the cab of the truck, ready to fight. Turning to Bishop, he said, "I'm good. Let's get the fuck out of here."

After pausing for a moment to make sure his friend was stable, Bishop jumped from the bed and hurried back to the cab. As he drove out of their hiding spot and back on course, he couldn't help but think about where he would dig a grave.

It had been some time since he had to excavate the final resting place for another human being. The defense of his old Houston neighborhood had resulted in casualties, and that had led to digging in a nearby empty lot. He had also lost neighbors during that time, those memories adding to what was becoming a deep sadness.

"Now what the fuck am I going to do?" he said to himself as he drove the truck through suburban Memphis. "We have one man down, another at 50%, and our cover story is completely blown."

The population density of the metropolitan area thinned as Bishop slowly progressed to the north and east, away from the Mississippi River. He had no idea if he were getting any closer to where Grim's family resided or if he were adding distance to what had already been far too long a journey.

The safety of the countryside didn't improve Bishop's mood. He had respected Deke, despite the operator having once kidnapped and threatened his wife. That episode, a misunderstanding cleared long ago, had allowed Bishop to appreciate the contractor's contribution to the efforts of reestablishing society in West Texas.

Deke and his seven security men had been the absolute best soldiers Bishop had ever seen. The fact that such a man fell victim under such unusual circumstances didn't bolster Bishop's confidence. He had always felt like he was the weak link in this rescue team, that if anyone were going to be hurt or killed on the current mission, he would be the one. Now that weak link was the sole survivor at full operational capacity. Now the guy with the least amount of skill and experience was the last man standing.

Sure, luck played a role, and every man who had ever taken up arms understood the impact of random events and virtual situations. But for Deke to die at the hands of such a lackluster force shook Bishop to the core. *Be the professional*, he reminded. *Be an operator.*

He also experienced a sense of loneliness. He would give anything to talk to Terri right now, to see her smile and smell her hair. He wondered about his son's future, the father's survival now seriously in question. Grim's voice interrupted the session of self-pity, evidently the man riding in the back was paying more attention to their surroundings than the guy controlling the truck's direction.

"Hey, Bishop, turn around. I recognized something back there, and I think it might be a good place for us to hole up and lick our wounds."

Bishop did as requested, reversing the truck in the abandoned roadway and slowly progressing back the way they had just come. He saw the sign this time, a brown and white affair declaring they were approaching a driveway belonging to the Patterson Rock Quarry.

"This place closed down a few years ago," Grim said. "No one would have any reason to be back there, and I think there are some storage sheds… maybe a good place to conceal the truck. If the army heard our gunfire back there, they might send up a bird with thermal sights to investigate. Besides, I want to build a fire, if possible."

After pausing for a brief moment to study the gate, Bishop decided it wasn't worth the effort to get out and try to pry loose the lock. Inching the already dented truck forward, he used the front bumper to bust through the opening. The gravel lane

169

twisted and turned for almost a half mile before the first signs of the now closed business showed themselves in the truck's headlights.

Large piles of rock chips, gravel, and other discarded stone began to appear on each side of the narrow, bumpy path. "Keep going. I remember there used to be some storage sheds where they stored the heavy equipment."

Grim's memory finally proved to be accurate, a huge facility of open bays, two stories in height, eventually coming into view. Yet again, Mother Nature had been doing her best to reclaim the area, with saplings and clusters of bushes growing through the otherwise smooth gravel surface surrounding the shed. It was behind one such concentration of growth that Bishop hid the truck, appreciating the camouflage provided in the isolation of the location.

Grim volunteered to sweep the area, no doubt feeling some measure of guilt for having missed the sheer number of attackers back at the cemetery. For a brief moment, Bishop paused, wanting to take the task himself and let the injured man gather his strength. On the other hand, redemption could be an important aspect of reestablishing morale – something both of the surviving rescuers needed badly.

Grim didn't wait for Bishop's answer, moving off into the night with his rifle dangling from its sling while he scanned the area with Deke's thermal imager held up with his one good arm. The scout returned 20 minutes later, declaring that they were indeed isolated, and this time, he was sure.

"We're only about five miles from my place," announced Grim. "It's going to be daylight soon, and I noticed you're favoring your arm, too. Let's try to get our shit in one bag, and then we can manage the rest of the distance to my place."

Bishop agreed, setting about removing his load vest and other equipment, Grim's observation of his arm proving more accurate than he would have liked.

After taking off his shirt, the flashlight revealed an inch thick welt and purple bruising across his upper triceps and shoulder. "For a bunch of guys near starvation, they sure could swing a baseball bat," Bishop observed gingerly stretching the sore limb.

"At least it's not broken. At least one of us is still at 100%."

"That may be true, but I still think we're in trouble. How in the hell are we going to get your wife and daughter past the roadblocks heading back into Arkansas?"

Grim didn't answer at first, staring down at the ground and shaking his head, his gaze moving back to the truck where the body of his friend still rested.

"I don't know, man. I'm not thinking real clear right now, and I don't think you are either. Let's hole up at my place for a day or two, and maybe something will come to us." Bishop couldn't come up with any better plan, so he nodded his acceptance deciding to try to eat while time allowed.

Grim made an attempt to pump some fuel into the truck's tank, his efforts handicapped by his injured wing. Both men found even the most basic activity was difficult, both extremely jumpy at sounds or noise in the vicinity.

"Where the hell did those guys come from?" Grim eventually asked, clearly replaying the entire episode in his mind. "What the hell were they doing in that cemetery? It just doesn't make any sense to me."

Bishop considered his answer quite a while, the same questions running through his mind over and again. "I don't know, and I don't think we'll ever know. My best guess is that they were grave robbers. I saw shovels, pry bars and axes to cut through roots during the dig. But there's no way to be sure. Maybe they were like us, thinking no one would ever bother looking in a graveyard. Some of those mausoleums were big enough to live in, as creepy as that might sound. Perhaps they were a gang of criminals, or just a random cluster of vagabonds who happened to find shelter in an isolated area away from the authorities. It was just bad luck that we bumbled into the hornets' nest."

Grim seemed to accept Bishop's logic, his head nodding slowly as he worked the hand pump on the 50- gallon drum of fuel.

Finally looking up, he said in a low tone, "We can bury him at my place. I know just the spot, a shady area underneath the big elm. Deke always liked the shade, and that way I'll be able to pay my respects if things ever get back to normal."

The two men continued the tasks at hand, each needing the chance to regroup. Bishop had been slashed by a machete attack, and an inspection of his shirt showed the cut material was repairable, but not something that he wanted to do in their current situation. Two of the MOLLE ladders on his vest had also been severed, as well as the hose of his water reservoir, the most critical damage to his kit. Patching the puncture using duct tape, Bishop then began redressing himself with the spare shit from his kit. It was the best repair possible. Reloading magazines was the next priority; the two empties retrieved from his dump pouch were soon full of 45-caliber rounds.

He then began the unwanted chore of inventorying Deke's equipment, any reservations over rummaging through the dead man's assets quickly dismissed by their desperate situation.

Grim started to protest Bishop's activities, but then realized the wisdom of the act. It was then that Bishop noticed the damage to Grim's rifle. Pointing to the weapon, Bishop asked, "Are you sure that blaster still functions? That looks like some serious damage.

A quick check revealed that indeed the rifle had suffered an apparently deadly blow from some sort of edged strike. Grim ejected the magazine from the damaged receiver, holding the rifle between his knees and working the charging handle. Looking up, he said, "It's a good thing you noticed that. This weapon is ruined, and now I'm really pissed. It has been with me on five continents... for 15 years. Now some amateur desperado with a pickax has ruined my lucky piece."

Bishop reached into the bed of the truck and retrieved Deke's carbine, giving the weapon a quick once over, checking for any obvious damage. Conscious of his partner's injury, Bishop worked the action of the rifle and found it fully operational.

Grim hesitated over exchanging weapons, but the logic of the move wasn't lost on him for long. Despite the damaged weapon having saved his skin on many occasions, Grim grunted and accepted the new unit.

"Deke would wanted it that way. I know he would," Bishop whispered.

Grim nodded, adjusting the sling and then letting the weapon rest against his chest. He patted the receiver with his good hand, and vowed, "I'll put it to good use if the need arises."

Each man then rested for 45 minutes while the other kept watch. It wasn't much sleep, but neither knew when they'd be able to rest again.

The yellow light of a new day guided them out of the quarry and into the Tennessee countryside. Grim's estimate of the distance to his home was accurate, Bishop pulling the truck to the side of the country lane just shy of being visible from his partner's property.

There was slightly more vigor in Grim's movements as he jumped from the bed of the truck and approached the driver's window. "I'm going to go up on foot so my old lady doesn't put a 12-gauge full of buckshot into someone's ass. She's probably a little jumpy these days."

Bishop chuckled, having little doubt that Mrs. Grim was fully capable of defending herself.

"You stay here for 10 minutes while I go check things out. That will give me plenty of time to make sure we don't freak her cookies."

And then Grim was off, half trotting into the distance

toward the homestead.

Bishop waited the prerequisite amount of time, and then slowly drove up the driveway. He hit the brakes when the property came into full view.

Rather than the modern home he expected, blackened timbers and piles of gray ash came into view. Grim's house had burned to the ground, the streaked outline of a bathtub and rusted shells of kitchen appliances the only identifiable objects.

Grim stood motionless, staring at the destruction without comment.

When he sensed Bishop at his side, the contractor looked up with sad eyes and responded, "Well, at least I know why she's not here."

Bishop's mind immediately leapt to the worst case – his expression showing the obvious concern over his friend's family being victims of the blaze.

Grim noted the look on Bishop's face. "They're not here," he announced, his voice growing angry. "I checked the ashes for bodies. Thank the Lord in heaven they got out."

"Would they have gone to a neighbor or relative's home?" Bishop asked.

"Maggie doesn't have any family locally. I can't find any evidence of foul play. I'm hoping she and Jana moved in with the Brewers down the road."

Bishop nodded, a bad feeling growing inside. "There's only one way to tell," he said, trying to sound positive. "Let's drive to the Brewers and see."

The rural countryside didn't warrant Grim riding shotgun in the bed of the truck. It seemed odd to Bishop, having someone seated in the cab after so many days of constantly being alone behind the wheel. The Brewer farm was only a mile and a half down the narrow lane from Grim's place. Again, Bishop stopped the truck some distance up the road while his partner dismounted to approach the neighbor's homestead.

Bishop waited the prearranged amount of time, and for the second time that morning guided his vehicle up a stranger's driveway. This time it was obvious someone was home, Grim and another man standing on the front porch of the traditional southern farmhouse, engaged in conversation. Bishop joined them a short time later, the expression on his friend's face indicating it wasn't the day for good news.

"Maggie stayed here with us for about a week after the house burned down. She thought a candle got knocked over while she and Jana were picking up walnuts," Mr. Brewer said. "Lily and I offered for both of them to stay, but you know that woman of yours – she's got too much pride to accept a handout from anybody. I suppose it didn't help matters that the wife and I are barely feeding ourselves, but the offer was genuine. About a week later, everything went to hell in a hand basket. We had a bad hailstorm about then, and it wiped out the garden she was keeping back at your place. We'd been sharing what little we had, but it was obvious that desperate times were heading down the road as far as food was concerned."

Grim didn't seem to be able to find the words to ask the next question, disappointment and frustration painted all over his face.

"Did they say where they were going?" Bishop inquired.

Mr. Brewer hesitated, glancing down at his boots, and then coming to a decision. Finally, meeting Grim's gaze, the farmer said, "Yes, she went to join the Circus."

"The circus?" Grim asked. "Do you literally mean my wife ran off to join the circus with the bearded lady and the clowns on those little bikes?" only a hint of sarcasm blended with doubt in his tone.

"No," the farmer continued, realizing he wasn't speaking to locals. "The Circus is what everybody calls a small community that follows the army units around. I'm not sure how it got its name. I've never seen it myself."

"Camp followers?" Grim hissed, not believing what the man was telling him.

"I don't know," Mr. Brewer continued, "Again, I've never seen it with my own eyes. Some people around here say it's like a recreation area for the troops. Others, well, you know how rumors are."

Grim was speechless, obvious thoughts of his wife and daughter's desperation running through his head, the conclusion not pretty. He visibly shuddered, and then again pleaded with his neighbor for more information. "Why? Why, would she do that? Were things really that bad?"

"The men who run the Circus put up signs all over Millington. 'Work in exchange for food. Come to the Circus.' They were posted all over the place, even at the end of our road."

"And where is this Circus?" Bishop inquired.

"It's in town, at the shopping center, or at least what's left of it."

Grim and Bishop tried to extract more information from Mr. Brewer, but it became clear after a while the man had relayed everything he knew about the situation. Expressing their thanks and moving back to the truck, the duo was soon pulling out of the driveway, unsure of their destination.

Bishop was exhausted. "Dude, I know you're probably anxious to see your wife and daughter, but I'm not going to be much help in my current state. Is there any chance we can rest and regroup at your place for a few hours before we head into another potentially dangerous situation?"

Grim started to protest, but then reconsidered. "You're right. I don't like it. I don't want to wait, but I'm afraid we might need to be at our best. My arm's throbbing like a bass drum. I guess a few more hours isn't going to make that much difference."

They pulled the truck back into Grim's driveway, navigating behind a surviving outbuilding to hide the truck. Bishop reclined in the driver's seat, his burning eyes appreciating the opportunity to close.

"There's a well over there," Grim announced. "Why don't you crash for a bit, and I'll bring up some water. I don't know about you, but my outlook on life might improve if I could wash at least one layer of this road grime off my skin."

Bishop opened his eyes and adjusted the rearview mirror, the reflection seconding Grim's observation. His face was filthy, his clothes tattered and soaked in the blood of the attackers and his late friend. "Whatever this Circus may be, it sounds as though there's some sort of organization. It might do us both good to look a little more presentable if we're going to be around polite society."

The quiet countryside and mild temperature were soothing, and soon Bishop nodded off.

His dreams were filled with the sound of Terri's laughter and images of playing with Hunter. Terri was setting out a picnic lunch while the guys were checking out the swings. The setting was park-like, a postcard pleasant Sunday afternoon. Deke was there too, enjoying the sunshine and mild breeze, laughing at the sight of the baby riding on Bishop's shoulders while the two toured the grounds. Suddenly, the calm was interrupted by the contractor coughing up streams of bright, red blood. The sight frightened Hunter. Just as before, the dying man's voice proclaimed his passing was okay, the same words repeated over and over again.

Grim's voice brought him out of the deep sleep, a quick check of the light outside the cab verified by a glance at his watch. Bishop had actually been asleep for several hours.

"Holy shit," he announced. "I didn't intend on crashing for that long."

Grim replied, "I went out like a light, too. We need to get moving, it will be dark in about an hour."

The two men wasted no time preparing for the next leg of their adventure. Millington was only about 15 miles away, and Grim doubted there would be any old traffic blockage on the rural route that meandered into the town.

They ate a quick meal, cleaned their weapons, and did their best to wash the dried blood and grime from their clothing. Grim produced a needle and thread, displaying a deft hand stitching up some of the tears and rips suffered during the battle.

The sun was just setting as they exited the driveway. The men rode in silence, unsure of what to expect as they traveled toward the small community.

Millington, Tennessee, had once been a pleasant, mid-sized city of approximately 10,000 residents. Like so much of the Volunteer State, the municipality had experienced growth in the decades leading up to the Second Great Depression.

Close enough to Memphis for commuters, the local leadership had struggled to maintain prosperity while attempting to maintain a dose of small town charm. For this reason, the new retail mall had been built on the edge of town - a small benefit for the rescuers as they could avoid travel through yet another potentially dangerous urban area.

It soon became obvious why everyone called it the Circus. The large parking lot of the once prosperous shopping destination was filled with campers, RVs and other miscellaneous civilian vehicles. Parked in a strategic formation designed to create a perimeter, they surrounded what was essentially a huge circus tent that had been erected in the open space.

Someone had strung Christmas lights, no doubt powered by a generator, into a complex webbing draped throughout the facility. The festive glow of the multicolored decorations reminded Bishop of Caribbean resorts trying to project a holiday atmosphere year-round.

Circling the establishment, the two men studied both the patrons approaching the obvious entrances, and the significant security forces that were in plain view.

Every 30 yards, a man stood on a camper top or other elevated perch, strategically placed like guard towers surrounded a prison – no approach was left unobserved. The newcomers noted two distinct entrances, gaps in the white barrier of the castle's fortress-like bastions.

The entryways were clogged with humanity, dozens of soldiers and civilians milling about while waiting to gain entrance to the facility. On their second orbit, Grim motioned for Bishop to slow down so he could read a large hand-lettered sign posted nearby the opening. It read, "No weapons beyond this point. No exceptions. All firearms and explosives devices must be checked."

"Well that sucks," proclaimed Grim.

"I wonder if they have a coat check to go along with the weapons check?" Bishop commented, trying to bleed a little of the stress out of the cab.

"Actually, it makes sense. It would be bad for business if a drunk trooper shot up the place every night. A zero tolerance firearm policy should help keep violence down to a minimum."

Bishop had to agree, "Guns and booze don't mix. Never have, never will."

The mall's expansive parking lot provided ample space for the multitude of both military and civilian vehicles used to transport soldiers and other patrons from nearby Memphis. At first, Bishop was hesitant for both of them to go inside as he did not want to leave the truck and its few remaining supplies unguarded, but the concern soon dissipated.

The presence of numerous armed men, obviously acting in a security role to guard the military's vehicles, alleviated Bishop's fear. There was no sense in locking the truck, the shattered passenger window making the effort futile. After verifying their cargo was covered by the tarp, the two men proceeded to the entranceway.

The procedure to gain access to the Circus reminded Bishop of passing through security for a pre-collapse airplane flight. Although they had joked about a coat check, the surrendering of their weapons was a similar process. A bored-looking man stationed behind the makeshift counter appeared not to even take notice of the make, model, or caliber of the firearms that he and Grim handed over. A piece of masking tape was wrapped around the stock of each weapon, a number handwritten with a black marker on each label. The clerk then copied down an identical set of digits onto small squares of paper, handing them over to the rescuers.

"Verify the numbers are the same," the man instructed.

Once they had tested the gentleman's copying skills, the two men from Texas proceeded to the next step required for entry.

After surrendering their firepower, they entered a section comprised of large tables, no doubt "salvaged" from a local church or community center. There were several rows, each having a queue of customers waiting to exchange goods for what amounted to the local currency.

Bishop had been wondering how it all worked, and it was no surprise to find a system in place that mimicked

Meraton's market back home.

He watched, fascinated as customers bartered with the employees seated at the tables. One man had two chickens in a wire cage, another soldier offering ammunition carried in a ziplock plastic bag. People carried all sorts of boxes, bags and other containers filled with valuables.

Taking the shortest line, the rescuers patiently waited for the soldier in front of them to negotiate his trade. The young private set a pair of boots on the table and opened the bargaining "Size 10, never been on a foot."

With a ho-hum attitude, the woman sitting behind the table picked up a sheet of paper and scanned the rows and columns of printed numbers. "Twenty credits," she eventually announced.

"That's all? Last week a good pair of boots was worth 30!"

The clerk didn't even bother arguing with the man, instead reaching for a wooden pole about the length of a broom handle. At the end was a white flag. She waved the signal into the air, and soon a man with a shaved head and wide shoulders arrived.

"This man is an evaluator," she said. "You can negotiate with him; his offer is final."

Obviously, the evaluator was conscious of the growing number of customers waiting in line. He quickly examined the private's offering, and then said, "Okay, 25 credits – take it or leave it."

Disgusted, the young soldier mumbled, "What choice do I have?" and then accepted the bid. Opening a small metal box sitting on the table in front of her, the clerk proceeded to count out what appeared to be poker chips.

Bishop and Grim were next, the woman not even looking up from her inventory sheet as they advanced in line. "What do you have to trade?"

"Ammo," Bishop declared.

"5.56 or 7.62?"

"5.56," Bishop responded.

The Texan didn't bother to haggle, not really anticipating to find much that he needed or wanted inside. He glanced at the handful of chips the clerk placed on the table, noting they were from a casino in Louisiana. He handed Grim his share, watching as the operator examined what amounted to the local currency.

"Makes sense," Grim observed. "These would be very difficult to counterfeit."

The next station was where the Circus collected a "non-refundable" cover charge. Bishop and Grim paid the required

178

sum, each man receiving a stamp on the back of his hand.

"It's like going to a dance club," Bishop observed, the comment not entirely in jest.

There was music playing in the distance and the ever-growing crowd carried an air of excitement, laughter and nervous chatter filling the air.

"I waited to get into a club in London once," Grim noted. "It was a similar atmosphere. Everyone all giddy about a new, cool place to drink and dance."

"A party is a party," Bishop observed. "Hell, didn't Nero play the fiddle as Rome burned?"

"They had fiddles back then? I think it was a flute – you're thinking of the devil and Georgia," Grim chuckled.

The final stage of the entry gauntlet was a security check.

Several large fellows were massed around the narrowing entryway, supported by even more serious-looking men with battle rifles, stationed slightly above in handmade wooden towers – each with his weapon at low ready and eyes darting over the gathered throng of wannabe visitors.

"But your hands on the wall and assume the position," a burly man ordered Bishop. He was wearing a t-shirt labeled Millington Police Department.

A moment later, rough hands frisked Bishop's person, searching for concealed weapons or other prohibited paraphernalia.

And then they were passed into the inner sanctum of the Circus.

Bishop's first impression was that of a carnival. His senses were assaulted at all levels. Music and the background hum of conversation and laughter filled his ears, accented by the aroma of food and people. There was motion and color everywhere, the dense mulling of the crowd, lights, signs and displays adding to the effect.

After gaining entrance, both men moved to the side, overwhelmed by the crush of it all. Bishop's head pivoted here and there, something constantly catching his eye or ear and drawing his attention.

There were two young, leggy girls, both scantily clad in short skirts and low-cut tops, dancing in cages that had been elevated to advertise. Another man, dressed as a clown, was walking through the crowd on stilts and carrying a sign touting an eatery.

It took them a few minutes to acclimate, but the layout of the place was fairly simple. The large tent was the obvious center of the action, covering a space half the size of a football field.

Surrounding that main attraction were corridors lined with small booths offering everything from laundry services to dry goods and finger foods.

The stall nearest Bishop displayed stacks of blue jeans and polo shirts, while its neighbor sported two very pretty women and a large sign offering "Massage – 100 credits."

They walked closer to the tent, peering over and around the passing sea of humanity that surged slowly around the outer corridor. Inside the Big Top, they discovered what was essentially a large nightclub. The rows of tables and chairs would have been right at home in any large bar or restaurant. Women carrying serving trays topped with tumblers plied the matrix of seated, smiling customers while taking orders and delivering beverages.

A huge bar constructed of timber and plywood resided at one end, mostly occupied stools lining its front. Behind the oversized structure, metal shelves held plastic milk containers, bottles and hundreds of mismatched glasses and mugs, the rainbow of colors making it obvious that the collection hadn't originated from a single source. About a dozen bartenders hustled about – pouring, wiping and conversing with customers.

"Let's circle around the outer edge and see if we can find my wife," Grim suggested over the loud rock 'n roll music.

Bishop swept the air with his hand, "After you, sir."

Whoever had organized the Circus obviously possessed extensive access to a wide range of resources, as well as significant management skills. The duo walked past stalls offering everything from open-spit chicken to packages of underwear and socks still wrapped in the factory cellophane.

Sex was obviously a big seller, no surprise given 90% of the customers were young soldiers deployed far away from home. Almost every other booth advertised some form of physical gratification or service, the offerings running the gamut of sexual appetites.

One area, cordoned off with Tennessee Department of Transportation sawhorses, reminded Bishop of pictures he'd seen of WWII USO dance clubs. One side was filled with anxious looking uniformed men, most of them sipping beverages and gazing across the dance floor at the available women. Between the gender-polarized groups, two dozen couples danced various jigs to the blaring music. If the tunes had included the melodic brass horns of Benny Goodman, rather than electric guitars, Bishop might have been convinced he'd traveled back in time

As they circled the perimeter, it became clear that profit was a motivator for those who ran the Circus. Everything, including access to the porta-potties, required credits. Hot steam baths were five credits, while a paper cup full of sliced pork required eight poker chips.

Concern over the bottom line was also evident in how commerce was allowed to proceed. Bishop was somewhat surprised at the morality enforced on the compound. While it was made clear that prostitution was a significant portion of the economy, the world's oldest trade was secluded – kept out of the open.

As their tour continued, Bishop began to worry about Grim, the man's thoughts obviously leaping to the worst-case scenario regarding the type of employment his wife and daughter might be engaged in. At one point they were solicited by a young lady to enter a sex show, the hawker promising both men they would see, "Things they had never imagined."

"I can imagine a lot," Bishop had joked, unaware that his ill-timed humor had run afoul with his partner.

Grim leaned close to Bishop, his whisper hard and mean, "She's not much older than my daughter. I need to find my family – let's pick up the pace."

Grim had described his loved ones in some detail, giving a description as he and Bishop had driven into town. Each man scanned the numerous stalls, booths, and tables, searching for the contractor's family. Bishop prayed they would find the women engaged in some innocent commerce – unsure of what Grim would do if that weren't the case.

That prayer wasn't entirely based on concern for his buddy. Armed security was everywhere, and it was clear they didn't tolerate the slightest misbehavior. Before they had reached the halfway point of the circuit, the two rescuers had witnessed the harsh discipline enforced by the local guards.

A young specialist had evidently consumed a little too much alcohol, or perhaps was simply overwhelmed by the spectacle before him. Bishop watched the man paw at a waitress, trying to slide his hand up the girl's skirt. She didn't appreciate the effort, asking him nicely to "Get lost."

Her rejection was ignored, the fellow persistent in his goal. After the second warning, Bishop saw the lady whisper to the bartender, who immediately turned to a nearby armed man of significant girth.

They came from three different directions. If the soldier hadn't resisted, Bishop believed they would have simply escorted him out. He wasn't that smart, or that sober. He resisted, the effort rewarded with a butt-stroke from an AR15 and two rabbit punches to the face.

In the span of a few seconds, the semi-conscious offender was being carried toward the exit, blood flowing from his nose and mouth. His now-unoccupied table was immediately wiped clean while another patron was shown to the still-warm seat.

If Grim finds his wife working the sex trade, there's going to be trouble, Bishop realized. I've got to have his back, but I sure do hope he doesn't get us killed by acting stupid.

They were three quarters of the way around the perimeter when Grim pulled up quickly, stopping so fast Bishop almost ran into his friend. Taking Bishop's arm, he extended a finger and pointed to a woman serving drinks at a table perched on the outer edge of the Big Top.

"There's Maggie! There's my wife."

Bishop studied the waitress, noting that she appeared unharmed, relatively clean and didn't seem to be suffering from malnutrition or any other noticeable ailments.

"Looks like she's waiting tables, dude. That's got to be a big relief compared to what some of these women might be asked to do in order to earn their keep."

Grim nodded, prodding Bishop to continue on their path, obviously hoping to spot his daughter at some point in the tour.

A few minutes later, he again nudged Bishop and pointed this time to a younger woman busy washing dishes in a huge tub of water outside of what was the center tent's kitchen. Grim's expression and demeanor drastically improved, the stress and worry obviously dissipating into the cool night air.

He wasn't the only one, Bishop feeling a sense of relief for both the women and his immediate future.

The rescuers entered the tent opposite where they had spotted Grim's bride. Their logic for not directly approaching Maggie was simple; they didn't know what was going on... how things worked locally. Her reaction might spark curiosity from a supervisor – might lead to extra scrutiny that could hinder any attempt to extract the two women.

Finding an empty corner table, well away from the better-lit areas, the two men took a seat and waited until approached by a waitress who could've been serving drinks in any pre-collapse bar or club.

"Hi guys, I'm Maryanne, and I will be your server this evening. What can I get you?"

Bishop responded, "We're new around here. What do you have?"

"We have beer, and it's almost cold. We also have moonshine whiskey, but I would advise you to take it easy on the hard stuff. This latest batch made some of the troops ill."

Images of Pete's homemade brew and bathtub gin passed through Bishop's mind, the seemingly endless need for alcoholic beverages no different now than before society fell apart. He wondered for just a moment if it'd always been that way. Biblical references to wine, the Romans' famous trade routes established for trading such indulgences, and other examples littered history where the taste for alcohol had shaped local politics and the habits of men.

"I'll take a cold beer," Bishop replied, Grim ordering the same. A few minutes later, Maryanne returned, carrying two mismatched tumblers that would've been an embarrassment for any reasonable tavern just over a year ago.

Bishop estimated each beer was between eight and ten ounces, the small portions made more insulting by Maryanne's demand for a significant amount of their chips. Some quick math allowed Bishop to determine that each of their beers had cost the equivalent of 10 rounds of ammunition. Not a good value from his estimation.

His consumer report took a nosedive over the weak, watered down brew. "It's no wonder we haven't seen more trouble around here," he commented to Grim. "I bet there's not enough alcohol in this beer to get a buzz, even after a dozen mugs."

Grim ignored the complaint, handing the waitress a few chips, including a tip. Before she could hustle off, he stopped her and asked, "Maryanne, do you have a moment? Like my here friend said, we're new here, and I'm really curious how all this works. We've not seen anything like this before... at least not since things went to hell."

Unlike pre–collapse servers, Maryanne's expression indicated she was in no mood to stand around and shoot the shit. Grim's tip helped ease the tension only a little.

"I don't know a whole lot," she responded, obviously wanting to move on and serve other customers, and perhaps collect more tips.

Grim was persistent. "I'm sorry, but I have some family that lives close by, and I was wondering if this is a good place to work."

The girl glanced right and left, checking to see if any of the establishment's other employees were within earshot. She then hunched over the table and pretended to be wiping up a nonexistent spill. In a hushed voice, she answered, "They lie to you when you first come to work here. We barely make enough to buy our food and rent a space in one of the campers. Unless you're willing to sell your body, no one makes enough to buy their way out." She stood back up and added, "But I guess it beats starving to death." And then she was gone.

Watching the girl scamper away, Grim mused, "I thought as much."

From their vantage Bishop and Grim could not make eye contact with Maggie. Trying to fit in, they slowly sipped the lukewarm beer, neither man thinking it was worthy of bottling, neither knowing exactly what to do next.

After observing their surroundings for a while, Grim's attention was drawn to a far corner of the huge tent. Indicating the area with a nod of his head, "That must be the VIP section over there. Check out all the muscle concentrated around those curtains. That's more protection than the Secret Service gives the president."

Gracefully, Bishop diverted his gaze where indicated, and had to agree with the assessment. Partially bordered by the end of the bar, a wall of drapes completed what was clearly meant to be an isolated, special oasis. He counted at least six very serious looking men, all equipped with carbines, all of their heads pivoting right and left as if scouring for threats. Their size and body language indicated a higher level of skill than the other private security. They concentrated their efforts in the same small area and were not mobile like the rest of the security personnel.

The party lights generated just enough glow to make out ambiguous shapes of other patrons sitting at the secluded tables. He was just about to comment when Grim pushed his chair back and stood.

"I'm going to casually saunter over that way and see what's going on. My curiosity is peaked."

And with that, the operator picked up his beer and slowly began meandering towards the exclusive section of the saloon. As Bishop watched, he had to hand it to Grim. Had he not known otherwise, he would've assumed that the operator was casually moseying around, perhaps seeking friends or colleagues. It took Grim almost 15 minutes to manage the scouting expedition, his progress constantly interrupted by clusters of soldiers, waitresses hustling beverages, and the packed compression of tables and chairs hindering the way. When he finally returned to his seat, Grim was smiling with confidence. "I think I know the guy who is running this show," he announced. "It's been a few years, but I think I recognized him from a stint at Fort Benning. His name is Major Beckworth."

"No shit?"

Grim nodded, "I always thought that guy bent the rules a little too much. He worked behind the green door in Intelligence, and was always involved one spooky op or another."

As if on cue, the security guards surrounding the retreat suddenly became alert, three of the armed men moving toward the nearest exit of the facility. Their action was immediately followed by a stocky, medium-height man with a shaved head appearing between the parted curtains. Closely tailed by an exceptionally beautiful woman and another guy with thick glasses who appeared to be some sort of clerk. The ex-major followed, making for the exit with a curt, military-esque stride. Before Bishop could comment, Grim was moving to intercept his old acquaintance.

Deciding he didn't want to be left out of the loop, Bishop stood to follow, having to hustle in order to match his colleague's pace.

"Major Beckworth! Major Beckworth!" Grim yelled.

The man paused, almost ignoring the hail, but then glanced over to catch Grim approaching through the maze of tables and humanity. Two of the security guards immediately moved to intercept, their carbines raised slightly higher than normal, their weight shifting forward to the balls of their feet.

Eventually, the major smiled, recognizing Grim with a slight tilt of his head. "It's okay boys, I know him. Let him through."

After the exchange of a handshake, Grim and the head honcho sized each other up. Bishop, anxious to join the party and wanting to support his friend, was stopped cold by the security guys.

"Grim, my gawd man, it's been what? Fifteen years?"

"Yes, sir, at least. I see you're doing well."

The ex-major glanced at the woman draped on his arm and then grinned slyly. "I've had my share of luck. Right place and right time... What brings you to my Circus?"

Grim looked around, deciding there were too many ears close by. "That's something we should probably discuss in private, sir."

The former army officer was nothing if not perceptive, catching Grim's meaning immediately. "Of course, of course. Why don't you join me for dinner this evening? ...Say around nine."

"Why, I'd be honored, sir."

"We can break bread and exaggerate old war stories," Beckworth added. Then he turned to one of the security men and ordered, "Give my old friend directions to my RV, and see to it that he is taken care of."

After receiving an acknowledgment that his wishes were understood, he returned his gaze to Grim and said, "I've got an important meeting to attend right now, but I look forward to speaking with you later."

And then the man in charge of the Circus was off, his entourage struggling to keep up. As he neared the edge of the Big Top, Beckworth again paused and motioned his security chief closer. "That son of a bitch Grim used to hang around with some pretty interesting people. Take a picture of that man with him. I don't think I've ever seen the other guy before, but maybe Washington can shed some light on who my old friend is keeping company with these days."

"Yes, sir... I'll take care of it."

"Send it right away," the boss added. "If we can get something back before dinner, it might help spice up my conversation."

"Consider it done, sir."

Chapter 13

Beckworth's security man peeled off the detail surrounding his boss after they arrived in a safer area of the compound.

After making sure his charge was well protected, he returned to the Big Top, working his way around the perimeter until his angle allowed for a clear view of Grim and Bishop's table.

The two strangers were talking, occasionally glancing around at the activities, the man they called Grim checking his watch to make sure he didn't miss his dinner date.

Despite months without operational towers, the head bodyguard still kept his cell phone fully charged, having found a multitude of uses for the handy device. One such task was taking pictures that could easily be transferred to any computer.

After adjusting the focus, he quickly snapped a series of photographs of both men and then made for the main office.

It took a few minutes to cross the grounds, several of his security forces issuing greetings, a few men needing clarification about this or that. Eventually he arrived at the one functional door leading into the actual mall. The major had wanted bookkeeping, communications and other critical infrastructure set up inside a real brick and mortar building.

Through his connections with both the military and the bigwigs in Washington, the boss had acquired an operational satellite communications system identical to the one used by Special Forces teams on remote missions.

Using a codebook residing next to the sophisticated machine, he punched in the prerequisite information and then swiveled to a nearby computer. A few seconds later, the images stored on his cell phone were traveling into space, almost immediately redirected to a similar unit at the Pentagon.

Finished with his task, he reset the transmitter, secured the computer, and then headed back to his primary job – making sure the major survived another day.

While full network communications hadn't been

reestablished, the airwaves used by the military machine were far from empty. The sergeant working the night shift saw the transmission come in, noting nothing special or urgent about the request.

The National Security Agency handled all such inquires asking for identification and background file information, so he followed procedure and forwarded the request to that agency.

It took only 11 minutes for the massive banks of computer servers to match Bishop and Grim's photos. An automated computer algorithm measured eight different points of each man's face, those dimensions as unique as fingerprints.

A database was then searched, the binary code identifying a match within a few seconds. Once each man's name was known, a less powerful machine took over, gathering data about the subjects from various sources throughout the massive amount of information stored by the federal government.

Military, tax, social and diplomatic archives were queried, the returned information consolidated and then eventually retransmitted back to the Pentagon. The entire process took less than 15 minutes.

Back in the basement of the military's Washington headquarters, the sergeant's console again indicated incoming traffic.

He noted the NSA's normal efficiency and again followed procedure, giving the packets a manual check for completeness and content.

One of the numerous items returned was a history of other such inquiries for each of the subjects. If the FBI or the IRS had shown interest in either man, it would be noted on the records.

His eyebrows rose just slightly when he noticed a recent inquiry on one of the files. Switching to another program, he verified that his memory was correct.

Someone had recently pulled a similar file on one of the men. The access code used only a few days ago began with the prefix "01." Only the Commander in Chief or one of his top advisors could use that code.

Anything to do with the president invoked a completely different protocol. The sergeant immediately reached for the phone residing next to his computer. It was time to call in an officer.

A gruff voice answered on the second ring. "Colonel Peterson."

"Sir, this is Sergeant McConnell in the communications room. We just received a type six information request from the Memphis region of Operation Heartland. The request generated a duplicate hit on one of the subjects – the original request instigated by the president."

The colonel didn't respond for a moment, obviously trying to determine how to handle the unusual situation. Finally he responded, "Send me the file, Sergeant. I believe General Owens is still at Camp David with the president. I'll let him handle it."

"Yes, sir."

General Owens was just about to turn in, finishing up the seemingly endless number of status reports, correspondence and other paperwork required of the rank.

Groaning when his computer indicated yet another message had arrived in his inbox, he opened the new correspondence with a grimace.

For a moment, he didn't understand why he had been forwarded what appeared to be a standard request for information from one of the units assigned to Operation Heartland.

Once he realized the reason, he printed the first few pages of the attached file and left his quarters, heading directly for President Moreland's cabin.

He was shown in immediately by Agent Powell, the prompt admittance evidence that Owens didn't just drop by unless it was something critical.

"What's so urgent, General?" Moreland greeted.

"Sir, one of the leaders from West Texas... one of the men we've been researching... he has shown up in Tennessee."

The statement heightened the chief executive's attention. "Which one?"

Handing over the printout, Marcus replied, "Bishop."

Moreland didn't react at first, studying the papers in detail. He finally looked up with a puzzled expression, "This is the man who shot Wayne," he mumbled, quickly adding, "He is also their leader's husband. What the hell is he doing in Memphis?"

"Unknown, sir. Protocol dictated you be informed of the duplicate request. Other than that, I have no additional facts."

The president's gaze returned to the documents in his hand, but it was clear he was thinking through the implications of the situation. "General, I want to talk to the person who submitted this request. I want to find out why this man has left his wife and newborn child and is roaming around inside our territory. And

189

whatever they do down there, don't let him out of sight until I've had a chance to think this through."

"Yes, sir. I'll get right on it."

Just as Bishop thought he was going to have to go barter more of his ammunition in order to remain at their table, Grim returned.

"Like my daddy always said," Grim began. "It's not what you know, but who you know."

"So I take it your ex–CO was glad to see you?"

Nodding, Grim replied, "Yes, and I got invited to eat dinner with him this evening. I'm hoping to be able to reach an arrangement with Beckworth in order to secure release for Maggie and Jana."

"That would sure solve a lot of problems," Bishop noted. "Still, do you think that's possible?"

"I can only hope… otherwise, getting them out of here is going to be a serious challenge. I don't think he'll give them up without some sort of deal. He's just not that type of guy. Back in the day, Beckworth was always on the edge of something shady. He ran with CIA and other spook-types, and there was always a hint that he was involved in some sort of dark enterprise of one kind or another. Rumors abounded… One time I heard the major was running a prostitution ring at Benning, another that he was knee deep in black market weapons running through Baghdad. He's the type that won't give up anything unless he gets better in return."

Bishop had anticipated as much, Maryanne's reaction indicating just such an employer.

After a few more swallows of beer, Grim tapped the face of his watch and announced that he was going to go and freshen up for dinner. "I'm going to go pay for a hot bath," he declared, grabbing a handful of casino chips. "At least I can smell civilized while dining with the uncivilized. I'll meet you back here in three hours."

Slightly pissed that Grim had not included him in the dinner plans, Bishop remained at the table and ordered another beer, of which he had no intention of drinking.

He dawdled, sipping the puny brew and watching the comings and goings of both the customers and the employees. He noted that there were officers and enlisted men, both partaking of the local libations. It was just like the army he remembered, an unspoken separation between the ranks. Soldiers tended to cluster with their own classifications, seeming to ignore those who were not members of the same group.

Movement beside his table interrupted Bishop's analysis, the sudden appearance of a young lady drawing his attention.

"Buy a girl a drink?"

"Sure, have a seat. Maryanne is my waitress; she should be by shortly."

The lady now seated at Bishop's table wasn't unattractive. He had made the invitation, snap judgment as it was, to invite her based mostly on a desire for more information with a small dose of boredom also to blame.

Their conversation started off casually enough, Bishop having experienced dozens of such encounters back in his single days while stationed at Fort Bragg. Like any town close to a major military base, Fayetteville had possessed its fair share of local watering holes, often frequented by young females who weren't opposed to conversing with the locally stationed soldiers.

Bishop had often wondered if the troops attracted the girls, or if the girls brought in the troops. Deciding the question was unanswerable, he'd given up seeking the truth early on, and focused his energies on the courtship of a variety of young ladies.

This, of course, had been years before he met Terri. Now, tinges of guilt tugged at him, despite the innocence of merely buying a young lady a drink in order to gain local knowledge.

"I'm new around here, and I'm surprised that the military lets this place exist."

"I was too," the girl replied. "I think the general in Memphis looks the other way in order to help morale."

Bishop raised his eyebrows, surprised at the depth of her answer. *These girls probably know more about what's going on than most of the officers in this place*, he thought.

Maryanne appeared, her nod indicating Bishop's guest was well known. "The usual," the waitress prompted.

Bishop decided to use Grim's line of inquiry on the young woman. After Maryanne had delivered the doubly expensive drink, he began, "So I have relatives that live nearby. They're running out of food, and I was wondering if this is a good place for them to find employment."

Just like the waitress before, his companion glanced around, as if she wanted to make sure their conversation wasn't overheard.

"It's okay, I guess. I was desperate, eating little scraps

191

and tidbits as I could find them. My mom got sick and died. There was no way to get help. I really didn't have any choice, but most of the guys are pretty nice to me, and I do have a warm, dry place to sleep and enough food to eat."

Despite his best efforts and another very expensive drink, Bishop could not extract any more information from the woman beside him. She demonstrated deft skills of redirecting conversation, never appearing rude, but never exposing any real facts. She eventually grew tired of his ceaseless questions, finally asking if he was interested in any extracurricular activities back at her camper.

When he declined the invitation, she politely smiled, thanked him for the drinks and then rose to go, intent on seeking customers at other tables.

The skirt-distraction no longer present, Bishop set about people watching. The multitude of uniforms circled his thoughts back to Deke, his friend's body still resting in the back of the truck. Burial on Grim's property was now in doubt. Just digging a hole anywhere was out of the question.

When presented with such a problem, Bishop always tried to consider a pre-collapse solution. In the old days, there would be several options available to surviving friends and family. Given his years of service, a military funeral would have been one such option – a resting place of honor among other warriors.

As he inventoried options, his concentration was interrupted by the presence of a man standing at his table. "Are you using this chair, sir?" came the polite inquiry.

"No, help yourself."

"Thank, you."

As the guy leaned forward to pick up the seat, Bishop noticed the patch on his arm. It was identical to the insignia attached to the uniform provided by Matt, now on the sleeve of his dead friend lying in the bed of the truck - the 377th Military Police.

As Bishop watched, the man carried the chair a few tables over, joining a small group of young officers gathered there. Bishop could make out the butter-bars of a second lieutenant on a couple of them. Given their youthful appearance, he guessed a few of the junior officers were out on a short pass, relishing the opportunity to get away for a few hours and wet their whistles. He smiled, the scene reminding him of his own early years while stationed at Fort Bragg.

The appearance of that patch gave the Texan an idea. Surely the military units occupying Memphis would have a proper procedure in place to lay their causalities to rest. It was a standard operational requirement for any significant deployment.

192

Armies had learned long ago that the respectful, honorable handling of the dead was critical. Warriors and families alike, wanted to see their fallen sons and daughters taken care of with dignity. Bishop started thinking of how he could use this standard to give his friend a proper burial.

Mulling over the options, Bishop decided he needed more information. The young man borrowing the chair had seemed friendly enough. Perhaps if approached from the right angle...

The Texan rose, picking up his glass as if headed to the bar for a refill. His intent was to pass close to the officer's table and eavesdrop as much as possible. He hoped to hear some snippet of conversation that would open an approach – give him a reason to strike up a conversation with the strangers.

His path was suddenly blocked by another man who appeared out of nowhere, making a beeline for the same table. The guy cut Bishop off, the rude act raising his ire. Were he not trying to remain low-key, the Texan would have most likely have commented, but he kept his tongue.

And then the asshole did it again. As he passed by the young LT who had borrowed the chair, Bishop watched the guy bump into the officer's shoulder, causing a significant spill of beer. It almost looked like the offender had purposely rammed the kid.

The hair on Bishop's neck bristled. Something wasn't right.

Surprised by both the assault and a lapful of cold beer, the lieutenant shot to his feet quickly, the chair toppling into the aisle.

"I'm sorry; how clumsy of me," immediately offered the offender, suddenly polite and concerned.

As he bent to pick up the overturned chair, Bishop saw the offender's hand move to the table for support, a stack of poker chips covered by his palm. A pickpocket!

Bishop was only three steps behind the thief, clearly seeing the empty tabletop where only a moment before had been a significant number of the brightly colored disks.

The crook moved the now full hand toward his pants pocket, but never completed the act. Bishop was there, grabbing the bandit's wrist with both hands and twisting hard.

Letting out a bark of surprise, the thief dropped to his knees immediately, Bishop twisting with considerable force, not caring if he dislocated a shoulder.

By that time, all of the officers at the table were standing, a natural reaction to the fast moving sequence of events.

"Hi, Lieutenant," Bishop opened. "You might want to check on your money."

The kid blinked, obviously confused. After Bishop's comment soaked in, the young officer glanced back at the table, then to Bishop, then to the guy on his knees.

"What the fuck," he mumbled.

Bishop applied additional force, twisting and pulling up. The leverage toppled his captive over onto his face, a moan of anguish sounding from the pickpocket's chest.

"Open your hand, asshole, before I tear off your arm and throw it away."

The man did as Bishop instructed, opening his clenched fist. A small river of casino chips tumbled across his back and onto the floor.

Bishop looked up at the LT and explained, "I saw him swipe those from your table. He bumped into you on purpose – to cause a distraction."

Before the shocked officer could respond, two security men pushed through the crowd. "What the hell is going on here?" one of them demanded.

"Pickpocket," replied Bishop. "I caught him red-handed."

Raising his weapon slightly, the guard ordered, "Let him up."

Bishop released his hold, standing upright and immediately moving his hands into the traditional, "Don't shoot," position.

Before the thief could rise, the security man grabbed him by the hair and twisted, looking hard at the face of the accused man. Recognition filled the bouncer's eyes. "I warned you the last time - never show your face in here again. Now I'm pissed, you thieving piece of shit."

The bandit was hauled roughly to his feet, two rather large gentlemen hustling him toward the exit. It was clear the pickpocket's new friends weren't overly concerned with being gentle.

Turning to Bishop, the guard mumbled, "Thanks," and then motioned to a nearby waitress. "These men all get a round on the house." And with that, the episode was over.

Still charged-up by the incident, it took the young soldiers a while to settle down. A few of them offered Bishop a handshake, thanking him for catching the crook. The kid who had borrowed the chair invited Bishop to sit and have a drink.

He accepted.

For a few minutes, Bishop filled the anticipated role. He questioned where the men were from, how long they had been deployed and heard about their families back home.

While the casual conversation was in progress, Bishop pretended to notice the LT's unit insignia, his eyes growing wide. "Are you missing a man?" he asked with low, serious voice.

"What do you mean?" the kid responded, looking around at his colleagues.

"I came across a dead man on the way here. He had on a uniform and a patch just like yours," Bishop informed. "I found this ID on the body."

Bishop dug around in his pockets, producing the identification card Matt had given to Deke. He passed it over to the lieutenant.

It took the young man a moment to comprehend. He glanced at Matt's picture, then handed it to one of the others. "I know this guy, he deserted a while back. He's on the watch list."

As the card was passed around the table, someone asked Bishop where he'd found the body. After telling a small white lie in response, the Texan added, "I'm not sure what to do with the corpse. I was going to head into Memphis and ask after I'd finished my business here."

"Where's the body now?"

Acting embarrassed, Bishop looked at the floor and responded, "I've got him wrapped up in a tarp out in my pickup. I couldn't just leave a soldier lying there and didn't know what else to do."

As expected, Bishop's expressed respect for the fallen seemed to touch the men seated around the table. Things grew quiet after the confession.

"Well, first of all, you probably have a reward coming. Anyone who turns in a deserter is eligible. I don't know why this man left the unit without authorization, but these days, I don't judge them as harshly as I would if we were at war."

"He died violently," Bishop added. "He died fighting someone. I must have gotten there just as it was all over, because his body was still warm."

Bishop's news was sobering, the combination of the pickpocket's failed attempt and now a member of their unit found dead. The oldest of the group looked around at his friends and said, "I don't know about you guys, but I'm not in the mood to party tonight. Let's save our money for another time." The man then looked at his watch and said, "Besides, we've got to get back soon."

There was agreement all around, a few of the men emptying their glasses at the suggestion.

The senior man looked at Bishop and asked, "Can you follow us to our unit? We can take the sergeant's body off your hands and process the reward there."

Bishop hadn't thought about any compensation, but then an idea flashed into his head. "I don't really want a reward. I didn't do anything to deserve it." He then paused as if thinking, and added, "But it sure would help me out if I could travel around without being stopped and having to tell my story at every checkpoint."

"And exactly what is your story?" asked one of the more cynical of the group.

"I own a farm out in the country. I was lucky... I saw what was coming and prepared for the worst. I've done better than most. I've got family spread all around these parts, and I'm on a quest to gather them up and take them back to my place."

Again, Bishop's story filled out the persona he was building. It would explain the fuel and supplies in his truck.

"I can't promise anything, but maybe my CO will grant you a pass. It would move you through the checkpoints a lot faster."

"That'd be great!" Bishop responded. *That would help get us home with Grim and his loved ones.*

A few minutes later the group of officers, Bishop in tow, exited the Circus and made for the parking lot. The men from Memphis had arrived via three small pickup trucks, the kind commonly used to motor troops around the larger military bases all over the country.

"Follow us," one of the men instructed. "It's about 20 minutes from here."

And then the convoy was off, Bishop's larger truck inserted in the middle of the four-car parade.

The class-A motorhome reminded Grim of the similar unit being used by Terri as her portable office back in West Texas. The accommodations, mobility and built-in infrastructure were just hard to beat in a post-SHTF world. Parked in an area with restricted access, Grim had to pass another ring of security before being allowed entrance to the section comprising the luxurious living quarters. Beckworth greeted him with open arms and a huge smile, none of which mellowed the contractor's attitude towards his ex-commander.

"I retired six years ago," the former officer announced. "The idea for this operation came to me as I was reading a history book on the Roman Legions. Since the beginning of organized armies, bands of regular citizens have followed warriors wherever their campaigns have taken them. When I found out about Operation Heartland, I decided I could provide a valuable service to our loyal soldiers, and I began organizing all that you see around you."

"Camp followers," Grim summarized.

Beckworth shrugged. "Call it what you will. At first, those tight asses in Memphis HQ declared our little community off limits. But that changed over time. As morale worsened and desertions began to rise, the stuffed shirts running that show began to loosen up. They now look the other way, and even cooperate with our endeavors now and then."

After two glasses of wine, poured by the man Grim assumed was a steward, Beckworth continued. "Now, morale has improved, and in addition, we're helping the local civilians with trade and employment."

And so the conversation went. Grim was served a medium rare steak, complete with baked potato and canned corn. The food was of much higher quality than anything he'd seen in the surrounding stalls, but then again, rank always did have its privileges.

Just as Grim remembered, the man across from him focused most of the conversation on himself. Terms, like *egotistical ass*, and *self-centered shitbird* rolling through the visitor's mind as his host droned on and on. Despite his distaste for the man, the food wasn't bad, and he managed to keep a polite smile painted on his face.

They were practically finished with the meal before Beckworth got around to asking, "So, what have you been doing since everything went to hell?

Grim didn't see any reason to lie or hold back from his host. He began relating the story of his employment guarding the man who eventually became the new president of the United States. The dinner guest even managed to entertain, passing along a few humorous stories about working at the West Virginia mountain retreat of the then Senator Moreland.

"And so what brings you here?" Beckworth finally got around to asking.

Here we go, thought Grim. "My house burned down while I was away. I guess my wife and daughter didn't have any choice and came to work here at your place of business."

The man across the table tensed, staring deeply into the serious eyes across from him. Like both Grim and Bishop, the ex-major immediately entertained thoughts from the dark side. This line of reasoning made him glance toward the door, wondering how close his security was.

He's scared of me, thought Grim. *He thinks my wife and*

daughter are selling their bodies, and I'm here to kill him. Taking advantage of that fear might be fun.

Beckworth cleared his throat, "You know I don't personally hire anyone... for any role. I'm sorry about your home, Grim. I had no idea any of your loved ones were working here."

I bet you're sorry, you piece of shit, Grim thought. "I just want to take them back with me," Grim replied, leaning forward for emphasis, and adding, "without any trouble."

Beckworth smiled, waving off his guest's concerns. "No problem, Grim. You know that..."

A knock on the door interrupted the rest of his statement. Annoyed, the host glanced in the direction of the offending noise. "Yes."

The security chief opened the door, not shy about his intrusion. "Sir, there is an urgent matter that requires immediate attention. My apologies for barging in, but this couldn't wait."

"Go on."

The large man glanced at Grim, and then back to his boss. "This matter is sensitive, sir. Private."

With a grimace on his face, Beckworth folded his napkin and rose. Looking at his guest, he apologized, "Business calls. Pardon me for just a moment," and then made for the door.

When they were outside, the guard glanced back at the camper and then spoke. "I ran pictures of your guest and the man accompanying him. Five minutes ago, a Blackhawk landed outside our perimeter and discharged a rather unhappy colonel from the Memphis HQ. He informed me that a man named 'Bishop' is traveling with Grim, and he is of 'special interest' to those at the highest levels in Washington."

Beckworth was clearly taken aback by the news. He knew Grim had worked on some very sensitive prerogatives during his time with the military, but there were thousands of such operators, all having similar backgrounds.

The security man continued, "We are to wait for instructions, but under no circumstances are we to let this Bishop character out of our sight. Our messenger from Memphis made it clear that our continued 'good standing' status was in danger if anything went wrong."

"Shit. Go put a man on this Bishop fellow," Beckworth replied and then glanced back at his RV. "I think I might be able to occupy our guests for a while... at least until Washington decides what to do."

"Well, that's a problem. He left via the front entrance 20 minutes ago," the bodyguard said, and then relayed the story of the pickpocket to his boss.

"Shit! Go see if you can find out anything more about

where our new friend Bishop might have gone. I doubt he wandered far, given his partner is still here."

When Beckworth returned from his emergency, Grim could tell something had changed. His host was now stressed. The man across from him was now so intense, for a moment Grim thought he had done something wrong.

"Are you traveling with another man, Grim?"

Oh shit, thought the operator. *What the hell has Bishop done now?*

"Yes... yes I am. Why do you ask?" he answered, his mind racing with next steps.

"There was an incident in the big tent. Your partner caught a thief and detained him for my security people. He seems to be a man with certain skills."

"Bishop does okay. He's not bad for a man who never served with any of the Special Forces. One of these days that Texas swagger of his is going to get him killed, if you ask me."

Beckworth tilted his head, "Texan?"

"Yes. I live in West Texas now. I hope to take my wife and daughter back there. The people there have organized... managed to get a lot of infrastructure up and running, and it's a pretty good place to hang your hat – at least compared to anything else I've seen so far."

Now it all makes sense, the major thought. *Now the pieces of the puzzle are coming together. West Texas is quite the hot topic of conversation in Washington. Bishop must be someone important.*

Beckworth seemed to relax, his facade reverting to its pre-interruption smug.

Something in Grim's answer had obviously pleased his host. So much so, he ordered his assistant to break out two cigars. After clipping and lighting the stogies, Beckworth leaned back in his chair and exhaled a fog of blue smoke. "I've heard quite a few stories concerning your friends down in the Lone Star State. What is really going on down there, Grim?"

Grim hesitated before answering, unable to figure out where Beckworth was coming from, why was there such a sudden curiosity about Texas. "I'm nothing more than a security guard, major. I only know a few of the people there. Most of my time is spent training their militia and setting up security for their key facilities and infrastructure."

"And your traveling companion?"

Warning bells erupted inside Grim's head. The question came to fast – almost eager. Besides, the man sitting across from him wouldn't normally give a rat's ass about some stranger, let alone inquire about him twice. Something was going on, and the operator suddenly felt like he was in over his head.

"I don't really know him that well," Grim lied. "He is just a guy assigned to help me retrieve my family. Other than that, I've only seen him around a few times."

Grim felt the ex-spook's eye boring in on him, trying to peel back the layers of the deception onion. Eventually, Beckworth shrugged his shoulders as if pronouncing the matter unimportant.

"Let me pull up the records on your wife and daughter. I am running a business here, and I need to verify my investment before reaching a decision. I'm sure everything will be fine, but I have to double-check. In the meantime, I'll reschedule their day off, so you three can have a happy reunion. I'll also make housing arrangements so you can all stay in the same unit."

Grim smiled, the anticipation of finally seeing his loved ones more satisfying than the steak he'd just consumed.

"Oh," Beckworth added as Grim rose to leave. "How rude of me. I'll also make separate arrangements for your friend. All on the house, of course."

"Thank you, major," Grim replied, and then made for the door.

As the retired officer watched his guest being escorted back to the main compound, he shook his head. "I don't really know him that well... He was just a guy..." he mocked. "Bullshit, Grim. Absolute, 100% farm fresh bullshit. Never try and deceive a professional liar."

"Frankly, I would have issued you this pass without returning the deserter's body," the captain said, sliding two pieces of paper across the desk to Bishop. "It's fewer mouths we have to feed. I wish everyone would come and retrieve their relatives and get them away from here."

Bishop accepted the documents, holding them up to read.

"This first one gives you permission to travel through the region for 10 days," the JAG officer continued. "The second allows for you to carry a personal firearm. I wouldn't have normally granted that privilege, but my junior officers relayed what you did for them at the Circus."

"Thank you, Captain."

Bishop left the building more than happy with his little scheme. He had to stop himself from whistling as he passed through the barbwire perimeter and guard shacks that had been erected around what had once been a middle school.

One small set of lies had achieved so much. He now had a way to pass back over the Mississippi with Grim and his family, managed a proper burial for Deke's body and, just for icing on the cake, insured that the army wouldn't be looking for Matt. They now thought the missing sergeant was dead.

The drive back to the Circus passed without incident. Bishop's only remaining concern was the release of Grim's family, but that seemed to going their way as well.

Passing through security went smoothly, and he found Grim sitting at their original table, teasing Maryanne about the weak beer.

It wasn't unusual for the Colonel or General Owens to be called to the president's quarters at such a late hour. As a matter of fact, given the state of the union, it was quite common.

Other than serving their country, the two men didn't share much of a background. Owens had come up through the ranks, making a decision to join the Independents before Moreland had become Commander in Chief. His performance during the brief, but intense, civil war had earned him a promotion and secured a role advising the chief executive.

The Colonel had achieved his position as advisor via an entirely different path. He had long ago rejected Washington's politics as well as her military. Instead, he chose to enter the corporate world, where he had managed a life of partisan seclusion until things had fallen apart.

Desperate for knowledgeable, trusted advisors, the former president had pulled the Colonel back into the political machine, playing on the man's patriotism and sense of duty.

The Colonel had rejected joining the Independents, instead advising negotiations and a joint effort to save the nation. "You all can fight it out with the voters after the country has healed," he'd recommended. "For now, we need to make sure there is something left to fight over."

Despite the different routes taken, the Colonel and General Owens found themselves allies, sharing a similar philosophy as well as being kindred spirits in what they believed was best for the nation. Both men knew they were in the minority, especially when it came to dealing with West Texas.

Walking together after being summoned by the

president, Owens quickly informed his friend of Bishop's presence in Tennessee, and what little else was known.

"I wonder what the hell he is doing there," the Colonel pondered.

"I have no idea, but I've got a bad feeling about all this. The president accepted our plan because there wasn't any other valid option. When I informed him of Bishop's presence, his eyes changed. I think your friend's travels have opened a door, and I don't like what's on the other side."

The two men entered the conference room unsure of what to expect. They found the president seated with another man they didn't know.

"I'm sorry to call you in at such a late hour, gentlemen, but new facts have come to my attention. I wanted to revisit our current operation concerning West Texas... to make sure we're still taking the right steps."

Motioning for his two subordinates to be seated, the president continued. "As I'm sure you are aware, Colonel, Bishop has been spotted outside of Memphis. We still don't know what he's doing there. I wanted to call you in and get your impressions."

Moreland then switched his attention to General Owens. "I've asked you to join us, general, because I'm concerned there might be a tactical reason why one of the leaders of their little group has ventured so far away from home. To be frank, I have concerns that our friends might be plotting some sort of strike against us and wanted to include your expertise."

The Colonel had to admit he had similar thoughts after hearing of Bishop's location. He wouldn't put it past his old employee to attempt a preemptive action – to take the fight to the enemy.

Owens disagreed, "I've already done a quick analysis of that, Mr. President. There's nothing critical in that immediate area. If they were after nuclear facilities, there are far more lucrative locations. If they wanted to sabotage our infrastructure, I can think of 50 different targets that would cause us more harm. Memphis is very low on the list of critical assets."

The Colonel added, "Besides, sir, It wouldn't make any sense to start a fight. They've agreed to our offer. All reports indicate they've already began making preparations to meet the terms. Why start a war now?"

The stranger sitting with the president finally spoke. "It could be they accepted our proposal in order to buy time. Perhaps there's been a change in leadership on their side? Maybe the new authority doesn't like the deal made by the old regime. Our estimation of their leadership was shaky at best. You gentlemen underestimated them once, we feel it would be a mistake to do so again."

The Colonel couldn't hide his expression, an intense storm brewing behind his eyes. It broke. "And just who the fuck might *you* be? The only underestimation that has occurred concerning this matter is how little you believe I'll kick your ass, right here in front of the Commander in Chief, God and General Owens. We advised the president to negotiate with the Alliance, advice that was contradicted."

The stranger bristled at the statement, partially because of the threating tone, mostly due to the vulgarity. Still, he remained unapologetic.

"Oh come now, Colonel. I know you are an educated man. Surely you understand the calculus involved in these types of decisions. We are negotiating with a woman who used to be a bank teller for God's sake. The key figures running this so-called alliance read like a Who's Who of Failures. There's not a doctorate in the mix, captain being the highest military rank achieved by any of them. Their actions are as predictable as common street criminals."

The Colonel grunted, staring down and shaking his head. "Calculus? Regime? Estimations? You answered my question, even if indirectly. How are things over at the CIA these days?"

The president spoke before the exchange could continue any further. "Gentlemen, may I remind you we're dealing with the future of our country, not ancient inter-agency feuds. I asked Mr. White to join our little skull session because he is a specialist in counter-insurgency. You'll all do well to respect each other's positions and work together. No more spitballs. That's an order."

Despite the words from his boss, the Colonel was through. "Sir," he began, looking the chief executive right in the eye, "my recommendation is to treat this new information as merely a footnote. There could be a thousand reasons why Bishop is in Memphis, 999 of them completely unassociated with our agreement or future relations with the Alliance. We should ignore this sideshow unless some incriminating facts are discovered."

General Owens nodded, "I agree, sir. Our people are going to be moving into place in two days. I say we keep an eye on Bishop's activities, but make no changes other than that."

The President looked back and forth between his two advisors, remembering his dismay at not following their advice the first time. Nodding, he signaled his agreement. "All right gentlemen, I'll stay the course. Thank you, and good night."

Mr. White intentionally lagged behind, waiting until he was alone with his boss. "Sir, I believe we have an opportunity here – that circumstances have presented us with an opening that could end this little rebellion and advance your plans significantly."

"Go on."

The CIA man cleared his throat, "I wasn't overstating my impression of the rebel's leadership. They are single dimensional, unsophisticated, and suffer from overconfidence. Yet, they are very popular with the people of the region – a fact that would be unwise to ignore, both now, and in the future."

"What are you suggesting?"

"If we could expose the true nature of those leading the rebels – make them publically display their inner weaknesses for all to see, the reintegration of that territory would go much smoother."

"I've already made my decision. You heard it – we are going to honor our agreement and proceed as planned."

Mr. White was not deterred. "Sir, I'm not suggesting anything to the contrary. I believe we can accomplish both."

"What? Are you suggesting we take out their leaders? Assassinate them... or some other illegal act?"

"No, sir. All I want to do is cast a little bait – see if any sharks come to bite. If they do, we will have won this little contest before it even gets started. Your legacy might be as potent as Lincoln's, at least when it comes to preserving the union."

The president's head snapped up, the comparison peaking his attention. "So what is this plan, Mr. White?"

"To begin with, sir, I need to travel to Memphis, right away." the mysterious man began.

Ninety minutes later, an armed military escort pulled into Andrews Air Force, its sudden appearance at such an early hour surprising the sleepy guards.

Chapter 14

Millington, Tennesee
July 11, 2016

Bishop went first, sharing his story of the evening's events. Grim smiled after reading the documents Bishop had obtained. "Good," the operator said, "Damn good job."

"And you? How did your dinner go? I'm ready to go home – I miss my wife and kid."

"I think he'll let my family go tomorrow. He's setting us up a place for this evening, arranging for a reunion. He's going to give you someplace to crash as well."

"Me? Why me?"

Grim thought about his response, not wanting to speculate. "He was aware you and I were working together. Our dinner was interrupted by your antics with the pickpocket. After that, I felt like the evening was more about you than me."

Bishop didn't know the major. Had never seen the man before in his life. It all didn't make sense.

Before the two rescuers could dissect the strange events further, Grim noticed Beckworth's head of security striding toward their table, behind him were Maggie and Jana.

Both of the women were absolutely shocked to see him. Hugs, kisses, half questions and partial answers dominated the next few minutes.

"I hate to break up such a joyous occasion," interrupted the security man, "but I need to show you folks to your quarters and get back to work."

They were lead through a maze of campers, tents and other portable outbuildings that comprised what was essentially a small city. Eventually arriving at a small camping trailer, the Circus employee indicated it was Bishop's home for the evening.

The Texan had to smile as he watched Grim and his family stroll off, all three of them excited about the latest turn of events. He maintained his vigil as they were being shown to a larger unit parked nearby. Bishop grunted, hoping it was equipped with a little privacy for Grim and his wife.

Bishop entered the small motorhome, the facilities more than acceptable. The camper had electrical power, which meant hot water, and the thought of a long, hot shower put him in a better frame of mind.

As he prepared to bathe, Bishop couldn't help but peek out the thin blinds. He didn't trust the environment, nor their host.

Regardless of his nagging suspicions, the Texan wasted

no time in filling the sink with hot water and soap, dousing his filthy clothing repeatedly in the cleaning fluid. Padding around the camper stark naked, he hung his wardrobe on numerous, available knobs and handles, sure the makeshift clothesline would provide him with dry clothing in the morning.

The bathroom was equipped with shampoo, body soap, and a razor. After enjoying a shave enhanced by actually being able to use a mirror, he then proceeded to relish in the hot shower flowing over his head and shoulders, lathering up time and again until the small heater ran out of the refreshing liquid. The fluffy towel was appreciated as much as the water.

The hot soak, clean skin and busy day all combined to help Bishop into REM sleep in record time.

Perhaps it was the excitement of finding his wife and daughter safe and unharmed, or maybe he had just grown used to getting very little rest. Whatever the reason, Grim couldn't get out.

With his wife sharing his bed for the first time in months, the contractor lay as still as possible, trying to remain quiet so his bride could rest. His mind was racing at 100 mph, the words of his ex-CO circulating through his thoughts.

Something had changed in the middle of his dinner with Beckworth, the transition occurring immediately after the security guy had barged in.

Afterwards, the conversation had focused more on West Texas and Bishop than his attempt to free his family.

Grim had no doubt his ex-CO was connected. The scale of the operation surrounding him was evidence of that. The major's role, back in the day, had been as a liaison between the intelligence apparatus of the US government and the military. Beckworth ran with the spooks from the CIA, DEA and other government agencies.

How many of those relationships had the man nurtured? How many did he still retain? Grim knew he would never get any answers to those questions, at least not tonight.

Since the day the rescue mission had been approved by the council, Grim had looked forward to holding his wife and child in his arms. That special moment had been a motivator, making the pain, risk and broken arm all a reasonable price to pay for keeping his loved ones safe.

Now, he dreaded the morning, unsure of what it would

bring for his family and for the people of West Texas.

Beckworth awoke to a loud pounding on the RV's door, the lack of light filtering into his cabin a clear indicator it was early – way too damn early.

"This had better be good," he mumbled, just as the obnoxious rap was repeated.

Throwing on a robe, he had built up a fury by the time he padded to the threshold and flung open the door. "What the hell is…"

He instantly recognized the man standing next to his security chief, despite the overcoat, fedora, and thick glasses. Not too many men embraced the retro-1960s look, especially around Washington. But it wasn't the man's wardrobe that enabled the recall. There was an aura about the visitor - the unforgettable veil of a predator. He had always reminded Beckworth of a shark – a constantly hungry, extremely lethal, and exceedingly crafty shark. The man was a legend in the intelligence community.

Since the beginning of time, there has been a hierarchy within the ranks of those that prey upon others. Engrained as a core aspect of survival, the Velociraptor no doubt recognized the Tyrannosaurus as the superior killing machine, respecting the larger animal's position on the food chain or becoming a meal. Beckworth knew he was staring at a very dangerous animal, a beast that could devour him in the blink of an eye.

"Good morning, Major. I'm sorry to interrupt your beauty rest, but urgent matters of state demand the hour."

The ex-officer was stunned. The appearance of a man on his doorstep he hadn't seen in 15 years caused his mind to experience a rare paralysis. It didn't help that this was a man he truly feared.

"Major?" the voice called, a slight hint of impatience creeping into the interrogatory.

"Sorry… I… the early… come on in Mister… Mister," Beckworth stumbled.

"Mr. White."

"Of course it would be… Mr. White. Please come in."

More like Mr. Great White, he thought.

The man from Washington didn't need to present his credentials. Beckworth understood his authority. After entering the RV, the CIA guru scanned his surroundings and asked, "Are we alone?"

"We are."

"Good. I want you to brief me on everything you know about Bishop. Leave no detail out. I've already verified with your security personnel that he is still here, at this... this facility. Please proceed."

Beckworth had delivered such debriefings a hundred times and knew the drill. He started at the beginning, relaying even the smallest facts.

Mr. White didn't comment, take notes or ask for coffee. He didn't even remove his coat. Taking a seat at the dinette, he sat silently and absorbed all of the major's words.

"And that's all I know," Beckworth finally finished.

"Take a piss, make coffee, fry eggs, or whatever your morning routine is, Major. Just keep it quiet. I need to think."
The man running the Circus was far too pumped to execute any sort of ritual, yet his visitor projected a need to be alone. Beckworth settled on getting dressed, the informality of his bathrobe causing discomfort.

When he returned from the rear bedroom, Mr. White was exactly where the major left him, eyes focused on some point in space and time. Unsure of what to do, the ex-officer sat in a nearby recliner and remained silent.

Mr. White finally came out of his trance, blinking once and then turning toward his host. "I have a very simple, yet delicate task for you. It will only take a few moments of your time, and then I'll be on my way."

Beckworth wasn't thrilled, to say the least. He'd operated at the higher level of intelligence and black ops enough to know that often a "simple, delicate task," was neither. Still, he didn't have much choice. He nodded, signaling his willingness to cooperate.

"I want you to call in this former subordinate of yours... this Grim fellow. Here is what I want you to say..."

Bishop awoke to the strange sounds. The thin metal walls of the camper did little to filter the racket associated with preparing for a new day of business at the Circus. As the early morning wore on, the din continued to grow in volume, pulling the Texan out of his half-awake state, and finally away from the relished softness of the berth's mattress.

He rose to find himself in a unique situation – there was

no place he had to be, no task demanding his attention. It was weird. Back in Alpha with Terri or on the road traveling, he always had a seemingly endless list of jobs that needed to be addressed. Now, while he waited on word from Grim, there was really nothing for him to do, nothing that required his presence. It was like being on vacation.

Deciding to embrace the holiday theme, Bishop savored another hot shower, skipping the shave. He found his clothing close enough to being dry and proceeded to dress.

Bored already, he exited the camper and began wandering around the perimeter of the Circus, taking in the hustle and bustle as the employees prepared for the day.

Breakfast soon became his top priority, and he immediately began a search. Visions of bacon, eggs and perhaps even coffee filled his head. It was not to be. After a careful forage, he had to settle for two slices of thick, bland bread, the doughy white meal salvaged only by the discovery of a vendor selling locally harvested honey.

The natural sweetness greatly enhanced the flavor of the bread. Coffee was the next order of the day.

Evidently, the resources available to the Circus weren't limitless, his favorite morning beverage beyond the reach of the local procurement specialist. He came to this conclusion after asking a man who was clearly a person of authority where he might find a steaming cup of joe.

"I have no idea," the man responded. "If you find any, make sure and let me know."

All was not lost however, as Bishop decided to take the opportunity and kill two birds with one stone. Exiting the secure walls of the Circus, he made for the parking lot without retrieving his weapon. It was only a short walk; the process of rechecking his rifle didn't seem worthy of the effort.

He found the truck exactly where he had left it, the tarp and contents of the cab appearing undisturbed. After quickly rummaging in his pack, he retrieved a small bag of coffee grounds he had brought with him from Texas.

Reentering the facility was a much more streamlined process than his first passage through security, the treatment now as if he were an honored guest. It bothered Bishop just a bit, but he shrugged it off, thinking the guards were becoming familiar with his face.

Entry was also expedited by the relatively low number of visitors milling around the entrance. The only people present were those who were trying to barter goods. Bishop spied several horse-drawn wagons, a few people-powered carts, and several folks just carrying boxes of valuables. He paused for a bit, watching the evaluators circulating among the small crowd, inspecting produce, meat and other assorted trade items.

He made his way back to the camper, heating water on the units of the small electric stove. After finding a cup in the cabinet above the sink, he settled at the small dinette, taking advantage of the great view to do a little people watching. It was relaxing to sit back, enjoy his brew, and observe the various activities occurring outside his window.

He was halfway through his second cup when he noticed one of the security guards escorting Grim through the throng.

"We'll know something soon," he predicted.

Grim entered Beckworth's RV, his nerves on edge. This morning was going to determine if the rest of their odyssey were going to be easy or hard. With his arm still in a sling, he prayed for easy.

"Good morning, Grim," the major greeted. "I have good news for you."

Those words lifted a portion of the heavy burden from the operator's shoulders, allowing his stomach to slow its churning. Not trusting the man seated in front of him one bit, he was wary that the other shoe still hadn't dropped.

"You and your family are free to go. I decided last night that our friendship outweighs any financial consideration on my part. Perhaps I'll ask a favor of you one day."

Grim waited, an uncomfortable pause ensuing, finally bumbling out with, "That's it?"

"Grim, my old friend, why do you have such thoughts? Of course, that's it. No strings attached."

The operator's face broke into a huge smile, relief flooding through his expression. "Thank you, sir. Thank you very much. I owe you one."

Waving off the gushing family man's appreciation, the major waited just a moment before continuing. "Where will you go?"

"Back to West Texas, I suppose."

The ex-intelligence officer played it perfectly, looking over Grim's shoulder, as if to make sure they were still alone, he lowered his voice. "I would reconsider that option, my friend. I have it on pretty good authority that there is some serious trouble headed that direction. Some very serious trouble indeed."

"What do you mean?"

"Just between us, I recently found out that a few of your old comrades are staging for a mission soon. Word is the president has ordered a covert insertion to take over key facilities, and eliminate some of the leadership. I don't know all the details, but I do know enough that I would avoid that area if I were you."

"What? What the hell are you talking about, Major?"

"Two teams passed through here a few days ago. I knew a couple of the senior NCOs from the old days. You know the same people, I'm sure…. teams out of Bragg. They were taking a little R & R before heading west. They drank a little too much, ran off at the mouth."

"What are they doing? Trying to start a war? That's crazy," Grim observed.

"I know, I know," the major played on. "I said the same thing. Their justification made sense though. They believed the people out there wouldn't be so feisty and uncooperative if they didn't have electricity. The other team was charged with removing the head of the area's leadership snake."

Grim turned away from his host, the move initiated to disguise his emotions as well as to give him time to think. It didn't take long for it all to soak in. He spun back around, anger painted all over his face.

Grim took a threatening step toward Beckworth, his fist balled into a tight knot. "Do you know when and where, Major?"

He's taken the bait… hook, line and sinker, the major thought. *Now to land him.*

"Not specifically," he lied. "My read on the conversation was in the next three or four days. There are high-level negotiations scheduled soon. I'd be willing to wager a considerable sum the op will go down before then."

Grim muttered several curses under his breath. Remembering the original purpose of his visit, he bowed slightly and thanked the major, his thoughts occupied with telling Bishop what he'd learned.

Before he could leave, Beckworth stopped him. "You and your family are welcome to stay here and work with me," he started. "I can always use a man with your skills, even with that broken arm. I've received nothing but excellent reports concerning your family's work ethics as well. You should consider it, Grim. West Texas might seem like a nice place to live now, but I have little doubt that is about to change. Do you really want to take your family into a war zone?"

Nodding, Grim uttered a low, "Thank you again, Major. I'll talk it over with my wife."

"Oh, and one more thing I just remembered. I kept hearing those men talk about a place called Chamber's Valley. Given the little things I picked up on, I'm pretty sure that is the jump-off point for the operation. If you and your family do decide to return, I would avoid that area, for what it's worth."

Grim exited the RV in a hurry, the major rising to watch him proceed on a direct line to Bishop's camper. Out of the back room, Mr. White joined Beckworth at the window, tracking the progress of the seed the two men had just planted.

"Satisfactory?" Beckworth inquired, not taking his gaze away from the window.

"Yes. Now let's see if my equations are as balanced as I believe."

Bishop knew something was wrong before Grim threw open the camper's door and stormed inside. He could tell by his friend's gait as he approached.

"You're not going to believe what Beckworth just told me," Grim opened. "He overhead some conversation about a pending operation against the Alliance."

"What? What are you talking about?" Bishop asked, almost spilling his coffee as he rose.

Grim repeated what he had heard just a few minutes ago, placing special emphasis on that statement about "Cutting off the head of the snake."

"Terri," Bishop stated, the word dripping with concern.

"Do you know where someplace called Chamber's Valley is?"

Bishop had to think for a minute, trying to recall the place. "Yes, yes I do. It's north of Fort Davidson as I remember. There used to be a rock climbing school that gave lessons up that way. I visited it once. I always wanted to attend, but never found the time."

"That's going to be their jump-off point, or so the major claims."

Bishop considered the information for a bit, drawing a mental map of the area. "Makes sense," he finally announced. "Secluded area, strategically located between Alpha and the electric control station at Fort Stockdale."

Bishop began pacing, his mind reeling with the news. A strike, such as the one being described, would make sense. Without electrical power and a few key personalities, the Alliance would crumble in short order.

He had to fight down the anger and injustice that insisted on invading his thoughts. He needed a cool head – needed to ignore the fact that Terri was one of those who would be a target.

Grim wasn't so logical. "You know they'll go after your wife. Probably her, Diana and Nick at minimum. I hate to say it, but I would if I were them."

It didn't take long for Bishop to reach a conclusion. "We've got to get back and warn them. I've got to get back and protect Terri."

The Texan began hustling about the camper, gathering his belongings. When he noticed Grim wasn't doing the same, he looked up and prodded, "We've got to hurry. Every minute counts."

Grim reached out and clutched Bishop's shoulder with his one good arm. "We would just slow you down. Maggie and Jana aren't good travelers, and I can't leave them again. Besides, with this one bum arm, I'm not going to be much help."

The concept of traveling back alone stopped Bishop cold. Trying to reason it all out, he asked, "But what will you guys do? Your house burned to the ground."

"Beckworth offered me a job here. Said the wife and kid can keep working as well. We'll figure out a way to go west after everything settles down. You go on. You've got that pass, and there's enough gas and food left in the truck for one guy to make it easy. Drive straight through, and you might get there in time."

Bishop nodded, accepting his partner's logic. "I understand. I mean, after all, you're talking to a guy who wishes he hadn't left his wife and child in the first place. If someone else had come along, Deke might not be dead, and you might still have both wings."

Grim looked Bishop in the eye, his expression sincere. "No one could have done better, dude. No one. When Deke called you an operator on his death bed, I had to agree. Sometimes we don't like to admit a guy to the club who hasn't made the sacrifice, but you've earned it. Now go and fight for what you people have built back there... go and protect that good woman who tolerates your sorry ass."

Twenty minutes later, after retrieving his checked weapon and giving the truck a good once-over, Bishop was speeding through the Tennessee countryside.

213

Concealed nearby, Beckworth and Mr. White watched the Texan race out of the parking lot. Feeling good about his successful role, Beckworth let his curiosity get the best him, venturing a question that he normally wouldn't have dared. "What is that man going to find waiting for him in Chamber's Valley?"

If death had a look, Mr. White mimicked it perfectly. The target of his gaze actually took a step backwards, so hostile was the experience. "Do you really want me to answer that, Major? Do you really want to be on the short list of those who know?"

"Sorry... I shouldn't have..."

Mr. White stepped close to the ex-officer, poking the frightened man in the chest. "Forget everything that happened here today, Major. Erase it from your mind, and seal your lips for eternity. If you don't, I, or one of my kind will come. We will come in the middle of the night, and you will die badly. We will extract revenge for your indiscretion using methods you can't even fathom. Your heart will explode from the pain during the final seizures of your brain."

And then Mr. White was gone, driving out of the parking lot at a rapid pace, on his way back to the Memphis International Airport and the waiting Air Force shuttle.

Bishop felt exposed driving in daylight. Were it not for the urgency associated with a threat against his wife, he would never use such a tactic, especially when traveling alone.

Memphis looked worse by day, the details of decay more visible than when they had passed through in the darkness. Little things drew the Texan's eye, like the abundance of graffiti painted on every overpass, abutment and countless relic cars. Evidently, spray paint hadn't been in short supply after the collapse.

He supposed the liberal use of color was logical. After all, you couldn't eat it. As he drove closer to downtown, the effect grew more intense. He wondered what physiological motive had inspired the artists. Was it a need to mark territory? Warnings? Directions for lost loved ones? There was no way to tell – maybe all of the above.

He reached the bridge spanning the Mississippi without incident, finding himself the only person waiting to cross at the army checkpoint. Evidently the other side wasn't a popular vacation destination. *And who wouldn't want to visit the*

214

badlands, he thought.

Surprised to have a customer, the MP who strolled to the truck was actually talkative and friendly. Bishop handed the man his pass.

"What's your destination?" the specialist asked, more from curiosity than any official need to know.

"Little Rock," Bishop lied.

"Really? I hear some really bad things about that city. It is strictly off limits to any military personnel, not that anyone ever crosses the river these days."

"You know how scuttlebutt gets all blown out of proportion," Bishop chatted. "Next thing you know someone will spread a rumor that there are cannibals over that way."

The kid's face got all serious, "Actually, sir, that's exactly the reason why I heard it was a no-go... cannibalism."

"No shit?"

"No, sir. Best of luck to ya."

And with that well wish, Bishop was waved through.

From the peak of the bridge's rise above the mighty river, Bishop thought the world looked the same as always, at least at a distance. Were it not for the burgeoning lanes of rusting cars blocking most of the crossing, he wouldn't have suspected anything was wrong on the other side.

Like much of Memphis, the Arkansas side of the river was clogged with remnants of what must have been a massive bug-out. Technically, the small community bordering the west side of the waterway was named West Memphis, but the town was a mere fraction of its namesake's size.

After dodging wrecks and the burned out skeletons of what were once family sedans and minivans, Bishop found himself on open road, increasing his speed to over 70 mph.

Knowing he'd have to cut off of the interstate before reaching Little Rock, the Texan decided his situation resembled that of a fighter pilot – speed was life.

On their trip east, he'd been overly cautious, fearing bushwhackers, local warlords and humanity in general. Now heading west, he went to the opposite end of the paranoid spectrum – blasting down the road with apparent abandon.

It wasn't just the urgency of getting home. Driving by himself made it very difficult to fight. Even the simple act of exiting the truck with his rifle was slow, the carbine bound and determined to become entangled with the steering wheel, bang into the doorframe or poke him in the crotch. For this reason, the weapon was unslung and beside him on the seat. The same was true of his sidearm.

Not that shooting and driving at the same time was

affective. Other than suppression, keeping someone's head down, it was rare such a tactic accomplished little more than to waste ammunition.

So Bishop determined speed was the best strategy, keeping his foot on the accelerator and his eyes scanning ahead for potential trouble. The miles flew by.

A sign, now partially covered by a honeysuckle vine that had climbed up the supports, indicated Little Rock was 71 miles ahead. Not that the distance marker was really necessary. For the past several minutes, the number of relics in the outbound lane had been steadily increasing – a sure sign of civilization ahead. By the time this was confirmed by the green sign, the grass median was beginning to fill with its share of discarded cars and trucks. "Time to get off this road," he said, just to hear a voice.

There were only a few cars at the exit, once operated by polite drivers as they lined up along the shoulder of the off-ramp. The parade of vehicles ran along the edge of the two-lane highway, the bumper-to-bumper queue stretching a quarter of a mile to the single gas station located there.

Bishop couldn't help but slow his pace, gawking at the scene as he drove closer. Reliving that horrific day sent shivers down his spine – like touring a historic battlefield where so many men had lost their lives. He didn't need a tour guide or literature to show him what had happened - the forensics weren't difficult to analyze. He could almost feel the ghosts, restless spirits still waiting for fuel that would never arrive.

As the service station grew closer, the polite line of cars widened and became erratic. *Panicked drivers*, thought Bishop. *They didn't want anyone cutting in line*. The two islands containing pumps were completely blocked by empty, lifeless metal, the parking lot filled to capacity with sedans, luxury cars and pickup trucks. The car at the forward-most aisle had actually been rammed by the driver behind, evidently taking too long or pumping too much gas.

The chrome bumpers were still interlocked, the impact disabling both cars. A black tail hung from the gas door of the first vehicle, the pump's hose having been torn away as the car was pushed from behind. Words like desperation, riot and anarchy filled Bishop's mind. He was glad he wasn't there that fateful day, thankful not to carry the memories.

Bishop stopped, right in the middle of the road – unconcerned about oncoming traffic. He needed to refuel himself, and this was as good a place as any. Despite his eerie feeling about the location, the truck wouldn't stand out as much here among the sea of steel and glass.

As he began working the barrel's hand pump, he studied the scene in more detail.

The windows of the convenience store were mostly shattered, birds nesting in the sign above the door. He could see barren shelves inside, many toppled over – one large display partially lying halfway out the door as if someone was going to drag it home... or maybe use it as a barricade, Bishop decided. Perhaps the owner was trying to keep people out of his store.

Through the windows he could see one bank of freezers lining the back wall. Once filled with every conceivable flavor, type and size of beer, soda pop and juice, their racks were empty as well, one door completely ripped off its hinges.

There was a sign, hand-lettered and still visible behind a small section of window glass that remained. In bold, black print it read, "Cash Only – No Credit Cards." Bishop wondered if that display had been prompted by the power failing and bringing down the credit card machine with it, or if the owner knew it was the end and was trying to gather all the cash he could. Probably the later, Bishop thought. They couldn't pump gas without electricity.

Pivoting his head, he scanned the pumps, looking for what the price of gasoline had been that final day. They were newer, digital models, so there was no way to tell.

The lot's surface, what little was visible between the rows of packed cars, still held evidence of the violence that occurred here. The cash register, drawer open and lying face down, rested under the bumper of a minivan. A few feet away was the remains of a coffee machine, dented and banged like someone had been using it as a shield.

Trash had piled up in a corner nook of the building, faded wrappers of candy bars and bags of snacks entangled with leaves and twigs, gathered there by the wind. There were bullet holes in the building's exterior, just above the garbage heap.

As Bishop finished his fill-up, he noticed three different cars with similar bullet wounds. Someone had started shooting, either trying to maintain control, protect himself, or perhaps even going insane under the stress of it all. The story would never be told.

Bishop emptied the remaining gasoline and then rolled the empty drum out of the truck's bed, the clanging impact causing him to cringe at the noise volume. Removing the now-useless container decreased the size of his supply cache should anyone notice the load in the truck bed, making travel among locals less risky.

Before entering the cab, he glanced around one last time, his mind pondering a new mystery. Where had the people gone?

He mentally inventoried the number of cars, averaging out two people per unit. He tried to visualize almost 300 people milling about, waiting on electricity and gasoline that would never arrive. There wasn't any nearby town… no water, food or law enforcement. Just an isolated gas station on a seldom-traveled rural highway.

Bishop imagined the debates. A husband and wife, growing frustrated and paranoid as they slept the first night in their car. Hunger aside, thirst had probably been the most nagging issue. They had witnessed violence at some point… gunfire erupting up ahead. Screams, shots, yelling… confusion. Had the wife said, "We have to get out of here," first, or was it her spouse?

Had the husband convinced his mate that it was time to start walking? Had they waited until they were too weak to travel far? How embarrassed had the woman been when she had to walk to the weeds to use the bathroom?

A nearby minivan was equipped with two car seats, their size indicating small children. The sight made him think of Hunter and Terri, forced him to the realization that children would have compounded the parents' stress a dozen fold. He could almost hear the debate of who got the final sip from the diaper bag's juice box. Was the last handful of animal crackers rationed out?

He found himself experiencing a morbid curiosity. Needing to stretch his legs, he pulled the rifle and keys out of the cab and went exploring.

The bones weren't obvious, the hollow, dark eyes of a human skull being the first to draw his attention. Buzzards, animals and bacteria had picked it clean, the off-white remains looking more like a teaching tool for a college anatomy class than a victim of violence.

He strolled to the front of the station, looking inside through the glassless window. *Which had been looted first*, he wondered. *The cigarettes or the beer? Those with addictive habits would feel the pinch before anyone else*, he supposed.

As he stepped over a pile of rubbish, his boot caught on something heavy. Looking down, he saw a cloth money bag that was commonly used to deposit store receipts at the bank. He bent and picked it up, surprised at the weight. A faded label on the outside matched the sign on the building.

Expecting to find quarters, dimes and other coins inside, Bishop hefted the bag in his hand, but didn't hear the expected jingle of loose change. His knife made quick work of the rotting cloth. Inside was a significant collection of watches, rings, bracelets and other jewelry.

That makes sense, he thought, reliving those fateful days. People would have grown so desperate, many not having enough cash for water or beef jerky. They would have started offering anything of value to the station's clerk.

"I'll trade you my 18-karat Rolex for that last box of crackers," Bishop said to the empty lot, imagining a desperate father. "Please, sir, my kid won't stop crying."

Once the clerk had accepted the trade, word would have spread throughout the community of stranded motorists. "Hey, take my wife's wedding ring. It has a big diamond – it's worth more than that watch!" someone else had probably countered.

Bishop didn't begrudge anyone nice things. Jealousy wasn't part of his nature. Still, he had to wonder about the utility of some folks' discretionary income prior to the fall of society. The watch he held in his hand would have purchased several years' supply of shelf stable food, perhaps more. The huge diamond ring would have easily paid for three or four good rifles and a thousand rounds of ammo. *They never thought it could happen*, he decided.

He shook it off, realizing he was working his mind into a funk over misery and problems that had happened over a year ago. There was nothing he could do to help those that were here, suffering badly on a lonely road with few options.

He returned the bag to its original spot, having no interest or need for the memories it contained. It belonged here, a memorial of sorts for the people who had lost their lives at this place.

Bishop returned to the cab and started driving.

After leaving the interstate, his progress slowed. Despite following the same route they had traveled east, it was impossible to maintain the same speed.

Tree limbs had fallen here and there, probably the victims of thunderstorms or high winds. Without county clean-up crews, the debris remained exactly where it had landed, natural impediments to Bishop's urgency.

He didn't stop at the bridges anymore, settling on the opposite tactic and pushing down on the gas pedal where the roadway allowed.

There were other speed-robbing distractions as well. Scanning for smoke was a constant requirement. Campfires, wood-burning stoves and outdoor ovens all meant one thing – people. Alone and in a strange world, Bishop wanted nothing more than to avoid humankind.

Just like the trip east, returning home didn't produce much of a cultural exchange with the residents of the Razorback State. Eating up the miles on secondary roads, bypassing towns depicted on the map and keeping up as much speed as possible, Bishop managed to avoid trouble and make excellent time.

The light was fading when the map indicated he was approaching the Arkansas River, the incident at Toad Suck Dam still fresh in his mind.

He decided to use a regular bridge, the decision bolstered by the fact that there just weren't that many folks around. Darkness would thin their ranks even more.

He pulled over two miles short of the big river, stretching his legs and nibbling at a light meal. Indecision over abandoning the truck and scouting the chokepoint nagged at Bishop while he chewed. If someone found his supplies in the unguarded truck while he was checking out the bridge, he was screwed. If he bumbled into a bad situation while crossing, he was screwed.

He concluded Toad Suck had been the exception, not the rule, and settled on driving directly to the crossing with his fingers crossed. It ended up being the right decision as he managed the span right before total darkness fell, not a soul in sight.

Using the night vision while driving was becoming second nature. His route was gradually increasing in elevation as he climbed through the foothills that would eventually become small mountains. Petit Jean was the destination.

He hoped Frank had been a man of his word. Hugh's final shuttle flight had delivered two last 50-gallon drums of fuel, the plan calling for the rescuers to drive back into Texas with Grim's family along for the ride. That trip across the Lone Star State would take 100 gallons of fuel, so the stash had been hidden inside the airport's sole structure.

Bishop recalled his conversation with the head ranger before they had departed. "If we're not back in four weeks, you should go forage around in the airstrip's building. You'll find a little treasure trove of goodies there. It would be a sin for them to go to waste."

He was counting on Frank, and everyone else, to have left that cache of fuel alone. If it wasn't there, again, he was screwed. It would take months to walk the 1000 miles to home – if he survived the journey.

Bishop's anxiety built when he saw the first sign indicating the park's distance was 31 miles ahead. He was fidgeting when another pointed to a Petit Jean with an arrow. His nerves were raw as a third informed him he had officially entered the facility.

It was after 2 a.m. when the green and black outline of the airstrip's building came into view through his monocle. He switched to Deke's thermal, scanning the surrounding forest and finding nothing suspicious.

With great trepidation, he entered the building. There in the corner, right where he'd left it just a few days before, was the stash of fuel and food. Undisturbed.

Bishop sighed audibility with relief. Sleep became the next priority.

Hunter's cranky cry rousted Terri from her slumber, the new mother slow to respond due to a dream that left her believing she was already feeding the lad.

"How can he be fussing and nursing at the same time," she asked herself in a state of half-sleep, quickly realizing she hadn't moved from her bed.

The vision of his primary provider appearing over the crib's rail settled the infant down. His rapidly developing mind happily recognized the routine and sensed food was soon to follow.

As she nursed, Terri gently rocked in a corner chair, humming a soothing melody to the child. She had no idea where the song came from or what it was called. For a brief moment, she longed to ask her mother if it were a family tradition.

While swaying back and forth, Terri couldn't help but consider the new day's calendar. The highest priority was a meeting with the council, an important discussion covering the negotiations with Washington. The tone of the meetings had changed significantly during the last session, and it was troubling.

Until yesterday, things had been progressing at an incredibly slow pace, the team from the nation's capital hammering on every little detail. Diana had commented that she felt like they were haggling over a nuclear arms treaty, not a trade deal. Every little detail had to be argued, pinched, poked and mutilated before agreement could be reached. It was maddening, time consuming, and she had to admit, necessary.

Then yesterday, something changed. The delegation representing the feds began acting as though they had been instructed to accelerate the process. Terri didn't know what was motivating that tactic, but the change was so abrupt, it made her suspicious. At one point, the men across the table had even approved one clause without reading it. That made her feel like they weren't taking the agreement seriously, like they didn't care.

Terri shook her head, the act causing Hunter to pull off her breast, thinking she wanted to play. It took her a bit to convince him otherwise, and soon he returned to filling his belly.

Like a dozen times before, Terri inventoried the events leading up to the drastic change by the other side. She couldn't think of anything that had been said or done to justify their newfound enthusiasm. *It must be something internal*, she concluded. *We've been consistent.*

Hunter finished topping off his tank, his eyes so droopy she hesitated to disturb him with a burp. As she adjusted to return her son to the crib, a robust belch escaped the lad's tiny mouth and eliminated any parental concerns over gas pains later in the night.

She kissed his forehead and inhaled, enjoying the aroma that was unique to newborns. Hunter was breathing rhythmically as she laid him down and pulled the tiny blanket over his chest.

Terri returned to her bed, hoping to catch another two hours of sleep before addressing the new morning. She tried to figure out what possible event could have changed in Washington, quickly realizing it was a question without an answer.

Maybe we should just take the money and run, she thought as sleep tugged at her mind. *Maybe they have finally realized we don't need them, they need us.*

Chapter 15

Alexandria, Virginia
July 13, 2016

Most Americans were aware of the Special Forces serving as members of the US military. Countless movies, books, and songs had depicted the ultra-skilled, elite warriors in numerous roles. Green Berets, Navy Seals, Marine Recon and other selective units were commonly known military components representing the best fighting men in the world.

But there existed another tier in the hierarchy of lethality, only known to only a select few individuals and rarely addressed in film or word.

In reality, they didn't have a name or unit designation. This was by design. Many weren't even assigned to a specific government organization or agency. Those that did know of their existence commonly used phrases like Intelligence Field Operators, or Clandestine Assets.

Possessing skills of part warrior, part spy, these field operators didn't master firearms to the level of a Delta Force commando, and wouldn't survive as long in the field as a Green Beret. They had no hope of matching the stamina of a Navy Seal.

But in some situations, they were just as deadly to the enemies of the United States – often doing more damage with a camera or small amount of explosives than an entire division of armor. They represented a select tool of violence – a scalpel of mayhem and disarray.

They didn't practice the espionage tradecraft so often credited to CIA spooks, but they often infiltrated hostile territory and delivered devastating results. Spies preferred to remain anonymous and gather intelligence, rarely resorting to overt violence or direct force.

The Clandestine Assets had no problem with confrontation. These operatives were trained in explosives and booby traps, often applying their expertise in creative fashion. Bishop had heard how a rogue country's nuclear scientist was killed by a small, sticky-bomb placed against his car window by a passing motorcyclist. In another case, a cartel leader was engulfed in flames after his, and only his cell phone came within range of a detonator.

While physical stamina and mental discipline were the hallmarks of military operators, intellect and creativity separated these men from the masses. They didn't seek military schools or formal training – they studied, visited labs and designed their own devices. The spent as much time learning a language as practicing with a firearm, could be found reading a book as often as running an obstacle course.

It was two of these men that Mr. White approached. A package containing their instructions, required authorizations for travel, and other important items was tucked under his arm. One of the men he knew only as Alastair, the other as Eris.

There were no greetings or introductions, no secret code exchanged. It was pure business for everyone involved.

"Use the normal procedure to contact me, if necessary," Mr. White instructed as he handed over the two envelopes. "Otherwise, I hope not to see you again."

And that was that. Mr. White continued on his way, brushing by the two operatives without another word.

No offense was taken by Mr. White's seemingly rude behavior. In fact, both men would have considered anything else as inappropriate.

Eris watched Mr. White for a few moments and then turned to his companion who was already opening his package. "Where to this time?"

After scanning the documents, Alastair looked up with a grin. "West Texas. Do you like rock climbing?"

Petit Jean State Park, Arkansas
July 14, 2016

Bishop grunted, inhaled sharply, and then kicked the barrel, a gong-like reverberation spreading across the airfield. He'd been rolling the 350-pound drum of fuel to the back of the truck by himself, and managed to run over his own toe after slipping in the gravel.

The kick, born of frustration, now left him with two hurting feet. *It's going to be one of those days*, he decided.

The now-throbbing foot elicited a string of inventive cursing, most of the foul dialect directed at his own clumsiness. The barrel, however, received part of the blame.

Taking a seat on the offending drum, he removed his boot and checked for broken bones. The diagnosis was uncertain, but he knew it hurt like hell.

"You all right?" Frank's voice sounded from the woods as the ranger appeared at the edge of the growth. "That looked like a painful experience."

"That's no shit. I don't think it's broken though."

Frank looked around, "Where are your helpers?"

224

"Grim stayed in Memphis with his family," Bishop began, and then let his eyes fall to the ground. "Deke didn't make it."

"Oh, no. I'm sorry to hear that. He seemed like such a competent man."

The Texan shrugged, "It was a risky deal from the get-go. We all knew that. Now I'm trying to get home as fast as possible. While we were out there, word came that the US Army is sending someone to try and kill my wife."

"What! That's crazy. Why would someone want to kill your spouse?"

"She's kind of the leader of our little alliance of towns. I guess they think removing her would cause our union to crack and allow the government to come in and take everything we've built up. I know it's not that simple, but in a nutshell, that sums it up."

"So you're trying to get back to Texas and warn her? Stop the assassins?"

"Yes, sir. I sure am."

Frank thought it over for a moment. "Let me go get some clothes and my rifle. I'll go with you. I'm not as good in a fight as your friends, but I can shoot."

Bishop was stunned by the man's offer. "No, sir. I can't let you do that. While I appreciate the willingness to go, and respect the guts it took to make the offer, you can't leave the people back at the lodge. They need you, Frank. You've got a wife and extended family here. Thanks, but no thanks."

The ranger scuffed some soil with his boot, finally looking up and responding, "Okay, I won't argue. But if you change your mind, I'm willing. At least let me help you get the truck loaded."

"Now that's an offer I can't refuse," Bishop answered, pulling his boot back on and tightening the laces.

The two men worked for 30 minutes lifting and arranging the contents. After finishing, Bishop wiped his brow and retrieved a map from one of the boxes.

He spread the gas station fold-out map, flattening the creases on the tailgate. "Now the real challenge begins," he commented.

"What's that?"

"Texas... more specifically getting to West Texas. I can't chance the urban areas like Dallas or Houston. Even the smaller cities might spell trouble... Texarkana... Nacogdoches ... they're all a no-go. I've got to plot a route that will bypass any town big enough to be listed on the map."

Frank glanced over Bishop's shoulder, studying the chart. After a bit, he whistled, indicating he understood the

225

problem.

Pulling a marker from his load vest, Bishop began tracing a route, occasionally writing alternatives in a small notebook.

"Do you have to take back roads the entire way?"

"No... at least I hope not. Once I'm past the Hill Country... Austin... I think I-10 will be okay. Where I'm headed isn't far off the big interstate."

"When is the attack supposed to take place?"

"I'm not sure about that. I was told two or three days, but I don't know when the clock started ticking. It seems our trusted federal officials are going to sneak in some teams and hit several different targets at once. I heard where their jump off point is supposed to be located, and I'm going to try like hell to disrupt there little foray."

"Alone?"

Bishop looked up from the map, staring into the distance for a moment. When he turned to face the ranger, Frank inhaled sharply.

It was if a mask had been pulled from Bishop's face, revealing a fierce, beast-like predator beneath. Bishop's pupils were dilated - dark pools, void of humanity or mercy, exposing an interior of ice. The operator's voice matched his expression – a robotic response from a killing machine that neither boasted nor experienced fear. "I can be very disruptive."

Frank didn't know what to say... how to respond. He watched carefully as Bishop seemed to relax and then turn his attention back to the map. When the Texan looked up again, it was the same man who he'd first encountered a few days ago.

"Frank, I left a few boxes of supplies inside. I'm sorry, but I need all the fuel. There's some food and ammo in there... not much... but some."

"Thank you. Every little bit helps."

"I'm going to be heading out of here in a bit," Bishop said, extending his hand to the ranger. "Our paths probably won't cross again. I wish you the best of luck."

There was just a hint of hesitation before Frank accepted the handshake.

The ranger watched Bishop climb behind the wheel, remaining in his spot until the truck had faded from sight. "I actually think he'll pull it off," he whispered.

Texas was going to require a lot of zigzagging, back tracking, and rechecking of the map. Three hours after leaving the park, Bishop crossed into the Lone Star State, experiencing a small sense of relief over entering his home turf.

Reality soon set in however, the comprehension occurring during one of his many roadside references to the chart. Since leaving Memphis, he was less than halfway home. It was frustrating.

His anxiety was further bolstered by the fact that he was driving through territory he'd never traveled. He'd already driven most of the route from Memphis to the park and felt reasonably secure that the path was unoccupied.

Now he was traveling virgin territory, and it wore on his nerves.

Bishop was somewhere west of I-45, having dipped below Dallas but staying well north of Houston. He was angling back to the northwest in order to avoid Austin and the cluster of villages, bergs and almost-cities that surrounded the state capital.

He found a lane, a thin line of trees offering some protection from prying eyes. Bishop needed the stop, partly because his vision was blurring, partly because he was getting stupid and impatient. His bladder's unrelenting protest was the clincher.

After poking around a little, he stretched and relieved himself. The thought of sleeping in the driver's seat was unpalatable, so he climbed into the bed and rearranged the tarp and boxes of supplies so he could get reasonably comfortable.

Setting his watch alarm was next, hoping an hour of rest would improve his judgment. With his hand resting on his rifle, Bishop was out before the truck's exhaust cooled enough to stop its gentle pinging and popping.

Terri and Hunter met him there, a red and white tablecloth spread across the greenest grass imaginable. There were ham and cheese sandwiches on paper plates, each accompanied by a towering stack of potato chips. Large Styrofoam cups were brimming with ice tea, the air full of happy laughter.

Terri was holding Hunter by the armpits, supporting the infant as he pumped chubby legs trying to walk across the cloth. The expression on the cherubic face said, "Look at me, dad! See how amazing I am?"

Dad had to agree, his cheeks hurting from the girth of his smile.

Over Terri's shoulder, something glinted in the sunlight – a flash of brightness that Bishop had seen before. Someone was up there on the hill... someone with glass... a rifle scope. He knew exactly what it was, but his throat wouldn't form a warning, his body wouldn't answer the desperate commands being screamed by his brain.

A small puff of gray smoke replaced the reflection on the hill. Bishop knew what it was, a sniper's gunshot, but he couldn't move. Everything was so slow, a horror movie watched frame by single, painful frame.

Terri's sternum exploded, a shower of gristle, tissue and bone erupting in a fountain of gore that suspended in mid-air. An identical wound appeared on Hunter's tiny body, the bullet passing straight through both of his loved ones. Both his wife and child showed bewilderment, unsure of what had just happened, unclear of the source of their pain.

Their eyes clouded dark as Terri fell over, pulling Hunter's lifeless body down with her.

The dream-chains released Bishop, allowing him to finally move while time accelerated to its normal pace. He crawled to his wife's side but knew it was too late. Hunter fared no better.

He looked to the sky as if to ask his Maker why, but only a prolonged cry of agony escaped his throat. "Nooooooo!"

The Texan bolted upright in the bed of the truck, fury and rage painted on his face, the scream stuck in his mouth. It took a few moments to realize he'd been dreaming. He was soaking wet, heart pounding in his ears. The images of the nightmare proved stubborn - difficult to shake.

He was just reaching to climb out of the bed when two gunshots rolled across the open field. Pausing for a moment, he decided they weren't a concern. The reports were very far off, so distant he wasn't sure of the direction.

"Probably somebody out hunting for a Sunday meal," he said to the truck, his voice croaking and hoarse. There just wasn't enough volume of gunfire for it to be anything else. Then it occurred to him that his dream might have been feeding off of previous shots. His level of anxiety increased.

Without giving himself much time to clear the fog of sleep, Bishop climbed back in the cab, urgency fueled by frustration dominating his mood. He ramrodded the stolen vehicle out of the lane, screeching to a halt and then jamming the shifter into a forward gear. The rate of gasoline consumption was the last thing on his mind as he jammed the accelerator to the floor.

He couldn't remember the town's name and actually didn't care. It was just another detour in what had become a journey filled with such bypasses.

The town's label was something like Birch... or Birchwood... or Birchville. He couldn't remember and didn't want to bother checking the map again, already frustrated with the number of references to the paper chart required by this trip. He was sure the ink coloring would be worn white before he could get home.

The two-lane highway he'd been traversing ran right into the middle of Birch-whatever, and he didn't want to do that. With the nightmare and gunshots still occupying his mind, he cut south, down a gravel surfaced, narrow country road, hoping to avoid the fine citizens of... of Son of a Birch.

"I'll have to remember that one," he joked with the truck. "Terri will love it."

Had Terri been along, she would have known Bishop's apparent jovial mood was anything but. He always dealt with stress by using cornball humor as a safety valve. The driver's primary frustration was due to many sources. Watching the time pass by without gaining much distance was one agitation, constantly fretting over the ever-declining supply of gas, another. The icing on Bishop's pissy-cake was the constant, ever building worry about his wife and son. The nightmare had provided the lettering on the icing, in black, bold letters – *Get the fuck home and save your family*.

His physical condition wasn't much better. The blow he'd taken to the arm still sent searing bolts of pain up and down the limb. He hadn't managed much sleep in two days. After that last dream, he wasn't sure he ever wanted to sleep again.

So it was an exhausted, short-tempered man who crested the small rise in central Texas, instantly tapping the brakes when he realized something was blocking the road ahead.

Creeping forward, his head was on a swivel - sweeping for any sign of an ambush, almost hoping someone would try. The fields bordering the road were empty. As Bishop approached closer to the obstruction, he thought his tired eyes were seeing things. It looked like someone had built a small house right in the middle of the road.

Normally, caution would demand stopping a considerable distance away, followed by scouting the activity ahead in detail. Not today, not in his frame of mind.

He drove right up, seemingly unconcerned, almost daring anyone to fuck with him.

The house blocking the road was actually an overturned wagon, complete with harnessed team and passengers standing around gawking at the wreck. The chaotic scene was further complicated by two other horse-drawn buggies and their occupants. One had run into a ditch, the other's animal lying on its side in the road.

Bishop was mumbling, "What now, an Amish accident? A Mennonite mangle?" as he exited the cab, pulling his rifle sling over his neck. An older man was standing nearby, watching as several other people milled about, pointing while exchanging hushed conversations. A few of the interactions weren't so soft, one sounding downright heated.

"What happened?" Bishop asked as he approached the gent.

"Those hoodlums took over the VFW and started shooting. We all were trying to get out of there in a panic, and these three buggies got tangled up," he replied, pointing toward a distant building. The single-story structure looked like a ranch style home, only the flagpole and two Korean War artillery pieces sitting out front indicating it wasn't the normal homestead.

"We've been having a sort of food bank once a week," the old timer continued. "Everything was going just fine until that bunch of assholes showed up. They shot the place up, took Marty's daughter hostage and chased us off."

Marty, as indicated by the witnesses' nodding heads, was the source of the angered voice, two men apparently restraining the distraught man from returning to the VFW.

Bishop shook his head, not believing his bad luck. He moved to examine the traffic jam, then over to look at the injured draft horse.

One of the wagons had evidently run over two of the animal's legs, both fractures compound and grisly. The injured mare's eyes were rolling in the back of her head, spasms of pain racking her body. Bishop knew the animal was finished, a boyhood spent on a working ranch leaving no doubt.

"Someone put this animal out of its misery," he instructed, scanning the onlookers.

A nearby mother, holding a scared, teenage girl was the only person who answered. "How? No one here has any bullets."

"Fuck," mumbled Bishop, pulling his pistol from the holster.

"Noooo!" screamed the girl, realizing Bishop's intent.

After he verified the mother was still in control of her child, Bishop knelt beside the suffering beast and covered its eye with his hand. He put the barrel an inch from its head and pulled the trigger.

The horse jerked once, twice, and then its pain was over.

The shot drew everyone's attention, and Bishop took advantage of it. "You men over there, come get that wagon out of the ditch so we can push this one upright. I'll help."

Again, the old timer approached. "That's Marty's wagon, and his mule won't move for anyone else. He refuses to do anything until those thugs set his daughter free... not that there's going to be much left of her after they're done."

Bishop glanced at the distraught father, two large fellows holding him back. "Marty! Marty! You can't go up there," one of the burly men said. "They'll kill you on sight."

Bishop's patience, already stretched taunt, snapped. Glancing between the VFW and the restrained father, logic was overwhelmed by rage. Turning to the old man, he mumbled, "I'll fix that," and then he stormed off, making a beeline toward what his brain registered as the source of his latest obstacle.

The VFW was only one quarter of a mile down the road. Like so many small towns across the country, the small building had been constructed on the outskirts of the community it served. This was due in part to availability of cheaper land, coupled with the fact that Saturday evening dances could go late into the night without disturbing the neighbors. There might have been a hint of some customers enjoying the occasional libation without prying eyes knowing their business.

None of this mattered to Bishop at the moment, his course unwavering, his stride evidence of grim intent.

"Check this asshole out," commented one of the invaders, standing on the front stoop of the VFW and chewing a mouthful of pillaged food. "What the hell does he think he's gonna do?"

"I got this one," his partner responded after swallowing. He reached for the pistol tucked in the small of his back.

Bishop kept coming, his steps almost robotic – pneumatic pistons closing the distance.

With his pistol still pointed down, the brave fellow stepped forward, holding up his empty hand, signaling for Bishop to stop. "Just what do you think you're doing ... "

He never finished the statement. Without saying a word or breaking stride, the ACR appeared from behind Bishop's back, the motion smooth... and very fast. He didn't even bother shouldering the weapon, firing four shots so quickly they were difficult to count. Each target took two in the torso, staggering backwards in shock, surprised looks of pain and torment on their faces.

Bishop charged. He covered the remaining 20 yards in five steps, his boot splintering the front door at the same moment as the first two men hit the ground.

There were four of them in there, surrounding a corner pool table with a struggling girl held down on the green felt surface. All of the men looked up in surprise, the violence of Bishop's entry causing their mouths to open in protest.

The first two fell instantly, grasping their chests where Bishop's rounds tore flesh and crushed bone. The third man managed to reach for a revolver lying on a nearby table, but his grip never closed. The 68 grain hollow-point, flying at 2900 feet per second, struck the man's temple. The bullet expanded to twice its original diameter before exiting the skull in a fountain of crimson and white. The results were immediate.

Number four managed to dive behind the bar, but it didn't do him any good. Bishop began firing into the wooden structure, spacing shot after shot only six inches above the floor, walking the rounds up and down the length.

Shards of splintered timber filled the air, mixing with dust from the pulverized concrete floor and the boiling cordite exhaust from the ACR's barrel. The empty cartridges, bouncing across the floor with a musical jingle, contrasted the stream of relentless thunder produced by the weapon, an unyielding hammer driving high velocity lead nails.

While his bullets tore through the thin wooden veneer, Bishop was sidestepping to the opposite end of the long structure. The cadence of his trigger finger never stopped until he rounded the corner. He found the target lying face down, unmoving with an expanding pool of red beneath. Bishop kept his rifle trained on the man, walking forward, wary the guy might be playing possum. After a couple of steps, he reconsidered, firing two more rounds from where he stood – just to be sure.

He then moved to the pool table, each body on the floor receiving an extra bullet or two as he passed. Without uttering a word, he scooped up the terrified, shivering girl, throwing her roughly over his shoulder.

Turning back to walk outside, Bishop stepped carefully through the gore between him and the exit, the floor already slick with the blood, urine and gristle of the dead.

The rescuer and rescued appeared in the sunlight, Bishop's stride identical to his approach as he crossed the lawn and made for the intersection.

He carried the young woman directly to her father, lifting her effortlessly from his shoulder and depositing her on the ground.

"Now move your wagon... before I move it for you."

The man's eyes darted between Bishop and the returned child at his feet. Ignoring the seemingly harsh request, he bent to check on his child, "Baby... baby... are you okay?"

An animal-like growl came from Bishop's chest. He reached down and grabbed Marty by the hair, lifting the poor fellow back to his feet. "I said move the fucking wagon... and I'm not going to ask again."

"Yes... yes... sir."

Two women rushed up, intent on attending to the victim at Bishop's feet. Marty staggered back toward his rig, glancing in fear over his shoulder at the crazy man who just delivered his daughter. Bishop stepped over the prone, sobbing girl and began walking to the middle of the gathered throng. He fired the ACR into the air and then began shouting, "I want every able-bodied man on this overturned wagon. Right now."

With fear plastered on their faces, the males eventually stepped forward, each taking his place in line and bracing against the up-facing side. "One, two, three... push! Push!" Bishop yelled, his own back protesting the effort as he flexed against the heavy object.

With groans of human straining, the wagon began rising, eventually falling upright onto all four wheels. "Now somebody get this piece of shit out of the road," Bishop commanded, scanning the group, making sure his request was understood.

He began walking back toward the truck, without saying another word.

A minute later he passed through the intersection, speeding off to the west and never looking back.

The trip across north central Texas passed with Bishop in a daze. A warning light on the dash broke the trance. The annoying icon indicated he needed fuel, so he begrudgingly pulled over and began pumping.

Taking the now dog-eared map with him, Bishop flattened the folds on top of the fuel barrel and studied his future route while moving the pump handle up and down. Using his thumb to measure, he realized it was almost an equal distance to either Midland Station or the canyon.

While the gasoline flowed from drum to tank, he pondered changing his plans and heading for the distant city. Midland Station was part of the Alliance, and he could contact Nick – give his friend warning of the impending attack.

It occurred to him that the US forces might be monitoring the unsecured transmissions of the Alliance. His mind was too tired to think up a clever cipher or code that Nick was sure to understand. It was something they should have thought of long ago.

There was also the time involved in finding someone who knew him, rousing the ham operator and then repeating the same process back in Alpha. If Nick were in the mountains with a training class, he would be wasting precious time.

A squirt flew from the tank, signaling the truck was again full. Bishop secured the all but empty drum and hose, pausing to think before climbing back behind the wheel.

The entire situation was maddening. The trip was taking far longer than he'd ever anticipated, each passing minute decreasing his chances of saving his family.

Even the brief pause, standing on the empty roadway made him feel guilty. What if he arrived at Chamber's Canyon five minutes after the army unit had left? What if just a few minutes made the difference between the life and death of his family?

No, he decided, *I have to go with the known – can't risk the unknown. I'm going to drive straight there and take care of business.*

Any concern Bishop experienced over being able to locate Chamber's Canyon was wasted worry. All he had to do was follow the helicopters.

Once in the general area, he saw no less than three of the military birds, all following the exact same route. It was a stroke of luck, as the truck didn't have enough gas for an extended search.

He found a good spot to conceal his chariot about two miles from the canyon. While it had been over 20 years since he'd visited the area, some familiar images reassured him he was on the right track.

It was with a sigh of sadness that he drove the screwdriver through the bottom of the gas tank, essentially driving a stake through the heart of the beast that had loyally carried him so far. He'd extracted a little petrol via the siphon hose, but not enough for his needs. The resulting hole in his beast's skin produced another half-gallon, not as much as he'd hoped, but it would have to do.

Despite his sense of urgency, covering the distance to his objective was extremely difficult. Bishop had his full pack, an extra rifle and two gallons of gasoline to carry. He had filled every nook and cranny of his gear with as many supplies as possible, doubting he'd be able to return to the truck any time soon.

The terrain proved to be more of a challenge than the extra weight. Rugged, sharp and hilly, Bishop had to climb, descend, and bypass an obstacle course of rock formations. More than once he had to backtrack, arriving at a dead end and having to retrace his steps. He was exhausted, scraped, and bruised by the time he reached Chamber's Canyon.

He'd found an overlook, nestled in a crevice between two car-sized boulders. Just over the crest of the cliffs surrounding the valley floor, it provided a full view of the activities below. As Bishop swept the area with his optic, he found a small military unit setting up camp.

The rocky crags and steep-sided cliffs surrounded a small patch of sandy soil – the only reasonable place to bivouac. The valley floor was crawling with activity, the sounds of hammering and shouted orders rising from below.

He didn't know how much time he had left, or exactly what he was to face. It was a safe assumption, given what he was witnessing, that he was vastly outnumbered and outgunned, but he did have a few advantages.

The element of surprise was on his side, and he would have to utilize that factor to the best of his ability. The goal wasn't to kill every man down there, but merely to disrupt their mission. He had determined this could best be accomplished by making sure they knew their plot had been discovered, and by inflicting significant casualties.

He also had the advantage of terrain.

Studying the area, he was reassured that his memory of the place was accurate. Basically a dead-ended canyon formed over thousands of years as wind and rain had eroded the softer rock away, leaving the granite and dense pumice.

The narrow gorge snaked along for over a quarter mile, never any wider than a football field. That ravine ended in a vertical wall of smooth stone that reached over 200 feet into the air, a draw for those who wanted a challenge scaling rock.

The valley floor was split down the middle by a small creek that was fed by a spring originating somewhere under the granite cliffs. It was the water that separated this location from the dozens of similar formations in the area.

The water enabled vegetation, both banks of the narrow stream lined with mature trees, including cypress and pine. Old man Chambers had originally thought to make his park-like property into a campground, but the endeavor had failed financially. After his passing, one of his children had taken up the hobby of rock climbing, and thus a new business was eventually formed. Now the military was using it as a place to launch an attack – a vicious strike aimed at those he loved.

In years past, people came from far away to camp and climb. Whoever managed the operation had seen fit to leave the area as pristine as possible, with only a block-walled bathhouse/restroom and a small, out of the way storage shed constructed on the premises. Now, large tents were being erected, bundles of supplies distributed throughout.

Whoever had selected the property as a staging area had made an excellent decision. Having a local water source would save a lot of weight as the teams were transported in. The valley was secluded, easily defendable and geographically close to the primary targets. Bishop visualized some officer in the Pentagon having attended the climbing school at some point in his youth. "I know a great place we can use to go assassinate new mothers!"

It was the perfect jump-off point - if the mission remained undiscovered. Bishop intended to turn the placid valley into a death trap, and he didn't feel the slightest bit of remorse over the carnage he hoped to deliver. These men were assassins and soldiers – this was war.

He pushed down the rage that was building in his chest, knowing now wasn't the time to let emotion guide his actions. He had to be calm, cool and professional. He had to be an operator. Time to get to work.

Given he was outnumbered, Bishop had to overcome a huge obstacle – firepower. He considered sniping from the rocks, but quickly dismissed the option. The men below would rapidly figure out he was a lone assailant and eventually would hunt him down for the kill. He had his long range rifle, but not a lot of ammo for that specific weapon.

He had flirted with creating a series of booby traps, but doubted their effectiveness. He might manage one or two victims, but the targets would catch on and eventually dismantle the devices.

A dozen pounds of military C4, or other high quality explosive would have made the job easier, but he had no such resource.

The one substance available was gasoline. He glanced down at the two plastic milk jugs, each almost full of the flammable liquid.

Combatants had been using gas-bombs for over 100 years. Often called Molotov Cocktails, petrol bombs had a long list of attractive features. They were cheap, readily available, and could be extremely effective against soft targets. Bishop hankered for a case of small glass bottles, but would have to do without.

Gasoline, by its very nature, was a powerful substance. One pound of vaporized fuel contained the equivalent of energy of five pounds of TNT, given containment and proper mixture of oxygen.

There were two way gas could be fatal – either by the heat produced by burning, or the pressure generated by a blast wave. The valley below was too open... too well ventilated to inflict harm by burning the substance.

Exploding the petrol was easy, given some sort of container. Containment was the key word. If a mixture of fuel and air was restricted inside of a pressurized vessel and then ignited, the gas would burn rapidly and cause an explosion, similar to what occurred inside of a car engine's piston. Again, given enough time and resources, he could have manufactured anti-personnel bombs. The frantic activities below eliminated that option.

Still, burning the gas might have a place in the evening's activities. If something important was burning, those men would try and fight the fire. They would be preoccupied – their attention drawn to the flames.

So it was down to the plan with the highest risk of his death. He would sneak down there, a single rifle against so many. He would pour the gasoline on their supplies, try and trap them in their tents, unaware. His weapon would spray death until their numbers eventually overwhelmed and brought him down.

It would be worth it, he determined. Terri would raise his son to be strong and independent. She would provide for the child, cherish him both as her offspring and in memory of their love. He hoped Terri would someday learn of his sacrifice... why he had charged into certain death. He prayed she would understand.

He began preparing his equipment. Hiding the backpack, exchanging as much weight as possible for magazines of ammunition. He hoped he would use most of it before they took him down.

It would be dark soon, and then he would descend into the valley – the valley of death.

Chapter 16

He waiting patiently, taking comfort in double-checking his equipment. His weapon was clean, well lubed, and as ready as he could make it. The pouches of magazines covering his mid-section and chest were full, ready to feed deadly lead as fast as he could manipulate the trigger.

His optic, night vision, and thermal imager were all supplied with fresh batteries. His Camelbak was full.

Every buckle and strap was secured and pulled tight. *The slightest noise might mean the difference between a short life, and a short, wasted life*, he thought. The reasoning elicited a low grunt. The end of his time on earth wasn't in question, the only unresolved issue being how long he could last and how effective that time would be. He prayed he could stand long enough to save his wife and child and the Alliance he cared so deeply about. Anything less would be a squandered sacrifice.

The feeling of his body armor, chest-rig and ACR bolstered his confidence, a soothing, known entity offsetting the fear and uncertainty of looming combat. He wondered if it had always been so.

Did the knights of old gain a sense of wellbeing, a boost as their squires hustled to strap on their armor? Did the men of Caesar's legions realize a calming effect after donning their breastplates and sharpening their broadswords? He thought about the paratroopers, flying across the English Channel on D-Day. Had they found faith in their kit to suppress the nagging fear that filled their chests before dropping into France?

Bishop supposed so, assumed it had always been that way. Men facing death needed both spiritual and physical reassurance. Many, including himself, had only their gear as a pacifier.

As he verified the contents of his blow-out bag, the faces of his friends began rotating through his mind. He wondered how many times Nick had experienced these same thoughts and fears. Pete and Betty were so dedicated and caring. They would help Terri recover and rebuild her life.

Deacon Diana Brown – her leadership skills natural and honest. The Alliance wouldn't be nearly as strong without her hand at the helm.

He pulled one last mouthful of water from the Camelbak,

the cool liquid helping fight the dryness that persisted in his mouth.

It was time.

He didn't move far before encountering the first problem. He couldn't find the sentries. Scanning with both light amplification and thermal imaging proved fruitless. *Either these are the stealthiest guards I've ever seen, or someone is way, way overconfident*, he thought.

His descent into the valley was slowed by the lack of security. Bishop was positive they had to have posted sentries… any competent officer would. He kept searching and scanning, eventually giving up the quest.

Flashlights, two campfires, and a few battery-powered tent bulbs illuminated the outpost. It was an easy approach given the number of rock formations providing cover.

While observing the activity from above, he had noted most of the supplies were being stored in a large tent on the north side of the compound. Bishop wanted to get rid of the gasoline and its anchor-like weight, so he made for that area first. If possible, he'd love to get his hands on a case of hand grenades before the shooting started.

He found the tent unguarded, moving to within 20 feet of the shelter without being challenged or noticed. He was amazed at the ease, always looking behind him to see if operators were closing in. None were; his egress remained clear.

As he scouted the crates, boxes and pallets full cardboard wrapped storage, Bishop noticed most of the materials were denoted with a red cross – the universal sign of medical equipment and supplies. *Now that's strange*, he considered. *I would have expected ammo, hand grenades, and claymore mines.*

Was it a ruse? Were the teams of assassins and saboteurs disguising their tools of destruction as medical supplies? Checking all around, Bishop didn't see anyone close by. He decided to enter the tent, and see for himself.

He found a pallet of supposed "pharmaceuticals," each container marked with the category of drug it claimed to contain. Bishop unlatched the container's hinges and opened the top. Again his head pivoted; again he found no one approaching his position.

Using the red lenses of his flashlight, Bishop tried to hide the torch with his body while checking the contents. He found rows of small boxes stacked inside, each of the two samples he pulled containing bottles of pills.

Replacing the lid, he moved on to another pallet two rows over, a container of bandages and medical wraps filled with exactly what its stenciled exterior claimed. The discovery was troubling.

Bishop was puzzled, his determination to deliver mayhem to the camp beginning to waiver - ever so slightly. Why would combat teams need such huge quantities of medical supplies? Why would a mission calling for quick insertion and extraction need a full case of diarrhea tablets? *Maybe Nick's defenses have them scared shitless*, he mused.

He needed to learn more.

His pre-dusk observations had identified the primary personnel tent located on the south side of the canyon. Withdrawing carefully from the supply depot, he worked his way around slowly, always watching for the expected sentries.

Again, he was stunned at how close he could approach the temporary structure. Voices carried through the canvas walls, the normal sounds of men in the field. Bishop listened for a few moments, learning nothing useful for his effort. There were too many conversations and secondary noises for him to make out anything.

He skirted around to the tent's primary opening, a space about eight feet wide covered with mosquito netting. The interior was brightly lit, a series of cots along one wall, the normal assortment of duffle bags, olive drab chairs and even a small desk with its own lamp. What he could see looked normal, like any military unit setting up a forward base in the field.

It was what he didn't see that caused him to pause.
There wasn't a single weapon in sight. Ignoring the fact that combat units rarely set up shelters unless they intended to be in the field for a significant amount of time, he fully expected to see M4 rifles, belt-fed weapons and other lethal tools of the trade. There were none, and it didn't make any sense.

He directed his attention to the men themselves. A few of the troopers were preparing to hit the rack, wandering around shirtless in the desert heat of July. Bishop studied these examples of humanity. These were not combat troops, let alone elite Special Forces.

Stomachs overhung belt lines. He didn't see a single man who had defined muscles. One guy had gray hair and looked to be almost 60 years old. Bishop backed away, retreating to the boulder field to gather his thoughts.

Something wasn't right, the whole setup not what he would have expected from hunter-killer teams. It just smelled bad. It was possible that what he had seen was all a ruse – a tactic to hide in plain sight or integrate the killers in with a benign unit, like a Trojan horse.

Before he started chopping people to pieces, he needed

to investigate further.

On the opposite side of the valley, elevated at the crest of the canyon wall, Alastair and Eris sat behind a well-constructed blind. Similar to a portable deer hide commonly used by hunters, the two men had arrived a day before Bishop, using the time to build their den of observation and set up what amounted to a high-tech, field-mobile bank of cameras and communications equipment.

"It's a good thing you thought to bring along the thermal liner," Alastair whispered. "Who would have thought some cowboy from Texas would have an infrared device?"

Eris didn't respond, his eye glued to a complex camera, the large unit mounted to a stout tripod. The sturdy stand was required due to the length of the lenses extending off the main body of the digital recorder. It was capable both of extreme magnification, and recording thermal video.

"He's not going to do it," Eris finally spoke, watching Bishop as he moved around the camp. "He's down there poking around and is going to figure it out... if he hasn't already."

Alastair shrugged, "No matter. If he doesn't, we will. Does the Mark III still have a good angle?"

Eris moved his eye away from the camera for a moment, glancing down at a computer unit lying on a nearby rock ledge. The small, shielded monitor was accompanied by a keyboard and joystick. In order to lower the amount of light generated, the operative couldn't see the display unless he was directly aligned with the surface of the flat screen. He adjusted his position in order to get a good look at what was clearly an aerial view of the valley below.

Human shapes glowed white against the black background of tents, rocks and other objects. One of the man-images showed the dark gray outline of a battle rifle and had a green, flashing box surrounding the image – the designated target, Bishop.

The software controlling the orbiting drone was much more sophisticated than the early models used in Afghanistan and Iraq. Eris had initially piloted the drone's flight path and camera with the joy stick until the unit had Bishop clearly in focus. A few strokes on the keyboard then ordered the flying spy to keep its bank of instruments trained on *that* heat source - no matter where the target moved.

"Yes, the drone is doing fine," Eris reported, then added, "I think our man down there is about to reach a conclusion, and I don't think he's going to do the dirty deed. You had better get into your rig. With any luck, we'll be out of here before the sun rises."

Alastair shrugged, turning to the back of the tent-like structure and pulling on a load vest. The kit was similar to Bishop's, complete with a row of magazines extending from its carriers. He then pulled a baklava over his head and topped off the disguise with a floppy bush hat. He could pass for Bishop, the resemblance by design.

"The rifle isn't the same. I thought for sure this guy would use an M4. Besides, I didn't have an ACR at the house," he noted.

"There aren't going to be any defense lawyers or experts studying this video. I'll zoom out the camera to prevent picking up so much detail. It'll be fine."

Bishop was checking the last tent, his mind reeling from what he had found so far. If this were an elite combat team, it was the most pitiful excuse for one he'd ever seen. So far, he'd found nothing but a collection of poorly conditioned men who, without their uniforms, would barely pass as soldiers – at least from Bishop's perspective.

It wasn't just their physical conditioning. Most of the men he studied were older, more than one sporting gray hair, and a few near the end of having any hair at all. They didn't move or talk like fighting men, especially ones who were about to embark on a mission.

He didn't spot one rifle, Kevlar helmet, or chest-rig in the entire complex. The only thing that could fire bullets in the camp was a single sidearm worn by an officer. The man seemed uncomfortable with the pistol on his belt, constantly fidgeting and adjusting the holster.

One more tent, he told himself. *Maybe the real warriors are huddled there. What's behind door number three?*

It was empty… unoccupied… nada.

"Shit, shit, shit. Brimstone and damnation," Bishop muttered. "What the hell do I do now?"

He decided to pull back and think. Forcing the adrenaline drain made his stomach hurt. After all the preparation, the hair-raising scramble across half the southern United States… the risk… the danger, the dead men in his wake.

His internal rant was disturbed by the sound of footsteps. A quick scan with the night vision identified a soldier, making for the edge of camp and eventually fumbling with his fly.

While the trooper finished his business, Bishop was moving. After completing his task, the soldier turned to see a shadow directly behind him. He started to greet what he thought was one of his comrades, but instead found himself on the ground, Bishop's knife held against his throat.

"Make a sound and die," hissed Bishop, increasing the pressure of the cold steel.

His prisoner was just a kid – maybe 19 years old, tops. Wide-eyed and clearly terrified, the private remained silent, not even chancing a breath.

"Real quiet now... what is your unit?"

"The 410th Mobile Surgical – New York National Guard," was the hushed response.

Bishop pretended anger, his eyes bulging in the kid's face, the knife pressing down just a little more. "Bullshit! You've got one more chance – what is your unit?"

"I... I told you, sir," the kid stammered, "I'm from Albany, and we just got here."

Bishop felt for the private's shoulder patch, ripping off the Velcro backed designation. With his knee in the kid's chest, he held it up to the light from the camp behind him. Sure as shit, it matched the soldier's story.

Returning to his prisoner, Bishop asked, "Why are you here?"

"We were ordered here to set up a supply depot. Tomorrow, the doctors are being shuttled into the towns... to start seeing patients while the nurses do inoculations. That's all I know, mister.... I swear."

It all matched what Bishop had discovered. Either the government's plan had changed, or he had been misled. There was no one here that he needed to kill.

Bishop moved his weight off the frightened private. "Get up," he commanded.

As the kid stood, Bishop withdrew a nylon tie from his vest. "I'm going to tie you up and leave you over there. After pushing the kid behind a nearby boulder, Bishop bound the private's hands and feet with the stout stripes and then wrapped duct tape around his mouth twice. "Sorry," Bishop whispered, "That's going to hurt like hell coming off."

Bishop knew every minute the kid was gone increased the chances someone would come looking for him. He hustled away from the camp, climbing rapidly to retrieve his pack and other equipment.

244

While he strapped on the heavy load, Bishop actually felt relief for the first time in days. Yes, it could be the Special Ops teams had used a different camp. There was still the possibility that he was too late... that his family and friends were still in danger, maybe already dead.

But he didn't think so. Maybe surviving the night changed his perspective. Perhaps he was optimistic that he was not having to take additional life. Whatever the reason, Bishop began hiking out of Chamber's Canyon with a smile on his face. The walk to Alpha was going to suck, but he'd survived worse. He was going home.

Alastair waited, giving Bishop plenty head start. As soon as he was convinced the Texan was far enough away, he began snaking down the incline until he reached the valley floor.
He didn't like killing Americans, but orders were orders. He'd done it before.

While waiting, he had decided to inherit Bishop's original plan. He found the two jugs of gasoline, right where the Texan had left them. He began dousing the flammable liquid throughout the supply tent. A flick of a disposable lighter caused a loud whoosh, and then the area was illuminated by towering flames.

The operative withdrew to the shadows, ducking down in a predetermined spot where he knew Eris's cameras had a clear view. Taking a knee and waiting on the guardsmen to respond to the blaze, he flicked the safety off his M4 and inhaled.

Bishop was almost a mile away when a sound resembling distant gunfire bounced through the rock crevices and gorges of the area. He paused, holding his breath and tilting his head in order to listen more closely.

He waited several minutes, trying to decide if the noise had really been gunfire or just a figment of his exhausted mind.

The momentary pause in his pilgrimage caused him to realize just how drained his mind and body were. He was emotionally, physically, and mentally done. *There's no great rush to get home*, he thought. *I'm going to find a good place to curl up and sleep for a bit. Maybe the nightmares won't come tonight.*

Chapter 17

Terri's morning routine with Hunter went off without a hitch. After both had finished breakfast, the new mom strapped on her constant companion and began trekking toward the courthouse.

She was looking forward to finishing her estimations for some of their local projects, the effort having been delayed by the series of negotiations being conducted with the team out of Fort Hood. It was two days before the next calendared meeting, and she was behind schedule.

Rounding the corner onto Main Street, she was surprised to see a military Humvee parked in front of the courthouse. *Odd*, she thought. *They're not supposed to be here today.*

Concern replaced curiosity as she walked closer. Rather than the assortment of officials from Washington, she could see General Owens, as well as three armed men. The guards noticed her approach and moved to intercept – their weapons in a ready position.

"Are you going to shoot me or the baby first?" she asked the nearest soldier.

"Sergeant, it's okay. Let her pass."

"What's this all about, General?"

"I was getting ready to ask you the same thing, Terri. Why on earth did you people murder all those men?"

"What? What men? We didn't murder anyone. What are you talking about?"

Clearly angry, Owens pulled a folder from under his arm, his actions curt and short. Inside were a series of 8x10 photographs, each depicting what looked like the aftermath of gory battle.

Terri managed to look at the first three before having to turn away. "Why are you showing me these pictures?"

"Yesterday, shortly after midnight, someone attacked one of our units. An unarmed medical platoon - men who were preparing a supply depot about 110 miles north of here. We informed you we were staging there over a week ago. Why, Terri? Why kill them all?"

"We didn't kill anyone! And I don't appreciate your tone of voice or the accusation of wrongdoing."

The general shook his head in disgust, reaching into the folder and producing a fistful of photos. "Are you saying you don't know *this* man?"

He held up a picture of Bishop, the image slightly grainy, but clear. Before Terri could answer, he produced several more photographs, including a few that showed her husband shooting a rifle. "Our security system took these pictures at the site of the massacre. This man killed over 20 of our soldiers and destroyed tons of medical supplies. Isn't this your husband?"

Terri was stunned and speechless. She suddenly felt light-headed, her legs weak. Nick appeared behind her, Diana at her side. "What's wrong, Terri? You don't look so good."

The emergency council meeting, like all such functions of the Alliance, was open to the public. Word of the massacre had spread quickly throughout the territory, rumors compounded by exaggerations. By the time the news had reached the far corners of the union, the story had grown to the point where war was being declared.

It was standing room only in the courthouse chambers, the walls lined with idling men, most of whom had left the seating to the women in a gentlemanly show of manners.

General Owens, accompanied by his three nervous bodyguards, sat at a table facing the gathering council members, his face stoic, body language reserved. Medals covered the breast of the commander's green jacket, many of them earned in combat. He seemed to sense every eye in the room was focused on him.

Here was the face of the enemy, a contradiction to what most of the audience thought they would see. He was a calm, professional-looking solider, not the fire-breathing demon many had expected. Honor sat in his chair – a life of service and sacrifice waiting to address a hostile entity. There was almost a sadness about the fellow – a projected regret.

When Diana's gavel finally called the meeting to order, a hush fell across the crowded room, the remnants of a few final whispers fading quickly.

Looking around the crowd, she began. "Ladies and gentlemen, may I introduce General Owens? He is in charge of the delegation from Washington that has been negotiating a trade agreement with our community. This morning, he delivered terrible news. There has been a mass killing at the edge of our territory, and the general has requested a public hearing to present the evidence gathered by the army investigators. General, you have the floor."

Owens stood, initially facing the council. "Thank you, Madam Chairman," he stated calmly. His next action surprised Diana. Instead of speaking to the governing members of the Alliance, he turned and faced the gathered crowd.

"My fellow Americans," he began, and then paused, eyes sweeping the room. "I don't use that opening lightly. It was not an accidental statement. I honestly believe all three words. All of you... are Americans."

The speaker paused for a moment, letting his words sink in before continuing. "As most of you know, there has been a disagreement between the federal government in Washington and your locally elected officials. There have been threats exchanged, as well as a few overt actions that have served to escalate the tension."

The general again swept the room, clasping his hands behind his back. "No one wants a war. No one wants to abuse the rights and privileges of any freeborn American citizen. Our disagreement involves material assets and perceived liberties. That is the key word to this entire debacle – perceived."

Diana watched the crowd, their attention rapt like a jury, willing to hear the man out.

Owens continued, his voice clear, his tone honest. "The president of the United States ordered me here. I'll be blunt, I didn't want to accept the mission. In my heart and mind, I am more closely aligned with your leaders than anyone in Washington. During countless meetings held at Camp David, I was always the voice crying out for the protection of each individual's rights. So why did my Commander in Chief send one of the few dissenting voices on such a critical assignment? Why did he choose me to lead our delegation? Because I have seen the results of American fighting American with my own eyes. These hands... my own hands... have spilled American blood."

After waiting for the shock of the statement to wear off, he continued. "I commanded the rebel forces at Scott's Hill, my friends. I ordered men to fight their brothers and cousins. Why? Because of how strongly I felt about a cause... my sense of right and wrong. So it was with this knowledge that President Moreland ordered me to lead these negotiations. He confided in me that if anyone had the motivation to avoid a civil war, it was me. I've been there, I heard the screaming of the wounded, watched the life fade from men's eyes. I know what war would mean."

Oh, he's good, thought Terri. *He's very good. But where*

After taking a drink of water, the general cleared his throat and resumed. Sweeping his hand toward the council table, he said, "And we were there. We had an agreement that avoided war and benefited both parties. Not everyone on my side of the table was happy, I'm sure these fine people behind me had their issues as well. Evidently, some people within your community were seriously displeased. Evidently, there were factions among you who decided reaching agreement with Washington just wasn't in the plan, and took it upon themselves to sabotage our proceedings... to kill the deal."

Owens then stepped to the table occupied by his men. He reached down and picked up a single sheet of paper.

"Two nights ago, at 0100 hours, this man attacked a forward operating base that was in the process of being constructed," he said, holding up an 8x10 photo of Bishop. "This base was outside of your alliance's territory, the location agreed to only three days before by your own council. This base was staffed by the unarmed soldiers of the New York National Guard. Medical personnel, ladies and gentlemen – doctors and nurses who were staging there in order to treat your friends and neighbors."

Moving back to the table, Owens then picked up a stack of photographs, walking to the edge of the crowd and holding the first up for everyone to see. "Private First Class, Mitch Benton, Medic" he announced, displaying a gory image of a dead man lying on the ground. "Captain Henry Phillips, Internist," he continued, showing another blood-filled image. "Major Becky Holland, Nurse," the general announced, presenting the image of a dead woman, her uniform blouse covered in purple.

"In total, 21 of our people are dead. Butchered."

Again a pause for effect, giving the audience time to absorb what he was saying. "So why do we believe this was the work of the Alliance? Why am I here addressing you? Because we were monitoring the construction of the camp with an observation drone. This is common practice when forward bases are being constructed in distant locales. We have pictures of the culprit; we have video of the man executing this crime. And that man is the husband of one of your most important leaders. That man, Bishop, has been involved in the assassination attempt of an American president. He has had multiple warrants issued for his arrest, and is still a wanted man associated with crimes committed on a federal installation. He has committed assault against a treasury employee and is known throughout the territory as a man capable of killing. Even if we hadn't been monitoring this location with an observation drone, we would have suspected this individual. As it is, we have proof who committed this atrocity."

Turning to one of his subordinates, Owens nodded. The sergeant reached to the table and turned on a projector, a large, illuminated square appearing on the front wall of the chambers. Turning back to his now-captive audience, the general continued. "I know you don't trust Washington. I know there is a long and difficult healing process ahead of us all. For this reason, I'm not here asking anyone to take my word for it. I want you to see the evidence and judge for yourself. Sergeant, play the video, please."

The projector displayed a series of still photos, all of Bishop. The accused was cleaning his weapon, loading magazines, and adjusting his gear. Then the display changed to motion video, taken from a thermal camera. There was Bishop stalking toward the camp, carrying two milk jugs, moving toward a tent.

The brightness of the footage suddenly changed. The clear outline of white-hot flames was visible in the center of the tent, the image of Bishop nearby, raising his rifle.
Other human shapes began to appear, rushing as if to look at the fire. Bishop's rifle began firing, the barrel glowing thermal hot in the images.

The soldiers, responding to the fire, began to fall. Some clutched their chests, others simply dropped to the ground in disheveled shapes. After several had fallen, the survivors began to run away. The image of Bishop chased them down.

The last ten seconds of video evidence showed the clear outline of a woman, holding up her hands in surrender. The rifleman walked up and calmly shot her in the head, a geyser of hot liquid spray graphically depicted on the wall of the courthouse.

The women of Alpha turned their heads away, the audience filled with gasps and moans. A few of those gathered whispered prayers.

After a nod from the general, the projector was switched off. He gathered himself, clearly touched by the evidence. His voice was shaky, a Herculean effort required to keep the anger from dominating his next statements.

"Ladies and gentlemen, put yourselves in our place. What would you do? The president is irate, his advisors begging that we immediately send tanks, gunships and infantry into West Texas to avenge our causalities. Wouldn't most of you do the same?"

Several heads were nodding in the audience, many of the citizens casting hard glances at Terri, a few at Nick and

251

Diana.

"But hope is not lost. If this man is apprehended and turned over to us, there is still a chance that war can be avoided. If the good people of West Texas see fit to accept the legitimate government in Washington, and immediately cease all of this Alliance nonsense, then death and destruction on a massive scale can still be avoided."

The crowd interrupted the speech, murmurs, side conversations, and rumblings sounding throughout the room. The general was patient, remaining statuesque and expressionless. Diana's gavel was required to restore quiet, her voice sounding above the din. "Order, please! Order in these chambers!"

The general nodded his thanks to the chairperson, and then returned to address his audience. "Tomorrow, I'm going to arrive here at zero-eight-hundred with four busses. I will take anyone who still has doubts to the scene. After that, if this situation doesn't come to resolution, the next time any of you see me, I will be riding on a tank, and I won't be alone. I will now leave you all to decide your future. I don't want to use critical assets to take more American lives, but I will do so if ordered. As I stated earlier, I've done it before. God help us all if it comes to that."

And then the army officer turned to his comrades and said, "Let's go." After a quick gathering of their paper and equipment, the four-man procession filed down the center aisle and exited the building.

The place erupted. Voices rang out and fists shook in the air, some pointed at Terri, others gesturing where the general had just passed. Everyone seemed to want to voice an opinion at once, some at the top of their lungs.

A few people, trying to be heard above the throng, tried to approach the council's table, but Nick and three of the Darkwater contractors were there, keeping the agitated citizens back.

Diana, her hammering gavel doing little more than adding to the dismay, slammed the device down so hard the handle broke.

It was a single gunshot that broke through the chaos, producing immediate silence. All eyes turned to look at Terri, standing on her chair. One of her arms was pointed to the ceiling, smoke still rolling out the pistol in her hand, the other hand covering Hunter's ears. "Enough!" she screamed at the top of her lungs. "You can run us all out of town later if you want, but we will have order right here, right now. Take a seat. Everyone will get a turn."

And they did.

The meeting lasted into the wee hours of the morning, with three intermissions. Two of the breaks were to feed Hunter, the third for bathroom necessities.

As the sleepy team of Diana, Nick, and Terri walked home, the new mother summed it up best. "Our people are divided into three camps," she stated. "One group believes my husband is a villain and that the entire council ordered the attack so we could keep our jobs. The second group thinks the government is lying and wants us to hold our ground, even if it means war. The third group is undecided. I bet we'll see a lot of the third group on the busses tomorrow."

Nick had been practically silent most of the evening, as if something was on his mind. Without warning, his head popped up, "Terri, how many rifles did Bishop take with him?"

"Oh… I don't know, Nick. It seems like so long since he left. Two, I think."

The big man seemed to ponder the answer for a moment, Diana interrupting his thoughts. "What are you thinking?"

"I don't know… it's probably nothing, but, those videos the general showed… something just wasn't right about them. I can't put my thumb on it, but something was strange."

The trio continued to trek toward Terri's home, Hunter fast asleep in his papoose. As they got closer to the bungalow, Nick's frame went stiff, his hand reaching for the rifle strapped across his back.

"What's wrong?" Diana asked, her head scanning all around.

Nick nodded toward Terri's front porch. There, along the front wall, someone had written "Killers!" in red.

The two women stayed back while Nick cleared the premises. The graffiti was still wet. Nick poked his finger in the runny substance and then held it up to his nose.

"Chicken or pig blood," he announced. He then turned to the girls and said, "Terri, I think you and Hunter should sleep over at our place tonight. I'll send someone over to wash this off tomorrow."

Terri seemed in shock, the cumulative effects of the day finally catching up with her.

Diana took her friend by the arm and said, "Come on, girlfriend, I've been hoarding some hot cocoa. I'll make you a cup while Nick gathers up some things for you."

Alpha, Texas
July 17, 2016

Bishop's knees and back were singing a song of pain with every step, the blisters on his feet adding to the chorus. The tune kept repeating over and over again, a seemingly permanent fixture of the morning.

He was so focused on putting one foot in front of the other, he almost didn't notice Alpha's small airport, only a few miles north of town. It was the first sign of civilization he'd seen in two days. The song of punishment faded, its jingle replaced by an upbeat rhythm inspired by almost being home.

He managed another half a mile when the sound of a car engine caused him to turn. There, sure enough, was a citizen of the Alliance rolling into town. Bishop stuck out his thumb, more as a joke than an actual signal that he wanted a ride. Normally, passersby would stop and offer him a lift, even if he were on a short stroll around Alpha.

The driver, who he recognized as one of the church volunteers, slowed as if preparing to stop and offer a lift. When she was close enough to identify the pedestrian, she looked straight ahead and sped on by.

Bishop was initially shocked, but then justified the woman's reaction by his appearance. He knew he would not be making new friends with three days of beard, two rifles, and clothes that were soiled, to put it mildly. *Maybe she got a whiff of me*, he thought. *I probably smell so bad a pig farmer wouldn't stop. He wouldn't want to offend the swine.*

He had forgotten about the incident by the time he reached the outskirts of town. The hour was still reasonably early, not many folks up and about just yet. He encountered the first pedestrians a few blocks north of the courthouse.

"Good morning, Mr. and Mrs. James," he greeted with a cheery voice. "A fine morning, isn't it?"

The older couple stopped, turning to see who had spoken to them. The husband's eyes betrayed a flicker of recognition, and then something totally unexpected happened.

Rather than a greeting, a frown flashed across Mr. James's face. Pivoting without a word, he pulled his spouse closer and then began walking off at a brisk pace, almost as if Bishop were some sort of criminal eyeing his wife's purse.

"Odd," he whispered to himself. "I wonder if they're mad at Terri over something the council did while I was gone."

As he turned to continue home, his question was

partially answered. There, tied to the pole of a stop sign, was his picture. Above the black and white photograph were the bold letters, "WANTED." Beneath the image was the statement, "By the US government for murder. Please contact any US representative. This man is responsible for the massacre at Chamber's Valley. He should be considered armed and dangerous."

At first, Bishop just stood and stared at the poster. *It has to be a joke*, he told himself. *Nick's really getting sophisticated with his stunts.* He even looked around, expecting to see a couple of guys with a video camera filming his reaction.

But then, it began to tie in with the morning's unusual events. The volunteer who wouldn't give him a ride. Mr. James's reaction.

He turned back to study the photograph, trying to determine where the picture had been taken. "Chamber's Valley?" he questioned to no one. "I just left Chamber's Valley. Oh, shit... Nick would have no way of knowing I was there... nobody would."

Not wasting any more time trying to dissect the "Wanted" poster, Bishop hurried the remaining few blocks to the bungalow. He noticed the truck was gone before entering the house. Another weird thing... Terri rarely drove anywhere, and he'd just passed the courthouse, checking the parking lot to see if anyone was at work just yet. No Terri and no truck.

Bishop entered, finding an empty nest. Most of their possessions were still there, but the bed wasn't made. *She must have been in a hurry to get somewhere*, he reasoned.

He tried to make the best of it, convincing himself it was actually a positive thing. He would have time to take a shower and change clothes before seeing his wife for the first time in days.

He had just finished dressing in clean duds when the squeaky brake of an electric golf cart sounded from the driveway. Poking his head out the front screen door, Bishop smiled to see Nick and Diana exiting their ride.

"Good morning," he greeted. "Would you folks know where my wife is?"

"Bishop," Diana said sharply, "What the hell is going on? What happened out at Chamber's Valley?"

Puzzled, still trying to fill in the blanks, he responded honestly. "Nothing happened up there. I left two days ago, and everything was just fine."

"So you were there?" Nick asked, his voice more worried than accusing.

Bishop shrugged his shoulders, "Yeah, I was there.

What the fuck is going on, Nick? Where's Terri?"

Diana pointed south, "Terri left yesterday for the ranch. Things were getting a little testy around here... there was even a protest of sorts. She and Nick thought it would be safer if she stayed out there."

The look on Bishop's face was helpless. "Testy? Safer? Protest? What the hell is going on, guys?"

Diana replayed the story of the military arriving two days ago. She repeated their claim that Bishop had butchered a bunch of military doctors, killed them in cold blood.

"No one believed it at first, Bishop," Diana continued, "We all thought it was preposterous. Then they showed us the video of you going into the camp with your rifle."

"I still didn't buy it," Nick chimed in. "So they took a bunch of us up there in a bus. I saw the dead with my own eyes. The pictures they had matched the background and landmarks."

Bishop was in shock. Turning away, he started blurting out unrelated statements, his arms waving in wild gestures. "I was there, but I didn't shoot anyone. The guy at the Circus... he told Grim... they were going to assassinate the council and Terri. They were going to take over the electrical sub-station. But all I found were medical supplies... not a Special Forces Team. I just assumed something had changed... that they had called off the mission after you guys had reached a deal. So I just left and walked home."

"Slow down, partner. Take it easy. Start from the beginning," Nick soothed.

For the next 20 minutes, Bishop paced the living room floor, recounting the events of the rescue mission. He told the story of Deke's death in the graveyard, details about the Circus and the information provided by the former army officer.

After he had finished, Nick looked at Diana and said, "I thought as much. A setup. They killed all those men out at Chamber's Valley to set Bishop up."

"Why *me*?" a confused Bishop asked. "Why go to all that trouble to make *me* look bad?"

Diana stared at the floor, her voice cold and monotone. "It wasn't you, Bishop. It was our government. After the US delegation showed the evidence of your crime, the news spread around the Alliance like wildfire. The people had been so relieved to avoid war... so upbeat that we were going to have a new trading partner. When Washington announced that the deal was off until you were apprehended and turned over to them, people felt like the rug had been pulled out from under them."

Nick cleared his throat, adding to the story. "Terri supported you 100%, but their proof was very convincing. People started gathering in the square, demanding that she be arrested and held until you were captured. Rumors spread; stories were exaggerated. That's when we decided it was best if she head for the ranch. I'm sure she and Hunter are okay. I escorted them there myself."

"I had people demanding we do something… anything to restore Washington's faith in us. The whole thing began to spiral out of control. We even had a bunch of folks form a committee and drive toward Fort Hood, probably trying to cut a side deal. The council members all traveled back to their hometowns, trying to get everyone to calm down. There's even been a call for new elections."

It all fell into place for Bishop. It had been a clever, well-planned ruse, and it was working. He started to turn to Nick when the picture window glass exploded inward, a brick landing on the rug. "Murderer!" someone yelled as a car sped off down the street.

After recovering from the shock of the incident, Bishop turned and asked, "Nick, can you give me a ride to the ranch? I think Terri and I need to pack up and head out of here."

Nick turned and looked at Diana, the mayor nodding her agreement. "That's probably not a bad idea. You and Terri could take a vacation for a while, let things cool off, and give us some time to prove the truth."

After the meaning of Bishop's words had soaked in, Diana's thoughts turned to Terri and the baby. "Bishop, where would you go?"

"I've always wanted to see the Rocky Mountains," he responded calmly. "I hear they're beautiful this time of year."

Bishop indeed felt like a criminal. As he and Nick drove through Alpha, he kept low in the seat to avoid being spotted. His "WANTED" poster was everywhere.

Despite Nick's insistence that he and Terri could remain at the ranch, Bishop wasn't buying it. No one knew for sure how Pete was reacting to the ploy, and the mayor of Meraton had a map to the otherwise off-the-grid home. Bishop had faith in the man, but only for as long as the bartender believed his friend was worthy of such trust. If Pete bought the government's story, he might give up the map.

Deke's team of contractors had been able to pinpoint the ranch as well. Using tax records from the courthouse basement, they had discovered the location with little effort. While Bishop thought he had removed any such trail, that basement was stuffed to the gills with archives. He might have missed something.

Then there was Nick himself. While Bishop believed Nick would die before revealing the site of the couple's homestead, he didn't think the man would allow his son, Kevin, to perish in order to keep the secret.

"What if some bounty hunter kidnaps your son, Nick? What if a group of vigilantes take Diana and demand you spill the beans?" Bishop had asked his dear friend. "No, it's better for everyone if we bug out. We did it once; we can do it again."

"But the baby," Nick protested as they left the outskirts of town. "You didn't have Hunter then."

Bishop shrugged it off. "This place was becoming too damn crowded anyway. A man needs some elbowroom. I was thinking about heading out after Terri got tired of being in the government anyway," he pretended.

The rest of the short trip passed quickly, both men clouded by the uncertainty of the future. When Nick finally negotiated the tricky, booby-trapped approach to Bishop's property, the two men looked up to see Terri stepping from the camper, Hunter riding in his papoose.

Bishop had to smile, noticing the pistol on his wife's belt. *She's learned so much*, he thought, *and it's a shame she has had to.*

Bishop jumped from the truck, running to meet his wife and son. Their reunion was joyful, but marred by an overhanging fog of the unknown. Nick stood by in silence, waiting for the hugs and kisses to end.

"I'll be heading back into town, Bishop," he stated. "I want to start working on your side of the story right away."

"Before you go," Bishop said, "Can I ask you to gather up some supplies and other odd items? I'd like to head out in a day or two."

"Sure, buddy. Just name it."

Bishop pulled his notepad from his vest and began jotting down a list. He tore off the page and handed it to his friend.

Nick scanned the paper and smiled. "No problem, brother. I'll be back tomorrow with everything."

"Thanks, man. I owe ya."

After watching Nick leave, Bishop turned to Terri and said, "Let's go have a seat. I've got one hell of a story to tell you."

After playing with Hunter and then sleeping for several hours, Bishop began packing the truck. The effort was heartbreaking, the bed too small to hold all of their belongings. The addition of a third family member and all of the necessary supplies adding to the lack of storage space. *Holy cow*, Bishop muttered to himself, *who knew something so small could require so much stuff?*

Terri split her time between caring for the baby and gathering necessities. There were several friendly discussions over what to take and what to leave behind.

"You know what saddens me the most?" Terri asked, pausing over the box of canned goods she was filling. "I don't think the Alliance can survive. We had such a good thing going, and now there are cracks forming in the dike. It could all fall apart at any time."

Bishop nodded, understanding his wife's remorse. "But it was always that way, Terri. The façade of society is always thinner than what we like to think. Besides, I wouldn't underestimate Nick, Diana, and Pete. They're good people and strong leaders. If anyone can hold it together, they can."

"I suppose," she responded. "Besides, I need to concentrate on us now. I need to keep my mind focused on our survival."

Bishop nodded, appreciating his wife's common sense attitude toward what was no doubt a shocking turn of events. "Do you remember when we decided to leave Houston? We were out on the back porch, making jokes about being Bonnie and Clyde. Seems kind of ironic now that we're going on the lam, doesn't it?"

Terri laughed, recalling that day which now seemed like a lifetime ago. She tilted her head, staring for a moment and then said, "I was scared then... really scared. Now, so much has changed, and I'm not frightened at all, not like before. I feel like we're both stronger... better prepared for something like this."

"I'm sure Bonnie and Clyde felt more confident after each bank robbery," he teased.

"You may think I'm all strong and tough, but that's not entirely true. I thought we had a future for Hunter. School, society, food... I thought we had it all worked out. Now I feel like we're starting all over again. I am worried for Hunter's future."

Bishop moved to hug his spouse, pulling her close and patting the 9mm pistol on her belt, "You are so much stronger now, and I love you more than ever. We have to have faith that

259

Nick and our friends will bring the truth to light. We have to believe that as much as anything. If we do, then this little journey is just a vacation, a trip to the mountains during the tourist season."

Finishing the hug, Terri returned to her packing in silence.

The sound of a horn honking in the distance alerted the couple that Nick had returned. As they left the camper to meet him, Bishop smiled when seeing the bed of his friend's truck was full of supplies, including two 50-gallon drums of fuel.

It was what Nick was towing that really drew his attention, however. There, tagging along behind the approaching pickup was a small, lightweight pop-up camper.

Bishop noticed Terri's attention was drawn to the trailer as well. "Our new home," he announced.

"It's so cute... does it have a hot tub?" Terri inquired with a wink to her mate.

Nick exited the cab, walking back with the couple to examine the camper. "I found it at that RV dealer over by Midland Station. The looters had concentrated on the big units and had left this little jewel alone. It's brand new."

The trio spent the rest of the afternoon packing and learning how to operate their new abode. Bishop was amazed at the amount of space inside after the top unfolded and the sides expanded. They would at least avoid sleeping on the ground or in the truck.

After transferring the fuel and supplies from Nick's truck to Bishop's, the two men then set about loading the gold and other valuables stored in the Bat Cave into the big man's empty pickup. The effort brought back memories of a darker time – when bank robbers ruled Meraton with fear and intimidation. Still, Bishop was happy to shed responsibility for the treasure.

Dusk was threatening by the time the backbreaking work was complete. Bishop's pickup sat low on its springs, the weight of fuel, ammunition, rifles, and all the other necessities they could stuff inside, stressing the stout suspension.

"If you go slow, it should handle the weight in the bed, as well as towing the camper," Nick judged.

"We're not in any hurry," Bishop replied. "Got no place we have to be."

"I'm officially retired," added Terri. "I'll send you an address where you can forward by pension checks."

The hard work involved in preparing for the bug out was nothing compared to what had to come next. When it was clear there was nothing else left to do, Nick looked to the west and announced, "I probably should be getting back. Diana has her hands full trying to keep the council together. We've even had a minor rebellion within the security forces. It's going to be an interesting few weeks – that's for sure."

And then it was time. Time for the heart wrenching goodbyes, hugs, and handshakes.

There wasn't a dry eye in the canyon as the three friends exchanged repeated embraces and promises. It was the worst Bishop could ever remember feeling, despite the reassurances of reuniting in the near future. None of the three felt overly optimistic at the possibility, all were afraid to say it.

Nick finally managed the cab of his truck, Bishop ready to follow his friend off their property for what was most likely the last time.

As Bishop moved to put the truck into gear, Terri reached across and grabbed his arm, a horrible look on her face. "We'll be back," he reassured, assuming his wife was having second thoughts. "It will be fine."

"It's not that," she said, nearly choking while trying to subdue a laugh. "We forgot Hunter."

"FUCK!" Bishop snapped, embarrassment all over his face. He threw the transmission into park and raced for the camper. He returned quickly, the still-sleeping child cradled in his arm.

A few moments later they were off, Hunter secure in his car seat, oblivious to the melancholy mental atmosphere that clouded the cab.

Epilogue

They exited Alpha heading north, the act of slinking through town, like escaping convicts, worsening Bishop's mood.

During the drive from the ranch, there had been some debate over detouring to Meraton, a quick stop to say their goodbyes to Pete and Betty. They finally decided against the act – afraid their presence would poison their friends politically. In truth, both were unsure if they could handle any more emotion.

Terri rode in the backseat with Hunter, the baby's safety chair buffered on one side by his mother, the other with boxes of supplies that dad had deemed most likely to stop a bullet. Bishop's spare body armor was strapped onto the back of his son's seat.

It was an odd scene, Terri riding back there next to her child, a diaper bag on one side, her rifle on the other. Bishop sensed prophetically that it was an image he would get used to. "Don't clean the carbine with the burp rag," he wanted to say, but held his tongue.

The front passenger seat was filled with boxes as well, with space reserved for his rifle and handgun so the weapons would be within easy reach. A newer model than what he'd recently been driving, Bishop was happy to see the truck's GPS functioned properly, the technology replacing the need for the dreaded paper map.

Terri watched the lights of Alpha fade behind them, eventually turning to face the front windshield. "So Magellan, where are we heading?" she asked, her humor cheering Bishop up.

"Have you ever been to Utah?"

"No. Do they still have the choir?"

Bishop grunted. "I don't know about that. Isn't that in Salt Lake City? Anyway, a long time ago I visited an area everyone called 'The Canyon Lands.' It's an entire corner of the state, thick with National Parks, reserves and open territory. It was beautiful, and there weren't very many people or towns. I thought we might head that direction first."

"Sounds good to me. Lead on, my love. As long as we are together, I'm a happy camper… no pun intended.

~ *The End* ~

From the Author:

Holding Their Own VII is scheduled for release in early 2014. Please visit us on Facebook (Joe.Nobody.Author) or at **www.holdingyourground.com** for the latest updates.

51594397R00148

Made in the USA
Lexington, KY
30 April 2016